# THE PROPHETEERS

*Also by Max Apple*

THE ORANGING OF AMERICA

ZIP

FREE AGENTS

# THE PROPHETEERS

A NOVEL BY

## MAX APPLE

PERENNIAL LIBRARY

Harper & Row, Publishers, New York
Cambridge, Philadelphia, San Francisco, Washington
London, Mexico City, São Paulo, Sydney

*Designer: Barbara DuPree Knowles*

*Copyeditor: Robert Hemenway*

---

Library of Congress Cataloguing-in-Publication Data

Apple, Max.
  The propheteers.

  I. Title.
PS 3551.P56D5 1987      813'.54      86-45637
ISBN 0-06-055056-2
ISBN 0-06-096158-9 (pbk.)

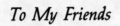

*To My Friends*

# THE PROPHETEERS

**F**rom the outside it looked like any new 1964 Cadillac limousine. In the expensive space between the driver and passengers, where some installed bars or even bathrooms, Mr. Howard Johnson kept a tidy ice-cream freezer in which there were always at least eighteen flavors on hand, though Mr. Johnson ate only vanilla. The freezer's power came from the battery with an independent auxiliary generator as a backup system. Although now Howard Johnson means primarily motels, Milly, Mr. HJ, and Otis Brighton, the chauffeur, had not forgotten that ice cream was the cornerstone of their empire. Some of the important tasting was still done in the car. Mr. HJ might have reports in his pockets from sales executives and marketing analysts, from home economists and chemists, but not until Mr. Johnson reached over the lowered Plexiglas to spoon a taste or two into the expert waiting mouth of Otis Brighton did he make any final flavor decision. He might go ahead with butterfly shrimp, with candy kisses, and with packaged chocolate-chip cookies on the opinion of the specialists, but in ice cream he trusted only Otis. From the back seat Howard Johnson would keep his eye on the rearview mirror, where the reflection of pleasure or disgust showed itself in the dark eyes of Otis Brighton no matter what the driving conditions. He could be stalled in a commuter rush with the engine overheating and a dripping oil pan, and still a taste of the right kind never went unappreciated.

When Otis finally said, "Mr. Howard, that shore is sumpin,

that one is um-hum. That is it, my man, that is it," then and not until then did Mr. HJ finally decide to go ahead with something like banana-fudge-ripple-royale.

Mildred rarely tasted and Mr. HJ was addicted to one scoop of vanilla every afternoon at three, eaten from his aluminum dish with a disposable plastic spoon. The duties of Otis, Milly, and Mr. Johnson were so divided that they rarely infringed upon one another in the car, which was their office. Neither Mr. HJ nor Milly drove the Cadillac, Milly and Otis understood little of financing and leasing, and Mr. HJ left the compiling of the traveling reports and the Howard Johnson newsletter strictly to the literary style of his longtime associate, Miss Mildred Bryce. It was an ideal division of labor, which, in one form or another, had been in continuous operation for nearly forty years.

While Otis hummed or occasionally listened to the radio behind his soundproof Plexiglas, while Milly in her small, neat hand compiled data for the newsletter, Mr. HJ liked to lean back into the spongy leather seat looking through his specially tinted windshield at the fleeting land. Occasionally, lulled by the hum of the freezer, he might doze off, his large pink head lolling toward the shoulder of his blue suit, but there was not too much that Mr. Johnson missed.

Along with Milly he planned their continuous itinerary as they traveled. Mildred would tape a large green relief map of the United States to the Plexiglas separating them from Otis. The mountains on the map were light brown and seemed to melt toward the valleys like the crust of a fresh apple pie settling into cinnamon surroundings. The existing HJ houses (Milly called the restaurants and motels houses) were marked by orange dots, while projected future sites bore white dots. The deep-green map with its brown mountains and colorful dots seemed much more alive than the miles that twinkled past Mr. Johnson's gaze, and nothing gave the ice-cream king greater pleasure than watching Mildred with her fine touch, and using the original crayon, turn an empty white dot into an orange fulfillment.

"It's like a seed grown into a tree, Milly," Mr. HJ liked to say at such moments when he contemplated the map and saw that it was good.

They had started traveling together in 1927: Mildred, then a secretary to Mr. Johnson, a young man with a few restaurants and a dream of hospitality, and Otis, a twenty-two-year-old farmer and former driver of a Louisiana mule. When Mildred graduated from college, her father, a Michigan doctor who kept his money in a blue steel box under the examining table, encouraged her to try the big city. He sent her a monthly allowance. In those early days she always had more than Mr. Johnson, who paid her $16.50 a week and meals. In the first few years they traveled only on weekends, but every year since 1938 they had spent at least six months on the road, and it might have gone on longer if Mildred's pain and the trouble in New York with Corky had not come so close together.

They were all stoical at the Los Angeles International Airport. Otis waited at the car for what might be his last job while Miss Bryce and Mr. Johnson traveled toward the New York plane along a silent moving floor. Milly stood beside Howard while they passed a mural of a Mexican landscape and some Christmas drawings by fourth-graders from Watts. For close to forty years they had been together in spite of Corky and the others, but at this most recent appeal from New York Milly urged him to go back. Corky had wired, "My God, you're sixty-nine years old, haven't you been a gypsy long enough? Board meeting December third with or without you. Policy changes imminent."

Normally, they ignored Corky's wires, but this time Milly wanted him to go, wanted to be alone with the pain that had recently come to her. She had left Howard holding the new canvas suitcase in which she had packed her three notebooks

3

of regional reports along with his aluminum dish, and in a moment of real despair she had even packed the orange crayon. When Howard boarded Flight 965 he looked old to Milly. His feet dragged in the wing-tipped shoes, the hand she shook was moist, the lips felt dry, and as he passed from her sight down the entry ramp Mildred Bryce felt a fresh new ache that sent her hobbling toward the car. Otis had unplugged the freezer, and the silence caused by the missing hum was as intense to Milly as her abdominal pain.

It had come quite suddenly in Albuquerque, New Mexico, at the grand opening of a 210-unit house. She did not make a fuss. Mildred Bryce had never caused trouble to anyone, except perhaps to Mrs. HJ. Milly's quick precise actions, angular face, and thin body made her seem quite birdlike, especially next to Mr. HJ, six three with splendid white hair accenting his dark blue gabardine suits. Howard was slow and sure. He could sit in the same position for hours while Milly fidgeted on the seat, wrote memos, and filed reports in the small gray cabinet that sat in front of her and parallel to the ice-cream freezer. Her health had always been good, so at first she tried to ignore the pain. It was gas: it was perhaps the New Mexico water or the cooking oil in the fish dinner. But she could not convince away the pain. It stayed like a match burning around in her belly, etching itself into her as the round HJ emblem was so symmetrically embroidered into the bedspread, which she had kicked off in the flush that accompanied the pain. She felt as if her sweat would engulf the foam mattress and crisp percale sheet. Finally, Milly brought up her knees and made a ball of herself as if being as small as possible might make her misery disappear. It worked for everything except the pain. The little circle of hot torment was all that remained of her, and when finally sometime in the early morning it left, she felt that perhaps she had struggled with a demon and been suddenly relieved by the coming of daylight. She stepped lightly into the bathroom and before a full-length mirror (new in HJ motels exclusively) saw

4

herself whole and unmarked, but sign enough to Mildred was her smell, damp and musty, sign enough that something had begun and that something else would therefore necessarily end.

Before she had the report from her doctor, Corky's message had given her the excuse she needed. There was no reason why Milly could not tell Howard she was sick, but telling him would be admitting too much to herself. Along with Howard Johnson Milly had grown rich beyond dreams. Her inheritance, the $100,000 from her father's steel box in 1939, went directly to Mr. Johnson, who desperately needed it, and the results of that investment brought Milly enough capital to keep two people busy at the Chase Manhattan with the management of her finances. With money beyond the hope of use, she had vacationed all over the world and spent some time in the company of celebrities, but the reality of her life, like his, was in the back seat of the limousine, waiting for that point at which the needs of the automobile and the human body met the undeviating purpose of the highway and momentarily conquered it.

Her life was measured in rest stops. She, Howard, and Otis had found them out before they existed. They knew the places to stop between Buffalo and Albany, Chicago and Detroit, Toledo and Cincinnati, Des Moines and Minneapolis, they knew through their own bodies, measured in hunger and discomfort in the '30s and '40s when they would stop at remote places to buy land and borrow money, sensing in themselves the hunger that would one day be upon the place. People were wary and Howard had trouble borrowing (her $100,000 had perhaps been the key) but invariably he was right. Howard knew the land, Mildred thought, the way the Indians must have known it. There were even spots along the way where the earth itself seemed to make men stop. Howard had a sixth sense that would sometimes lead them from the main roads to, say, a dark green field in Iowa or Kansas. Howard, who might have seemed asleep, would rap with his knuckles on the Plexiglas, causing the knowing Otis to bring the car to such a quick stop that Milly almost flew into her filing cabinet. And before the emergency brake had settled into its final prong, Howard Johnson was into the field and after the scent. While Milly and Otis waited, he would walk it out slowly. Sometimes he would sit down, disappearing in a field of long and tangled weeds, or he might find a large smooth rock to sit on while he felt some secret vibration from the place. Turning his back on Milly, he would mark the spot with his urine or break some of the clayey earth in his strong pink hands, sifting it like flour for a delicate recipe. She had actually seen him chew the grass, getting down on all fours like an animal and biting the tops without pulling the entire blade from the soil. At times he ran in a slow jog as far as his aging legs would carry him. Whenever he slipped out of sight behind the uneven terrain, Milly felt him in danger, felt that something alien might be there to resist the civilizing instinct of Howard Johnson. Once when Howard had been out of sight for more than an hour and did not respond to their frantic calls, Milly sent Otis into the field and in desperation flagged a passing car.

"Howard Johnson is lost in that field," she told the surprised driver. "He went in to look for a new location and we can't find him now."

"The restaurant Howard Johnson?" the man asked.

"Yes. Help us please."

The man drove off, leaving Milly to taste in his exhaust fumes the barbarism of an ungrateful public. Otis found Howard asleep in a field of light-blue wild flowers. He had collapsed from the exertion of his run. Milly brought water to him, and when he felt better, right there in the field, he ate his scoop of vanilla on the very spot where three years later they opened the first fully air-conditioned motel in the world. When she stopped to think about it, Milly knew they were more than businessmen, they were pioneers.

And once, on her own, she had had the feeling too. In 1954 when she visited the Holy Land there was an inkling of what Howard must have felt all the time. It happened without any warning on a bus crowded with tourists and resident Arabs on their way to the Dead Sea. Past ancient Sodom the bus creaked and bumped, down, down, toward the lowest point on earth, when suddenly in the midst of the crowd and her stomach queasy with the motion of the bus, Mildred Bryce experienced an overwhelming calm. A light-brown patch of earth surrounded by a few pale desert rocks overwhelmed her perception, seemed closer to her than the Arab lady in the black flowered dress pushing her basket against Milly at that very moment. She wanted to stop the bus. Had she been near the door she might have actually jumped, so strong was her sensitivity to that barren spot in the endless desert. Her whole body ached for it as if in unison, bone by bone. Her limbs tingled, her breath came in short gasps, the sky rolled out of the bus window and obliterated her view. The Arab lady spat on the floor and moved a suspicious eye over a squirming Mildred.

When the bus stopped at the Dead Sea, the Arabs and tourists rushed to the soupy brine clutching damaged limbs, while Milly pressed twenty dollars American into the dirty palm of a cabdriver who took her back to the very place where the music of her body began once more as sweetly as the first time. While the incredulous driver waited, Milly walked about the place wishing Howard were there to understand her new understanding of his kind of process. There was nothing there, absolutely nothing but pure bliss. The sun beat her like a wish, the air was hot and stale as a Viennese bathhouse, and yet Mildred felt peace and rest there, and as her cab bill mounted she actually did rest in the miserable barren desert of an altogether unsatisfactory land. When the driver, wiping the sweat from his neck, asked, "Meesez . . . pleeze. Why American woman wants Old Jericho in such kind of heat?" When he said

"Jericho," she understood that this was a place where men had always stopped. In dim antiquity Jacob had perhaps watered a flock here, and not far away Lot's wife paused to scan for the last time the city of her youth. Perhaps Mildred now stood where Abraham had been visited by a vision and, making a rock his pillow, had first put the ease into the earth. Whatever it was, Milly knew from her own experience that rest was created here by historical precedent. She tried to buy that piece of land, going as far as King Hussein's secretary of the interior. She imagined a Palestinian HJ with an orange roof angling toward Sodom, a seafood restaurant, and an oasis of fresh fruit. But the land was in dispute between Israel and Jordan, and even King Hussein, who expressed admiration for Howard Johnson, could not sell to Milly the place of her comfort.

That was her single visionary moment, but sharing his moments with Howard was almost as good. And to end all this, to finally stay in her eighteenth-floor Santa Monica penthouse, where the Pacific dived into California, this seemed to Mildred a paltry conclusion to an adventurous life. Her doctor said it was not so serious, she had a bleeding ulcer and must watch her diet. The prognosis was, in fact, excellent. But Mildred, sixty-one and alone in California, found the doctor less comforting than most of the rest stops she had experienced.

California, right after the Second War, was hardly a civilized place for travelers. Milly, HJ, and Otis had a twelve-cylinder '47 Packard and snaked along five days between Sacramento and Los Angeles. "Comfort, comfort," said HJ as he surveyed the redwood forest and the bubbly surf while it slipped away from Otis, who had rolled his trousers to chase the ocean away during a stop near San Francisco. Howard Johnson was contemplative in California. They had never been on the West Coast before. Their route, always slightly new, was yet bounded by Canada, where a person couldn't get a tax break, and roughly by the Grand Canyon as a western frontier. Most of their journeys took them up the eastern seaboard and through New England to the early reaches of the Midwest, stopping at the plains of Wisconsin and the cool crisp edge of Chicago where two HJ lodges twinkled at the lake.

One day in 1947 while on the way from Chicago to Cairo, Illinois, HJ looked long at the green relief maps. While Milly kept busy with her filing, HJ loosened the tape and placed the map across his soft round knees. The map jiggled and sagged, the Mid- and Southwest hanging between his legs. When Mildred finally noticed that look, he had been staring at the map for perhaps fifteen minutes, brooding over it, and Milly knew something was in the air.

HJ looked at that map the way some people looked down from an airplane trying to pick out the familiar from the colorful mass receding beneath them. Howard Johnson's eye flew over the land—over the Tetons, over the Sierra Nevada, over the long thin gouge of the Canyon flew his gaze—charting his course by rest stops the way an antique mariner might have gazed at the stars.

"Milly," he said just north of Carbondale, "Milly . . ." He looked toward her, saw her fingers engaged and her thumbs circling each other in anticipation. He looked at Milly and saw that she saw what he saw. "Milly"—HJ raised his right arm and its shadow spread across the continent like a prophecy— "Milly, what if we turn right at Cairo and go that way?" California, already peeling on the green map, balanced on HJ's left knee like a happy child.

Now, close to twenty years later, Mildred settled into her eighteenth-floor apartment in the building owned by Lawrence Welk. Howard was in New York, Otis and the car waited in Louisiana. The pain did not return as powerfully as it had appeared that night in Albuquerque, but it hurt with dull regularity and an occasional streak of dark blood from her bowels kept her mind on it even on painless days.

Directly beneath her gaze were the organized activities of the golden-age groups, tiny figures playing bridge or shuffleboard or looking out at the water from their benches as she sat on her sofa and looked out at them and the fluffy ocean. Mildred did not regret family life. The HJ houses were her offspring. She had watched them blossom from the rough youngsters of the '40s with steam heat and even occasional kitchenettes into cool mature adults with king-size beds, color TVs, and room service. Her late years were spent comfortably in the modern houses just as one might enjoy in age the benefits of a child's prosperity. She regretted only that it was probably over.

But she did not give up completely until she received a personal letter one day telling her that she was eligible for burial insurance until age eighty. A $1000 policy would guarantee a complete and dignified service. Milly crumpled the advertisement, but a few hours later called her Los Angeles lawyer. As she suspected, there were no plans, but as the executor of the estate he would assume full responsibility, subject of course to her approval.

"I'll do it myself," Milly had said, but she could not bring herself to do it. The idea was too alien. In more than forty years Mildred had not gone a day without a shower and change of underclothing. Everything about her suggested order and precision. Her fingernails were shaped so that the soft meat of the tips could stroke a typewriter without damaging the apex of a nail, her arch slid over a 6B shoe like an egg in a shell, and never in her adult life did Mildred recall having vomited. It did not seem right to suddenly let all this sink into the dark earth of Forest Lawn because some organ or another developed a hole as big as a nickel. It was not right and she wouldn't do it. Her first idea was to stay in the apartment, to write it into the lease if necessary. She had the lawyer make an appointment for her with Mr. Welk's management firm, but canceled it the day before. "They will just think I'm crazy," she said aloud to herself, "and they'll bury me anyway."

She thought of cryonics while reading a biography of William Chesebrough, the man who invented petroleum jelly. Howard had known him and often mentioned that his own daily ritual of the scoop of vanilla was like old Chesebrough's two teaspoons of Vaseline every day. Chesebrough lived to be ninety. In the biography it said that after taking the daily dose of Vaseline, he drank three cups of green tea to melt everything down, rested for twelve minutes, and then felt fit as a young man, even in his late eighties. When he died, she read, they froze his body—and Milly had her idea. The Vaseline people kept him in a secret laboratory somewhere near Cleveland and claimed he was in better condition than Lenin, whom the Russians kept hermetically sealed, but at room temperature.

In the phone book she found the Los Angeles Cryonic Society and asked it to send her information. It all seemed very clean. The cost was $200 a year for maintaining the cold. She sent the pamphlet to her lawyer to be sure that the society was legitimate. It wasn't much money, but, still, if they were charlatans, she didn't want them to take advantage of her even if she would never know about it. They were aboveboard, the lawyer said. "The interest on a ten-thousand-dollar trust fund would pay about five hundred a year," the lawyer said, "and they only charge two hundred dollars. Still, who knows what the cost might be in say two hundred years?" To be extra safe, they put $25,000 in trust for eternal maintenance, to be eternally overseen by Longstreet, Williams, and their eternal heirs. When it was arranged, Mildred felt better than she had in weeks.

Five months to the day after she had left Howard at the Los Angeles International Airport, he returned for Mildred without the slightest warning. She was in her housecoat and had not even washed the night cream from her cheeks when she saw through the viewing space in her door the familiar long pink jowls, even longer in the distorted glass.

"Howard," she gasped, fumbling with the door, and in an

instant he was there picking her up as he might a child or an ice-cream cone while her tears fell like dandruff on his blue suit. While Milly sobbed into his soft padded shoulder, HJ told her the good news. "I'm chairman emeritus of the board now. That means no more New York responsibilities. They still have to listen to me because we hold the majority of the stock, but Corky and Dibble will take care of the business. Our main job is new homeowned franchises. And, Milly, guess where we're going first?"

So overcome was Mildred that she could not hold back her sobs even to guess. Howard Johnson put her down, beaming pleasure through his old bright eyes. "Florida," HJ said, then slowly repeated it, "Flor-idda, and guess what we're going to do?"

"Howard," Milly said, swiping at her tears with the filmy lace cuffs of her dressing gown, "I'm so surprised I don't know what to say. You could tell me we're going to the moon and I'd believe you. Just seeing you again has brought back all my hope." They came out of the hallway and sat on the sofa that looked out over the Pacific. HJ, all pink, kept his hands on his knees like paperweights.

"Milly, you're almost right. I can't fool you about anything and never could. We're going down near where they launch the rockets from. I've heard . . ." HJ leaned toward the kitchen as if to check for spies. He looked at the stainless-steel-and-glass table, at the built-in avocado appliances, then leaned his large moist lips toward Mildred's ear. "Walt Disney is planning right this minute a new Disneyland down there. They're trying to keep it a secret, but his brother Will bought options on thousands of acres. We're going down to buy as much as we can as close in as we can." Howard sparkled. "Milly, don't you see, it's a sure thing."

After her emotional outburst at seeing Howard again, a calmer Milly felt a slight twitch in her upper stomach and in the midst of her joy was reminded of another sure thing.

They would be a few weeks in Los Angeles anyway. Howard wanted to thoroughly scout out the existing Disneyland, so Milly had some time to think it over. She could go with HJ, as her heart directed her, to Florida and points beyond. She could take the future as it happened like a Disneyland ride or she could listen to the dismal eloquence of her ulcer and try to make the best arrangements she could. Howard and Otis would take care of her to the end, there were no doubts about that, and the end would be the end. But if she stayed in this apartment, sure of the arrangements for later, she would miss whatever might still be left before the end. Mildred wished there were some clergyman she could consult, but she had never attended a church and believed in no religious doctrine. Her father had been a firm atheist to the very moment of his office suicide, and she remained a passive nonbeliever. Her sole belief was in the order of her own life. Milly had never deceived herself; in spite of her riches all she truly owned was her life, a pocket of habits in a burning universe. But the habits were careful and clean and they were best represented in the body that was she. Freezing her remains was the closest image she could conjure of eternal life. It might not be eternal and it surely would not be life, but that damp, musty feel, that odor she smelled on herself after the pain—that could be avoided, and who knew what else might be saved from the void for a small initial investment and $200 a year? And if you did not believe in the soul, was there not every reason to preserve a body?

Mrs. Albert of the Cryonic Society welcomed Mildred to a tour of the premises. "See it while you can," she cheerfully told the group (Milly, two men, and a boy with notebook and Polaroid camera). Mrs. Albert, a big woman in her mid-sixties, carried a face heavy in flesh. Perhaps once the skin had been tight around her long chin and pointed cheekbones, but having lost its spring, the skin merely hung at her neck like a patient animal waiting for the rest of her to join in the decline. From the way she took the concrete stairs down to the vault, it looked as if the wait would be long. "I'm not ready for the freezer yet. I tell every group I take down here, it's gonna be a long time until they get me." Milly believed her. "I may not be the world's smartest cookie"—Mrs. Albert looked directly at Milly—"but a bird in the hand is the only bird I know, huh? That's why when it does come . . . Mrs. A. is going to be right here in this facility, and you better believe it. Now, Mr. King on your left"—she pointed to a capsule that looked like a large bullet to Milly—"Mr. King is the gentleman who took me on my first tour, cancer finally but had everything perfectly ready and I would say he was in prime cooling state within seconds and I believe that if they ever cure cancer, and you know they will the way they do most everything nowadays, old Mr. King may be back yet. If anyone got down to low-enough temperature immediately it would be Mr. King." Mildred saw the boy write "Return of the King" in his notebook. "Over here is Mr. and Mizz Winkleman, married sixty years, and went off within a month of each other, a lovely, lovely couple."

While Mrs. Albert continued her necrology and posed for a photo beside the Winklemans, Milly took careful note of the neon-lit room filled with bulletlike capsules. She watched the cool breaths of the group gather like flowers on the steel and vanish without dimming the bright surface. The capsules stood in straight lines with ample walking space between them. To Mrs. Albert they were friends, to Milly it seemed as if she were in a furniture store of the Scandinavian type where elegance is suggested by the absence of material, where straight lines of steel, wood and glass indicate that relaxation too requires some taste and is not an indifferent sprawl across any soft object that happens to be nearby.

Cemeteries had always bothered Milly, but here she felt none of the dread she had expected. She had averted her eyes from the cluttered graveyards they used to pass at the edges of cities in the early days. Fortunately, the superhighways twisted traffic into the city and away from those desolate marking places where used-car lots and the names of famous hotels inscribed on barns often neighbored the dead. Howard had once commented that never in all his experience did he have an intuition of a good location near a cemetery. You could put a lot of things there, you could put up a bowling alley, or maybe even a theater, but never a motel, and Milly knew he was right.

Howard Johnson knew where to put his houses but it was Milly who knew how. From that first orange roof angling toward the east, the HJ design and the idea had been Milly's. She had not invented the motel, she had changed it from a place where you had to be to a place where you wanted to be. Perhaps, she thought, the Cryonic Society was trying to do the same for cemeteries.

When she and Howard had started their travels, the old motel courts huddled like so many dark graves around the stone marking of the highway. And what traveler coming into one of those dingy cabins could watch the watery rust dripping from his faucet without thinking of everything he was missing by being a traveler . . . his two-stall garage, his wife small in the half-empty bed, his children with hair the color of that rust. Under the orange Howard Johnson roof all this changed. For about the same price you were redeemed from the road. Headlights did not dazzle you on the foam mattress and percale sheets, your sanitized glasses and toilet appliances sparkled like the mirror behind them. The room was not just there, it awaited you, courted your pleasure, sat like a young bride outside the walls of the city wanting only to please you, you, only you, on the smoothly pressed sheets, your friend, your one-night destiny.

As if it were yesterday, Milly recalled right there in the cryonic vault the moment when she first thought the thought that made Howard Johnson Howard Johnson's. And when she told Howard her decision that evening after cooking a cheese soufflé and risking a taste of wine, it was that memory she invoked for both of them, the memory of a cool autumn day in the '30s when a break in their schedule found Milly with a free afternoon in New Hampshire, an afternoon she had spent at the farm of a man who had once been her teacher and remembered her after ten years. Otis drove her out to Robert Frost's farm, where the poet made for her a lunch of scrambled eggs and 7-Up. Milly and Robert Frost talked mostly about the farm, about the cold winter he was expecting and the autumn apples they picked from the trees. He was not so famous then, his hair was only streaked with gray as Howard's was, and she told the poet about what she and Howard were doing, about what she felt about being on the road in America, and Robert Frost said he hadn't been that much but she sounded like she knew and he believed she might be able to accomplish something. He did not remember the poem she wrote in his class but that didn't matter.

"Do you remember, Howard, how I introduced you to him? Mr. Frost, this is Mr. Johnson. I can still see the two of you shaking hands there beside the car. I've always been proud that I introduced you to one another." Howard Johnson nodded his head at the memory, and seemed as nostalgic as Milly while he sat in her apartment learning why she would not go to Florida to help bring Howard Johnson's to the new Disneyland.

"And after we left his farm, Howard, remember? Otis took the car in for servicing and left us with some kind of sandwiches on the top of a hill overlooking a town, I don't even remember which one, maybe we never knew the name of it. And we stayed on that hilltop while the sun began to set in New Hampshire. I felt so full of poetry and"—she looked at Howard—"of love, Howard, only about an hour's drive from Robert Frost's farmhouse. Maybe it was just the way we felt then, but I think the sun set differently that night, filtering through the clouds like a big paintbrush making the top of the town all orange. And suddenly I thought what if the tops of our houses were that kind of orange, what a world it would be, Howard, and my God, that orange stayed until the last drop of light was left in it. I didn't feel the cold up there even though it took Otis so long to get back to us. The feeling we had about that orange, Howard, that was ours and that's what I've tried to bring to every house, the way we felt that night. Oh, it makes me sick to think of Colonel Sanders, and Big Boy, and Holiday Inn, and Best Western . . ."

"It's all right, Milly, it's all right." Howard patted her heaving back. Now that he knew about her ulcer and why she wanted to stay behind, the mind that had conjured up butterfly shrimp and twenty-eight flavors set himself a new project. He contemplated Milly sobbing in his lap the way he contemplated prime acreage. There was so little of her, less than one hundred pounds, yet without her Howard Johnson felt himself no match for the wily Disneys gathering near the moonport.

He left her in all her sad resignation that evening, left her thinking she had to give up what remained here to be sure of the proper freezing. But Howard Johnson had other ideas. He did not cancel the advance reservations made for Mildred Bryce along the route to Florida, nor did he remove her filing cabinet from the limousine. The man who hosted a nation and already kept one freezer in his car merely ordered another, this one designed according to cryonic specifications. He presented it to Mildred housed in a custom-built twelve-foot trailer, as orange as a U-Haul and already connected to the rear bumper of the limousine.

"Everything's here," he told the astonished Milly, who thought Howard had left the week before, "everything is here and you'll never have to be more than seconds away from it. It's exactly like a refrigerated truck." Howard Johnson opened the rear door of the trailer as proudly as he had ever dedicated a motel. Milly's steel capsule shone within, surrounded by an array of chemicals stored on heavily padded rubber shelves. The California sun was on her back, but her cold breath hovered visibly within the trailer. No tears came to Mildred now; she felt relief much as she had felt it that afternoon near ancient Jericho. On Santa Monica Boulevard, in front of Lawrence Welk's apartment building, Mildred Bryce confronted her immortality, a gift from the ice-cream king, another companion for the remainder of her travels. Howard Johnson had turned away, looking toward the ocean. To his blue back and patriarchal white hairs, Mildred said, "Howard, you can do anything," and closing the doors of the trailer, she joined the host of the highways, a man with two portable freezers, ready now for the challenge of the Disneys.

# CHAPTER TWO

*A*s he traveled across the desert, Mr. Johnson took long naps. After lunch in Palm Springs, only two and a half hours out of Los Angeles, he put his head against the small down pillow that Otis kept on the front seat and handed to Mr. Johnson after each meal. Otis kept Mildred's pillow up front too, a firmer all-feather pillow that lay beside Mr. Johnson's on the front passenger seat, but in the desert, Mildred usually preferred to think rather than sleep. Sometimes, though, she would doze, or half doze, while Mr. Johnson was asleep. The back seat was certainly large enough for two naps, and Mr. Johnson in all his years of travel had never once asked to put his feet up and displace his companion to the front seat. He merely leaned his head sideways, dreaming while still awake, and within minutes fell into a strong silent sleep. His body seemed to regulate itself by population density rather than by the relation of the earth to the sun. He would sleep across Utah, take catnaps in Illinois. But this time he stayed in deep slumber even at the outskirts of Phoenix, within sight of two of his houses.

"He's saving up for something big," Otis whispered, "I can feel it."

Mildred told Otis to skip dinner in Phoenix and drive on. Mr. Johnson's slumber, as Otis recognized, was a sure sign of something powerful on the horizon. Mildred recalled a week in 1948 when she and Otis thought Mr. Johnson had been bitten by a tsetse fly. He slept almost continually for four days. They could awaken him only for one meal in the evening. As he ate, Mr. Johnson said he felt fine, and assured Milly and Otis that there was no problem. Then in the car, or in the motel room, without any sign of being tired HJ lapsed into such a deep slumber that Otis had to help him undress at night and during the day had to hold him under the shoulders at highway rest stops.

"I'm fine," Mr. Johnson would say, then he would smile and doze off again. He slept from St. Louis to Portland, Oregon, and then quite suddenly, when Milly and Otis had decided that surely in Seattle, their next stop on the way to Vancouver, British Columbia, they would take Mr. Johnson to a hospital, HJ awoke, refreshed and energetic. In the dreary, overcast Pacific Northwest, his vigor returned. Howard Johnson asked Otis to stop the car as they crossed the Columbia River into Washington. At the border, Mr. Johnson walked down the steep incline where a salmon fisherman in hip boots stood on the muddy banks. Mr. Johnson's wing-tip shoes and his blue trousers sank into the mud almost all the way up to his knees as he made his way into the clean waters of the Columbia. Mildred and Otis waited and watched from the small unpaved parking lot near the historical marker that signaled the end of the Lewis and Clark trail.

Otis shook his head from side to side in wonder. Mildred watched her companion and partner as he spoke to the fisherman. Howard Johnson was in his mid-fifties at that time, his hair was already gray, but he had not yet developed his stoop. From where she and Otis stood, several hundred yards above Mr. Johnson, Mildred could not see his face or hear his words. The waters of the Columbia River roared and in the background there was the hum of traffic moving across the wide bridge. Mr. Johnson removed his tie and loosened his shirt collar. He removed his wallet from the breast pocket of his blue suit coat, put it into his trouser pocket, then offered the jacket to the fisherman as if in trade for a pole. Mildred and Otis had never known Mr. Johnson to be a fisherman. Yet he expertly cast the borrowed line into the tight hard current of the river. Within minutes, Mr. Johnson had a bite. As the fisherman whose pole he had borrowed raised a net to help, Mr. Johnson easily brought up a three-pound Columbia sockeye salmon. After the fisherman removed the hook from the salmon's jaw, Mr. Johnson held the squirming fish in front of his face for a few seconds, then placed it into the fisherman's catch bag. The host of the highways rinsed his hands in the Columbia, then he bent at the waist in a solemn Japanese-ceremonial-style bow as if addressing the river, or asking permission. He placed his face completely under water. He dipped his arms in up to the elbow. He rubbed cool water into the small of his back, then took a breath and did a deep knee bend to completely submerge himself. The fisherman, alarmed, reached into the water to help, but Mr. Johnson's form in a few seconds arose easily from the face of the water, and shook itself. Three times Mr. Johnson submerged, to the alarm of the fisherman, who apparently was trying to discourage Mr. Johnson each time, fearing that the genial man was perhaps suicidal. On each immersion Milly and Otis, waiting at the historical marker, held their breath along with Mr. Johnson's. When he went under for the third time, the fisherman dropped his pole onto the surface of the water and went down to help. In a few seconds the two arose, laughing, their hands touching under the water. The Columbia carried away the Shakespeare pole, and the freshly caught salmon, and Mr. Johnson's suit coat. The fisherman accompanied Mr. Johnson up the steep embankment to the car park where Mildred and Otis awaited him.

"This is Mr. Strawn," HJ said. "I am indebted to him for the use of his fishing gear and for his interest in my well-being." From the cash box in the glove compartment HJ withdrew ninety dollars to reimburse Mr. Strawn for his equipment. He also took down Mr. Strawn's name and address. Before that year was out, John Strawn, now their old and dear friend, became the buyer of fresh fish for the HJ restaurants. Strawn never left his home in Portland, but he became, anonymously, the man behind the choicest fantail shrimp, and the originator of the all-you-can-eat fish fry which spread throughout the land and was so thoroughly and quickly imitated that when the Korean War began, the U. S. Army altered its menu to include, for the first time, a weekly fried fish. At Mr. Strawn's advice, the quartermaster, whenever possible, purchased the catch fresh from the South China Sea.

The four days in deep slumber before the awakening at the banks of the Columbia were in Mildred's mind as Mr. Johnson slept across Arizona. In the day after he caught that Columbia River salmon, HJ could not think of sleep. He wired New York to arrange an emergency board meeting within seven days. The three of them drove straight across the northern route, over the Grand Tetons, through the Bonner Pass, over the northern river of the Grand Canyon. There were none of their characteristic side trips, no searching out the landscape. During the speedy trip across the country, Mr. Johnson preferred not to be read to by Mildred as was their daily custom, nor to be engaged in any genial conversation. He was awake and wholly taken with an idea. At that crucial meeting his restaurants not only added fish, but the houses in one swoop installed swimming pools.

"How could we have forgotten water?" Mr. Johnson later wondered. "That should have come first, even before food and shelter." He felt ashamed of his oversight.

"We did offer water," Mildred reminded him. "Tubs, and free-standing showers, and a full array of beverages."

"But the pool, Mildred, it's the first luxury of the traveler. To sit down beside running water, to hear the murmur of the stream. I should not have forgotten that."

There was no opposition to Mr. Johnson's dream of pools or fish, but that was 1948, when HJ and Mildred still controlled 70 percent of their corporation, when there were no other motel pools anywhere in the country, nor were there Holiday Inns, or Disneylands, or resurgent downtowns cluttered with

Hyatts and Marriotts. The country itself was awakening from a long slumber, and Howard Johnson was there, waiting, in the evening and at breakfast. HJ felt the motions and the needs of travelers, and he translated his feelings into buildings and watering places.

Now, his vision had become a large public corporation, she and Howard were old, and people had forgotten that the all-you-can-eat clams, the twenty-eight flavors, the swimming pools were not given; they were created over a long career. They were the fruits of Howard's labor, and hers, and now that they were so full of years Mildred wondered what new awakening she and Otis might witness when, at the end of the desert, Mr. Johnson would surely arise, rub the sleep out of his eyes and scan the landscape before him and within him.

It was the habit of Otis Brighton to hum melodiously from time to time. The limousine was equipped with a radio which they used when they wanted reports on threatening weather, or when the news of the day held some particular interest, but by an easy mutual agreement reached early in their travels, they had decided to honor the necessary silence of Mr. Johnson's work.

Still, when Mr. Johnson dozed or Mildred read to him, or when the desire for slumber began to overtake him too, Otis Brighton livened up the car, and himself, with humming. He hummed because he was a hummer, not because Mildred or Mr. Johnson asked him to hum rather than sing. Had he been a singer, he would have sung out in the car. He had grown up humming alongside his harmonica-playing daddy in Tilton, Louisiana. His daddy played a bluesy harmonica as wet and spooky as the bayous around Tilton. Otis accompanied that hot sound with a dry intense contrapuntal hum. The neighbors and relatives thought the Brightons, father and son, were good enough to audition for the American Amateur Hour and prevailed upon the senior Otis Brighton to take his son and his harmonica up to New Orleans in April of 1927, when the NBC radio program was holding area-wide auditions for their national talent show.

Otis was twenty-two years old then and had never been to New Orleans. He and his father, mother, brothers and sister sharecropped a rice field owned by the LaToulette family of Tilton, the very family that had once owned Otis's great-grandfather and after some years of decline had reemerged with the ownership of its ancestral lands.

Only rice grew around Tilton. It was too wet for peanuts or soy. At least once a year the bayou flooded the fields, and the Brightons' cottage. A few feet of water did not harm the thirsty crop but it kept the family and their neighbors from acquiring immovable property or even the desire to possess items that couldn't easily be stored in a pocket. Otis and Violet Brighton and their two sons and one daughter moved to higher ground when the fall rain started, they moved to the cabin of their cousins in Winthrop to wait out the flood, and it was those cousins who insisted, after hearing the two Otises year after year during the high water, that this father and son ought to be on the radio. After a lot of coaxing, especially from Violet's cousin, Mary Muirhead, Otis Sr. and Otis Jr. took the bus to New Orleans for the first time in young Otis's life, and for the first time since the end-of-the-war parade for Otis Sr.

Not ten miles out of Tilton the bus came to a sudden stop. Howard Johnson and Mildred, with the front end of their Model T in an L-shaped ditch to the right of the highway, had waved down the bus.

The angry bus driver refused to help. "We've got a schedule to keep," he said, "and I'm already behind. If I stopped to help every fool who drove into a ditch we'd get to New Orleans on Thursday."

Although the Otises were at the back of the bus, and could barely hear the driver, it was not their custom to deny help to those in need.

"I'll take you to New Orleans if you've got the fare," the

driver said, "and that's it. Hop on, I ain't got all day."

"We have to be in Beaumont, Texas, by nightfall," HJ said, "or we'll lose an important land option. I would be forever obliged for any help you could offer."

Without a word spoken between them, the two Otises stepped off the New Orleans bus.

"I'm not gonna wait," the driver said, "and you two won't get your ticket money back neither." The doors hissed shut. The American Amateur Hour never heard the sweet mournful hum of Otis or his father's wet harmonica.

But Howard Johnson and Mildred, nervously carrying $4,-700 in cash for a man who wouldn't take a check, arrived in Beaumont in the nick of time to purchase the site of their first property west of the Mississippi. After that, Otis Jr. traveled with them and avoided the ditches that stood in their path.

Mr. Johnson never forgot a good deed. By 1937, the Brighton family owned the big LaToulette house and the rice fields around it. Otis Jr. sent his pay home accompanied by a very grand yearly bonus. And almost every year, HJ and Milly, with Otis at the wheel, visited the Brightons, often going hundreds of miles out of their way in order to pay their respects to Otis's family and to commemorate the good deed that had been done for HJ and Mildred in a time of necessity.

Otis Brighton never regretted getting off that bus to help a stranger pull his car out of a ditch. He had become a far richer man than any musician could hope to be. Otis, too, owned thousands of shares of the Howard Johnson Company but when he hummed in his still powerful basso profundo there was the deep melancholy of thirty-seven years on the road. He had married in 1930 and was the father of two grown children, though he had not seen them grow up. A month each summer, a few weeks at Christmas—Otis only had glimpses of his two sons. His wife was someone he knew less well than Milly and HJ. But it was almost over now. In Tilton, just the other side of Texas, Otis Brighton would hand over the keys to his nephew, Mel Briggs. The retirement had been arranged months before. At 59, Otis decided he had had enough. Come what may, the other side of Texas was, to Otis, the other side of Jordan, his promised land.

On the second full day of Mr. Johnson's sleep, just east of El Paso, Otis Brighton began to hum as he had not hummed in years. First, he hummed happy. He hummed "Sunshine," and "Camptown Races," and "Mocking Bird," and "Elbows." Then his humming turned inexplicably sad. He hummed "Old Black Joe," and "Days in the Delta." He hummed "Troubles," and as the desert began to pass away under the wheels of the Cadillac and Mr. Johnson made the sounds of awakening in the back seat, Otis hummed "Killing Floor" and then fell silent.

# CHAPTER THREE

*A*fter Howard Johnson's recognition of the pool and the fish, road travel entered a generation of consolidating Mr. Johnson's insights."

Mildred crossed the lines out though she knew them to be true. As they moved across Texas she tried to concentrate on finishing the next issue of her monthly "Howard Johnson Report," the newsletter that the corporation mailed to all employees and to travel agencies and travel journalists. She had been writing that newsletter each month for twenty-two years; it was a kind of genial postcard to the HJ family, an almost personal hello to the managers and clerks and maids and waiters whom they met on their continual journeys across the country. Milly used to write individually to so many employees that she finally decided to unite the effort in the "Howard Johnson Report."

Howard never liked her to write much about himself. She knew he would object to the statement regarding his insights. Sometimes, when they traveled, Howard still insisted on taking a room under a fictitious name. Mildred always identified herself as an employee of the HJ corporation; after all, they were not spies, just friendly owners, like parents, she thought, looking after offspring that had sprung and multiplied throughout forty-seven states. But Mr. Johnson, understandably, preferred not to be asked if he was *the* Howard Johnson. Now and then, when his identity became known, waiters asked him to autograph menus. Once, in Oklahoma City, a guest, learning that

Howard Johnson was actually staying down the hall, brought her pillowcase to him for a signature.

Mr. Johnson stood in a narrow corridor, caught between his desire to please a customer and his equally strong desire to deter theft of corporate property. He graciously offered to sign her nightgown or luggage instead. After that incident, Mr. Johnson began registering in HJ houses under the name Ernest Goodman, Colorado Springs. Mildred paid the bills for the three of them with her personal credit card or check. For a time she had been the treasurer of the HJ corporation, its first treasurer, but that was a job she gladly gave up since it would have confined her to New York.

Mildred understood the truth and historical accuracy of the sentence she had crossed out. By 1950 most of the pioneering work was over, the rest was expansion, consolidation, and the accumulation of ever more valuable shares of stock and a company increasingly run by Corky and the Board of Directors in New York. With the first public sale of shares in 1951, HJ stopped being the owner and became merely another shareholder. He still owned 11 percent of the corporation, but it was a far cry from the total control he and Milly enjoyed during the exciting years. Then he and Milly and Otis had been the Board of Directors, convening daily in the car, deciding over lunch or during a dull stretch of road whether to include Nebraska or Mr. Johnson's favorite out-of-the-way place, the Black Hills of South Dakota.

Feeling comfortable now, without her pain, and reassured enough by daily health, Mildred decided to pay no more attention to the orange trailer than to a spare tire. Milly tried to focus once more on the corporate future.

Howard had been murmuring about the Disneys for months, but because of her pain and her worry in Los Angeles, Milly had been detached, even unconcerned, about Howard's plans. While she struggled with the dilemma of her pain, Mr. Johnson and Otis had gone daily to Disneyland. They circled the periphery the first morning like shoppers seeking a parking place. Mr. Johnson noted the circumference of the park and its driving distance from the freeway ramps. He counted the number of city stoplights between the road and the amusement center. He concerned himself with the midday heat, and noticed with surprise that none of the parkgoers carried a sack lunch.

The black limousine, slowly circling but never parking, called attention to itself. It was exactly the kind of problem that Mildred would have foreseen and warned against. Disney security police stopped the car. Mr. Johnson and Otis had to disembark, then prove ownership of the vehicle and identify themselves.

"We are tourists," Mr. Johnson said.

"I suppose you are looking for a parking place," the policeman asked Otis.

"Yes, sir," Otis replied, amused that after all his years of driving he was pulled over for the first time while going eight miles an hour around Disneyland.

"You might have noticed," the policeman said, "there are about fourteen thousand vacant parking places on the lot. Any reason why you're not heading for one of them?"

"We are trying to get a general sense of the traffic flow before we park," Howard Johnson told the smirking officers. "Mr. Brighton was circling at my direction. I was not aware that we were violating any traffic ordinances."

"You're not," the officer said, "but you sure look suspicious crawling around here over and over. If you didn't have such an expensive car, I'd guess you were looking to avoid the parking fee. But that don't make sense, I guess . . . who knows . . . anyway, you boys decide, in or out. This is all private land, you know."

"Even the thoroughfares?" Mr. Johnson asked.

"Yep. The corporation owns this whole part of town, streets, sidewalks, everything. You're in Walt Disney country right down to your security force. We pay attention to the small things. We noticed you right away. Nobody circles Disneyland eight times without parking. When I called the chief, we thought you were a carload of Arab women. That's happened before. They'll come in a limo and wait while the men go to the park, but they pay the parking fee and wait on the lot. It's happened a few times. They caused a ruckus one time when they sent their servants out to make coffee—they tried to start fires right on the asphalt. We've got instructions now to just bring out a big stainless steel urn, some Styrofoam cups, and just leave them alone. That's why we pulled you over, really. We thought we'd have to phone in for coffee."

"No need," Howard Johnson said, "but we appreciate your interest."

"You either park it or move it," the officer said.

Otis followed the police car to a spot near the trolley pickup point.

"Arab women," Otis said, laughing until tears came to his eyes. "Wait until Miss Milly hears about that."

Mr. Johnson was not amused. Disneyland made him gloomy.

After purchasing admission, Mr. Johnson rented a golf cart and a teenage driver to carry him and Otis through the land. From his shaded perch he traveled from the Streets of Yesterday to the furthest edge of Tomorrowland, the point at which the Disney monorail intersected the undersea home of the eleven corporate submarines.

Howard Johnson sought comfort and amusement in Disneyland. He sought relaxation, he sought a good meal and a well-kept restroom. He sought in the faces of those who waited in line beside him some answer to the riddle of all this success. He sought shade. He sought a nice fresh ice-cream cone and a Coke with just a little bit of ice.

A young graduate of the Cornell Hotel Administration program showed Mr. Johnson through the central kitchen. Mr. Johnson introduced himself as a restaurateur from Cleveland interested in looking over the operation.

"You'll be surprised by the diversity," the proud young man

said. "We cover the territory from Tahiti Treats to Wild West barbeque. The difference is the sauce."

He showed Mr. Johnson an assembly line wherein hacked beef in paper trays crept along a conveyor belt to be squirted either dark red for Texas barbeque or light gray for Tahitian Treat.

"Eight thousand dinners a day," the young restaurant executive said, "and never more than a seven-minute wait once the patron is seated."

Mr. Johnson asked about the person of some appetite, the person who might prefer a wider selection.

"We've got pizza, of course," the Cornell man said, "and a straight-up burger. But we serve those at their own locations throughout Tomorrowland, Frontierland . . . everywhere. We think the people who choose the sit-down restaurant are either Barbeque or Tahitian Treat types and eight thousand times every day we're right."

Mr. Johnson seemed disoriented, Otis thought, as they continued their tour in the golf cart.

"Two meals," Mr. Johnson said to himself, "and we offer twenty-eight flavors of ice cream."

The driver of their tour cart played a prerecorded tape that gave Mr. Johnson and Otis colorful background information on the Magic Kingdom. They learned that there were eight hotels on the periphery of the land, a bus and taxi service in addition to the world's first monorail, and even a ferry boat to Santa Catalina.

Mr. Johnson stood in line for the Alpine Monster, though when it came his turn he ceded his place to a girl in pigtails. He kept a stopwatch in his pocket to surreptitiously time the wait, then he calculated the waiting time in relation to the duration of the ride. At the pirate-infested island and the submarine ride Mr. Johnson did the same, causing wonder and gratitude in those who took his place in the line, and no suspicion among the cheerful employees since he kept the watch either in his pocket or cupped in his large hands. Mr. Johnson calculated a four-minute pleasure for each thirty-minute wait in the warm sun: thus in a six-hour day, allowing a minimal one hour between sites and at least thirty minutes for food, the most dedicated thrill-seeker could hope to sample eight rides per four and one-half hours of patient endurance.

When he awoke near San Antonio, Texas, Mr. Johnson began thinking aloud to Mildred about his Disney experience. He was full of wonder at the patience of all those who stood so long in line.

"They were like pilgrims at Mecca," Mr. HJ said. "They kept their eyes on the end, they were gratified by small movements. They were kind to one another. I realized as I stood in their line, Mildred, that the Disneys understand the future as we once did. They think not of the single traveler but of the busload. For them the church or civic group has replaced the family. They have an animal notion of rest. It is not sleep they provide, it's merely lying low in the dark."

They were sixty miles from San Antonio, Texas, in the thirty-eighth year of their travels through the land. Otis was only a few days from retirement and behind their limousine they pulled a reminder of their frailty. But Howard Johnson spoke now of a new adventure as if he was a young man.

"I think we could take them, Mildred. I think our idea of comfort can go the week or longer. I think we can incorporate games and rides and satisfy the needs of a family. I think the Disneys have left out too much. I think we can move into vacations, Mildred. I think that's where we're headed."

Otis heard these words and hummed "Lightning."

Milly felt her stomach stir as if the pain might reappear with the next breath, but it did not.

Howard Johnson ran a hand slowly through the thin white hair, still carefully groomed even after his long sleep.

"I know it's not like anything we've done before, but I'm going to call New York at the next stop."

32

## CHAPTER FOUR

$C$orky did not take too seriously this idea for a Johnsonland, a nature-lover's park, an Audubon Society version of Disneyland where there were no mechanical rides, no waiting lines, only a large-scale game preserve dotted with small restaurants and lodges. The children could swing through trees on ropes, there would be a tree house for every lodge, and putt-putt cars for children to drive along yellow brick roads, a tiny steamboat to transport youngsters throughout the land. For mom and pop there would be saunas and natural pools beneath artificial waterfalls. There could be, Howard Johnson told the members of the board, a genuine vacation in the midst of a nature preserve.

For the past decade the board had endured rather than encouraged the traveling trio. Corky was unmoved as he listened to Howard describe a version of the Garden of Eden where children would ride on the backs of Tortuga Island turtles, where families would spend idle hours in lodges modeled upon Mayan or Egyptian splendor, where the spirit of the lost continent of Atlantis would replace Frontierland or the Seven Dwarves' Pub which had given Mr. Johnson a backache as he crouched for an orange juice cocktail.

"People don't need just a night off the road," Howard Johnson said. "They need the refreshment of a week, not just in another country, but in another world."

Corky had gone to the Wharton School of Finance. He understood the bottom line.

"HJ," he said, "when you come back we'll discuss all these plans and projections. You can't just jump into such a big capital outlay."

Mildred, in her close to forty years with Howard Johnson, had never before doubted his judgment on any matter of business. In the pioneering of matters like room-controlled air conditioning, king-size beds, and the enormously expensive color TV in each room, she had stood by Mr. Johnson in many a squabble among the executives in New York.

"Why the hell can't they all go to the lounge for color TV?" Keyes, a vice president, had said at a crucial board meeting. "Why can't they go where we can sell them a drink and then a meal too? Why put $500 plus upkeep into a gadget that will keep them in their rooms? Don't forget," he said, "that 24 percent of our revenue comes from nonroom charges."

Howard was magnificent that day. Corky and the other directors nodded in agreement as Keyes made his argument. Milly thought it would be only Howard and herself against the others until Howard Johnson arose in that boardroom. His voice was strong and the sun from the slightly open venetian blind cast an aura about him. The others, even Mildred, were surrounded by briefcases and papers. The table before Howard Johnson was as bare as the desert. He looked separately at each of the twelve directors.

"I want a color TV in each room," he said, then he paused and looked again at each director. Milly clasped her hands in suspense. "Because people have children." When he sat down the silence buzzed in the room. There were no other arguments. The vote was eight to four in favor of color.

In the San Antonio hotel room, Mildred saw the disappointment in Howard's face. She pretended to busy herself at the writing desk leafing through a tourist book on San Antonio nightlife, but it was apparent from the tone of Mr. Johnson's voice and the way he closed his eyes, as if summoning forth patience, that he wasn't going to have an easy time with the board.

Not that it had ever been easy. Nothing had been easy. The New York men always wanted a high return on their investment. Howard and Mildred placed profits further down on their scale of values; the confrontations were inevitable, and Howard and she did not win them all. They had lost on four o'clock tea for the restaurants and underground parking in the Southern states and most recently on water beds and shag carpeting. On the big issues they were always together, but this time Mildred averted her own eyes in the full-length mirror. This time she didn't know if she could support Howard.

A Howard Johnsonland did not appeal to her. On their map dotted with tiny orange successes there would have to be one monstrous orange blot. The proportions were all wrong. So was the product. What did she and Howard understand about entertaining people, especially children? She and Howard understood the rhythm of driving and resting; the Disneys must hear a different drummer, she thought.

For fear of another ulcer attack if she put it off, Milly confronted Howard with her objections that very evening. She knew that he was brooding about the telephone conversation but she decided not to wait.

"There is a difference," she told Howard, "between a trip and a vacation. Howard Johnson is the means, Walt Disney the end. You always said, Howard, that everyone has to stick with what they know best. The Disneys don't try to build motels beyond the range of their parks. They want vacationers. The travelers are ours, Howard, just as we, you and I, have always been theirs."

Howard entered her room from the balcony where he had been studying the horizon. He looked at Mildred and then at himself in the full-length mirror behind her. He sat down on the corner of the king-size bed. He sat gently, hardly disturbing the crisp polyester bedspread.

"I know what you're saying, Mildred. But what I have not told you is that I think I can understand their rhythm, too. All these years, Milly, we've known the day. What do you ask me each morning at 6:45 right after wake-up? 'Did you have a good night, Howard?' That's what you ask. And then you look at your calendar, Milly. Each day is a separate event. Do you know why we've built motels? Because we were tired, that's why. In all our travels, have we ever mentioned the word vacation? Yes, we've gone off separately a hundred times, but when we're together, when you and I are us, Howard Johnson, have we ever thought beyond the single day?"

Mildred realized that Howard was now talking about something similar to her own jarring experience with time during her recent illness. "Until I got sick, Howard, I never thought of more than the day, I admit that."

Howard Johnson rose from the corner of the king-size bed and held up his long slightly shaking fingers. "Seven, Milly, that's the big number for the 1980s, the 1990s and beyond. And after that it will be fourteen and twenty-one and twenty-eight. The day has been replaced like the county road. This is what's come to me in these last months. This is what I've been thinking about in California and in the desert. This is what I know in my bones."

"How odd," Milly said, "that Otis is retiring and that a few months ago we both thought it was almost over. Now here we are in virgin territory discussing something altogether new."

"Yes," HJ said, "something has bothered me for a long time, Mildred. I haven't enjoyed it like I used to, not the last few years. The high rises, the foreign franchises—those things, Milly, don't mean anything to me, you know that. This land could be a new start for us. We could stay down here and watch it go up just like we did with those early houses in Buffalo and

Erie." Mr. Johnson smiled at his reflection in the full-length mirror. "You know what I'd like to call, 'it'? 'Bryceland,' for you, Milly."

"Oh, Howard," she said, standing close to Mr. Johnson and full of admiration for him and regret that she would have to be less sympathetic to his new design than he had been to hers. She held Howard Johnson's hand as she led him on a slow walk through the moonless San Antonio night. Otis followed at fifty feet with the headlights on low beam. Getting Howard Johnson to change his mind was easiest when he walked. In a chair or in the back seat of the car she could never do it. Lately Howard had not been taking the walks they used to enjoy together. He confined his walking to the area around the front desk, the restaurant, and the cabana. He did not offer objections though, when Mildred led him into the humid Texas evening. Otis, in happy surprise, and knowing his role, walked quickly to the Cadillac. Although Howard Johnson's hand felt cold to Mildred, his eye was clear and alert. His pale shirt and smooth white hair lit up San Antonio. Mildred felt, as always, small and proud beside him. Even when he was wrong, he was still Howard Johnson.

After almost a block of silence Mildred began, "You are probably right about the week, Howard. We were young and in a hurry when all this started. Who could think about seven days anywhere? But you know something, Howard, I still can't. I'm ready now after six days to leave anyplace."

"Well, if it wasn't for Bryceland I'd be ready, too, but there's a reason to stay now. There will be for some time, once we pick the place."

"Yes, I know that, Howard, that's why I'm against it. If it starts we'll be settled all the time. Weeks, even months at a stretch. Otis will retire, the New York crowd will set up an office down here, all new capital spending will be concentrated in one place, there will be no point in looking for other spots."

37

Howard walked on in silence, holding her hand as lightly as ever. A group of boys approached them. As they came closer one of the boys, a redhead about as tall as Mildred, hit Howard Johnson in the face with a cold stream from his water pistol. Accompanied by wild screams, his friends opened up on Mildred. Otis put on the bright lights and gunned the engine, scattering them.

"You OK?" Otis asked as he toweled Howard Johnson's face. "Should I call the police?"

"We're all right, Otis," Mildred said; she was only slightly damp. Most of the spray had gone over her head to Howard's face and white shirt. Mr. Johnson shook his head no when Otis asked if they wanted to get into the car now.

"Mischief makers," Howard said, "won't stop us."

"They're the ones you'll have to please," Milly said as they continued, more wary now and with Otis almost directly behind. "Boys like these go on vacations to Disneyland. They are the kind who steal towels and carve their initials in the woodwork and drop whole rolls of tissue in the commode. Overnight they don't have the chance for major destruction. Their parents, up early, want them in the car and on the road. These are the people we'll have to entertain, Howard—not just make them comfortable, but give them something to do for seven days."

Howard Johnson was wet, but calm.

"Because of a single wanton act, Mildred, should I judge a whole generation?"

"No, Howard, don't judge them, but don't build for them either. Leave them to Dr. Spock and Dr. Seuss and baseball and gang wars."

"Do you mean," said a now solemn Howard Johnson, "do you mean leave them to the Disneys, Mildred?"

"I would have said it without these squirt gunners, but they have made the point better than I could. The Disneys know how to make people sit still for a long time—movies, cartoons, games, whatever it is. We know how to give people good food and good rest. A person can have good food and good rest for seven days and still not enjoy his vacation. I know this from experience, Howard. And the Disneyland children don't even want food and rest. They want to be frightened and amused." Milly took from her purse a newspaper article. "This was in the L.A. *Times* a few days ago. I bought it at a newsstand and have been saving this article for you. The headline is 'Sociologist Says Disneyland Similar to Nightmare." She put the article in the pocket of Howard's trousers. "You can read it later if you want to. The sociologist just says that the success of the rides and the strange creatures is the fear you have of the unusual at night. The Disneys have made a happy little nightmare. Making nightmares, Howard, even good ones, it's the opposite of what we've always tried to do."

"But what about the week, Mildred, and what about Nature which I want to make as restful as a motel?" Howard was biting his lower lip, a trait she had not seen since his anger in 1961 at officials of the Seattle World's Fair for failing to make HJ's peach, chocolate and vanilla the official ice creams of the Fair.

"The idea," Mildred said, "is one of the best you've ever had, but it's not a Howard Johnson concept. Do you think that someone like Einstein or Wernher von Braun never thought about a motel and restaurant chain? Think of Einstein making all those car trips between Princeton and Baltimore and Washington. He had a bad back, too, and was a light sleeper. With his name and reputation he could have raised the capital for a dozen houses just on his say-so. 'Einstein's Inn': wouldn't you give it a try, Howard? But if the idea came to him, as I'm sure it probably did, he just put it aside in favor of relativity. All I'm trying to say, Howard, is that man is limited. Especially limited are those blessed with a gift as singular as yours or Einstein's. Walt Disney has the gift, too. No matter what we think of their plans, Howard, we have to admit that Disney understands."

"Yes," Howard said, "he understands money and movement

and perhaps nightmares, too, but he doesn't understand Nature. Disneyland could have been built in Kansas and for what he's going to do here he doesn't need Florida or California. I've been thinking of Nature all through this trip, Mildred. I've thought of the games birds play and the pleasures of the jackrabbit. I've wondered about the turtle in his pond, the squirrel with a good supply of nuts and breadcrumbs; these are the things I have in mind. Walt Disney doesn't see Nature, Mildred. He sees the shadow of the revolving cocktail lounge and the waitress in the Mouseketeer hat. I would have instead a real rabbit hutch and an artificial Mayan ruin and a real Polynesian girl wearing a laurel wreath."

"It would be beautiful," Mildred said wistfully, "it would be like nothing else in the world. But still it wouldn't be Howard Johnson's. You must understand that, too, Howard. That's why you're thinking of calling it Bryceland. But even if we called it Bryceland, Howard, it wouldn't be mine, either. No matter how beautiful the week is, Mildred Bryce is content with the day. I will have them one at a time, Howard, or not at all. I want to tell you this before you say anything more to New York. To me recreation is as strange as a home and a family."

Mildred remembered some of her attempts at recreation. A month at St. Moritz where her 9:30 bedtime caused her to miss the social life in which she had no interest to begin with; Miami Beach; the White Mountains; Orcas Island; Machu Picchu; Acapulco. Throughout the world she had taken her two weeks or her month, hardly able to stand it until she could get back to Howard, Otis, and their regular travel schedule.

"Conrad Hilton," Howard said, "has his color portrait in every hotel and the Marriott biography is on each of their nightstands, and you don't want one recreation area named for you."

"Don't be angry at me, Howard. I am pleased at the thought. But you're the same way. Where are the Howard Johnson portraits or your story which is so much more interesting than

Hilton's? I remember how hard it was to convince you to give the ice cream your name. You held out so long that our first five thousand quarts were printed 'Jim's Smooth and Deluxe.' You and I, Howard, we're not like the Disneys and the Hiltons so let's stay out of their business, too. If you want a Natureland let's endow a fund and let the National Geographic Society or the State of Florida create the thing."

On frail legs Mr. Johnson walked through downtown San Antonio. Along the river and past the Alamo he walked. The day and the week, the vacation and the rest awaited his judgment. Mildred, too, was silent now. She had said what she had to say; the decision, as always, would be his.

It would have been a wonderful battle, she thought—Walt Disney's Art and Howard Johnson's Nature, with the customer making the choice. Maybe there would be enough customers for both enterprises, maybe Howard would enjoy spending his last years on a single project. If he decided to do it, she knew that she would stay too. In spite of her many objections, when Milly thought about alternatives she hurried her steps to keep up with Howard Johnson. Otis had the car in parade gear, which let him control speeds below five miles per hour. They used the speed control not only for walks, but when they wanted to circle some large open properties or sometimes just to go around the blacktop of an HJ lodge off the turnpike and see how people behaved toward the picnic benches and the vending machines. When they traveled so slowly near the grass, people sometimes thought they were pulling a lawn mower, or playing games with the traffic. Otis was unmoved by the taunts of fast drivers, and Howard Johnson never heard an insult.

When, after several blocks of silence, Mr. Johnson held his arm straight up as a signal to Otis, he made no mention of a decision, nor did Mildred ask. "I'll have to rethink Florida," Howard Johnson said quietly, "and maybe the Carolinas, too."

# CHAPTER FIVE

*J*ust west of the Louisiana border, the black limousine pulled into the parking lot of a Hardee's restaurant at lunchtime. Their standard rule of the road was never to drive more than thirty extra miles to an HJ location. When there were no HJ restaurants, the three of them, without shame, ate the food of their competitors. They tasted, they judged, they were not ungenerous in their praise of French fries at a Holiday Inn or the bun at a Hardee's, the sauce at a Big Boy. Mildred took notes on the virtues as well as the flaws of their competitors, though neither she nor HJ ever doubted the superiority of their entire menu. Though he knew that there was no HJ facility between San Antonio and Tilton, Louisiana, Otis was still hoping that his last stop would be at one of their own places. He wanted to pull that long black car under the orange roof one more time before handing over the keys.

While Mr. Johnson and Mildred ate lunch, Otis, who rarely ate at midday, gave some final attention to the vehicle. He checked the oil level, the transmission fluid, the air pressure of the tires, then he looked over the surface of the car, and underneath as well, for tiny nicks in the undercoating. He trusted his nephew Mel, but he knew that the young man would never take care of a car the way he did.

This Cadillac was not his favorite. Otis remembered the first Packard, a 1947 dark-blue Clipper with a running board and mud flaps. It was their first new car after the war. There was no air conditioning in those days, no ice-cream freezers, no electronically controlled Plexiglas panels. There was a big old back seat, a high roof, those soft gray wool seats, and a lot of rubber on the road. The tires were a big change after the war. The '39 Buick and all of the earlier cars had thin tires, but not that old Packard. After the war, when rubber wasn't scarce, they really made some old tires. Those tires were as plump as bayou roaches, and they had tread down to his second knuckle.

Don't make tires like that no more, Otis thought—don't make Packards at all. He was sorry now that he hadn't bought the Packard when Mr. Johnson offered it to him at far less than the trade-in value, but his wife wanted a station wagon.

"How's it gonna look," Estelle said, "me driving through town in a fancy old limousine. You're the big shot driver, not me."

So Otis bought his family a Plymouth wagon with wooden panels. He wished he still had that one too—but he didn't miss it like he missed the Packard. The Packard had overdrive as quiet as a church. It had rims that you could drive fifty miles on even if the tire blew out and a defroster for the rear window.

Otis had given Mr. Johnson a good year's notice of his coming retirement. He told his boss in January 1963 when he returned from Christmas at home. It was his decision, not Estelle's. He could have quit years before. Otis Brighton didn't stay on for the money. He didn't even know how much money he was worth. The HJ stock that Mr. Johnson gave him every Christmas was locked away in a bank vault in Winthrop. Mr. Johnson told him that it kept on splitting and doubling every so often so that each one of his shares was quite a lot more than one. And he understood that on any day he could look in the newspaper toward the back near the want ads to see how much a share cost, but Otis never looked. He knew better than the newspaper that the restaurants and motels were doing fine, he saw it firsthand almost every day of his life.

No, he hadn't come to work for Mr. Johnson for the money and he wasn't stopping because of money. Through the rearview mirror he had watched Mr. Johnson grow old, and lately he had seen Miss Milly grow sick. He had always been a good watcher. While he was keeping his eye on the back, Otis knew that the driver of the car in front was watching him and driving and watching. He wasn't old yet, at least he didn't feel old, and he wasn't sick, but something told him on that New Year's Eve that it was getting to be time.

He and Estelle were home alone on the Fourth; both boys lived in New Orleans. Jerome was a disc jockey and Harold owned an insurance agency. Mr. Johnson's Cadillac was the first car Harold ever insured—wrote the policy out when he sat in the front seat next to me, Otis thought.

Otis had sent both the boys to college. They can sell insurance and read the news on radio good as any white man, he thought. The boys had grown up in the big house in Tilton, the house that never flooded. They didn't know what it was like to hum with a harmonica-playing daddy while it rained day after day so that you couldn't go to work in the fields. His boys had never picked a crop.

When Harold graduated from Alcorn A. & M., Mr. Johnson and Milly were there right beside Otis and Estelle. Mildred cried. So did Otis. Mr. Johnson offered the young man a job in New York, but that Harold, he said he wouldn't leave Louisiana, not for nothing, not even for Howard Johnson.

"You've been a good father, Otis," Mr. Johnson told him. "You deserve the rewards of parenthood and you have them. Your sons are independent young men. They don't need you. That shows how well you've done your job."

Otis hadn't much thought of being a father as a job. He was gone so often that Estelle did as much of the fathering as the mothering. The boys, Otis thought, were mostly her doing, but he was proud of how they had turned out. You could never know about that for sure, except in a way, he thought, maybe you could.

Whenever he'd be home for a while when they were little

ones, they'd always bring out the wax and help him put on a good Simonize job and they'd get their little fingers into the cracks of the seats and pull out dust and crumpled papers.

They never lorded it over anybody that they lived in the big house and had plenty of money. They were good boys. Otis bought each one a four-door Chevy when he graduated from college and they both still had those Chevies and kept them real clean.

Yes, he'd always known his boys were going to turn out all right and he imagined that his daddy hadn't worried too much about him either. It had been his own choice to go with Mr. Johnson and Miss Milly. Daddy didn't tell him yes or no, though he knew that when Daddy got on the bus back to Winthrop, his playing and humming days might be gone forever.

It was one heck of a ditch Mr. Johnson had put that Model T into. Of course it wasn't all his fault. They didn't repair the roads much in those days. You were lucky if you had any kind of an even surface. Mr. Johnson had just veered to the right to avoid a pot hole in the blacktop and there went the front end into the ditch, leaving the back tires spinning in the air.

Miss Milly with a big bump on her forehead sat there holding a purse full of money and it was raining cats and dogs.

"I'm much obliged, gentlemen," Mr. Johnson told the two of them when they got off the bus. But try as they might they couldn't get that Model T out of the muddy ditch. The three men lifted the front end right up in the air but they needed a push from behind too. Finally, sweating and full of mud, Otis Sr. walked across a field of okra to a small farm and borrowed a mule. The two Otises tied a rope to the mule. The mule pulled, Mildred sat at the steering wheel and the three men lifted and pushed and just like that they were out of there.

Mr. Johnson put his arm around the mule and thanked him. It was raining even harder by then and they had to get on to Beaumont, which was the other way from New Orleans.

After they returned the mule, the two Otises joined Mr. Johnson and Milly for the ride to Beaumont. The men had no choice unless they wanted to stand in the rain and wait for the night bus home.

Otis Jr. was feeling bad about missing out on the amateur hour audition. He wanted NBC to hear his daddy's harmonica. He didn't have much to say all the way to Beaumont, neither did Mr. Johnson and Milly. Mr. Johnson just said that he would make sure at Beaumont to take care of their return trip. When he offered to pay them, Otis Sr. just shook his head.

"No reason to pay for helping folks out. Money ain't good for that." Mr. Johnson understood.

"You're right, Mr. Brighton, thank you," he said, "from the bottom of my heart. Thank you for helping a stranger. And thank you for reminding me of what can't be bought."

At Beaumont, the two Otises and Milly waited in the car while Mr. Johnson went to the bank with that purse full of money. He carried it under his arm like a woman does.

"It's a lot of money," Milly told them, "but if we buy this land and it works out, then we can open up our business throughout the west. It's a big step. We're going to open a restaurant right beside the new highway, and someday all the way to California."

When Mr. Johnson came back and handed the empty purse to Mildred, he was as happy as could be. He jumped in the air and clicked the heels of his wing-tip shoes. He took the four of them to Galatin's, the finest restaurant in Beaumont, for a late dinner. Otis Sr. tried to tell him no, but he wouldn't listen. Even at the restaurant Mr. Johnson didn't understand what the manager told him. Mr. Johnson just stared like he was realizing for the first time that the two Otises were colored. Like he didn't know that colored and white ate separate.

"It's just not done, sir," the manager said. He was a polite white man. He apologized. He told them the name of a good

colored folks' restaurant and Otis Sr. and Jr. were ready to go
—but Mr. Johnson was something standing there in the lobby
of Galatin's saying "Mr. Brighton's need for food is no less than
mine."

"That may be true," the manager said, "but he'll have to
satisfy that need elsewhere."

"Sir," Howard Johnson said, "if you do not serve my friends
at this hour, then I promise you, as surely as it rained today,
that a year from now this establishment will not serve anyone."

That manager looked around at his big old fancy restaurant.
He had maybe fifty tables, all with blue linen tablecloths, and
waiters in tuxedos, and chandeliers hanging from the ceiling,
and he looked at that tall thin Mr. Johnson and little Milly and
two colored men, one with a harmonica in his pocket, and he
said, polite but kind of smirky, "That's a threat that I can live
with, sir."

The four of them then drove over to Leon's Ribhouse in the
colored section, which Mr. Johnson said was probably a much
better restaurant anyway. And after he wiped the barbecue
sauce off his fingers, Mr. Johnson said that it would take him
six months to build a restaurant and less than six to drive
Galatin's out of business.

Even if Mr. Johnson hadn't done what he did, Otis Jr. would
have been ready to go to work for that man on the spot. And
he said so. He didn't ask his dad's permission, he just said he'd
like to join them and maybe help with the car and whatever
hard work there was. At the time Otis thought they were going
to need him to work in a restaurant. He had not even driven
a tractor when Mr. Johnson handed him the key to the Model
T and demonstrated the shifting technique.

They drove past Galatin's sputtering and stalling the next
morning on their way to deliver Otis Sr. to the bus station. The
manager and some of the waiters were just opening up. They
turned to watch Otis learning to drive. The manager tipped his
hat to Mildred. Otis was so nervous that he let his foot slip off

the clutch and the Model T shuddered to a halt in front of Galatin's.

"You folks droppin' by for breakfast?" one of the waiters asked.

"No sir," Howard Johnson said, "we will not enter your restaurant again."

"Well, that's a doggone shame," the waiter said. "I was gonna fix those darkies some grits that would make their eyes pop out even more."

Otis Sr. looked straight ahead through the windshield. Otis Jr. kept his shaky foot on the clutch but he couldn't get the gears to engage. Miss Mildred patted his shoulder and told him to relax. She said there was plenty of time to get to the bus and driving under pressure was a good way for him to learn.

Howard Johnson, however, understood the insult to his companions. In those days, Otis recalled, Mr. Johnson looked as solemn as now, but he was much faster of foot when he wanted to be. He opened the door and swung his long legs out of the Model T. With the noise of the stalled car attracting the attention of passersby, people stopped to watch the white man in the blue suit leave his woman in the automobile with two black men and approach the steps of that splendid mahogany exterior of Galatin's restaurant.

Mr. Johnson walked up close to that waiter who was making a nasty face and was not polite the way the manager had been the night before. Otis Jr. stopped trying to start the car and felt his right hand become a fist. He had never hit a white man but he thought that this might be the time a'coming and he wished though it hurt him to admit it that he and his daddy had stayed on that bus and were right now auditioning in New Orleans instead of about to get run out of town in Beaumont, Texas, because this Mr. Johnson didn't have the sense to know that colored folks couldn't eat in white restaurants.

"He's a good man, though," Otis thought and he heard Milly say, "Oh my," and then it was all over.

Howard Johnson walked up the steps, looked at that sassy waiter and then at the crowd of eight or ten people that had surrounded the porch of the eating establishment, and said clear and loud,

"All men are created equal." Then he turned and walked away. He opened the back door of the Model T, Otis stepped down on the clutch, the car moved without a jerk and Otis knew that he was going to be a chauffeur.

In other households and schools across America children learned that Abraham Lincoln said those famous words, and maybe he did, Otis thought, but he taught his sons that Howard Johnson said them in Beaumont, Texas, in April of 1927 and he, Otis Brighton, was there to witness and to hear those words spoken about him and his daddy. Daddy stayed at the bus station and Howard, Otis and Milly headed west from Beaumont toward those points where the southern routes would meet the highways slipping down from Chicago to the long road across the empty quarters of America, the road called Route 66 that Howard and Milly knew would soon be created, even before the waiters in Beaumont, Texas, came to know the wrath of Mr. Johnson and the truth that all men are created equal.

Waiting outside Hardee's for Mr. Johnson to finish his milk-shake, Otis remembered their return to Beaumont. It took Mr. Johnson longer than he thought it would. Otis had never expected anything more to happen, but when Mr. Johnson said he would do a thing, then he did do that thing. Bad times held him up three years, though they had been back through Beaumont a number of times. They always ate at Leon's Ribhouse and stayed at the St. George where Otis had a room the same as any white man's.

Otis didn't know what Mr. Johnson had in mind when he told Otis one day that they would be stopping for a few days in Beaumont so why didn't Otis drive on home and bring his daddy and his mom and his brothers and sister back on Tuesday. Otis was excited to show his family the HJ roadhouse with its orange roof and turquoise chairs but when he drove up with Momma and Daddy and LeRoy and Robert and Elvira, Mr. Johnson showed them the beautiful HJ house and then he and Milly climbed into the car with the Brighton family and Mr. Johnson told Otis to drive to Galatin's restaurant.

Otis Sr. looked at Otis Jr.

"You're sure, Mr. Johnson?" Otis Jr. asked.

Mr. Johnson nodded. "It's OK, Otis, I know that none of us has forgotten."

Otis parked in front of Galatin's and waited in the car.

"Please," Mr. Johnson said, "I'd like to take your family to dinner. I failed once, but this time you need have no fear." The Brightons followed Mr. Johnson and Mildred into the restaurant and just as Otis figured there was the same manager.

"A table for eight," Mr. Johnson said and without waiting any more than they did at Leon's Ribhouse, there they were all sitting down under a chandelier at Galatin's.

Mr. Johnson ordered wine and steak for everyone. Otis didn't remember if that smartass waiter was there but he knew the manager was the same one, yesiree, that fellow kept coming over to see if everything was all right but you could tell that he knew it wasn't.

After dinner Mr. Johnson called him over, and asked did he remember any of them and he said yes he did. And Mr. Johnson said, "Why did you serve us tonight, sir, when three years ago when we were in greater need you refused us?"

"Three years ago," the manager said, "you didn't own the place. The boss told me today that you bought the place, so what you say goes. If you own the place and you tell me to feed the beef to the dogs out back, then I will."

"That won't be necessary," Mr. Johnson said, "nor will this restaurant be necessary."

And that was it. The next morning while Howard and Milly

and Otis and the rest of the Brightons watched, two bulldozers leveled the Galatin restaurant. They leveled it intact, the dishes, the silver, the chandeliers, the mahogany tables, the electric sign, the blue linen napkins and tablecloths. Otis was wondering why Mr. Johnson didn't salvage anything, it seemed like such a waste.

"Don't worry," Mildred said, reading Otis's thoughts, "in the long run it will be good for business. The Galatin customers will eat at our restaurant and as for this . . ." she looked at the rubble being created before her eyes—"Howard wants no profit from evil."

"Amalekites," Mr. Johnson said as he and Mildred squeezed into the Model T for the ride back to Tilton.

More than thirty-five years ago, Otis thought, but he remembered the details of the restaurant and the color of the napkins, the rich grain of the mahogany wood, he recalled it as if the destruction had happened yesterday. He checked the tires on the orange trailer too, and the lock and the hitch. Everything was set for his last drive home. In the restaurant, Howard Johnson wiped his lips on the napkin and left a 20 percent tip. Otis put on his leather driving gloves and, for the last time, felt the long black car slide along the entrance ramp and then speed into the line of traffic.

# CHAPTER SIX

*M*anny Vincent remembered his parrot. Every few weeks he would awaken in the middle of the night and recall his loss. He recalled it as a film, frame by frame, though his life since then was a blur. He saw again the gray-green tree, the lustrous celluloid feathers, the curved but still almost snubnosed beak. He heard the wisecracks in the parrot's clear baritone.

"Perky doesn't want a cracker. Perky wants to bite Mickey Mouse's ass." And he had. Perky bit Mickey's ass and his wallet, he bit the mouse and the whole Disney studio, that's why they ruined him, the parrot and his maker. . . .

Manny Vincent couldn't believe they were striking again. They had already destroyed him once. Thirty years ago he had moved to the other coast, changed his name, given up his love of drawing, and now, here Disney was again.

When Vincent came to Orlando it was hardly more than a swamp with orange groves. He drained some of the swamp and sold campsites to refugees from the North. He built a tiny fairgrounds for folks too poor to go to Havana. He drained more swamp and built a ballfield. He paid a few ex-major leaguers twenty dollars a game and the rest of the team was local kids playing free hoping a big league scout would give them a look. During the day the ballplayers worked for the Jones Construction Company. At night in July and August they played Class D baseball. Bones Jones and his Orlando Pirates. The team logo, Perky Parrot with an eye patch on a gray-green tree. A bird in the bush. That is what he had become. Manny Vincent, cartoonist, now known as Bones Jones, a land developer.

They ruined my negatives, he thought, so I developed myself.

He developed a few houses around Kissimmee, Florida. He developed the Orlando Pirates. He developed his hatred, still fresh thirty years later. He was a pirate along with his team, living in the swamps, building stucco bungalows while they took Beverly Hills and the big studio in the valley and made a killing on Disneyland.

Bones Jones was already in his baseball uniform having an early dinner, as was his custom before home games. He picked up his copy of the afternoon Orlando *Times*. He looked over the headlines as he ate his salad. By the time Carol, his regular waitress, brought his hamburger steak, Bones Jones had no appetite. It was a rumor, the *Times* said, but Walt Disney didn't deny it. They were putting their show on the road.

In his fantasies of vengeance he had always come to them. Now, in reality, they were coming to him. Perky Parrot's last words were "Bite Mickey Mouse's ass." Never heard, never seen, those unanswered last words lived only in Bones Jones's mind.

It was his own fault, but as he relived it he couldn't blame himself. How could he have thought to insure the value the negatives would soon have? The insurance company paid him $30 for his future, the burned reels, the simple value of the film. They gave him $9,000 for the building and he sold the land for $15,000 more. He was not broke, $24,000 in 1934 was a lot of money. He was not broke, but he was ruined. Disney hired away his four artists. He had no product and no distributor. Pathé dropped him when he couldn't fulfill the product as promised, and he had had it all done. The two demonstration reels and all but the final cut on the six seven-minute cartoons that would have driven Mickey Mouse to the wall. "Forty-two minutes between me and a fortune," Bones Jones said. It was a fact. He knew it and so did Walt Disney.

"Not hungry tonight, Bones?" Carol liked him. Everyone in Orlando liked him. He belonged to the Chamber of Commerce. He lured a few pensioners to the area, and he owned the baseball team. They called him Bones because he was so thin. He had melted down like his burned negatives. When he arrived in Orlando, you could see through his flesh. He weighed 111 pounds when he got off the bus. He wasn't strong enough to carry his own suitcase. His wife had divorced him. He had no more friends. When he checked into the St. Clair Hotel he called himself Mr. Jones. He planned to kill himself. He got off at Orlando where the Greyhound line switched to a bigger bus for Miami. He didn't need another bus, he didn't need Miami.

When he listed no first name and refused to answer the clerk's request for one, the man wrote in "Bones" because he was so thin. "Room 14, Mr. Bones Jones, and we've got a good restaurant here at the St. Clair. It looks like you could use it."

He slept for a day, then he had dinner at the St. Clair Room. He signed the check Bones Jones. It felt like a real name. He liked the sound, the ring of it. "I'm Bones Jones, from Orlando." He said it aloud a few times.

He had a twenty-thousand-dollar cashier's check in his pocket. When he opened his account at the bank that afternoon everyone thought of Bones Jones as a rich man. In Orlando, he was.

The temperature was 104. He had broken his glasses six months ago and hadn't bothered to get new ones. The buildings on the street all merged together. When he took off his shoes and looked at his bare toes, with his eyesight they seemed webbed, like Donald Duck's.

He couldn't get the Disneys out of his mind. He couldn't prove that they did it, accidents happen to everyone, every day. His friends thought he had gone crazy. Nobody believed that Walt Disney burned him out. The police said there was no proof. It was not arson. An electric wire shorted. Everyone was sorry. Why didn't he start over?

How could he start over when he couldn't even eat or sleep? He'd lost forty-seven pounds. He stopped talking. He didn't care if the Depression ruined everyone else, he hoped it would. He hoped for an earthquake. He imagined drawing one. Walt Disney slipped into a volcano, shot up, holding the cheeks of his burning ass as he turned to dust, gray-green dust, the color of Perky Parrot's tree—the tree of life that Walt Disney had cut out at its roots. Walt Disney knew thirty years ago that Woody Woodpecker and Bugs Bunny couldn't destroy him, but Perky Parrot could. The first three finished cartoons took over Disney bookings as soon as theater owners saw them.

It was a new and tiny operation—Disney had a big head start, but Perky was the real thing. A wise-ass bird. Now, Manny Vincent, known as Bones Jones, was an old man in Florida, the chief of the Pirates, and Walt Disney was approaching Bones's swamp with his millions.

Bones Jones still lived in the St. Clair Hotel. He could have owned it by now if you added up all the rent. He paid his bill by the week. He had no phone. He refused to buy any insurance. He built bungalows one by one and sold them. He was reasonably well-to-do. The Pirates averaged six hundred fans a night. The lights were so dim that he used a flashlight to signal his coaches. Some teams refused to play on the Pirates' field. Bones listed those refusals as Pirates victories. His team won the Florida Class D Championship each year. He was the statistician for the league and when nobody else wanted the job he became the Commissioner as well.

But baseball was not his first love. He had given up color, motion, speed, animation—the celluloid flicker that he loved. He watched the Pirates run the bases in the dusk. He had no car. In Orlando he could walk to his own construction sites. In town they thought of him as a lovable old eccentric. He patted babies' heads, he still liked anything that looked like a cartoon character. But he never went to the movies. How could he? Disney owned the world, and Bones Jones scraped along, sucking the water out of a Florida swamp.

His wife had remarried—one of his former cartoonists, a man whom he had taught. They had children. He had the Pirates. The fire had burned his soul, the negative of himself, and he knew it. Bones was his true name, that was all that was left—bones, and pirates, and Disney was coming.

"Would you rather have the sirloin," Carol asked, "or the New York strip?"

They were still trying to fatten him up. He had been a steady 145 for a generation but his skin still had that bluish transparent look. His veins seemed pasted on the outside of his arms. He looked like he was wearing a loose striped baseball uniform even when he wore his regular trousers and a short-sleeved shirt.

He could have been mayor. Everyone in Orlando knew Bones. They respected his privacy. They knew him as an honest businessman, a semirecluse who came out of his room for baseball. In the winters he hibernated. He paid everyone in cash.

In one of the six burned cartoons, Perky Parrot and his dog, Silly Sam, had tried to build a perfect city, and it was that for birds and dogs, but others wanted it. Silly Sam tried to write down rules—migrant cats and rodents invaded. Silly Sam and Perky tried to be fair and include everyone. There were no taxes, no immigration laws. Not much labor either. Everything grew on trees or lay twinkling in the gray-green dust. Sam couldn't get dirty. Rolling in it made him glow. Perky hung from all the branches until a jealous cat, waiting for his chance, pounced. That was one of the unfinished ones—you couldn't kill your hero. As it had happened it didn't matter—he burned before his release. Death by fire, worse than the claw of a fellow celluloid character. Uninsurable loss, loss of character.

"Bones." Carol touched his shoulder. "If you're taking a nap, my friend, do it after dinner."

She took away the hamburger and brought sirloin and French fries and custard and iced tea.

He ate but the food tasted like straw again.

She knew Bones's schedule. He ate at five, put down his tip before she gave him the bill. He left the dining room at five thirty-five so he could be at the ballpark by six. He didn't care if the food was undercooked. Nobody else came down to dinner before six.

Carol tasted a French fry to make sure it was warm enough. She sat down to watch the news and to keep Bones Jones company. On the TV they were showing Martin Luther King being arrested in Birmingham.

"What you think of that nigra?" Carol asked Bones Jones. "What you think of that whole business? Pretty soon they'll be coming into the St. Clair Room too, you watch. Everything is changing. I said when President Kennedy was assassinated that that was it. Ask Bob and the other waitresses if you don't believe me. I said that very day that things would never be the same again. If any old Communist can shoot the President then everything else is possible too. And you know what, Bones? I don't give a damn. I don't care if Lyndon Johnson sends the whole damned NAACP into the St. Clair Room, I don't care if there are nigras on the moon itself. The whole thing is too crazy for me. All I know is that the Russians killed Kennedy and nobody's doing a thing about it."

Bones was not listening. Walt Disney was the only news. Disney was coming. Bones Jones remembered how it had been after the fire. The feeling was returning. Disney was coming for what was left—the swamp, the Pirates, the stucco houses, the St. Clair Hotel. Nothing was enough. Bones Jones knew they had forgotten him, knew they didn't care about his fiefdom in Orlando. He understood that he was the gravel of history. But they were coming, and he was here now, old and with nothing much to lose. Just Bones—meaningless Bones Jones, who had been rotting in the swamp for thirty years.

Carol ate the French fries. The custard was too soft for her.

"Disney is coming," Bones Jones said aloud to Carol.

"Yeah," Carol said. "Ain't it great?"

# CHAPTER SEVEN

*B*y the time the Pirates took the field that night, everyone in Orlando knew about the new Disneyland. One of the popcorn vendors bought out Woolworth's supply of Mickey Mouse caps. Starting in the bleachers he worked his way down the third-base line. When Bones Jones looked up from the dugout he saw the ears of his enemy atop the heads of his fans.

He sent Elmo Wylie, the third baseman, into the stands to capture the vendor and confiscate the product. "I bought out the dime store," the fourteen-year-old told him.

Elmo was a classic third baseman, short, bowlegged, good at lunging to his left. He brought the vendor to the dugout, squeezing him like the last out.

"Why are you selling this shit?" Bones Jones asked the nervous fourteen-year-old. "Where's the Pirates caps?"

"I haven't sold the Pirates caps in months, Bones . . . I've been selling playing cards and magazines and today with everyone talking about Disneyland this seemed like a natural."

The boy smiled. He put on his mouse ears to demonstrate their beauty.

"They're selling like hotcakes, I sold almost a hundred, mostly to adults. Maybe we should change the name of the team to the Mickeys or something, you know? To take advantage of what's coming."

Bones's pitcher, Al Rivers, had loaded the bases again with

three consecutive walks. He had walked in four runs the previous inning. Elmo, who served as an unofficial assistant to the manager, nudged Bones.

"Maybe Al should come outta there."

"Kid," Bones Jones said, "you wanna pitch?"

"Are you kidding?"

"I'm not kidding."

The St. Petersburg Cards had scored nine runs in the second and were already up 11-2. The fans with and without mouse caps were reading and playing cards or checkers. The kid put down his tray of mouse ears and accompanied Elmo to the mound. Elmo gave him the ball and Al Rivers's glove and cap as well. The boy handed Elmo his brown Sportservice jacket.

"What's your name?" Bones yelled toward the mound.

"James 'Dutch' Henderson," the boy yelled to his manager. "Should I throw all fast balls?"

Bones Jones pulled up the microphone and announced that Henderson was now on the mound for the Pirates. While the boy glared at the catcher, Bones, with his bare hands, tore the ears off all the remaining caps.

The boy gave up two hits, then struck out the side.

When Henderson came back to the dugout he spat between his front teeth and slapped his thigh with his glove. "We took care of 'em," he said.

Bones snatched Al Rivers's glove from the boy and handed him the tray of earless beanies.

"What's going on?" Henderson asked. "I struck out the side, didn't I?"

"Get outta here," Bones Jones said. "And if you ever come back with any of this Mickey Mouse stuff, I'll shove a bat up your ass sideways."

"Jesus, Bones," the kid said. "What'd I do wrong? I struck out the side."

"Get out." Jones pointed toward the exit under the bleachers. Henderson took his earless caps toward the parking lot.

"I'm not through," he said. "I deserve another shot at it. It ain't fair."

"What does he know about fair," Bones Jones said aloud.

"You all right, Bones?" Elmo meant it as a baseball question. If Bones was not all right Elmo would replace him as manager. It had happened a few times when Bones had the flu during the season.

"I'm all right," Bones said, but between innings he announced on the loudspeaker that it was a rule at Pirates Park that no Walt Disney paraphernalia be worn in the stands.

The fans booed the announcement. Nobody took off their ears. Between innings they waved the ears at the Pirates dugout.

By the sixth nobody was watching the game. They were chanting for Henderson to return with mouse caps. They wanted him to sell from the mound. The crowd was cheering "We want Mickey," the name they had given to Henderson.

In the seventh Bones Jones told Elmo to take over. The manager walked as fast as he could back to the St. Clair Hotel.

In his room he took off his spikes and his Pirates cap and lay down in his uniform. He felt like he did the day he got off the bus and came up to this very room, though it now had new curtains and draperies and a TV.

"What do they want," he said to himself, "why are they everywhere? Why Orlando, why the last stop on the bus? Why pick a town that draws only retirees, most of whom can't afford a stucco bungalow? Why put an amusement park here?"

He barely knew Walt Disney. They met once in 1933 at a party before the first Perky Parrot was released. Manny sized up his competitor. That's all he was then, competitor, not enemy. He looked at the Disney ears and knew where Mickey's came from. Walt, he thought, had a rodent-type face too, long and pointed, with eyes always looking for food.

Disney was pleasant to Manny. He said he looked forward to seeing the Perky work. He said he hoped there would be many more cartoonists. He wanted an industry, he said, a lot of motion, a lot of speed and color and good camera synching. He left the party early. Manny never saw him again. Eleven months later Perky Parrot lay in ashes and Manny Vincent was ruined.

He went to the sheriff's departments of L.A. and Orange counties and to the Los Angeles Police Department. Nobody gave him the time of day. They looked at him as if he was a crazy man. The cops had girlie calendars behind them. Nobody cared about six rolls of celluloid film. It was the Depression. Others had lost more, ruin was everyone's destiny—the country needed Mickey Mouse to cheer it up. After weeks of filing reports and accusations, Manny finally got an appointment to see Bill Lawrence, the chief investigator for the Sunset Insurance Company of North America.

It took a lot of explanation to get the appointment. The secretary could see no reason to tie up an executive on a claim that was only contested on a thirty-dollar segment.

Manny sat down. The investigator was grim. He had no eyebrows. Manny was used to looking at eyebrows. They gave big behavior clues to his cartoon characters. Manny liked to see eyebrows moving; he made Perky a little bit in the image of Groucho Marx.

"Walt Disney had my studio burned and my films destroyed." Manny said it bluntly, matter-of-factly. His hands were hot and he felt his feet swelling inside his brown shoes. "It wasn't a simple fire," he said. "He burned my future. He's not afraid of Walter Lantz or the Bugs Bunny stuff. Perky Parrot scared him. Without the Parrot Disney's got it all, the whole cartoon industry. I want you to go after Disney and get damages. I'll need my artists back and enough capital for six months of operation and I'll need to use Disney's studio, nobody else has the facilities. If he'll agree to all that, then you don't have to put him in jail."

Inspector Lawrence took no notes.

"Mr. Vincent," he said, "how am I going to put Walt Disney in jail because you had an electrical fire?"

"Because he caused it. I told you I'm his only competition."

"If everybody put his competitor in jail there wouldn't be capitalism would there, Mr. Vincent. There'd be a police state, with every man accusing anyone in his way."

"But I know he did it."

"You may know but nobody else does."

"My burned building, my films destroyed only a few weeks before release—do you think all that is a coincidence—you think there's no reason behind it?"

"Mr. Vincent, I can tell you from my experience that people's lives are ruined every day for no reason whatsoever. We insure risks. There are no sure things. It sounds like you wanted a sure thing."

Manny's feet were throbbing. He bent to loosen his shoelaces. The eyebrowless face glared at him.

"Go home, Mr. Vincent, and forget this vendetta. You've had a stroke of bad luck, pick up the pieces, it's what life is about. Forget Walt Disney and think about Manny Vincent."

He stood, shook hands and pointed Manny toward the door. On swollen and heavy feet the cartoonist walked out.

"Gone," he told the receptionist, "gone—there will never be another Perky Parrot."

In his bed in Orlando he remembered his swollen feet and the hairless brows of Inspector Lawrence. He remembered every word of their conversation. In the swampy lowlands of Florida at the end of his bus route, Manny Vincent did pick up the pieces. He made a new life out of new houses and a baseball team, but the old life still hung over his heart. He hadn't made a drawing since the day of the fire, hadn't seen a cartoon since then, not even a movie. He read mysteries and kept his baseball statistics for the Florida State League. The stats, he thought, those were his characters, you put them all together and you had a season, a league, half a lifetime, but no motion, no color, no voices, no laughter. Disney took all of that from him—left him numbers and the St. Clair Hotel and the Orlando Pirates and now they were coming after his new life too.

"It's at least the top of the ninth for me," Bones Jones said to himself, "and I'm down twenty million runs or so—what've I got to lose? They took it all once—Manny Vincent's been gone a long time. Bones Jones is just Bones." He thought of Ezekiel in the valley of the dry bones. He remembered his swollen feet in the insurance company office. He saw the mouse caps in the bleachers.

Too old for a third life, he thought. This time they won't run me out. This time I'll be ready.

# CHAPTER EIGHT

*T*he crowds in downtown Orlando excited about the Disneys did not disturb Margery Post. The townspeople had been excited about the moonport too. They would forget. They were always excited about what was good for business.

"My business," she thought, "my only business is staying out of everyone else's business."

Margery knew that people would sell their souls if it was good for business. She had no sympathy for the merchant class, neither had her father. In all his success, C. W. Post never once did what was good for business. He did what he thought was right. He wanted animals to live without fear of slaughter and men to live like angels, without blood on their hands and flesh in their bowels. Money meant no more to him when he had it than when he was without it. All her life the world had envied her. The society pages referred to Margery Post as Queen Ceres. She was the heiress to Corn Flakes and Grape-Nuts and Post Toasties and Raisin Bran. Grains adorned with her father's name were as common throughout the world as mosquitoes.

Yet C. W. Post had gathered his fortune without ever trying. When the corn spoke to him he was at prayer. And Margery's life had been similar. When Clarence Birdseye spoke to her she was sitting in a park in Central Asia. By opening her eyes and listening and tasting she had earned her own fortune. Although it added nothing to her life, she sat in seclusion in her Orlando mansion, the mistress of two great fortunes, Post Cereals and

Birdseye Frozen Foods. Her father flaked grain and she and Clarence Birdseye froze some Russian blackberries. It was that simple, though to the vast hordes of the envious, the seekers of their own fortunes, she seemed like a magical being, a true queen of the earth turning nature into profit. Margery knew herself to be what she was, a lonely old woman who was sick of public adulation. In her years in Orlando she had enjoyed what was left to her—solitude mingled with the occasional company of a close friend.

Orlando, far from New York and Paris and Rome, was the perfect place for her. Nobody was just passing through Orlando. Nobody came unless she invited them. And the locals now had their hands full envying the rich in Palm Beach, so they left her alone, hardly even knew she was there. The mansion her father built had been uninhabited for so long that when Margery finally moved there in 1958, people thought she was only a new caretaker.

Around town, most everyone still thought the house was empty. Nobody really believed that the heiress of Post Cereals lived with a small staff in the midst of swamps and orange groves so far from the centers of culture.

President Kennedy himself had commented on her isolation when he visited Margery in 1961 to discuss the moonport.

"You don't know Battle Creek," she told the young President. "Where you grow up matters. I spent the first twenty-four years of my life living in a shack beside a cereal factory. When you grow up that way you're never comfortable in high society."

President Kennedy said he knew what she meant, though Margery knew he did not understand. Nobody could know what it was like to be C. W. Post's only child. Kennedy understood having a fortune, no doubt, but he and his big family had lived all over the world. C. W. Post hardly took her anywhere. Once to Madrid to buy art, once to Arizona to buy a town. The rest was Battle Creek, up at five, to bed at nine, once a month fasting, new shoes twice a year. Clouds of grain dust every-where. Prayer morning and evening.

A millionaire in cash, C. W. Post was richer still in grief and in guilt. His fortune was a burden, a constant reminder of the true fortune that he might have gathered had he remained a Nazarite.

"Mr. President," Margery told John Kennedy, "you'll just have to put your rocket city elsewhere. I'm going to stay in Orlando and I don't plan to spend my declining years near rocket ships and news reporters."

"I don't blame you," the young President said, "and as a citizen you have every right to register your protest. I'm here to tell you that your protest is being heard at the highest levels of government."

Margery smiled. She knew the President had come to charm her, and he could. But not enough to move her from her home. If the only way to get to the moon was from Orlando, then mankind which had waited so long already would have to wait until she was out of the way. However, as her lawyer, Treat Gilbert, told Vice President Johnson, Mrs. Post would reim-burse the public treasury for its expense and would even do-nate to the government thousands of acres at Cape Canaveral on the east coast of Florida.

She and the President were discussing the problem over tea in her observatory. The President was looking at the moon through the telescope.

"Your father must have been interested in the stars to have built such a room."

"No," Margery said, "my father was interested in the ground. He never looked up. When he had this house built, he just told the architects to build him one each of every kind of room they could think of. There's a smoking room—he never smoked—and a gun room, though he never had a gun."

The President laughed. So did Margery. "My father never lived in this house. He just had a mansion built so that people would stop bothering him about living in a shack in Battle Creek when he was so rich."

"Why did he pick Orlando?"

"You may not know it, Mr. President," Margery Post said, "but you're standing atop the Fountain of Youth. He consulted the old Spanish maps and had this place built on the exact site that Ponce de León said was the location of the Fountain of Youth. So here I am retired, growing old at the Fountain of Youth. I'm living proof that superstitions are just that."

"But you haven't sampled the fountain, have you?"

"There are no waters, just the swamp all around us."

"And"—the President smiled at her again—"you want to keep the Fountain of Youth clear of rocket ships."

"Precisely," Margery said. "Let the rockets' red glare glare elsewhere."

"Do you know," the President said, "that very few individuals are ever mentioned in a cabinet meeting—I mean as private citizens—and you were."

"I'm honored," Margery said, "but only if the cabinet agreed not to build the moonport in my backyard."

"Would I be here if we were going to be enemies?"

"You're here because you're visiting your family in Palm Beach and it's an easy helicopter ride. You're probably curious about who this rich old witch is too. And maybe you think you can even charm her into realizing what she can do for her country."

The President pretended to be shocked by her candor. But he was still smiling.

"Right on all counts," he said. "I was going to see how much influence a visit from the President had."

"I am impressed," Margery said, "don't misunderstand me."

"But . . . ?" the President asked.

"But I won't change my mind about anything no matter how charming you are."

The President again put his eye to Margery Post's telescope.

It was early evening, too soon to gaze at the stars, but the moon, three-quarters full, leaped into the telescope atop her mansion.

"It's really something," the President said. "When you cut out all the political bullshit about where to locate the moonport and all the competition from the Russians . . . when you just put your eye to the telescope and look at it, it reminds you of what all of this is about. . . . I think there ought to be an observatory in the White House and one in the Kremlin, too. It would remind all of us how insignificant we are."

The President was wearing a checked sport shirt and pale-blue trousers. He took his eye from the telescope and looked at the moon through the window, as if trying to see it just as clearly through his own eyes.

"I wish my father had bought us a telescope," the President said. "We had plenty of things, but not this."

The telescope that Margery had made and was going to deliver to the White House took over a year to construct. Her gift to Mr. Kennedy arrived in Orlando a few days after his assassination. She didn't have the heart to press it upon the widow. It sat in one of her warehouses. One of these days, she meant to send it to the President's children, but it was so big that it needed a motor to turn it and had to be platform mounted and aimed through a roof. She spent over a million dollars on it, a kind of thank you to the President for putting the moonport at Cape Canaveral instead of Orlando.

In a letter the Secretary of the Interior told her that it was geographically and economically more reasonable to build the facility at Cape Canaveral, but she never doubted that her protest made the difference. She had spoken and John F. Kennedy had listened. When she spoke again Walt Disney would listen. If she could persuade the government she would certainly persuade Disney.

"It won't be easy," Treat Gilbert told her. Gilbert was her chief lawyer. When his firm assigned him to Margery he had to give up his practice in New York and his home in Connecticut. He had to move to Orlando to oversee her Florida holdings and be close by if she needed him. At first Gilbert resented the forced move. He was an Easterner and a Yale Law School product. Six years after his relocation he stood before her as portly and pompous as any Chamber of Commerce type in Orlando.

"It will be good for business," Treat Gilbert told her.

"I don't care about business. I care about what's good for me. And if you're thinking that makes me selfish, fine. Let's just get on with it. I want you to stop this amusement park at all costs."

"Do you just want to buy them out?"

"Is that a possibility?"

The lawyer walked around in her eighteenth-century sitting room. "I don't even know," he said. "I'll just have to talk to them. Apparently Disney has been buying land on the sly for years, slowly, to keep the prices from skyrocketing. He's been accumulating under various names and has let farmers and growers stay on the land for minimal rents. I don't know how committed they are to this property over any other."

"We convinced the government."

"I don't know about that," Gilbert said. "I think they were going to go to Canaveral all along; we just made it a sure thing by donating the land. Anyway Walt Disney will be harder to deal with than the government. He doesn't have to pretend to be concerned. You saw the letter. He's offering seventy-five dollars a square foot for the house, and plans to use it as Cinderella's castle, the place where she and the Prince settle down to live happily ever after. I guess Disney thought you'd like that detail. They've got twenty-seven thousand acres and have already signed contracts for the hotels and the food concessions and the builders. I think they'll say that it's a lot easier for you to move than for them to start over."

As Treat Gilbert droned on in his lawyerly manner about the Disney assets, Margery was remembering the day she met her husband.

———

On the day that James Merriweather, Woodrow Wilson's personal friend, came to Battle Creek, C. W. Post was cleaning the world's largest corn shredder. The machine had to be blown clean once a week or the accumulated corn dust slowed down the gears so much that the machine processed and cut unevenly. When that happened, some cornflakes came out thick as steaks, made as much of cob as of kernel. The machine, made to Mr. Post's own specifications by the Precision Tool Company of Chicago, could, when it was clean and operating properly, process nine thousand ears of corn an hour. It was the most expensive piece of machinery ever brought into the State of Michigan. Mr. Post himself put on a blue coverall and a gauze surgeon's mask for the weekly cleaning operations. It became part of his ritual of preparing for the Sabbath, which he celebrated on Saturday in the mode of the ancient Hebrews.

Each Friday at 2 P.M. Post Cereals ceased operation. C. W. Post donned the mask and the coverall and entered the belly of the corn slicer. He carried upon his back a seven-pound blower, a kind of reverse vacuum cleaner equipped with a long wand designed to caress each sharp blade and each gear with just enough force to loosen the corn starch accumulated from the processing of hundreds of thousands of ears that week. The blades and gears were so delicate that Mr. Post insisted on doing the work himself. Hundreds of pounds of corn starch and dust blew into the main processing room. The hazards of fire were great. During that process, a spark could cause the entire factory to explode. Some grain elevators in the area had done so.

C. W. Post never allowed Margery near the building when he cleaned the blades. Each Friday she stood along with the small group of the faithful employees of the plant who declined to return to their families until they saw that Mr. Post was safe. They stood a few yards from the factory. They watched through the big glass windows as Mr. Post donned his coverall and took up the blower. They prayed for the safety of their boss and benefactor. Margery often stood among the crowd watching her father's slow movements until he disappeared within the gray cast-iron machine. For three or four minutes nothing was visible to the watchers, then the billow of white began to engulf the room. The dislodged starch clouded the window and steamed out into Battle Creek. It fell from the blades and gears propelled by streams of air like snow moving upward. Within minutes the machine was completely invisible in the cloud of white. The dust that escaped even through the closed windows choked the onlookers. Some put handkerchiefs over their mouths, others departed when the dust became extreme, trusting that their boss would emerge safely from his dangerous encounter with the corn.

James Merriweather was in Battle Creek in order to learn some grain technology before becoming Ambassador to the Soviet Union. He had come on the New York Central Line, unloaded his baggage at the Central Hotel and walked the four blocks from the hotel to the Post factory. He carried a letter of introduction from former President Wilson. He had never before been in Michigan and only the week before had sampled for the first time a dry breakfast cereal. Mr. Merriweather was a meat and potatoes man, but as interested in exotic culture as C. W. Post was in vegetarianism. When he came upon a group of women with covered faces standing before a cloudy building, Mr. Merriweather took them to be Muslim ladies at a shrine. He bowed low to the earth as he knew the custom to be in certain Muslim lands.

"Salaam aleichem," said the tall ambassador. He removed his black derby hat and took three steps backward to indicate his respect for the divinity of the place. His nostrils, flared and strong and unusually gifted for discerning rare scents, sniffed at the strange aromas in the wind. The local incense tickled his membranes, made him sneeze. Mr. Merriweather, annoyed by the odor, pulled out a Havana cigar to create a more pleasant aroma. He bit off the top of his cigar, then struck a large wooden match on the bottom of his shoe and took three quick starting tugs. Before he had completed the third puff the ladies were upon him like Harpies. He did not understand the hysterical babble of their voices. They knocked him to the ground and pulled the cigar from between his teeth.

"Ladies," the ambassador tried to say, "I come among you as a friend, a fellow believer in Allah." They tore the match from his hand and one dark-haired woman placed her lips upon his and in one swift action sucked the smoke from his mouth.

"Idiot," one of the women finally said to the ambassador who lay in the dust, "you could have killed Mr. Post. Any spark from your cigar can set off the particles. Get out of here." As she spoke she kicked Mr. Merriweather sharply in the shins. "Get out of here before you hurt someone."

Margery Post bent down to the ambassador. Silently, she gave him her hand and helped him up. "Come with me," she said.

Margery led the stunned man to the Post cottage only fifty yards from the factory. She gave him water and a wet cloth to wipe the dirt from his face.

"I'm very grateful to you, Madam," Merriweather said, "and I offer a thousand pardons. I meant no religious offense nor did I intend to harm Mr. Post." Merriweather knew Post was a zealot, but nobody had warned him about smoking in the presence of women.

That evening at the supper table Merriweather whispered in her ear what were for Margery the words of love. "I'm not a vegetarian," he said. "I'm a man of the world."

Margery Post wanted to leave Battle Creek and she wanted to eat meat. With Merriweather she gained a full diet and a trip to the Soviet Union.

Although Margery was the heir to millions of dollars, she never ate in a restaurant until after her marriage. C. W. Post did not allow it. He wouldn't even taste his own products in the restaurants. He called public eating places fleshpots.

C. W. Post never trusted Merriweather.

"You can marry him if you want to, Queen Ceres," he told his twenty-four-year-old daughter, "but there's something about this man I don't like. He's smart all right and he's a big man in the government and you'll travel with a lot of fancy people—but Merriweather seems to be the kind of person who's eaten too much canned food."

Halfheartedly the cereal king led her down the aisle of the glorious Battle Creek Seventh Day Adventist Church that he had built for the community. Margery's wedding was a paid holiday for all Post Cereal employees. Even some of the Kellogg's people came. There was no enmity between the empires, their common foe was meat.

Margery's white gown was as plain as a flour sack, but for that glorious day, C. W. Post created the single-serving box that could serve as its own bowl. Every guest received a variety pack. The church only seated two hundred but guests stood on both sides of the street, down two entire blocks. The bridal couple marched between the townsfolk. Neighbors threw rice and rose petals. Margery was wearing her first high-heeled shoes, Merriweather wore a black tuxedo and a top hat. Woodrow Wilson sent a telegram congratulating the couple. C. W. Post, who had hardened his heart since the day he decided to live, shed tears for the memory of his beloved wife and for his failure as a Nazarite.

On his daughter's wedding day, he also remembered his own father, Abraham Post, and the way in which he, a failed Nazarite, had found such an unexpected way to do the Lord's work. C. W. Post stood amid his employees and neighbors watching his little girl walk down Sixth Street on the arm of the ambassador to the Soviet Union and he remembered how the corn spoke to him.

# CHAPTER NINE

When the corn spoke to him on the day that he went to the beggars' field hoping to disappear from the face of the earth, on that day C. W. Post was finally ready to understand what he had heard. The corn stretched two feet above his head and bent to the north. He made his own path where only rodents and rabbits had gone before in a field thick with God's plenty, the field wherein C. W. Post's own body moved like the wind, causing the stalks to bow like the brothers before Joseph. The heavy ears drummed against his rib cage, the silk cascading from the ripeness caressed C. W. Post's cheeks and lips. He walked so quickly that the angel of death could not see the cornstarch trickling from between his toes. On his head he wore the high black skullcap that he bought from the Jew in Battle Creek, in the pocket of his dungarees was the leather purse, the profits his father had awarded him for selling fodder to the neighbors in the year of the drought that the Posts had anticipated because of the seven-year cycle of famine and plenty chronicled in Genesis 41.

C. W. H. C., Child Whom He Called, his father had named him on the night that Abraham Post held his infant up to the moon. On that luminous night his father vowed that neither wine, nor woman, nor razor would defile the purity of this infant whom he anointed with oil from the casing of his Winchester. The oil Sarah Post immediately washed off with lard soap and a gallon of heated salt water because her infant son was so cold from his exposure to the blessing of the Nazarite that his little blue lips, Sarah thought, might never again taste even milk.

When she had warmed her son at her bosom and removed the oil of his anointment, she also shortened his name to C. W., Charles William, she said, not Child Whom, and she also warned Abraham Post that she would take the child and go back to Niles and spend the rest of her days working at her father's printing press before she would let her infant be raised a Nazarite in western Michigan in 1875, long after the days of the Bible.

"No angels speak in this house," she said, "and no prophets, and my boy is just going to be a boy, not a Nazarite." She reached for her sewing scissors on the low table beside her to violate the hairs on the head of her month-old child but just when her fingers spread the steel blades and Abraham Post turned aside his glance so he would not see his wife violate the Nazarite creed, just then the cat, Gingham, sprang from the darkness and landed upon Sarah Post's shoulder so that she clutched her C. W. with both hands and dropped the scissors into the pot of boiling water where it hissed and spoke like the cat's ancient ancestor. The frightened child spread out his arms for his father and Abraham Post took the miraculously spared Nazarite in his arms while the angels that his wife heard not sang Hosannas so gloriously that the soul of the cat, instantly and long before the death of the beast, entered the highest rung of the Heaven that has no end.

There were no mysteries. Everything was known, only not yet to C. W. Post, who trampled through his own fields as the avenging angels had trampled through his life not long after Father Abraham lost his voice and began communicating with his son through simple stick figure drawings on the backside of wrapping paper which C. W. saved in order to savor over and over the words of his beloved father, that were not words because the Nazarite child was no more a Nazarite, because without tasting wine or feeling the razor's steel C. W. as a young man had succumbed to the white flesh, to the soft throat, to the even teeth, to the limbs of Josephine Forbes where he forgot his mission and his father and all else until the avenging angel smelled deceit upon his plow and hardened the earth first and then caused mange upon the herd and finally crept into the lovers' cottage, into the lungs of Josephine until his lovely innocent young wife breathed her last cold breath never knowing why eternity had come for her in its fine carriage before she even heard their little girl say a word, before her spring garden showed a sprout, before she knew for sure the kind of man C. W. Post who slept beside her for barely a year would turn out to be when finally he understood the plan of his life.

More than Biblical Jacob mourned his Rachel did the young farmer mourn his Josephine. He gave his child to his mother and his ever-silent father to raise as their own. He ate only bread and muffins that his sisters brought to the cottage. He tilled the soil behind Flag, more resigned than the beast. He brushed and fed the animals. He harvested the crop for Abraham to sell in Battle Creek but he allowed no joy to cross the stormy threshold of his heart, no smile to break the teeth's barrier. He waited for the word that he understood would come through the field—through Nature, more trustworthy than man, Nature unpolluted by lust passing seed in the winds—not through the milling of flesh.

C. W. Post thought he had robbed his father of speech and his wife of her living soul, because he, the chosen one, turned out to be just another farm boy as Momma and his five sisters always had known he was and not the chosen one whom his father anointed and expected with every new dawn.

But the signs were there; the night of the anointing, the Jew's cap, the ever full purse—what were these signs if not marks of his marking? "I ran from Thee," C. W. Post spoke to the corn,

"I ran as Jonah ran, as even Moses the magnificent servant of your will fled into the desert when he feared his awesome mission before Pharaoh."

C. W. Post lived in the best of times. His five sisters married and were blessed with offspring. His father's acreage spread all around the new city. His little daughter Margery hardly knew her young father who never played with her when he came in to sit by Grandpa near the piano and watch the older man make marks and drawings on the long brown paper which they never gave to her.

Her father was a mere hand on the farm, a stranger who could not look at her because he saw Josephine's toes in the little girl's and the small white teeth and brown curls and he was reminded of the wreckage he had made of himself and she whom he loved by not heeding the bidding of an angry God whom he now hated but obeyed though it cost him his joy.

In all the lands around the Kalamazoo River only C. W. Post had suffered the wrath of an angry God. Prosperity reigned in the land. Houses sprang up like flowers. Cohen, the Jew, built a store with three winding staircases. One of C. W.'s brothers-in-law became mayor. The railroad passed through Battle Creek and soldiers and teachers settled. To the east of the town, though C. W. and Abraham hated the sight and stench of it, there arose a slaughterhouse where frightened cattle were turned upside down so that their spittle ran into their crazed eyes clouding the thick instant of their death.

All of the Posts were and remained vegetarians. They could no more eat beef than one another. They sold no farm animals to slaughter. Their chickens had many generations of kin. Theirs was a farm of milk and honey and cheese and eggs and bread of every sort. Each of the girls married only after her man took the vow of abstention from meat.

"My lips are clean," C. W. spoke to the corn as he passed through on his day of decision. "My lips are clean and my bowels, nor has my voice been lifted in profanation."

"You were no Nazarite," Sarah said when she held her 22-year-old boy in her arms after his wife died. "That was just silliness your father planted in you. My God, boy, stop torturing yourself that you've done wrong by marrying. If your father had a voice left even he would tell you that Josephine dying like this has nothing to do with you not being a Nazarite. She died of the influenza. There is no such thing as a Nazarite. Your daddy used to wash the feet of travelers just in case they were angels and expected it. There were no angels, they were just machinery salesmen and blacksmiths and new neighbors, people who didn't know what to make of having their feet washed. And you were never a Nazarite. I cleaned that rifle oil off of you on the day he did it. Take hold of yourself, boy. You've got a little girl to raise. Find another woman and go on like the rest of us. It's what the world is about."

But C. W. Post could not just go on and he didn't until the day he saw Cohen standing beside his buggy holding a whip in one hand and a top hat in the other and looking C. W. Post straight in the eye as the young man trudged past on the muddy road following Flag through a new furrow. The Jew was out riding, looking at the world. C. W. noticed the velvet seats of his buggy and the fine linen of his black suit. He hardly recognized in the prosperous merchant the little man who had swept the counter clean with a feather whisk and rolled up his fabric and then spread open a Hebrew book before seven-year-old C. W. Post and his anxious father.

Together the Posts looked at the Hebrew characters. At their request, Cohen showed the book to them as nonchalantly as if he was showing a bolt of muslin. He went about his business. He washed his hands, pouring water from a two-handled cup, he put on a high soft black skullcap, he broke bread and poured salt upon it and offered sustenance to the two vegetarians who had called upon him to teach the Hebrew tongue to young C. W. and to circumcise the flesh of the lad.

The word of the Lord in all its beauty in its mother tongue

lay before them. The Posts believed in no church. The Pope was Antichrist but even Moses had mistaken the great moment in history, the making of the golden calf.

"These people who had seen miracles," Abraham told C. W., "would they make an idol that was not a divine image—could they who crossed the Red Sea and left slavery in Egypt do so?"

The golden calf must have shimmered more than the sun on the Kalamazoo River before the logs jammed it. The calf itself was a holy emblem against eating flesh. The mistake of Moses was not to see this.

"Because of this mistake he did not live to enter the Holy Land," Abraham Post told his young son.

The Jew continued his display of holy vessels. He spread a white cloth over his counter. He pulled beaten silver cups out of drawers lined in blue wool. He spread out the phylacteries to show the Posts the wood and leather ornaments to God and he was about to pour wine into the lambent vessels when Abraham Post stayed his pouring with an outstretched arm and mighty hand.

Cohen did not know he was in the presence of a Nazarite. He spoke of the wine of sacrifice, the wine of the Christian mass.

"Not for C. W.," Abraham Post told the only Jew in Battle Creek, "not for the Nazarite who will lead us against the Philistines."

Cohen wondered who the Philistines were. He had moved to Battle Creek after a disastrous storm had crushed his goods and his wagon near Chicago. He told the boy how the banks of Lake Michigan foamed and turned brown and rose up like whirlwinds and tore bed linens from the hands of customers and wound the cloth around bystanders, wrapping them tight as mummies. He talked about icicles growing from the small strands of hair in the noses of men, icicles that broke and tinkled with speech when the lips were still able to move, but in the deepest frost grew like elephant tusks upon the men of the Windy City forced to go about with uncovered faces when the wrath of God made itself felt on the shores of that lake full of speckled fish in the summer which Cohen never saw because he traveled at that season to do business elsewhere, finally Battle Creek, where he decided to stay. But not, God forbid, among Philistines.

Cohen refused to circumcise. Only in Chicago, he said, could this be done in a holy ritual; but elsewhere it could be done by doctors. The boy, afraid of the elephant men of Chicago—holy men circumcising by tusks, by knives, by cunning alone—and of the wound of circumcision, begged the Jew for another sign of his anointment.

Cohen, whose father had been a peasant on the estate of Count Sobieski near the city of Riga, had known many righteous gentiles. They littered the continent that he had wandered since his father left him penniless and with a sick mother in New York while he went to seek a cousin in Beaver Falls, Pennsylvania, and was not heard from again, not even when his wife died and the police telegraphed Beaver Falls where nobody knew a Yacob Cohen. After that his eleven-year-old son became a merchant, first of tin cookware as thin as a tubercular's arm and then of musical instruments to make gay the life of isolated folk in villages of Missouri and Southern Illinois and finally of the one-piece shirtwaist dresses that ladies buttoned in the front without the help of servants, shirtwaists that were stitched in New York by Polish immigrants just like Cohen, only happier than he because they lived among other Jews.

"You know," Cohen said, "I think a skullcap would do the trick." In twenty minutes the merchant made a new one for C. W. out of stiff muslin, high in the middle, high as a Sephardic rabbi's forehead. He placed the head covering on the long brown stringy hair of the anointed one and recited the prayer for bread in the ancient tongue. The prayer moved Abraham Post to warm tears of gratitude and forever after allowed C. W.

Post to believe himself invincible before men. The high skull-cap blessed in Hebrew represented a sign on, if not exactly in, the flesh. A sign that he could take upon himself, a sign more powerful than magic because it worked nothing other than the will of C. W. Post, who willed for three years deep mourning and abstinence and mortification of the flesh and did not once in those awful years put the skullcap on his head.

Nightly he rubbed the soot from the fireplace on his feather pillow, the pillow that had been part of Josephine's dowry and was still covered by a percale case she had embroidered with small yellow flowers that looked like none C. W. had ever seen. He rent his undergarments so that people would not be able to see his mourning in the second and third year after her death. He continued to mourn and to grieve long after he had forgotten the sound of Josephine's voice and the feel of her feet against him at night and the deep sighs of her lovemaking which seemed to him like asthma but were the motions of her feelings. He forgot how to stop mourning as his father had forgotten how to talk on the day of C. W.'s marriage and walked among the wedding guests in a blue wool suit smiling and accepting silently the congratulations of all those who knew not that C. W. was to be a Nazarite.

Abraham had promised his son to the Lord if only the Lord would open the womb of his barren wife.

Sarah refused to think of herself as barren because she had not conceived in two years of marriage. Until the night of the anointment Abraham did not tell her his prayer to relieve her barrenness. When she gave birth to five daughters in the next eight years, the girls too seemed heaven-sent, bonuses from a barren womb because the Lord was pleased with C. W. Post and his upright father.

The corn was ripe. The corn lay upon C. W.'s shoulders when he stopped. Ears dropped from his pockets, ears so full of new sugar that the stalks dripped like tree syrup. Some of the unpicked ears were already rotting underfoot. All harvests now were bitter harvests to Post but the corner where he now walked was the spot where they had conceived his daughter when he took Josephine to walk through the Post acres so recently her own. The field was newly planted that year, just cleared of the Dutch elm trees with their pointed leaves and still unsteady to the feet in places where the roots once went deepest. This was the corner of their field that would never be harvested, he told Josephine. It belonged to the poor, to the beggars, the wanderers, those without sustenance. He marked it off with thick rope, as his father had already marked off his own fallow lands, and he posted a sign over the neck of the scarecrow. Take, it said, and be satisfied.

None took. The corn rotted on the stalk. The poor of Battle Creek were less poor than C. W. Post. They had their own acres and shops, their own granaries. "What," Josephine had asked, "would a poor man do with an ear of corn? He couldn't use it for feed if he had no animals, nor could he eat it like the fruit of the tree to satisfy himself."

The poor did not eat of his produce, the Lord had not accepted his sacrifice, his father had lost speech and his wife breath and now C. W. Post in the fourth year of his grief lay down among the other unclaimed gifts of the earth ready to spit out his soul.

He had fasted for three days and nights. In the clarity of hunger he understood fullness. He deciphered the language of the birds; they sang of the glory of the Creator and the splendor of food. "No mysteries," C. W. spoke aloud to himself, "only hallelujah and digestion."

On her wedding day, Margery Post, nicknamed Queen Ceres when she was fourteen by the Battle Creek *News*, remembered the day C. W. took his only child to the beggars' field where she had been conceived and told her how the voice came to him there as he hovered over the slough of despond.

"I wanted to give up the ghost," he told Margery, "I had no

more use for myself, I wanted you and everyone else to forget me and let me sink into the earth, just another uneaten ear."

But the corn spoke to him. From beneath the shell of his body he heard the earth groan though the heavens remained silent. The voice of the corn was sweeter even than praises of starlings. "The corn is ripe," it said, "and the wheat immortal gold." Nature sang out to him the words he had placed upon the breast of a scarecrow, "Take and be satisfied." He opened one of the fallen ears, stripped the husks and the silk, and with the folding bone-handled knife his father had given him C. W. Post sliced into thin strips one majestic raw kernel of corn. He held the hard fragment upon his tongue where it softened even before his teeth ground it to sustain him. One after another C. W. Post sliced and softened slivers of corn.

The southerly spring wind blew the stench of the slaughter-house over his abundant field and C. W. Post realized that his life was not yet over.

The way Jacob wrestled with an angel, the way St. Paul understood truth and threw off the garb of the world, so C. W. Post understood that he would live not as a failed Nazarite and a bereft husband, but as keeper of the world's granary. The corn that he sucked while lying on his belly at the gates of Gehenna would save all the animals on the face of the earth. The food was here rotting underfoot while men slaughtered and pillaged and desecrated themselves with blood and lacerated flesh, holy flesh, in order to lie with full stomachs and murderous souls upon God's sweet earth.

C. W. Post arose. He took water from his well, honed his knife and with that knife and a scissors he burrowed through to the skin of his face. No more would he wear the face of a Nazarite. With his skin ragged as the scarecrow's and smeared with his own half-dried blood, C. W. Post walked toward the Bank of Battle Creek. The idlers on the street did not recognize the bloodied beardless young man who had not been among them since his wife's death. They thought he was a stranger who had been robbed and beaten about the face. They followed the trail of his blood into the bank until he turned his raw face, bleeding everywhere except at the eyes, to the gathering multitude and told them, "I am C. W. Post and I'm going to start feeding the world."

Margery Post was thinking of that story which she had heard from her father and from so many others, the story that had become a legend in Battle Creek where within a decade Post Cereals sucked up the grain of an entire continent. She thought of her father arising from the field to feed the world while her hair dried in a soft white Turkish towel at the Hotel Del Prado in Madrid, Spain, where her father had taken her to learn some of the ways of the world while he began the work of effacing the image of wine and meat from art.

She thought of the strange and wonderful career of her father while she listened to the art historian James Robinson and the young Spanish painter Dali talk about killing C. W. Post in order to save the paintings he wanted destroyed.

The cereal man and his daughter went by the New York Central line to New York. There they joined James Robinson, whom Post had hired the year before to tell him how to rectify the mistakes of past art.

With Robinson they sailed on the great ship *Mauretania* to Madrid, Spain. There Margery slept in a bedroom larger than the cottage she and her tycoon father still shared in Battle Creek. The cottage remained as it was while Josephine had lived, but there were no more empty fields around them now. Beside the cottage stood the first Post Cereals building where eight hundred women shucked corn for twelve hours a day every day except the Sabbath—and even that day the corn grew. Margery, from the window beside her bed, looked out at rows of workers as endless as the blue-white ocean that she looked at through her luxurious porthole on the *Mauretania*.

"Queen Ceres riding on the *Mauretania*," C. W. told his daughter. He liked the name the newspaper had given her, he wanted her to be the Queen, for he knew that her reign would be long and just and that all the years that had been robbed from Josephine would come to settle in their beauty and riches and splendor upon her only remnant, this daughter for whom he acquired every week of his life more riches than Midas ever dreamed of.

Just as the earth produced, so did Post Cereals. His flaked corn and his hard-toasted grains swept over the land faster than locusts. Everywhere that the railroad went, it carried thousands of cases of Post cereals, and even to remote spots far from the railheads wagonloads of Post cereals went out to rural America.

C. W. Post had a letter from a Navajo chief telling him that he ate nothing else, that because of Post's Corn Flakes he had reconciled himself to the loss of the buffalo. Teddy Roosevelt ate two bowls a day and so did his enemy William Howard Taft. Among the governed it became the custom to eat it for breakfast although Post continually emphasized that his flaked corn was a meal in itself, a full supper designed to spare the lives of cattle and hogs and sheep and bring merriment back to meadows and speed the coming of the day of redemption of all souls—human and animal alike—the day in which the lion would lie down with the lamb and man would not ravish the helpless cud-chewing herds who trusted in his mercy.

Her skin softened by the Spanish bath oils and the perfumed water of the Hotel Del Prado where Margery reigned in even more luxury than on the *Mauretania*, the young woman from Battle Creek, Michigan, heard the plotters against her father's life. She covered her thin boyish limbs with a silk robe and wrapped the white towel more tightly around her head so that she looked like a Queen of Araby in silk and turban come to mete out terror among the lawless.

The two men were drinking well water from a crystal pitcher when Margery walked into the drawing room. They did not know she had stayed behind to bathe while C. W. Post took his daily three-hour walk through the narrow streets of Madrid, paying along the way his deep respects to the land and the people of Columbus. Her feet burned from those walks and she was already weary of the crepuscular atmosphere of Madrid where everything smelled like sewage to her and people had such long thin faces and fleshy lips and sucked on olives and spit the pits in front of them, where the pits seemed in the sunny places like monuments designed by the insects.

The enturbaned maiden who stood before the two art fanciers was nineteen years old, and since the day her father came from the bank with the face that made her scream and took her back to the cottage of her birth he had been a father like no other. The fortune that engulfed them belonged to the Lord. C. W. Post taught his child that money was offal. He brought home crisp new bills, $100 and $50 and $20 bills with pictures of famous men, and let his little girl color upon them and cut them into shapes and forms that delighted them both. He showed her the little leather purse that Abraham had given him during the drought of 1892 when the Posts, who always put aside one-seventh of their crop for bad years, were the only farmers on the Kalamazoo River with grain to sell. Young C. W. meted out the grain as Joseph had in Egypt, selling to his neighbors and giving to those who lacked cash. No animals in their neighborhood starved that summer because of the foresight of Abraham Post. The profit of those grain sales C. W. placed in the little leather purse that his father told him would never be empty.

"If it ever gets to the last dollar it will just refill itself. Like the mouth with spittle, like the kidneys with urine, the purse will fill itself all the days of your life. Use that money to build the New Jerusalem."

While the world heaped riches upon him, C. W. knew that it was merely the filling up of the purse, the law of nature, the way of the world. The goal of his life was the creation of the New Jerusalem, not the accumulation of gold and colored paper. The corn was the way the Lord had chosen to rebuild his lost capital. The money was the Lord's, the time and the place were the choice of C. W. Post. To advise him he hired James Robinson of Harvard University and the Sorbonne and the Louvre Museum and the companion of Post's fellow tycoons who kept mansions in Newport and New York and London and wondered at C. W. Post in a rude cottage in Battle Creek when he could have taken his place beside the Vanderbilts and Goulds and Mellons where Mr. James Robinson told him he belonged when that eminent historian arrived in Battle Creek. He came because C. W. Post had sent a woman from the factory who took ten $1,000 bills out of a pocket of her blue shirtwaist and a ticket to Battle Creek where Robinson expected to be given a grand commission to furnish a mansion or two with the beauties of antiquity that he would select at his leisure, during a year among the museums of Europe at the expense of Mr. C. W. Post.

At the headquarters of the Post Cereals Company Robinson was taken with such a fit of sneezing that he was within a half-dozen sneezes of giving up the commission and returning to New York before he even met his employer. The dust from the flaked corn and wheat filled each room of the factory like a cloud of unknowing. Fans blew the particles upward where they stayed suspended during the workday while the tall employees walked hunched over and employees of all sizes put handkerchiefs over their mouths. On the days that they worked three shifts with no time for the fans to be shut and the grain dust swept away, the eight hundred women stood ankle deep in vegetable fluff, their mouths covered like bandits, their eyes reddened, watching the cereal boxes slide along a wooden conveyor, four thousand each hour.

Robinson hung his head out the window of C. W. Post's office, though the air beside the factory was scarcely less clogged. It was as if Post owned the air too, straight up to the heavens where the dust of his product rose like blown incense.

With tears already pouring from his irritated eyes, James Robinson met his employer and learned that Post wanted him to become the executioner of everything he loved.

"At first," Margery heard Robinson telling the Spaniard, "I thought he was joking. It was just too preposterous to believe that anyone would be willing to spend a fortune to change the great paintings of all time, for any reason.

"But when he started talking about the New Jerusalem he would build, I saw that he meant it. There I was, in his office, choking to death on corn dust while he was telling me how many cubits long the altars would be. The man is obsessed and is earning so much money so fast that he can spend virtually any amount for the paintings he wants to buy. He wants the meat and wine out of the *Last Supper;* after that he wants a list of all meat paintings since the Middle Ages.

"I told him the catalogue alone would cost $100,000. 'Fine,' he said, 'Let's get at it.' "

Margery heard the Spaniard laughing through the blue plaster wall. She already knew that Robinson hated her father's plan. On the *Mauretania* one afternoon while Post took his nap Robinson gave Margery trinkets as if she was an Indian princess and asked her to help him convince her father not to buy the *Last Supper.* He handed her a golden brooch in the shape of a goose with emerald eyes and a pin of ivory formed into a stalk of bananas and a pink coral necklace which he showed her on his own neck could be wound around three times.

While he still had the coral beads dangling beneath his short black beard Robinson fell to his knees and put his forehead against her kidskin shoes. Margery was going to call for the ship's doctor, a man with false teeth and more ribbons than the captain, but Robinson grabbed her foot to tell her he was begging, not dying, though die he surely would if C. W. Post succeeded in ravaging the museums of the Old World to buy and then clean up the great art of Europe in order to make beautiful his New Jerusalem.

The historian wiped his eyes with the hem of her dress. He touched his pockets as if he was a Catholic until he pulled from inside his jacket a sketch of Jesus and the disciples and the food and drink on the long table in front of them. He begged her to save the painting as if he was begging for the life of a child.

"No matter what your father thinks, Jesus probably ate meat," he told her. "Who in history ever thought to ask the question? I have reread the Gospels and Flavius Josephus and the early church fathers—loaves and fishes, bread upon the waters—but nothing against meat. Nobody cared, Miss Post, and nobody cares now except your father. The *Last Supper* is about the sadness of men and God, it is not about what Jesus ate and drank."

Robinson kissed her hand. He told her how Leonardo's mother had gone without olive oil in order to buy her son paint, how Leonardo more than anyone had his eye on God while he sketched the forms of this world. When Margery bent to help the eminent man arise the ivory bananas fell from her grasp and cracked at the stalk on the rubbed mahogany floorboards of the *Mauretania*'s deck.

"I'll buy another," Robinson said, "anything you'd like." He went to his knees again to retrieve the pieces of the stalk. While he groveled before her Margery wondered what could be so important about art.

Many years later, when she knew the answer to that question, she remembered that sketch of the *Last Supper* and that sunny day on the deck of the *Mauretania,* she remembered it when Walter Disney's agent casually placed on the coffee table in front of her an architect's drawing of Disneyworld and told her that only she stood in the way of this great wonder and happiness that awaited all the children of the earth. The Disney man had neither the passion nor the manners of James Robinson. He represented the mice and the rodents and all the base noisy instincts that art left out because everyone knew about them while only the few came to know, in their own brief spans, the life we live in spite of ants and rodents.

She had liked the tearful historian that afternoon aboard the ship and had agreed to help him convince her father, but when she heard Robinson talk of murder, Margery Post forgot art and hurled herself into the midst of the conspirators.

"If anyone lays a hand on my father," she said, "I'll buy every painting in Europe and burn them all at the Pope's own chimney. You'll see what will happen if my father is harmed."

Robinson began to shake and sob and was ready to fall to his knees again and beg forgiveness for what was, after all, only a passing thought mispoken among friends, when Margery grabbed him by his small beard and wrenched his face as far toward old Jerusalem as she could.

Robinson's gray cravat lay pinched in the crook of Margery's elbow when the Spaniard, still laughing, pulled the heiress off the throat of his companion by approaching from behind and touching her breasts so gently that it took her breath away. And when she turned to unleash her vengeance upon him as well Margery saw beneath the loosened collar of his wool shirt and along the lower portion of his collar bone a tattoo of a basket of fruit so vivid in its colors and so fresh that it seemed the morning dew itself fell from heaven upon the bosom of this young Spaniard who bowed at the waist and told her most gently that murder was not anyone's intention but that he would kill and then mutilate the body and eat the heart of any person who willfully changed even one line of his own work. "And I, mademoiselle," he said, "am no Leonardo da Vinci."

## CHAPTER TEN

For twenty-one years C. W. Post had been feeding the world as no one had ever fed the world before him. The profits from Corn Flakes and Grape-Nuts waxed in his bank account, but C. W. Post took no pleasure from his money. His greatest pleasure was the knowledge that every bite of his grain gave life to animals, and the goal of his life was to curtail the desire that had overtaken mankind somewhere early in the journey out of Eden, the disgrace of looking at animals and seeing not our brethren, but our meals.

Margery Post walked with difficulty on her high-heeled white shoes through the multitudes of Battle Creek. The crowds yelled "Queen Ceres" to her. Every soul in Battle Creek, she knew, wished her well, but her deepest wish was to go as far from the Post Cereal Company and its eleven hundred happy employees as she could. Moscow sounded just fine.

C. W. Post gave his daughter knowingly into the hands of a carnivore.

"The choice of life is always yours," he told her. How could he, a failed Nazarite, impose a code on anyone, even his own daughter? "In Russia," he said, "they eat bread but not cereal and not very much rice." As part of her trousseau C. W. Post gave his daughter two thousand boxes of Grape-Nuts to distribute in the Soviet Union. He also gave her a million dollars in gold and the Jew's purse and a tiny photograph of her mother in a golden locket.

"You'll always have everything," he told his daughter, "but

without peace of mind there is no pleasure."

At the corner of Sixth and Main streets while virtually every citizen of Battle Creek looked on, C. W. Post blessed his daughter and her new husband in the ancient words:

"May the Lord bless you with peace and make his countenance to shine upon you." C. W. Post kissed his daughter and watched her board the train to Detroit, the train that would take her from Detroit to New York, then on to a boat toward Russia. His only seed now sailed in the world's wind.

In Moscow, Margery Post ate meat but was not satisfied. In her husband's arms, her heart froze. James Merriweather had the gout. He spent most days shoeless, with his right foot elevated on a stuffed velvet cushion. He paid far more attention to his swollen toe than to his bride. Stalin, Beria, Radek, Erlinsky, Zinoviev . . . important Russians came every day to visit. They played Russian gin rummy with Merriweather and drank straight vodka. Margery walked the streets of this strange city. Pictures of Lenin floated over Moscow the way corn dust covered Battle Creek. Everyone was poor. When Margery took her morning walks, the streets were littered with frozen cats.

Her husband, Ambassador to the Soviet Union, was supposed to be an expert in agriculture. He had gone to Princeton and Oxford. He could read Greek and speak African dialects, but not Russian. The Soviets wanted advice on big farming projects. They wanted to turn peasants who had no cash into prosperous growers. From what Margery gathered listening to Stalin's bad English, they wanted all of Russia to be like Battle Creek. She told them it already was.

The Soviets admired C. W. Post. They didn't know his personal story, but they had heard of the flaked corn. They wanted it too. Stalin asked her to invite her father to the Soviet Union as Stalin's personal guest. C. W. Post cabled his daughter, "I stay away from the godless Communists, and you should too."

No matter how often Margery dissociated herself from Post Cereals, the Russians, disappointed in Merriweather's lack of practical knowledge, looked to his wife for help with agriculture. Erlinsky, who spoke a reasonable lisping English through his blue-black teeth, seemed almost obsessed with persuading Margery to help the Russian people.

She sat for hours in the overheated study of the ambassador's residence listening to Comrade V. R. Erlinsky talk about crop rotation, while her husband dozed, awoke every half hour or so for a sip of vodka, checked his swollen toe, and returned to his nap.

When she sat through these evenings of crop talk, Margery Post Merriweather found it hard to believe that she was in Moscow, married to an ambassador and living in a great mansion, and in the company of people who ruled a large part of the world. It was as boring as Battle Creek. The leaders of the Revolution talked mainly about crops and production, and her elegant cosmopolitan husband was such a dim presence that the gout seemed to have overtaken his character. Margery quickly learned that Merriweather liked small, manageable problems; one each day was his preference. The gout was perfect. He had his problem for the day and could ignore everything else, especially his wife.

Life for her husband, Margery came to realize, was a matter of avoiding accidents. Nothing more. He reveled in narrow misses. "Almost" was his favorite word. Contemplating his swollen toe, he would tell his wife adventure stories—how he almost fell off a sleigh, or almost ate rancid fish, or how his clever perception of a staircase saved him from almost stubbing his sore toe.

She slept with this man, and twice a week walked beside him as he hobbled to the opera. He wore an open-toed right sandal through the snowy streets. When they entered the opera house he put on a heavy wool sock, which he removed before the end of the first act. Margery understood neither the Italian opera nor the Russian language around her. She kept Merriweather's wool sock in her purse and wondered if there was such a thing as an adventurous life.

She knew that the people of Battle Creek thought she was going quickly and smoothly into the world of grand society. She had thought so too. When she left Battle Creek, Margery expected grand balls, charming statesmen, champagne, soldiers in clean blue uniforms. Instead, everything was dull and gray. She saw the glamorous buildings of Moscow, but most of them had no electric bulbs in the chandeliers and were closed by order of the State. The soldiers wore uniforms that looked like coveralls. The Russian leaders had bad breath, and dreamed of a good growing season, and everyone was always drinking vodka from breakfast to bedtime.

She wrote a long letter each week to her father. It was easy to tell him about the kinds of things that interested him. Crops, weather—that was mostly what she learned about in the Soviet Union. About marriage she learned that a wife was about as important as a good pair of sandals. Married seven months, Margery Post began to think about returning to Battle Creek.

When she agreed to accompany Comrade Erlinsky across the Ural Mountains to Uzbekistan and the Central Asian plains, she did so only to be able to last out the year. She didn't want her father to think she was too weak-willed to make her marriage last even one year.

"You'll see Russia," Erlinsky said. "You'll see the Russian land, the Russian people. Moscow"—he made a gesture to include everything around them—"Moscow is nothing. I wash my hands of Moscow. The daughter of cornflakes must see all of Russia, see our wheat fields and our hearty peasants."

Erlinsky seemed to think that all Margery had to do was look out the train window. He acted as if Margery was a talisman, a magical being who could make things grow better merely by her gaze. He thought of her father as a magician rather than a capitalist. He kept asking her for the secret of C. W. Post.

"He doesn't eat meat, and he prays in the morning and the evening. And he doesn't work on the Sabbath—that's Saturday, not Sunday. He doesn't try to earn a lot of money. He wants people to stop killing animals. He's a lot more revolutionary than anything I've seen over here."

"Russian people must eat meat," Erlinsky told her. "It's too cold here for vegetable protein. Without meat we would get sick and die."

"You mean without vodka," Margery said.

Erlinsky laughed. They were sitting in a private dining car on the Uzbekistan rail line. This was its first complete run since being repaired from damage caused during the war and the Revolution. The Whites blew out sections of track sporadically, Erlinsky told her, in a random pattern. The Reds, he said, were more systematic. During the Revolutionary years you could ride through a town and tell at a glance whether it had been attacked by Reds or Whites. Red damage was clear and complete, it had an end in mind. It was not simple destruction or punishment. Reds destroyed only what had to be destroyed, he told her, but they did so totally.

"In such a way," Erlinsky said, "we will build, too. The Red Army and our great communal farms to rival those of your brave father."

Erlinsky refused to believe that Battle Creek was not a battleround. He thought C. W. Post had fought some heroic battle and emerged victorious and the possessor of the secret of rapidly growing grain. Margery understood that Merriweather was glad to see her go off on a long journey to the Russian breadbasket. He hired Black Africans to work in the house. He spoke their dialect.

"Who knows," Merriweather told his young wife, "maybe you will be able to give them some farming tips. Erlinsky seems to think so. At any rate, there's nothing to lose. You'll get to see Russia, and they'll be grateful. With my condition as it is"

—he gazed at his toe—"there's no way I could take you on such a journey."

She packed everything she wanted to keep in her trunk. When she said goodbye to Merriweather she knew she had decided not to return to Moscow and her husband.

Margery slept most of the time as the train moved toward Central Asia. The heavy meals and the rocking motion of the cars plus her own lack of stimulating thoughts made sleep seem the best alternative. It was either going to her car to read and sleep or sitting with Erlinsky as he calculated agricultural data concerning the provinces they were passing through. Whenever they stopped, she and Erlinsky, bundled in coats and blankets, rode on a sleigh to look at snow-covered fields dotted with the huts of peasants. In her daydreams, Margery began to think of the world as composed of snow and corn. She had seen enough of each to last a lifetime and she was only twenty-five years old. She wanted something exciting to happen to her, and at Tashkent it happened.

Three weeks into her journey, Margery decided not to accompany Erlinsky across yet another snowy plain to listen to yet another conversation between a congregation of peasants and Erlinsky. She chose to stay in her hotel while Erlinsky took a three-day side trip. She wanted to look at the Asian buildings of Tashkent and the narrow Turkish faces of the people. She wanted a few days of simple tourism.

She rested momentarily on a cold bench in Pushkin Park. She watched a peasant in a round fur cap as he dug through the snow near a tree in the small park. Margery was fascinated by his precise actions, as if he was digging for gold and knew the exact spot. Only the two of them were in that section of the park. Though it was still mid-afternoon, the sun was already setting and the air was becoming too cold for a comfortable walk. Margery decided to watch the peasant seek his treasure before returning to the hotel.

As she awaited the peasant's find, Margery watched children

skating on the small pond at the far end of the park. She couldn't tell in the distance whether they were boys or girls; they all had dark knitted caps and mittens. As she watched them, she recalled her own pleasures as a skater on the Kalamazoo River.

For the three or four months of the year during which the Kalamazoo froze solid, C. W. Post did not mind if his daughter skated upon the solid water beside the empty fields that in the spring would bring forth grain for his mill. He did not permit her to go skating after dark, but on bitterly cold days, between the end of the school day and sunset, Margery in her sheepskin jacket and wool scarf liked nothing better than to speed across the ice, without thinking, only letting the wind and sometimes the snowflakes seek out the few uncovered places on her body. With her fingers stiff and her cheeks numb, she returned to the hot lentil stew or the baked sweet potatoes or the soybean casseroles that C. W. Post cooked for the two of them each evening. C. W. Post never had a chef nor a maid, nor a chauffeur, and though he scoffed at Communism, he gave every worker in his mill shares in the Post Cereals Company.

The Post Cereals Company had no strikes, and C. W. had no enemies. In the evenings he dozed over the Bible. He taught Margery to knit, which she did profusely and well. All of their sweaters and caps and scarves were the work of her hands. At Christmas every poor child in Battle Creek received a hand-knitted gift from Margery and a box of Grape-Nuts and a silver dollar from C. W. Post.

And the citizens of Battle Creek and employees of Post Cereals made every sort of decorative item for their benefactor and his solitary child. What the Posts gave they got back tenfold. Mittens and wool blankets and rag dolls surrounded them, and hundreds of handmade angels and fondly whittled toys and religious objects, but never, Margery remembered with some bitterness, anything she really wanted.

Her only joy was the dream of escape. This she could not tell her father, nor did she know where else she might go. There were aunts and uncles and cousins, but they all lived in and around Battle Creek. C. W. would fetch her home in five minutes if she ran away. Had she wanted anything she would have gone after it, but C. W. Post had been such a nonmaterial capitalist, such a spiritual being, that he failed to give his daughter anything to long for except escape. He also failed, to his everlasting disappointment and grief, to pass on his religious fervor or his vegetarianism. Margery never believed in her father's foods or his God, though his simple goodness and his sincerity kept her bound to him until that surprising day when the handsome diplomat, James Merriweather, came to court her and found her easier prey than he expected.

I would have married just about anyone, she was thinking, berating herself for her own foolishness. The peasant had dug up his treasure. He approached Margery.

"Here," the peasant said, "taste this."

Before she could say anything, something cold and hard was in her mouth. She swallowed it without tasting.

"You're an American?" Margery's first thought was that she'd been poisoned. "What was it?"

"You're the second person on earth to have eaten a blackberry that is more than one year old."

His face up close was obviously not the face of an Uzbek—nor was it a fleshy Russian face. It was a long thin American face, the kind of face that looked at a bowl of cornflakes every morning.

"What is an American doing here?" she asked, more stunned by him than by his frozen blackberry.

"Working," he said, "same as you."

"How do you know what I'm doing?"

He pulled a mimeographed sheet from his pocket. "Isn't that you?" The newsletter told of her scheduled visit to Uzbekistan with Erlinsky.

"All of the embassy offices got a copy of it," he said. "It

makes Uncle Sam look good. I'm just like you," he said. "An adviser to the government of the Soviet. In fact, your husband is my boss. At least he would be if he ever worked. He's just as lazy as the Russians, and just as much of a drunkard, too."

Margery, about to defend Merriweather, decided not to. What the man said was what she felt. She liked him.

They walked down Lenin Boulevard. He told her about freezing foods. "Even the Romans knew how to do it," he said, "but the trick is to keep everything ice cold even in the summer. What I did here is what the Eskimos do. They stash meat in the cold ground. First they let it start to go bad. They like it better that way. If a Russian was doing this, he'd load a big drum full of berries, a drum that already smelled like fish or vodka, and then he'd probably be too lazy to bury it deep enough. What I do is freeze just a few at a time, like a pack of candy, and I get 'em on ice right away." He stopped walking and held another berry in front of his face. Together they looked at it.

"Solid as a hard-on," he said. He walked Margery back to the hotel. They ate the rest of the berries. He asked her to meet him in the park the next day. Margery understood that her new life, almost a year late, was finally beginning.

She met Clarence Birdseye the next day. They walked to his small house near the park. They made love with their clothes and gloves on. Birdseye's house was filled with blocks of ice. He kept the ice on logs and built an efficient drainage system under the logs. A sheet-metal trough carried the melting ice water under his door. The water froze all around his tiny house. An old peasant in a sleigh delivered fresh blocks of ice twice daily.

"I just want to prove that it can be done," Birdseye told her. "I've buried fruit all over town, but none of it will be good when the thaw begins. What I've got here in my house, under constant freeze, is last year's crop. I've kept it good throughout the summer." He gave her an icy strawberry.

"Here. You can be the second person in the history of the world to eat a fresh strawberry more than a year old."

Birdseye never undressed at home. He kept a stove in his bedroom but used only enough heat to allow him to sleep without freezing to death. Margery, though moved by desire and grateful for the relief of her boredom, wouldn't spend an Arctic night with him. But she decided on the spot to spend her warm days and hours with Clarence Birdseye.

"I'm only staying so that I can continue to experiment with freezing things," he said, "and I'd rather be here than the North Pole. Russians aren't much company, but the Eskimos are probably worse."

When V. R. Erlinsky returned to Tashkent to rejoin the cereal queen on her journey through Central Asia, he met Clarence Birdseye and became the third person to taste a fresh one-year-old strawberry. The man was unmoved by the historical event.

"Fruit, by its nature," he said, "is against the interests of the working class. It is expensive to transport and has a high spoilage rate. The only workers truly able to enjoy it are the growers or those close to the market. Yet they rarely taste this fruit of their labor because the market value makes it necessary to ship fruit immediately to the tables of the rich."

"All I asked," Clarence Birdseye said, "is if it tasted OK."

"Nothing, sir, tastes good that has been stepped on by class tyranny. This government is committed to grain—long-lasting, largely unperishable, easily transportable grain. The people need bread, not frozen berries."

"People have had bread for about a million years," Birdseye said, "and nobody's had frozen fruit. I've been freezing my ass out here for two years and you can't even give me a straight answer. How's it taste?"

"It tastes like ill-gotten gain," Erlinsky said. He held out his arm for Margery to join him. The train was scheduled to leave that afternoon.

"I'm not going," she told the chief of Soviet agriculture, "I'm staying here with Clarence."

Erlinsky, accustomed to crop failure, civil war, and the necessary tragedies of collectivization, did not understand the young woman's impulsive decision to abort her journey for a liaison with an idiot who froze berries. He urged her on behalf of the Soviet people and her husband to continue her journey, then urged her on behalf of common decency and good sense. At 3 P.M. he ordered the train delayed until the next morning and cabled Moscow for instructions. The Ambassador's wife, though traveling as a private citizen, was his guest and the responsibility of the Soviet government. Had she been a Soviet citizen he would have had her forcibly placed on the train.

In Moscow, Stalin, equally aware of the unusual and serious nature of Mrs. Merriweather's desire to remain in Tashkent, consulted her husband.

The Ambassador, slightly relieved of his siege of gout, was living contentedly with four African ladies whose dialect he spoke and who attended to his needs. He urged Stalin to allow his wife to do as she pleased.

"We Americans," he said, "are like that. We're roamers. We pick a spot now and then and just decide to stay—spend a season or two. That's how the West was settled. It's part of our character."

The fact that the Ambassador's wife was choosing to roam with another man and in the west of another country seemed of no consequence to Mr. Merriweather. "A man has his health and his career," he said. "Women come and women go. Diplomacy goes on."

Stalin, amazed by the behavior of the Americans, telegraphed Erlinsky to abandon Mrs. Merriweather to her fate.

V. R. Erlinsky was not a fool. Part of his plannings during the long rail journey had concerned his amorous intentions toward Margery. Because of his party standing he had been most discreet. He had been waiting until the return journey, secure in his feeling that by that time either he would be an esteemed man in her judgment, or two months of her repressed lust and loneliness would make up for his not being an esteemed man. The quick collapse of his daydream unnerved him.

As he arrived at the hotel to show Mrs. Merriweather Stalin's telegram, Erlinsky decided to bare his heart.

"Madam, when I told you the Russian farmer needed your approval, I spoke not in the abstract but of myself. This Russian farmer, Vladimir Radovich Erlinsky, so desires your company that the return journey seems impossible without your presence beside me. As I gaze at arable land with my left eye, the right takes in your sweet beauty. As my mind is taken with feeding our people, so my heart feeds upon you." The Minister of Agriculture put his head against Margery's bosom and sobbed.

Margery had never been spoken to in the language of courtship. Two days ago Birdseye had said nothing. He merely put his arms around her. He felt like a warm bath and she stepped in. Merriweather expended all his tenderness upon himself. In their amorous encounters he positioned Margery in an almost military fashion. These were the men in her life.

"I can't make love to a foreigner," Margery said, realizing only as she said it that it was true.

Erlinsky's desire turned to anger.

"Keep your American then, and freeze with him. Do you think your father's money can even get you out of here? When this train departs there won't be another for two weeks, maybe longer. And there aren't ten people who speak English in this entire region. The madman you've fallen in with lives in an icehouse. You would rather freeze with an American than ride in a first-class car with a citizen of the new Soviet."

Margery didn't even hesitate. For the first time in her life the world had stopped seeming as dismal as Battle Creek.

Clarence Birdseye walked out of the bedroom to join them

in the parlor of Margery's suite. He was dressed in a checked wool logger's shirt and long underwear. His frostbitten fingers were covered with cold cream. He placed his arm around Margery, being careful to keep the cold cream from smearing her sweater.

"Comrade," he said, "when I was fifteen I left North Dakota on a freight train. In Milwaukee I got off for something to eat. Then I went on to Erie, Pennsylvania. I've eaten moose that I shot myself and I've seen criminals and pimps in Buffalo and in New York City that would make you look like an honest man. You think Clarence Birdseye is afraid of being cold in a city in Russia?"

"He's a scientist," Margery said. "Clarence is doing important experiments."

"The grand experiment is the Revolution," Erlinsky said. He put on his fur hat, saluted the lovers and walked toward the station of the Uzbekistan railroad.

# CHAPTER ELEVEN

*W*hen Jerome, her butler, led the gray-haired man into her study, Margery Post thought immediately of Clarence Birdseye. Though his trousers were as loose as pajamas, she could see that the man had Birdseye's bowlegged strut. When he shook her hand she noticed the wide flat fingernails. A cousin, she thought, or an unknown half brother, someone bringing a message across the years. The thought of Birdseye still made Margery feel flushed, angry, guilty. She had not forgotten anything.

"Ma'am," the man said with the same kind of directness she remembered in Clarence, "I'm Bones Jones, owner of the Orlando Pirates. You don't know me, but we have a common enemy. I've come to help you in our battle against Walt Disney."

Two days earlier, Mayor Greener and several city councilmen had accompanied Treat Gilbert to her home, asking Mrs. Post to drop her objection to Disneyworld. She had refused and there had been something in the paper. But she did not expect or want every local grumbler to seek her out. That would be as bad as Disneyworld.

"Mr. Jones," she said, "I don't know who you are, or what you understand of my position regarding the Disney enterprise, but I am not seeking any allies. The matter of my property is entirely personal, I assure you."

Bones Jones looked at the splendor around him. From the

study he could see seven of the eleven indoor gardens that C. W. Post's architects had created.

Margery would have asked Jerome to show the man out at once, but his resemblance to Clarence Birdseye overcame her reluctance to talk about anything with a local ruffian. If Clarence is alive now, she thought, he's this man's age, probably looks like this. The thought of Birdseye as the owner of a baseball team made her smile.

"Mrs. Post," Bones Jones said, "there's nothing to laugh about." She thought he was foaming at the mouth, but it was only his chewing gum.

"Mr. Jones, if we're going to converse," Margery said, "you'll have to do so without your chewing gum. I have a deep aversion to the habit."

"OK," he said. Margery handed him an ashtray, but Jones put the sticky gum, unwrapped, directly into his pocket.

"Disney's a killer," he said. "He burned me out once, he'll do the same to you. Anything in his way doesn't stay there very long."

Bones Jones roamed her study the way he roamed the third-base line in a close game. Margery listened almost against her will to this pacing maniac. She was afraid he might attack her if he was interrupted. She couldn't judge whether the story of Perky Parrot was a madman's fantasy or the true story of Bones Jones's life. What she recognized in Bones Jones was hatred, the kind of hatred she heard from Russians raging against Stalin years after she had known them as his admirers in Moscow.

"I've got the Pirates and the stadium," Bones Jones concluded, "and you've got all this. Together we can make a stand. I won't back down, I promise you that. He ruined me once, now I'm a dangerous man."

An untidy one, she thought, with your pockets full of chewed gum. Has it come to this, Margery wondered—two foolish old people trying to stand in the way of what the world wanted?

"Mr. Jones," Margery said, adopting a tone of voice that her father would have slapped her for, "I don't think we have anything to discuss. Please excuse me."

"I know you're very rich and must think badly of me for such a hasty introduction," Bones Jones said, "but don't just toss me out. If you're gonna quit, fine, I'll stand up to him myself, but I've come to tell you, Mrs. Post, that if you fight you're not going to be up against a corporation full of lawyers trading words in a courtroom. No ma'am. If you're going against Disney you'll need guards and dogs and fire alarms and a tough hide yourself. If you stand in Disney's way he's not gonna settle for winning, he's gonna destroy you. You may have ten million bucks but you'll burn and wither as quick as Perky Parrot. There's not much difference between the melting point of skins and celluloid."

"Perhaps you should talk to my attorney, Mr. Gilbert."

"Treat Gilbert?" She was as surprised as Bones Jones that Gilbert should be a mutual acquaintance.

"Do you know Mr. Gilbert?"

"Everyone in town knows him. I didn't know he was your lawyer, I thought he worked for the Mafia. He owns every square inch of speculative land in Orlando County. I heard he's a pimp and a gambler, too."

Margery laughed to herself at the idea of Treat Gilbert as a pimp. Did that make her the whore?

"We must be talking about two separate Treat Gilberts. My attorney is not a criminal. As far as I know he spends all his time on my behalf."

"Well, do you own a whorehouse and a dog track?"

"Of course not!"

"Treat Gilbert does. And he lends money at twenty-five percent."

"That's absurd."

"That's true. I went to him last year to borrow eleven grand for new light towers. My outfielders were getting beaned by fly balls. He listened, then offered me a twenty-five percent loan. I told him to shove it. He told me he'd buy the team for ten bucks when I went bankrupt."

"I'll ask him about these allegations, Mr. Jones, but Treat Gilbert works for Hedges and Knowles, a major law firm in New York. He reluctantly transferred here some six years ago to look after some of my affairs. I can assure you that I own no whores or dog tracks."

"I'm not accusing you. I'm just recognizing as we talk that you're more helpless than I thought. If Gilbert is negotiating for you Disney already has you in his pocket. I thought you'd at least come up with the muscle in lawyers and influence. You're mighty lucky I came along. I'll bet Gilbert sold you out a long time ago."

"Mr. Gilbert doesn't make any decisions," Margery said.

"If there's money in it for him, you can bet he does."

Who knows, Margery thought, maybe it's true? She never received a bill from Gilbert. Hedges and Knowles paid him out of a yearly retainer paid by one of her trusts. She didn't know what business he actually conducted for her. She had only called him about the moonport and this Disney business and once in a while about IRS or charity matters that she didn't wholly understand. Maybe I own a dog track and don't know it, she thought, maybe I'm a madam.

"Between Gilbert and Disney there won't be anything left of you," Bones Jones said. "They'll steal your money and cut out your heart and leave you to wander about until you die."

"That wouldn't take long if they cut out my heart."

"You know what I mean. I just came to tell you who I am and to let you know that someone is on your side for his own reasons. But even if I didn't hate the name Walt Disney I'll be damned if I'd be going crazy the way this whole county is about a thing as silly as an amusement park. And it's not the kids that are excited. It's the adults."

"I know," Margery said, "that's what has amazed me as well

—how delighted this area is to become the receptacle of kiddie-land."

"It's sad," Bones Jones said. "The Pirates play hard and draw five and six hundred a night. Disney will suck in that many in a minute at ten times the price."

The manager walked around the circumference of the study. "I know, you don't trust me," he said, "but when you find out the truth about your lawyer maybe you will. Don't be afraid to call. I've got a few people we can trust—some of the Pirates and a few others, and Al and Hal the midgets. They hate him almost as much as I do."

Margery had seen the twin dwarfs often in downtown Orlando, though she hadn't known their names.

"Are they baseball players?"

"Management," Bones Jones said, "and during the off season they work construction for me. They're honest fellows, you can't say that about many in this county. I know people would sell their souls for a few bucks but I didn't know it would be just as easy to buy their kids."

## CHAPTER TWELVE

*A*t breakfast Howard and Mildred worried together about high-rise motels.

"When you can't see your car from your bedroom something strange happens," Mildred said. "You lose some faith in a building that takes you away from your vehicle."

HJ, who in all his travels had never used a parking ramp, nodded agreement and looked out at San Antonio. In his briefcase were the plans they had given him in New York, plans for what they told him were the next generation of motels.

"Things go in cycles," Corky said at the board meeting. "When you started out it was important to be small so you wouldn't look like all the hotels in town. You could do your L-shape or your rectangular sixty units, throw in a thirty-six-foot kidney pool, and if you wanted to go whole hog, double-deck her and put a lounge next to the coffee shop. That just won't cut the ice anymore. We can do six hundred units for only four times the cost of sixty. Once you're there, you're there. The only way is up."

At that time, with Milly sick and HJ anxious to get back on the road, HJ did not dispute the matter with his board of directors. When he asked about his orange roof and his ice-cream parlors they told him there was no point in putting an orange roof on a fifteen-story building where only the birds could see it. "And as for the ice cream," Corporate Vice President Dibble said, knowing that he had to be careful on this subject in the presence of Mr. Johnson, "Baskin and Robbins has really pulled the rug out from under us in ice cream. They went into the neighborhoods because they knew we were stuck on the outskirts. And when you have a choice of going say six blocks or six miles for ice cream, which are you going to choose? But don't worry, HJ, we're not about to drop the ice cream. It's doing fine along the highways, sales are still very good, only relatively it's now less than 2 percent of the operation. The ice cream is still good, but the pie around it has just gotten a lot bigger."

Since 1956, when Corky became president and the federal government began to drop the billions into the highway system, Howard Johnson had known it would come to this. "You and Mildred built the fifties and sixties thirty years ago, HJ," Corky said. "Now it's almost '64 and we've got to get going on the seventies and eighties." Milly's trailer was a constant reminder to Howard Johnson of what the seventies and eighties held, but still the desire was big in him to go out once more, always just once more, to feel his way around the country like a blind man in a new room.

From his balcony at the San Antonio house, Howard Johnson could see the whitewashed walls of the Alamo, smaller than a Beverly Hills house.

"Disney made history here," Howard Johnson said, "with Fess Parker and Buddy Ebsen. The coonskin caps, the records, the movie, the TV show. He never lets a thing go out. He bends it into all its shapes."

As they ate, Howard, Milly, and Otis reconstructed what they knew of the Disney saga. "David Crockett alone lasted years," Milly said.

"And then Zorro." Otis slashed a Z through the air with his butter knife. "I liked that fat Mexican, he was somethin' else. Old Zorro always got him though."

"He makes nature films out of waste footage," Howard said. "Do you remember 'Steamboat Willie'?"

Mildred remembered. It was the first talking cartoon she had ever seen. Mickey Mouse drove a tugboat and attacked a number of the female passengers. He sang bawdy songs. She thought of it as a rude and offensive film which reminded her to double check on the rodent problem in their houses.

"They started about the time we did, Milly, only in the opposite direction. From the Pacific toward the Atlantic."

"From sea to shining sea," Otis hummed.

The second night in San Antonio, Otis's last night as driver, was a restless one for all three. Milly felt her first pains in several weeks. They were not severe but caused her to inventory all that she had eaten since Los Angeles. Otis, as they headed toward his Louisiana birthplace, felt a quiet nostalgia for the heat, the bayous, the gumbo, and even the poverty of his youth which from this distance did not seem so bad. But Howard Johnson thought only of Walt Disney.

From his San Antonio balcony HJ daydreamed in the night air as he contemplated the Alamo in the moonlight. Without too much effort he imagined himself, Milly, and Otis entrapped in that small clean fort while Walt Disney surrounded them with the engines of war. The Disney wolves and dogs growled at the walls, mice skirted the parapets. Within the Alamo sat Howard Johnson after an excellent meal, satisfied, desiring a toothpick at most and ready to walk along the smooth stone path to his private boudoir. Outside the fort were the Disneys, like bus tourists lined up before a gas station urinal. O smug one come out, they yelled from their pissoir, O eater of ice cream, longer for calm sleep, make way for us who are the future.

We have a thousand musicians synchronized to our movements and ten million carefully framed actions. All possibilities are predrawn. Already, five minutes from now our banner in 35-mm. color overhangs your roof. Your Alamo Lounge will become a wax museum, your 28 flavors a single gray Tastee Freeze.

Within the Alamo Lounge HJ leaned his elbows upon his dinner table. As he tried to enjoy a quiet meal, the Disney creatures bombarded the walls with their popcorn machines and stormed the motel on ladders of pink and white peppermint sticks. Fess Parker led them singing the Davy Crockett anthem through the kitchen where with Bowie knives they diced stale caramels, cooked them in microwave ovens and dipped rotting apples in the hot mixture.

In the small dining room deep within the lounge, HJ sat calmly at his finished meal. A single loyal waitress remained at her station lest he should desire a final refill for his coffee. The looters dissipated themselves with souvenirs. "Whistle while you work," they sang. "Heigh ho, Heigh ho." Mildred and Otis too seemed to have vanished in the noise. "Waitress," Howard Johnson called, "my check please."

Instead of the waitress a shaggy Fess Parker appeared in coonskin cap, gold records dangling like scalps from his beige suede waist. He plucked the BankAmericard from Howard Johnson's grasp. His teeth were thin and sharp as an animal's. Spittle gathered in the corners of his mouth. He swung a long leg over a chair and sat grinning across the table. "The last meal," he said, "is on us. Eat up. Tomorrow it will be Tahitian Treat or barbeque."

Howard Johnson arose from his revery, closed the sliding door to the balcony and pulled the drapes to shut off his sight of the Alamo. And though he knew it was very late he picked up the Princess phone and buzzed Mildred in the adjacent room. Her voice as always reassured the host of the highways. Trembling slightly from his vision and the night air, Howard Johnson said, "Milly, I'm afraid."

# CHAPTER THIRTEEN

*A*s Otis watched, his nephew Mel Briggs closed the door of the Cadillac, turned the ignition key, placed the transmission into drive, and that was that. Otis Brighton, for the first time since they drove out of Beaumont, was not at the wheel of Mr. Johnson's limousine. He knew Miss Milly would be leaking little tears in the back seat and Mr. Johnson would be patting her hand and looking out the window—and Mel, though he promised Otis otherwise, would be eyeing that FM radio and thinking about driving that big old car through Miami Beach. Thinking about all those women looking at him driving such a car.

Mel promised to check the tire pressure every thousand miles and to keep the oil, transmission and battery fluid topped up and to look over the belts and hoses every time he filled the tank, but Otis suspected that his young nephew would not be so reliable. Oh, he would be better than a stranger, Otis knew that, he wouldn't have turned the vehicle over to a stranger at all, but he would have preferred one of his own sons to do it.

"You're not passing down a kingdom," his wife reminded him, "it's just a car, just a job even if it's for Mr. Howard Johnson. You've done your job and you got paid. Who could know all that stock would add up to so much? Mr. Johnson himself probably didn't know it when he started piling it on you."

She didn't understand what had been going on in that car. How could she know what it was like when Howard Johnson said, "Let's have a look over there," and disappeared for an hour or two while the engine cooled down and Miss Milly wrote notes in the back seat and Otis leaned against the back fender carefully and smoked a Chesterfield.

And then a year or so later they'd be going toward that spot again and almost where Otis dropped his cigarette butt there would be a building, a restaurant, sometimes with a motel. Otis knew other stuff went on outside the car, contracts and money and wood and steel and all that, but just passing by, year by year, it all seemed to happen just because they stopped and looked. Because Mr. Johnson looked and walked it out, and if it was OK, then you could put a town there and hook up the sewers. The man knew things you couldn't explain to a wife. Only Milly and Otis had seen it up close.

It pained Otis that strangers sometimes thought Mr. Johnson was a jerk. He couldn't do a thing with his hands, he couldn't even make the jack work when they had a flat. Once Otis watched Mr. Johnson check the oil. In an emergency, Otis had headed straight for the men's room. When he returned, there was Mr. Johnson holding the dipstick far away like it was a dead rat. He couldn't find the place to put it back in. He had black oil on his fingertips and a little soot on his upper lip. Otis never went to the men's room after that without checking the oil first. Mr. Johnson didn't like to trust the gas station attendants. Mr. Johnson believed in taking care of important matters yourself. They traveled. The car was important. They took good care of it.

To the world Otis Brighton was a servant. In the car, he was the vice president of transportation.

He tried to explain this to Mel, but how could you tell a twenty-five-year-old fella who had grown up seeing orange-roofed motels, how could you tell him what everything was about?

"Jesus, Uncle Otis," Mel told him when he handed over the keys, "relax, I'm not a dummy. I know this is an important job.

I'll be careful and safe. What more can a person do?"

That's what he couldn't tell the boy—it was a lot more than being careful and safe. That much was understood. That anybody could do. But you had to understand that Mr. Johnson and Miss Milly were not just out plucking greenbacks. Otis had seen Mr. Johnson tear down a restaurant to do honor to him, a Negro from Louisiana. You could not explain that to a boy who had come along later and any day now would be able to go into any restaurant he wanted, even in New Orleans.

Mel was his sister-in-law's boy. Lucy and her husband still raised rice only now it didn't flood every spring—there were drainage ditches to the bayous and Lucy and Tom had a fine house and an Avion camper too, and Mel Briggs had gone a year to Louisiana A. & M. before he decided that he'd rather talk about rice farming with Tom than with somebody who was supposed to teach him what he had known all his life.

Mel drove a Ford. The whole family had a preference for Fords. Nothing Otis could do about that. He told them what he thought, then they did as they pleased. Himself, he'd just as soon drive a Willys Jeep as a Ford. Mr. Johnson wouldn't buy a car without Otis's approval. If Otis said no Fords, that was it, no Fords.

He tried to explain to Mel but how could you tell anyone how it was all those years to park and then to watch Mildred check in while Mr. Johnson sat in a tiny lobby and leafed through Optimist Club brochures, acting like any old tourist. Oh, he was a sly one, Mr. J., fooled Otis at first. You'd think he didn't notice a thing, you'd think he had a nose cold or was half asleep or hungry and then he'd start telling Miss Milly about every loose tile in the floor and exactly to the second how long the check-in took, and how much dust there was on the plastic flowers. He kept his finger on a stopwatch the whole time he was inside anyplace. He liked to time things. Mildred always checked in in less than sixty seconds but Mr. HJ said the average was closer to three-and-a-half minutes for other people.

In larger motels after a slow check-in it could take you ten minutes or more to find your room tucked away someplace behind a garbage dumpster.

Mr. Johnson hated for anyone to get lost in his houses. He would sit there by the pool wearing his blue suit and keeping a watch in his pocket and observe a family all loaded down and tired after a day on the road looking for room 403 or something, which was still around two more corners and down a long hallway. And sometimes a baby would cry and the father would say, "Jesus Christ, I told you so," and go to move the car and then the mother would drop something and Mr. Johnson would know how bad those folks felt being lost and tired. He would bite his lip and keep his finger on the stopwatch and feel sorry for everyone but not do a thing except sit there and time their trouble while Milly was reading a book up in their room, and all those folks would be looking for their room in the dark and carrying little bags of potato chips and half-eaten sandwiches in case they got hungry during the night.

After a seven-hour ride, Mr. HJ could still put in five or six hours more watching people look for their rooms, which was even more frustrating after dark.

And then, at around eleven, Otis's phone would ring and it would be Miss Milly, worried that HJ had been down there too long, and Otis would put on his slippers and go down to where a few kids were usually still at it even though POOL CLOSES AT 9:00 P.M. SWIM AT YOUR OWN RISK! signs were posted in three different places and Mr. HJ would still be looking at the perimeters, watching people confused at the four corners and be sad about it all, and telling Otis that if those kids drown in that pool, that's a catastrophe, but if you add up all the minutes that people lose in a day looking for their rooms it would add up to lifetimes lost too. And Otis would say, "That's right, sir," and it would be right, too, because that's the way that man was, nothing was too small for him to notice.

One day, as Otis recalled, they were up in Maine and Mr.

Johnson said he had decided to use dogs. They were reliable and inexpensive and 100 percent accurate. So for a house in Maine as an experiment they bought four dogs, two retrievers and two terriers, and Mr. Johnson paid a lot to have them trained. And when a person in Bangor, Maine, in 1952 finished checking in, the clerk held a key under the dog's nose and gave that key to the customer and told him to follow that dog. And those dogs could tell the difference between room 101 and 102 just like you'd know your mother from your sister.

And if you think Mr. Johnson didn't take care of those dogs, you didn't know the man. They slept inside in little dog houses behind the manager's office, and the desk assistant had to take them out on an exact schedule and keep track of them just the way the maids kept track of towels and pillows, and those dogs only worked six hours a day each.

Mr. Johnson stayed in Bangor, Maine, a whole month to watch the dog experiment. It worked fine. Not one dog made a room mistake. It surprised a lot of people, though, to have a pet lead them to their door. They would joke and say to the desk, "Do I have to tip him?" So many people asked that question that Mr. Johnson realized that they really did wonder. So he had a little card printed to explain the dog experiment as a safe, inexpensive way to direct each person to his room, and he put NO TIPPING signs on each dog's collar.

"Dogs are our friends and helpers at home," Mr. Johnson said. "Why not at a large motel?"

The man was like that. If something worked at home he wanted it on the road too. He was always trying to make it seem like you were right where you wanted to be, even if it was a thousand miles from there.

Otis always was a thousand miles from home. When Harold was playing on the junior high football team Otis wanted to be there on Thursday afternoons to watch his boy play. When he shut the TV off and turned off the light each night he wanted his wife there and he wanted it to be Tilton, Louisiana, outside his window, not Bangor, Maine, or Pittsburgh or Mobile. But there he was, a traveling man. When he came home when the boys were little, they'd quiz him on the states. Had he been in Idaho, and North Carolina, and Kansas?

It was always a yes, and all those places seemed like another planet to Jerome and Harold and Otis too, when he was home, but after a while he didn't know what to do at home. He wasn't a farmer and he didn't have anyplace to go around Tilton, and you could only polish and tune up the car so much. After a week or ten days he had to be on the road again. It had got into his blood, it was where he belonged.

But not now. Now Mel Briggs was driving and Otis was 59 years old and doggone if he wasn't gonna see what it was like finally to stay put. He had the dogs; two of them, Butch and Ginger, were still alive. Mr. Johnson didn't want to send them to a kennel so he asked Otis if they could live on his farm where they'd be able to run around and enjoy life.

They never did become regular dogs, not after that motel training. The big terrier would still take everybody that walked into Otis's house right into the bedroom. He didn't wait for a key or anything. If you walked into the house you had to go directly to a bedroom no matter what. It tickled the whole family. The boys played along with him. If you didn't he'd stand by the door like a soldier at attention until you came back and went into that room. Once they had tested him and the dog stayed that way for the whole day so they never did that to him again. Everyone just got into the habit of going to a bedroom right off. They were still doing it even after that dog died. Butch and Ginger would lead you to a room but it didn't seem to bother either of them if you didn't go in. Old Scotty, though, was like Mr. Johnson. He didn't like to give up.

Mr. Johnson did give up on the dogs, though. He had to. Someone called the Health Department, and the Health Inspector said if pets can't stay in the rooms then pets can't work at the hotel. Anyway, the man said, who ever heard of dogs working except as watch dogs or something?

"They're assistants to the room clerk," Mr. Johnson told him.

The inspector wrote that in his report.

"I've heard everything now," he said. "Dogs working in hotels."

"Animals have always worked," Mr. Johnson reminded him. "There would be no civilization without working animals."

"All right," said the inspector, "but that's still different from bellboy dogs."

When Mr. Johnson was right he didn't understand other people. He told the inspector there could be no harm in his dogs —a dog could lead the blind, why not the lost?

The inspector filed the complaint and if Scotty had not bit a ten-year-old boy who put his finger in the dog's eye, then Mr. Johnson would have probably won on that one too. When the parents sued the motel Mr. Johnson decided to drop the dog idea, which pleased the staff at the Bangor house, who were tired of cleaning up after the dogs, but it made Mr. Johnson sad because, he said, "Lights and directional signals didn't help much, and a dog was a presence and a comfort. But you can't have everything," and Otis didn't have everything either, not right now, as he leaned against the fender of his Plymouth wagon and looked up at his big old house with six empty bedrooms and his big old empty station wagon filled and lubed with no place to go.

No sir, there was nothing like being on the road with Mr. Howard Johnson, nothing like it at all. Otis rubbed the short hair on his terrier. Together they walked into the house where the dog led him straight down the hall to his room.

# CHAPTER FOURTEEN

*N*one of them knew how hot it was. In the air-conditioned limousine, they glided along the palm-lined boulevards. Occasionally gardeners looked up from their weed plucking, moved by the funereal grandeur of the automobile and its orange caboose. The bells of a Spanish church accompanied the silent car. Barely a flicker of wind touched the leaning palm trees. The limousine rolled through Orlando as if the city no longer existed. Through four-way stops and blinking caution signals went the Cadillac, past the townspeople, asleep in ranch-style homes where thick Sunday papers gleamed like manna on smooth lawns.

On such a morning Ponce de León had come to Orlando. He took off his big steel helmet, wiped the sweat from his brow, fed his horse and settled down beside a quiet pool to conjure up life eternal. "Any place this comfortable," he thought, "has got to be close to paradise." The musty Indians he had left in the swamps of the south. His own ragtag Portuguese cohorts had deserted him for the dark nubile ladies of the Lower Indies. Alone, Ponce de León moved through the heat looking for what he knew must be a better world. Better beyond the thighs of Indian girls, better than hot crocodile steak and native wine. Better even than the imperial courts of the kingdoms from which he had gladly fled. Stout Cortez came hungry for gold, Columbus and Balboa barely stopped to look around, so keen were they for the short routes through the world. Only he,

Ponce de León, came to stay, perhaps forever, at least as long as his luck held out.

The Portuguese nobleman took off his boots and made a camp. He stayed until he was killed by Indians at the age of 61. Very near Ponce de León's original 1513 campsite, Milton Cambell, some 437 years later, built Orlando's first drive-in movie. Where the Spaniard washed his dusty toes, Cambell built a cement-block refreshment stand. When his small screen and bad speakers began to lose favor with the Orlandoites, Cambell closed the movie and turned the refreshment stand into a small pizza parlor. It was robbed too often to show a profit. In 1960 Cambell, then selling real estate in Tampa, happily unloaded his old drive-in for just about what it cost him in 1950. "Nothing ventured nothing gained," he said to Mrs. Cambell. They bought a condominium in Miami Beach.

At the site chosen by Ponce de León and later by Milton Cambell, the black limousine circled, vulture-like, the abandoned pizza parlor and refreshment stand. When it suddenly stopped, the back door of the Sedan de Ville opened and Howard Johnson, up earlier than usual, made his way over the scattered debris. The others stayed in the car, motor and air conditioners softly moaning. Howard Johnson took the heat, scanned the landscape. The padlock to the building had long ago been violated. Howard Johnson entered. A red glass Drink Coca-Cola sign lay smashed on the cement floor. Where the stools and the counters had been, there were now open holes. Cockroaches ran freely along the aluminum molding. There were no longer any pizza smells, but several cardboard trays curled and blackened by mildew lay among the litter of cups and glass and dust. The cement-block walls sweated in the humidity. Insects groomed one another in the larger cracks.

Shading his eyes, Howard Johnson looked out from the grim gray building toward the cracked and peeling screen upon which the people of Orlando had, in better days, seen *Bwana Devil*, their first three-dimensional movie. The distance from where he stood to the screen had once parked two hundred cars at two dollars each and at least another dollar for refreshments. Howard Johnson shook his head slowly. His hair gleamed in the tropical sun and beads of perspiration trickled from his thick white eyebrows. As well as he could, he closed the broken door of the pizza parlor and moved toward the screen in the path that had been invisibly formed by the white light of a 35-mm. projector. He touched the aluminized surface, aflame in the sun, bent to look closely at something in the debris, and with one last glance at the abandoned building moved slowly toward his limousine.

Before he reached the car, Mildred Bryce in a wide-brimmed hat joined him, shading Mr. Johnson with a parasol she held high. "Don't look down, Milly," Howard Johnson said. "The place is loaded with Coney Island whitefish. It must be a lovers' lane." Mildred narrowly averted her eyes.

"How can lovers come here?" she asked. "How can it be? Neither movies nor popcorn nor pizza, not a bed nor a TV, not a lounge or even a gas station nearby."

"Milly," Howard Johnson said, touching the warm sleeve of her print dress, "Milly, please stop. Don't torture yourself this way."

"What brings lovers here, Howard, to such a barren and dead place?"

"They don't want to pay the $18.50 and up, it's that simple."

"Can there be love in places like this?" Mildred Bryce asked in wonder.

"They're young and in a hurry, Milly. The ones that come here, they're not the ones we build for."

"In such desolation, Howard, what can come of it? And here in a place where you wouldn't put a Midas Muffler stand, here they're going to build a twenty-story hotel with glass elevators and a revolving cocktail lounge." Howard Johnson listened, and looked beyond the movie screen.

Together he and Mildred wondered at Walt Disney. "Maybe

123

he never looks at the land, Howard. Maybe he uses architects and designers. Maybe there are no personal touches in Disneyland."

"But, Milly," Howard Johnson said, shaking once more his head in disbelief, "he doesn't know the word 'vacancy.' "

Howard Johnson and Mildred walked the perimeter of the abandoned drive-in theater. Over the Coke cans, the broken glass and the crumpled Kleenex they walked. She no longer averted her eyes. The steel posts from which the speakers once hung stood out like the crosses on a military cemetery.

"They can't do it," Howard Johnson said. There was finality in his voice. He walked back to the car so quickly that Mildred almost had to run to keep up.

"Not even Walt Disney can do it here, Milly," Howard Johnson said when they were back in the dark coolness of the limousine. "They'll spend millions but it will be lemonade without sugar. Let them bring the crowds. We'll build our own world, in a place where grass grows and birds sing." As soon as he said this, Howard Johnson fell asleep with a look of content on his old pink face.

As the host of the highways dozed in his leather cushions, Mildred directed Mel to the Post estate where her old friend Margery Post Merriweather awaited them. Howard and Margery had only met a few times, usually at charity functions in New York, but Mildred had spent a rare two weeks with Margery Post in 1946 and they had not lost touch with one another since. When Mildred phoned from New Orleans saying that she and Howard would be in Orlando in a few days, Margery insisted they stay with her. Milly would have made an exception in this case but Howard Johnson, she knew, would never be anyone's house guest while he was on the road. In principle Milly knew he was correct. Their job was to study the motels. Their major work included an estimate of how well they slept, how fast the breakfast came, how cheerful the wake-up call. "If we stopped with our friends," Howard said, "we might as well never leave New York City."

Although she had turned down Margery's invitation, Mildred could not visit Orlando without going to see her old friend. Howard she knew would not begrudge her a few hours, especially if his mind was occupied with the Disneys, as it now seemed it would be for the foreseeable future.

She let Howard sleep in the car while Mel kept the air conditioner functioning. Alone, Mildred went up the many steps that led to the white-columned mansion of Margery Post Merriweather. The house looked to Mildred as if it were left over from the filming of *Gone with the Wind.* She had seen Margery from time to time in New York, and of course had virtually been her roommate for those two weeks in India, but she had never before seen the Post estate.

"The architects thought it should look antebellum," Margery told her over tea. "My father didn't care so they went all out. Anything good in the South is always antebellum. They call chicken stands plantations. You and Howard Johnson must have a bunch of plantation-style steak houses." Margery felt bad that Mr. Johnson was asleep in the car when she had over a dozen empty bedrooms.

"He sleeps best in the car," Milly explained. "He wakes up ready for work. Really he's an amazing man. The driver is used to waiting out the naps." Mildred knew that Howard would not want to stay long, and she was not anxious to explain the cryogenic equipment that now accompanied them, but fortunately Margery Post saw nothing unusual about a limousine pulling a trailer. Margery even understood the necessity for Mildred to stay in a motel.

"You're one of the lucky ones, Milly," she said, "you've had something to do all your life. Your work takes you places. You get to see what you've done."

Mildred remembered the despair of Margery Post more than

fifteen years earlier when they had been Gandhi's guests. Along with Margaret Sanger they had visited India to encourage the mass distribution of birth control information. To Milly and to Margaret Sanger alone, Margery Post confided the fact that she had undergone a secret abortion in 1926. "Clarence and I were not really in love anymore. I wasn't even thirty years old. I thought there'd be other men, even other children. But menopause came early to me," she said, "and love never again. Clarence wanted the child. That's another reason he left. He thought I cheated him out of a business and a family."

Margery tried in India to become passionate about the condition of the poor but could never move herself very far beyond disgust at their primitive habits. Mildred too wondered that they needed any birth prevention device more potent than their smell. Margery and Mildred withdrew themselves from some of the visits to the countryside which Margaret Sanger said would be the most inspiring part of their journey. While Miss Sanger distributed pamphlets and explained techniques to thousands of peasants who did not believe that the British had actually gone, Margery and Mildred stayed in Delhi, drank tea with the Brahmin intellectuals and in the loneliness of a strange land comforted one another for what seemed their failures at home.

Mildred thought Margery was honest, easy to talk to. Their fortunes made them, in a sense, equals. They both knew what wealth had not bought for them and were equally bleak in their feelings about hope for the Indian masses.

"I'm trying good works," Margery admitted, "because I've found no satisfaction in anything else. But preaching about rubbers to these peasants is about as gratifying as converting vegetarians in Battle Creek."

Mildred supported birth control and came to India for other reasons. She hated, above all else, clutter. A too cluttered earth seemed to Mildred as apocalyptic as the atomic bomb.

"We both have strange lives for American women," Margery

said to her in India. "No husbands, no families, no real homes."
When they met Mohandas Gandhi, Margery in a fit of playful-
ness introduced herself as "cereal" and an embarrassed Mildred
as "ice cream." In his calm British accent Gandhi replied, "As
the leader of a hungry nation, I welcome you to India." He was
a thin and spiritual man. Mildred was immediately drawn to
him. She could have listened for hours to anything that came
from his pale soft lips. He smiled often.

Margery did not like the slowness of speech in India. "The
Russians talk fast," she said, "like we do. It takes an Indian
twenty minutes to ask for a glass of water." She thought
Gandhi boring.

"Now that you've driven the British out," Margery asked the
small, thin man, "what do you plan to do next?"

"Next we must feed the people and educate the children."

"And then?" she asked, barely able to understand his low
lisping English.

"Then," Gandhi said, "I will go to the United States and
spend my days asking Mrs. Merriweather what she will do
next."

Margery was too depressed in India to appreciate Gandhi but
whenever they met subsequently she told Mildred how de-
lightful he seemed to her in retrospect. "If he were still alive
I'd probably go back there just to apologize for being so arro-
gant. I'm really not like that very much these days, Milly, living
in Florida has calmed me down. I'm still not happy but I don't
have that crazy desire to get away and do something the way
I had it in India. After thirty years of looking I finally decided
there is nothing for me to do."

After the jasmine tea that Margery remembered was her
friend's favorite, Margery innocently asked what brought
Milly to Orlando.

"Walt Disney," Mildred answered, "but Howard would prefer that nobody really finds out that we're here. Holiday Inn
once hired a detective just to tell them where we stopped. Since

Howard found out about that he hasn't trusted anyone."

"You mean you came because of that park the Disneys were going to build here?"

"They are going to build it. Howard has very solid information on that."

Margery Post Merriweather arose. "Milly, if you had one place on earth where you finally felt comfortable, would you let the Disneys build a park in your backyard?"

Mildred put down her tea cup and thought awhile.

"I suppose I wouldn't want a park, but a few motels and restaurants wouldn't bother me a bit."

"Don't worry, Mildred," Margery laughed, "it's not Howard Johnson I'm out to stop. I just found out about their plan for a new Disneyland last week. I've already begun the necessary steps against it. Stopping the Disneys will be the best thing I've done since frozen orange juice."

# CHAPTER FIFTEEN

*T*he Orlando *Times* announced the coming of Disneyworld in a 42-point headline—the same type used for the extra announcing the end of World War II. It was going to happen—Orlando was about to become a world city. A few people read the paper and pulled the For Sale signs off their front lawns. Others stopped worrying about orange-juice futures. Everyone who owned land considered himself a prospective millionaire. Laborers turned coy, carpenters and electricians gathered downtown in small groups, waiting to be plucked from the streets like high-priced call girls. Three million tourists a year for openers—employment for teenagers, a clean nonpolluting industry. The Orlando *Times* estimated four billion dollars for the area in the next decade. People with terminal diseases cursed their fate even more and rewrote their wills. Nobody could talk about anything else.

In the first game after the official announcement, the Pirates committed six errors against Durham, N.C., and still won. It looked as if luck and money had fallen all over Orlando. Fatty Wallen, the league's leading hitter, asked Bones before the Pensacola game for a $1,000 raise effective immediately.

"Mr. Bones Jones," Fatty Wallen said, "take the rubber band off your wallet, let the moths out. Don't you know that everything changed two days ago? Don't you know that God has smiled on everybody who owns land in central Florida? Your outfield is probably worth half a million now. If you had a big parking lot you'd be lighting my cigars with thousand-dollar bills. Loosen up, old man, the Pirates are a hot property. I oughta get paid by the hit. I shouldn't even be in baseball, there's big money in real estate."

Bones Jones looked his pudgy right fielder in the eye. "Get your ass into real estate, then."

"I will." Fatty Wallen took off his cap and unbuttoned his shirt. Bones scratched his name from the lineup card.

The right fielder left his number 34 jersey on the bench. He walked into the locker room and put on his madras blazer, gray worsted slacks and straw hat. He poked his head back into the dugout.

"You'll miss my bat, old man. But I've had it with this nickel-and-dime shit, I don't need baseball. I've got a real-estate license."

Dressed in his snappy street clothes, Fatty Wallen walked onto the field. He toed the right-field foul line, then he turned and walked back toward home plate.

"I've put a lot of years in," he yelled to Bones Jones. "I drove in a lot of big runs. I deserve better than this from you, old man."

Bones Jones was not listening. He had walked out of the dugout back into the locker room. The Pirates were finishing the infield warm-up. It was two minutes before national-anthem time.

Fatty Wallen walked up to the microphone that the plate umpire used to announce pinch hitters and pitching changes.

"Attention, ladies and gentlemen," Fatty Wallen said. Some of the crowd stood. They thought Fatty had put on street clothes to lead them in "The Star-Spangled Banner."

"I'm retiring from baseball," Fatty said, "I'm a licensed realtor. I'm gonna go right down the line to a third-base box seat and hope some of you will come to see me. I'd like to do some business, and thanks to all of you for being such good Pirates fans."

By the time Bones Jones had flushed the toilet and come back to the dugout with the lineup card, Fatty Wallen was already seated and talking to customers. He had a snappy ballpoint pen and a memo pad and was writing down names and addresses. In the eighth inning he walked into the dugout. His big face shone.

"Bones, you old miser, forget the grand. Let me write a little option on the stadium."

Bones threw a resin bag at the slugger's chin.

"Get off my field, and don't sit in that box seat without a ticket ever again."

"Tomorrow I'll have an office, Bones, and next season you won't have shit." He wiped the resin from his face with his sleeve. "Old man, you ain't in Walt Disney's league."

When Margery saw the headlines she called Treat Gilbert at once. He told her he was busy until noon.

"Whores?" she asked him. "Or dogs?"

Gilbert came at once. "We can't stop them," he said. "It's a free country. Anyway, the town is going crazy for another Disneyland. If you'd leave your house and go downtown you could see it for yourself."

Margery looked over her attorney. He wasn't much more than half her age but he already had the posture of an old man. His eyes sagged. He moved slowly. He thought before he spoke. Money weighed him down.

"What's your salary, Treat? How much do I pay you?"

Treat Gilbert hesitated, weighed his answer like a commodities future.

"I'm paid by Hedges and Knowles."

"I know," she said, "but I pay them. How much?"

"One hundred thousand."

"A year?" she asked.

"Of course."

"And when you travel to New York, or England, or anywhere else, who pays for it?"

"The firm."

"You mean they bill me?"

"I don't keep track of such things. I suppose they do."

"So you're paid one hundred thousand dollars a year essentially to keep me satisfied. Is that right?"

"You have a lot of interests in Florida, Mrs. Merriweather. You own orange groves, and land, and mineral rights . . . you have complex tax shelters. You're more complicated than most corporations."

"But I had all of that before you were born. I didn't need you here for that, did I."

Gilbert became suddenly proud. "If you're not satisfied with my service, you can tell the firm to replace me next week."

"I don't want to just fire you, Treat, I want to know what you've been doing for the last six years. I want to know how much I've contributed to vice in this county. I want to know whether Walt Disney has been paying you more than I have."

Treat Gilbert turned his back to his employer. "You can't stand a loss, can you? If everyone on earth wants something and you don't, you'll still try to stop it."

Margery Post Merriweather remained calm. She had learned from her father to save her anger for the big moments. Treat Gilbert was an experiment. By reading him, she could see what Disney had already accomplished. Treat Gilbert put his hands in his pockets. He looked out the window. He jingled imaginary quarters. His hair stuck to his forehead. He looked to Margery as if he was posing for a department store ad. "If I had paid you five hundred thousand, Treat, would it have been enough? A million?"

"It's not my salary, Mrs. Merriweather, you don't understand. I can't stop them and you can't stop them. They have the land and they have the right to do what they want. Your father went out and made cereal. He wanted to put meat packers out of business. Nobody stopped him. Nobody can stop Walt and Will Disney. They have what Orlando wants, what America wants. If you don't like it you can buy another house, literally anywhere on earth."

"And the Disneys can build anywhere else too. What about Tampa? St. Petersburg or Miami? They can buy whole islands in the Caribbean. They might even be able to buy Puerto Rico or Haiti. They can live without my backyard."

Gilbert sat down. He now acted patient, fatherly. He explained to his employer the Disneys' market research, the transportation grid, the climate.

"Disney needs 330 clear days a year to make a profit," he told Margery. "That puts three fourths of the country out of the picture. Disney needs a combination of semiaridity and the tropics. He needs the cooperation of nature. This is no puny investment. He's essentially building a new ultramodern city. Think of the Mayas and the Incas. It's on that scale."

As the professional lawyer made Disney's case, Margery understood that Gilbert had long ago decided against her. He was as knowledgeable about the other side as she had been when she paid Clarence Birdseye $800,000 to take away his company. Like Treat Gilbert, she too had made the right business decision. The lawyers convinced Margery that Birdseye Foods had to merge with Post Cereals. Clarence wouldn't go to meetings or sign contracts. He even refused to patent his process. He said ice was universal. He hated governments and boundaries and all manner of bureaucracy. "He's a genius," they told her, "but he can't manage a frozen-food empire."

Margery's return from Russia was as abrupt as her romance with Birdseye. It was still the middle of winter when the cable reached her in Uzbekistan. C. W. Post had contracted polio. His limbs were shriveling. He was in the Battle Creek hospital.

Clarence said he wouldn't leave until spring, until his experiment was over. But Margery couldn't wait. Her father in need was a new thing—an event that had never before seemed possible. C. W. Post in his daughter's eyes was invulnerable, eternal. When she left for the Soviet Union he had not even begun to age. His hair was still dark and his skin firm. He never wore eyeglasses or had the need of a dentist. Yet the cable said he was dying. Margery telephoned Moscow. When she needed him, Merriweather helped. He rented her a plane that flew all the way from Istanbul to pick her up in Tashkent. Until Clarence joined her on the icy runway she did not know that he would accompany her.

"I'm sorry your father is dying," Birdseye told her when they received the wire. "But it's not so sad. He's had his chance, now it's someone else's turn."

Margery was too sad and too stunned to hate him for his indifference. She went to the city administrative building to phone Merriweather in Moscow. She could not remember how she spent the three days waiting for the airplane. Clarence suddenly seemed a stranger to her, an American farmer living in an ice house, as odd a being as Merriweather elevating his foot in Moscow. In Battle Creek, where she belonged, C. W. Post was not arising at 5 A.M. to toast his wheat bread and read the barometer. He was on Ninth Avenue, in the big hospital, the place where her mother had died. Margery tried to telephone Battle Creek but there was no way to reach Michigan from Uzbekistan. The local party chief told her that she could be in Istanbul in two days and then in Paris four days after that. Then the boat ride and another train from New York to Detroit and a change to Battle Creek. It might take her three weeks before she could sit beside C. W. Post.

"No need to rush," Clarence advised her. "If he's going to make it, he'll keep, if not, what can you do? If you just want to listen to a priest tell you about how fine heaven is going to be for him, there's plenty of them right here."

It was only when she knew he was dying that Margery began to love her father. She wept for him. "He was a lonely man," she told Clarence, "he never enjoyed anything. He never laughed, he never went to a party. He thought all of life was suffering."

"He was right," Birdseye said. He continued to check his freezing samples, and remained in his ice house while Margery waited for her plane. She didn't even say goodbye to Clarence, didn't care to when he seemed so far from understanding her feelings. But there he was on the runway holding three burlap bags full of strawberries, asking the pilot if he could strap the bags to the wings to keep them cold. The pilot said no. In the cabin the ice melted around their feet. In Istanbul they ate tepid berries in the sunshine. Birdseye's grand experiment seemed a folly as extreme as her marriage to Merriweather.

By the time they reached Battle Creek, C. W. Post had been in an iron lung for a month. He couldn't move or speak, nor would he ever. The doctor, himself a former Post employee, cried when he told Margery how weak her father's lungs had become, how hopelessly paralyzed they were. His great heart beat on, fueled by will alone, the doctor told her, but it too had been weakened, it would only be days.

Margery walked to her cottage from the hospital. No person greeted her with words, but on the streets they all had tears in their eyes. C. W. Post was the city itself. She sent Clarence to the hotel. Everyone in Battle Creek wondered who he was, but she had no energy to explain that. How could they know that after barely eleven months in Russia she was already growing tired of her second man?

C. W. Post did not die until Margery's third day in Battle Creek, but as he struggled for breath, she couldn't be certain that he knew she was there.

C. W. Post was finally still, finally just there for her to look at, a dying man, her father alone in a big closet called an iron lung. She wondered what he would say about all this if he could talk. Maybe he would be interested in the mechanism itself, how it squeezed the breath through his body. More likely he would be thinking about meeting God and making amends for the sins of his life. He would be on his knees asking God for forgiveness and God would be all over the place, like cornflakes in milk. And C. W. Post would go on and on about his sins, about not being a Nazarite.

God would forgive him, that Margery knew. As she touched her father's cool forehead—he was already more dead than alive—she wondered if she could forgive him.

With God the rules were clear, but what had they owed to one another, father and daughter? What had gone so wrong that in the midst of her sadness, she felt that the struggling body beside her was no closer to her than to his employees and fellow church members? He cooked her meals, he gave her her cough syrup when she was sick. He was leaving her the richest woman on earth but he lived so close to God that she always felt like an intruder in her own cottage. What was happening between God and C. W. Post was the important thing and that was always none of her business. Without ever telling her so, C. W. Post made his daughter realize that she was a boarder in the Lord's house, a schoolgirl who found herself an unwilling observer of Biblical tales. She worried about another flood like Noah's, she thought that Niles and Kalamazoo might vanish one day like Sodom and Gomorrah. Her father never told her it would not be so. When she asked he told her that ten decent men could have saved Sodom, but he would not guarantee that Niles and Kalamazoo contained ten such upright characters.

God and C. W. Post left Margery out of their conferences. At first she thought it was because she was too young. Then she thought it was because she was a girl. Finally she came to understand that her father hated her. She was the impediment, the proof that he had failed as a Nazarite. Every day of her life was an affront to God, who had worked so hard to create an almost perfect citizen, C. W. Post, only to let a wife and a child come between God and man. The wife God had taken care of quickly enough, but why had he spared the child? Once, when she was fifteen and had figured all of this out for herself, she asked C. W. Post and he did not deny it. When she asked why the Lord had spared her when her mother died, C. W. Post knew the answer.

"To remind me," he told his daughter.

To her father she was a walking, breathing sin—the flesh of his flesh, the sin of his sin. Once he even told her she was his golden calf. How can you forgive a father that, even if he leaves you a bottomless purse and the granaries of the earth? As the wheezing machine worked its last mechanical hours on the stricken lungs of C. W. Post, Margery did forgive. She told him that it was his fault that she hated God and had chosen to eat meat. But she told him too in her silent parting that when he and God finally met in the fields of eternity, someone owed an apology to her mother who had died so innocently, and to Margery, who never should have been labeled her father's sin.

Battle Creek went into mourning. Within hours of C. W. Post's death two citizens of Battle Creek committed suicide. All the churches had special weekday services to mourn C. W. Post and to warn people against suicide and other excesses of grief. The Post and the Kellogg factories closed for the week. For the first time in a generation there was no cereal dust in the Battle Creek air.

Margery spent a week of mourning. She received visitors twelve hours a day. They lined up and waited outside the door of C. W. Post's tiny house. As much as his death, the simplicity of her father's life now overwhelmed her. In his closet she found only four shirts, two pairs of pants, and his winter coat and gloves. He carried his money in his zippered change purse. He had no personal checking account. On the day he entered the hospital her father had $3.50 in his purse. His shrunken body even in death seemed pure. He had asked that he not be embalmed. Margery and the leader of the Seventh Day Adventist Church agreed that he should be buried behind his cottage, so near the factory. They buried him two hours after his death. There was no need to wait for anyone to arrive. All Battle Creek was there. The minister spoke only briefly. He said that C. W. Post's entire life was a miracle. He said you didn't have to be any kind of a believer to believe that. He said that C. W. Post was the best proof he knew of the existence of the Almighty. He said there was a heaven and Mr. Post was there and the hard thing was going to be for the rest of us to live without him. He got down on his knees and wept. There wasn't a dry eye all the way to Niles and Kalamazoo.

# CHAPTER SIXTEEN

*W*hen Margery arose from mourning, the factories that were once more shredding grain were all hers. She greeted the managers of all the Post divisions and then could hardly wait to go to Chicago where Clarence had gone the day after the funeral, where he had rented a two-room apartment on the South Side, a dingy space near the railroad tracks.

Margery didn't even put down her suitcase. "I'll never live like this again," she told Birdseye. "I decided last week that when I left my father's house I was never going to live like that again. When I die I'm going to leave a big mess, not a tidy closet and a town full of crying people."

She told the cab driver to take her to one of the big hotels she had seen near the lake. Clarence stayed in his apartment. For the first few days she walked along Michigan Avenue looking in the store windows, buying whatever caught her attention. She bought a dozen large stuffed animals, things she had never had in her childhood. She bought all the dresses that one shop had in her size. She bought several dozen pairs of shoes and handbags in six colors. She rented a second suite for her possessions. But the shopping did not help. After four days she returned to Birdseye's apartment. He had rented a meat locker and filled it with asparagus, kale, spinach, all the dark green vegetables he could find. He was working on color. He wanted to see if he could measure how much green would be lost by quick freezing.

"Green is the health of the plant," he said. "It's like rosy cheeks. If it's green it's beautiful."

Margery was wearing lizard-skin shoes and a silk dress. She had had her hair washed and styled in the Marshall Field beauty salon. She wore Chanel perfume behind her ears. Birdseye did not notice. He bit her lips, reached under her silk dress, pushed her forward toward the army cot that was his only furniture. She wondered even as she returned his caresses what it was that drew her to such a simple-minded, obsessed, humorless man and then, in the midst of her pleasure, she remembered what her father had been.

She stayed in Chicago for six months. During that time she and Clarence formed Birdseye Foods. Their first product was kale. Margery rented warehouse space and bought ice chests. Clarence redesigned the chests to hold frost longer. He also developed a press to squeeze the moisture from the vegetables so that he froze a solid leaf. Margery paid for everything. The Post Cereals Company put frozen kale into every grocery store in Chicago.

"Nobody eats kale," the distributors told her. "It's like trying to sell frozen golf balls." In the first months, thirty-five packages sold in all of Chicago. Clarence didn't care. He went from store to store to see how the kale kept in the ice house or refrigerated cabinet of each grocery. He bought samples so that he could taste the quality himself. In one store he got into a fist fight with a merchant who had put the frozen product on the shelf among the canned goods.

"You can throw away your money any way you wish," the manager of Post's distribution system told her, "but this country's in a downturn. It seems a sin when people are going hungry to put thousands of dollars into frozen kale."

Juice was her idea. Clarence never drank it. The only reason he went along was his fascination with the idea of a machine that could strip the meat from the peel of an orange. When Margery said orange juice she meant only the juice. Clarence understood that he would have to freeze the orange itself.

"You can't sell water," he told her. "They can put that in themselves." In less than a month he made a machine that could strip an orange and press the innards, even the pits. Once they put the product in the stores, they couldn't make the orange juice fast enough.

Henry Muller, the new president of Post Cereals, told Margery she was a genius like her father. They had two-thirds of breakfast now. If she could find a way to freeze eggs they would have one-third of the American diet.

It took almost a year for the orange-juice system to operate smoothly without Clarence. By then Margery could do without him too. She'd grown tired of the hotel and now lived in a house on Lake Shore Boulevard. She had a maid and a gardener and could look out her window at the pleasure boats on Lake Michigan. In addition to her father's fortune the orange juice was beginning a second one; this one she shared with Clarence but it was becoming almost impossible for her. The instant success of the orange juice didn't surprise or delight him. He stayed in his awful apartment but he rented a laboratory downtown and began to experiment exclusively with liquid nitrogen. He told her he could freeze the warts off children and the spots off a leopard. He told her he could strip away an eyelash painlessly. He was only interested in what could be frozen and maintained at constant temperature indefinitely. One night in the midst of making love to her he withdrew to capture and freeze his own sperm. A few days later when she found out she was pregnant she decided that she would not tell Clarence. She did what Post management had been telling her to do all year, she exercised her option to buy Clarence Birdseye out of Birdseye Foods. She gave him $800,000, three times the fair market price of their new company. She went to Pennsylvania to find Margaret Sanger, the champion of birth control, then on to Nova Scotia for an abortion. When she returned to Chicago Clarence was no longer there. He didn't cash his check until

1928. She never heard from him again. For more than a decade she tried to find him just to make sure he was alive. She bought ads in rural newspapers around the country. She had not cheated him. Without her original investment he would have stayed in a Russian igloo. She made Birdseye a name, a company, then she bought him out. But $800,000 was just an elaborate goodbye. Clarence was too much like her father. She did not want to relive her childhood. At that time she still thought she would love other men. She still believed the world held something special for her, Queen Ceres.

Treat Gilbert continued to rattle off the Disney statistics. "In Southern California they've turned orange groves into gold. They will here, too. You've got to think of the public welfare."

"Treat," she asked, "do you really own women and dogs?" Margery's voice was soft. She did not accuse. She understood weakness and perversity. She never held the African women against Merriweather. She wondered only how they ever found passion in his tangle of bodily complaints. She had gone off from Battle Creek to Russia expecting love and found only Ambassador Merriweather's gout.

At first she didn't believe the rumors that began to circulate about him. Technically she and Merriweather were still man and wife. Neither sought legal divorce or separation, they traded Christmas cards and sent each other itineraries when they traveled. He favored Africa throughout the thirties, photographing big game and cohabiting with Nubian girls like those in the childhood books he had never outgrown. Franklin Roosevelt finally made him ambassador to an obscure African country where he contracted malaria, TB, and shingles. His aides one day shipped him to Washington against his will. He spent what he thought were his last weeks in the Walter Reed hospital. Four African women were at his bedside. Margery did not like her husband's appearance. Illness and approaching death had not hollowed his puffy cheeks nor had the hospital staff or the African ladies trimmed the ear hairs which gave to the sides of his face a furry entrance to the muff of his cheeks. She could hardly bear to look at him.

"How long do you have?"

"A matter of days, perhaps weeks." He sighed, became generous, expansive. "Everything is forgiven. Take care of my darlings, I plead with you." He motioned to the dark ladies in their bright native dress. "For me have they forsaken their homeland and their tribe. Love, you see, only entered my life after you left. You and Birdseye really did me a favor. I'd have been dead long ago if not for them."

The dark ladies hummed at his bedside and took turns spooning gruel into him from a native wooden bowl. "You and Birdseye were interested only in food. All the time you never cared about the people who ate it, just the thing itself. You're both selfish. Thus you have reaped the anguish of the lonely and the mean. I learned love from these people. From them I learned that it matters not what you eat if it is consumed with love."

"Your diction," she said, "is more primitive than your appearance. You're too hilarious to die quickly, please let someone record your wonderful deathbed homilies to these darlings of yours."

Merriweather smiled in pain. He coughed heavy phlegm into an orange cloth napkin that one of the Africans held beneath his chin.

"Oh Christian life, where are you in the wilderness," he asked, "where plunder stains the soul? My ladies cherish me in disease as you never loved Birdseye in your awesome lust. You thought to disembowel my days when you left me with Stalin and yet the good Lord has still graced my soul with beatitude."

Listening to him Margery Post Merriweather remembered with full force why she had deserted her husband. None of the social columnists understood how she could leave this handsome diplomat to run off with a mechanic from Erie, Pennsylvania. It was, some of them speculated, a kind of trend, an affection for the lowly inspired by Karl Marx. "Heiress Spurns Ambassador for Working Class Lover," the *Daily News* said. There was even an editorial appeal in the Washington *Star* for people of social distinction to remember their special obligations. If heiresses so tastelessly denigrate their positions, what about the rest of us? What about clerks and merchants and field hands and journalists? A decade later, when King Edward abdicated his throne to marry Mrs. Simpson, certain columnists blamed the English scandal on Margery.

But society writers did not know that Margery Post and Clarence Birdseye were bound in their affair by ties stronger than personal affection. Even Merriweather, who did know, still tried to ascribe to lust a decision that was essentially good business.

"You talk too much to be dying, Merriweather. What is that putrid mess they're feeding you?"

Merriweather wiped the gruel from his lips with the napkin and sat up straighter in bed. "Art thou still Queen Ceres after all these years? Hath time no sting for thee? Does the yawning abyss hold not the recognition of human worthlessness?"

In dialect he spoke to his companions, who offered the wooden spoon and cracked bowl to Mrs. Merriweather. With her gloved hand, Margery batted it from their grasp, staining the wall and the crucifix with the dark gruel. The four African ladies stood in wonder. A nurse entered from the hallway. Margery walked to the crucifix. Raising herself to her tiptoes she put her nose close to the waist of Jesus.

"It's nothing but oatmeal," she laughed, "and your ladies are probably from Mississippi. You'll live to be a hundred unless the gout kills you."

These were her last words to Merriweather, who did survive his afflictions but drowned accidentally in the bathtub of his Georgetown house a few days before he was scheduled to return to Africa. The State Department did not announce the death for several months since one of his brides without waiting for the medical examiner decapitated her benefactor and began the slow process of pickling and drying his head. The African ladies left the body in the tub where a maid found it. The State Department refused to bribe the maid for her silence but Margery gave her ten thousand dollars. Merriweather's body was discreetly buried in Washington and the four African ladies, after an autopsy and investigation ended all suspicion of murder, were handed over to Margery along with the Georgetown house and a few paltry bank accounts.

Remembering Merriweather's request, Margery offered the Africans their choice of a way of life. Two immediately requested a return to the hazards of their native country, one stayed on as a domestic on Margery's staff and survived without learning English until her death of natural causes in 1955. The fourth went to the Berlitz School, later to business college. With help from Margery she opened a Tarot and palmistry center in West Los Angeles and thrives to this day. It was she who upon leaving for the West Coast presented to Margery the dried and shrunken head of their husband. When she looked at the unrecognizable face Margery was moved to tears for Merriweather. She had the head buried alongside his body. Now only her last name was left to remind Margery of her husband. She liked the name Merriweather so much that it became her first great obstacle with Clarence. She wanted to call it Merriweather Foods and he, insisting upon the inventor's right, wouldn't budge from Birdseye.

Poor Treat Gilbert, she thought. All his idealism and youth gone so quickly. No real passion, either. He loved neither the women nor the dogs, not even the Disneys. He did everything just for profit.

"What will you do with your money?" she asked the lawyer. "Don't you already have all that you and your family want?"

"You don't understand money," he told her. "You don't know a thing about it. You make a phone call and you want the Red Sea to part. You think everybody has everything."

"I don't."

"You were raised in luxury. You spit on human ambition. You're not fit to carry Walt Disney's luggage. He made a fortune out of pen and ink. Because of him children, even on their deathbed, laugh. Because of him city children know about nature. He wants to bring life and children and activity and profit, yes, profit, to a swamp filled with old people. And you have the gall to stick your millions in his way. I might be a sinner and a conniver, Mrs. Merriweather, and I might even be embarrassed someday before the bar, but if I helped you to stop Walt Disney, I would be judged and condemned by God Almighty."

Tears were in the corners of her lawyer's eyes. He stood tall, glowing a little on her Oriental rug.

"Get out of here, whoremaster," Margery said.

Gilbert hardly heard her. Along with the rest of Orlando, he was already safe in the Magic Kingdom.

# CHAPTER SEVENTEEN

*W*alt Disney could watch an ant farm or a beehive with the attention other men gave a football game. He could gaze tirelessly at the tiny, faceless creatures, all leg and antenna, with their chocolate-drop bodies and pinpoints of color. His original idea of the animated cartoon came from the simplest secret of small-creature life: there is no stillness. Life is crawling, creeping, eating, listening, defecating, waiting with a few legs in the air while the footsteps of strangers echo all through your body. From early boyhood, young Walter could pick out specific ants on the farm. He needed no color coding or infrared markers, even if these had been available to him. A dragging of one leg, a birth defect perhaps, a slight discoloration upon an otherwise fine, deep-black body. Sometimes it was "personality" that shined forth the individual being, the way a particular ant whom young Walt called Marc would always stop dead in his tracks whenever a flashlight illumined his workday. The curious ant stopped to wonder at the sudden light the way primitive men might have marveled at an eclipse.

Will never shared or even attempted to understand his brother's hobby. If they caught some frogs together Will would try to sell them to fishermen, but it was always Walt's instinct to domesticate them. Walt was fascinated even by the night crawlers which they regularly collected and sold ten for a penny. All that motion under rocks, he thought. "Just jab at the earth anywhere," he told Will, "and you'll see a hundred things coming to life. When you put a shovel into the ground it's like sunrise for the worms."

Will Disney nicknamed his younger brother Birdhead when Walt won the 1914 Turner Street Elementary School Audubon Society award. At eight, Walter could imitate a canary, a parakeet, a sparrow, a starling, and a robin redbreast. Because they had him, the Disney household was devoid of pets. At Will's urging, Walter would go through the five-room frame house imitating a different bird in each room. In the basement coal bin, where his practice disturbed nobody, Walt tried out the larger, nonmusical animals: the roar of the jungle beast, the surprisingly mellow tone of the crocodile, the almost silent purr of the domestic cat always beside her master.

Father Disney was a mail carrier who allowed no dog imitations in his household and no noise whatsoever after his 8 P.M. bedtime. Mrs. Disney, tending her house and a small porch garden against the erratic Missouri weather, watched in almost total silence the swift spurt to manhood of her two sons. The Disney boys both lamented the fact that neither parent lived long enough to see Walter's peculiar talent become one of the great ideas of the century. "Constant movement and sound," Walt rambled in an interview years later, "what else is the cartoon?"

Will, who managed all the ventures, even the third-grade Audubon contest, thought the story was the most important element. "You can't just have a damn mouse moving around a screen," he told Walter when he saw and appreciated his brother's first Mickey Mouse frames. "The mouse has to be trying to get something. A cheese, a girlfriend, a job—something." Will's insistence created the earliest version of Minnie, a dowdy gray matron named Pearl whose round form and schoolteacher smile made her less alluring than Will had hoped she would be.

An initial philosophical premise separated the brothers on cartoons throughout their lives. Will wanted tits on Pearl

Mouse. "Mice don't have tits," Walt said laconically and refused to draw even the tiniest bulge on his standing matronly mouse as she tied her frilly apron strings and looked at the pies cooling on her mousehole windowsill. To Walt Disney a mouse was always a mouse. You could make him a railroad engineer, a ship's captain, a middle-class husband and father if you wanted to, but a mouse he was still. In the shadow Walter saw the substance, in the movement he perceived the constant. Mouseness, not humanity, was the heart of his creation. The business Disney saw it otherwise. The mouse was only a cute disguise for the man who lurked within. If you put tits on girl mice, then Mickey could walk up and squeeze one and everyone would get a kick out of that, even people who would be surprised or offended to see a human caricature do such a thing on a public screen.

Because Will saw the man where Walter saw the mouse, the early cartoons, the only ones the brothers actually made themselves, had a kind of schizophrenic duality. Will wrote a human script celebrating the continuity of thought and action, Walter drew creatures who in each of their thousand incarnations failed to remember the "self" of their previous drawing. "Mickey was taller than Pearl when they first met," Will would point out to his brother, who had forgotten as he drew the images that the two mice had indeed met and courted and made significant and promising gestures to each other only a few hundred drawings earlier.

To Walt Disney, the cartoon was like the ant farm. You just let your eye wander around the surface. You watched tiny actions, meaningless to you but interesting because of the motion under glass. What was the "story" in the activity under a rock or in a mousehole? His original mouse moved so quickly that Walt drew neither close-ups nor full-face angles for the camera. Mickey had long rodent teeth, dark blotchy fur. He moved around on four legs.

"Jesus Christ," Will Disney said when he delighted in the

movement but was appalled by the features, "why is the mouse so damned ugly? Why doesn't he stand up like a man?"

On this phrase, "like a man," the Disney Studios in 1932 almost faltered before they began. Walt was twenty-seven and drawing on a broken easel. He had a studio in a barn outside Kansas City. Will, thirty and married, sold space in a grain elevator to support his bride and gave whatever he could to his dreamy kid brother, who in five years had not held a job beyond three months.

"Like a man," Will Disney said in April 1932, "like a man, or I don't buy you another fucking paintbrush." From April through July, Walt Disney drew no creatures. His easel lay face down amid the strands of straw, his pigments lost their freshness, his brushes hardened. The brothers Disney, all their lives as close as testicles, barely exchanged greetings during these months. Walt took a job with a WPA road crew. At night he was too tired to miss his drawing. He cleaned up, ate, and went to bed. On weekends he picnicked with Lucille Walters, whom he would marry in 1934 but to whom he could not explain in the summer of 1932 why he suddenly stopped the drawings which for years had been his special hobby and were part of the great charm to which Lucille was attracted. He brought her drawings of flowers instead of the real thing, sketches of gifts he would have bought for her if he could.

"Walt Disney," she finally said, "I don't know what's happened between you and Will and maybe it's none of my business, but if you don't stop moping around and go back to your drawing, you can just stop coming around on weekends too."

The loss of Lucille and Will would have been too much. At the end of July, Walt Disney quit his job on the road crew and Mickey Mouse, for the first time, stood up like a man. He drove a steamboat and pulled on the whistle with childish delight. For his brother, Walt named the man-mouse Steamboat Willie. Willie smacked his red humanlike lips at female mice and felt them up in their tight-bodiced gowns. The two-footed mouse had ambition greater even than his lust. He longed to be a ship's captain plying his big steamer along the Mississippi, openly blowing his raspy whistle in the ports where his ancestors used to huddle beneath the docks drooling for the remnants of grain. He would not settle, this ballsy mouse, for being like a man, he wanted to be a big man, a leader, one whose actions changed the world, one who roused in women sighs deep enough to move sheets drying on the line. When Steamboat Willie, lunging from his whistle and salivating for big-city life, pulled into New Orleans, ocean liners made way and Creole girls tugged at their petticoats. He made for the waterfront jazz parlors, where respectful mice, dark as the ace of spades, laid oyster stew and shrimp gumbo before this man-mouse bursting with appetite. Barely off his sea legs, Steamboat pulled a lithe waitress to his hot lap and spoon-fed her those squiggly oysters and the down-home gumbo that had put such roses in her cheeks. "Oh, sailor boy," she cooed as his five-fingered mouse hand disturbed layers of crinoline. Not long did the sailor enjoy such bliss. A wart-encrusted first mate in a buccaneer's hat claimed the girl and flattened the ambitious sailor with a hard thump on the head. Walt Disney drew a rainbow for the unconscious mouse, a smooth curving arc that disappeared into the horizon and suggested opaque colors. Will later made him change it to stars.

The young mouse shook the rainbow from his head and pummeled the brute so mercilessly that the warts fell from the mean sailor's body and formed a small, independent mound that begged in the voices of suffering Negroes for an end to this beating. Steamboat did not stop until the girl rubbed herself against him like a cat. He lowered his fists and raised his passion. The warts jumped back on their man and led him from the tavern. Steamboat and Sweet Sue embraced. He tugged her beneath the oysters, which climbed out of their stew to peer at the sport. On the waterfront, Steamboat's now-quiet ship sat on smooth coastal waters awaiting the success that bloomed beyond even Will Disney's hopes. Steamboat Willie curbed his libido and became the innocent young Mick. Sweet Sue, no longer so easy herself but equally sweet, donned an apron and a more open-mouthed smile to charm the world as faithful Minnie, created in spite of the stubbornness of the creator by the worldly wisdom of his brother. To the applause of all mankind, Walt Disney's mouse had become "like a man," but his creator's vision stayed forever with that long-toothed, four-footed rodent who visited him regularly in the barn. Walt Disney never liked the plots and never cared what happened to the mice. When he gave his final approval to a cartoon he looked only for stillness. His sharp eye could spot a static one-sixteenth of a second. But if an editor were to put Franklin Roosevelt in the frame to replace the mouse, Walt Disney would have approved the plot as automatically as ever.

Because Will's insistence on human styles had unmanned him before his public career ever began, Walt Disney took no pleasure in the creatures who bore his name.

He OK'd Donald Duck at a casual luncheon with some draftsmen. The nephews, Pluto, Scrooge, the various deer, squirrels, and elk that sprang from Disney Studios were all committee decisions overseen by Will and later by a marketing specialist. Walt Disney never saw *Dumbo* until its commercial release. Because Walt himself had such prominent ears, Will didn't want to risk offending his brother before release. Perhaps because it was made completely without him, Dumbo became Walt Disney's favorite Walt Disney character.

Once the success started, Will left his brother alone to do as he pleased. Only the name Walt Disney became famous. The man married Lucille Walters and finally moved to Hollywood after World War II when Will said it was getting to be a big public-relations problem for Walt to stay in Missouri. Will chose his brother's house, his car, his wardrobe and, when it became necessary, even his toupee. The periodic Walt Disney depressions which Will tried to talk him out of had begun to occur almost as soon as Walt drew Steamboat Willie. The brothers loved each other wholeheartedly and Walt was as pleased as Will with most of the fruits of wealth, but he could never overcome his initial belief that mice ought to be as distant from people in cartoons as they were in real life. The success of Disney Studios and later of Disneyland were direct contradictions of this notion. Although after 1934 Will never rubbed it in, each successive Disney enterprise proved conclusively that everybody wanted human-type creatures. Almost alone in the civilized world was the taste of Walt Disney, fascinated by ant farms and aglow over random motion. For love and money he went along with Will on all the Disney ventures. But when Lucille died in 1955, Walt moped more than ever. He preferred to stay at home and draw as he always did the realistic creatures that nobody ever saw in a Disney cartoon. Will came over daily to cajole his brother out of the mansion, to get him to the studio or at least to the Brown Derby for lunch. For Will's sake he went to Orlando, just as for Will's sake he played the part of being uplifted by pep talks. At first it had worked a little, and the smile continued to fool Will over the years. Yet Walt Disney's melancholy had grown almost in proportion to his success. He carried his sadness with him shrouded in his personable, easygoing style so that it almost appeared as an enviable ease with the material world. Will brought him ventures, but since Steamboat Willie there had been no "adventures," no risks of his talent, no taste of the world. Walt Disney, lionized and admired since his late twenties, felt at sixty, as he hovered queasy-stomached over Orlando, like a bronze statue in the middle of a small town.

## CHAPTER EIGHTEEN

*I*n fact, for the cruise over Orlando the Disney brothers made one of their rare changes in itinerary. Usually they did not travel in the same aircraft or even stay at the same hotel. Walt could not leave California without being skeptical about all the past Mickey Mouse business.

"We did the goddamn mouse thing," he said often, "and that's enough. How many goddamn mouse things can a man do?"

Will Disney had the personality to complement his brother's genius. "Walter," he would say, "once you get people listening to a talking mouse you have got them, brother, by the nuts." Will called his brother's creation "Milky Mouse," because he could milk it for all it was worth.

Years after making it big, Walt still had no confidence. Money in the bank did little to bolster him. Becoming an international celebrity only made him think less of the world. "Sometimes I think, Will, that one of these mornings I'm just going to wake up and find out that it's all over. The Mouse, Donald, Pluto, Scrooge, Minnie, the nephews, the comic books, the whole drafting department gone like a flushed toilet."

"Yes," Will said, "but if that ever happens your shoes and your bed and your house and California and New York will all be gone too. When are you going to realize, Walter, that what we have is a product, the same as cars and food and clothes?

When are you going to stop whining about Mickey and Donald and wake up to the whole damn industry? Did Henry Ford worry that someday people would stop buying the Model T? The hell he did. For twenty years he wouldn't even give 'em a second color. Do farmers sit around on their butts not planting seed just in case there's going to be a drought next summer? And what about the whole damn clothing industry? On just about any day, people can stop buying new duds and make do for a couple of years. That don't scare the shit out of Seventh Avenue. Hell, no, it just makes people work harder, take bigger risks. It keeps things interesting, Walter, and you and I, brother, we're in the most interesting business of all."

Will could always bring him out of the dumps with his little pep talks. He had to remind Walter that they were part of a big, wide, profitable world.

"A few smiles for your brother, Walt. That old silver lining for Will, who remembers changing your diaper. There, that's the Walt Disney everybody loves. Not a moper, not a loser. Remember what Mom used to say, 'Shit smells and class tells'? Goddamn it, Walt, we got 'em by the balls. Who are you worried about, Woody Woodpecker? Lantz hasn't made a decent woodpecker in fifteen years. You worried about TV, about Hanna Barbera? Shee-it. They go three frames a second —that's not movies, that's stillies. You worried about the banks? Christ, we got up to forty million in credit already cleared with J. P. Morgan. The Bank of America thinks we're a better buy than Warner Brothers. Did you ever think, Walt, back in K. C., that someday you and I would be a better pick than the Warner Brothers, the Marx Brothers, or any goddamn brothers in the world? We're something new, Walt Disney, and don't forget it. And I'll tell you a secret, brother, we're not breathing hard yet. When Walt Disney, Inc., gets its second wind, just watch us go. General Motors, you better look out for your ass."

"How'd we come outta the same mom and dad, Will? We're day and night, the two of us."

"That's why we're winners, brother. Between us we cover all the shots."

Will smoked cigars and slapped backs. Walt gravitated toward corners. "You said the Dodgers would never leave Brooklyn. Walter, remember that, remember when you told me it was crazy to buy so much out here, remember. Well, Walt Disney, if all your movies disappeared like the athlete's foot, you'd still be sitting on a kingdom. This is not mice and ducks. This is *real estate.* It's magic, Walt. I always said fuck the stock market, fuck commodities, get us some land and let every poor bastard come over to have a little fun. You wanna leave it all for those Six Flags phonies? They've got three spots already. They're big with farmers, big in the South, you want peanuts like that to get all the benefit of what we did on the Coast? Face it, Walt. Do you want the real Disneyland or do you wanna let the imitators take it over?

"Sure, I've bought the land, but we can back out. It's not too late, just a few thousand bucks lost. We can plant oranges, tomatoes, anything you want, Walter. I'm not going to force another Disneyland. I thought I'd go under from all your worries before we ever opened in Anaheim. But once you decided to do it, little brother, you were all there. Who made the great choices? Who crossed out the Mississippi Steamer and changed it to Tomorrowland? Who said No to Frontier City and Yes to Cinderella's castle?

"Why do I have to keep reminding you that you're not some old Walt Disney at an amusement park, handing out the Teddy bears. When are you going to realize, Walt, that you're the tops? More kids know the Mouse than Jesus Christ. We could build a religion, a college, an atom-powered village—anything we want. But I say we need another Land, only this time with nothing held back—no nine-watt bulbs this time, no cardboard, no fiberboard. Plywood—glass—steel—aluminum. A railroad, an airport, a hotline the President will be jealous of. We'll be the Statue of Liberty for another planet. In the year 2064, when those men from Mars come down here, and you bet your ass they will, I want 'em to ask, 'Where's the Disneys' world? We read the lights in the stars and we picked your earth over a dozen other neat places because of Disneyworld.' That's what I want, Walt, and we'll have it, the Lord willing, right on schedule we'll float over Orlando like bees on a rose."

To celebrate the coming of the new world, the brothers Disney, just this once, got in a helicopter together to overlook Orlando. Walt insisted that they wear parachutes. A second company helicopter trailed them in case of any emergency.

Adolph West of the Sunset Insurance Company, uncomfortable in his parachute, and Virgil Nicolson, representing the Chase Manhattan Bank, accompanied the Disneys. Will couldn't hold back his excitement as they climbed into the twelve-passenger helicopter. He helped the bankers into their genuine leather seats. "Hughes just got a big government order for these for the Army. They strip them down, load 'em with cannons, and pop the Commies right out of the trees. In L.A. the talk was about one and a half billion for a three-year contract. We're still punks compared to the military business, aren't we, Adolph?"

The financier nodded in smiling agreement. "Had your Dramamine, Walter?" Will asked. "OK, let her rip." From a secluded corner of a private airfield west of Orlando, the Disney helicopters hovered and scanned.

"When we looked at Anaheim," Adolph West recalled, "there wasn't this kind of space. It was all oranges and avocados, not a plowed farm or a plain old nonfruit tree anywhere around there. Here it's like upstate New York with a little good weather."

"Yes," Will said, "it cost us a lot less for the acreage here, but it wasn't only the money. You know why I wanted Florida? I wanted it because we're like a belt around the country when we're here and in California. Same latitude, same climate, same kind of people, really: the kind that can't take the big cold cities. Miami is like L. A., too far gone in construction to buy what we need. Now the 'glades would have been good but then you hit the transportation problem in there. I believe I talked to you, Virg, or maybe it was to someone else from Chase, about financing a few dozen Hovercrafts to wheel the crowds through the swamp. That way we could have turned a nice profit and made it some fun just getting people from one Land to another. But the swamps aren't really deep enough for those big air boats, and someone said to me once, How would it look, Will, if a swamp buggy with about two hundred kids went down in the muck near Never-Never Land? After that you'd have ten years of mothers taking their kids waterskiing and skydiving and being scared shitless of Disneyland.

"So when we shelved the Everglades we started looking inland, and there was Orlando. When I saw it I knew how Columbus must have felt. You couldn't have asked for anything more perfect. Good superhighway, a new airport, dirt-cheap farms full of watermelons and okra. The whole place like a big old plantation with lots of sleepy coons and a few rich masters going to parties in Key West and Miami. It was in '57 when I first saw it and started putting the package together slowly so that nobody would suspect. I didn't even tell you New York people. If the word had been out, every watermelon farmer would have wanted ten times more for his land. No, we waited and it's been better than six years. The land that's left is mainly the big clumps, the ballfield and then there's a few hundred that some old heiress has and that's about the only big stuff left on the perimeter. Sportservice, I can tell you, is very interested in the concessions. I think we can clear as much as fifty percent from their gross, and the restaurants and motels, the gas stations and shopping centers will all be after us for space."

"Does it really have to be this big?" Adolph West asked.

"Virgil and I were both thinking about the same size as Anaheim might be enough."

Will chuckled. "You boys are just like Walt, you just can't stand to think a little beyond right this minute. How many people are there in the country, Adolph; about two hundred million, right? And more than half are kids, and three-quarters of their parents have enough extra cash to take two-week vacations and send the kids to camp. And there's also about one million Japs and Turks and Frenchmen and others coming to Anaheim every year right now. What we're planning is roughly three times the size of Anaheim, and I guarantee you that by 1980, maybe sooner, we'll wish it was three times that.

"Look at Walt. Sure he seems creepy and airsick this minute, but Walt could have stopped thirty years ago and still been the most successful artist in the history of the world. You know I get a kick now and then out of these art books talking about Michelangelo or Leonardo or some other Italian making their pictures seem like the people could really move. Hell, Walter and the boys in the drafting room are making people and animals that move sixty-three times a second and in color. And they do it mostly with their hands and their eyes and a pen just like the old-timers did. Suppose someone had told Michelangelo that in five hundred years Walt Disney Studios could take that Vatican ceiling which damn near broke his neck, put it all on celluloid, add as much color as it needs, and make the whole thing *move*. The hand of God *moves* right over to Adam's hand and shakes it. The breath of God *moves* right into the body of Adam. I've been talked out of religious cartoons by everybody, but I've thought for years that there's a market there right in those same Sunday schools whose ministers keep telling me it would be sacrilegious. If it's not sacrilegious to have the saints and the apostles and everybody in the picture books, why is it a sin to put them into Disney cartoons? Nobody's answered that one for me yet, but who wants to mess with the Pope?

"What if we made just one as an experiment, showing, say,

159

the loaves and the fishes or Jesus on the water, nothing sad or bloody, just some well-known miracle? I'd say one good seven-minute cartoon that we could put out for less than eighty thousand would revolutionize the Sunday schools."

Adolph West seemed as interested in the religious films as in the new Disneyland. "I believe you have something there, Will. I don't see anything irreligious about making the Gospels in fine, tasteful children's versions."

Will liked to impress the financiers with his ideas. After all, it was his ideas and their money that made everything happen right from the start. "Well, Adolph, if you think I've got something, see if you can put a little heat on Bishop Sheen or Billy Graham, or some of the big shots in the National Council of Churches. A few years ago, one of our creative men did go to Bishop Sheen with some terrific sketches. Jesus looked just like he always does. He was wearing a white toga with a rope belt and a pair of two-thousand-year-old sandals that we actually had made by a guy in L. A. so that our artists could watch a foot move in those old-fashioned things. They were goatskin. I mean, for the walking on the water you need some real close-ups of the feet. And you know the best effect of all and the easiest is this incredible glow you can get around his head just by leaving some white space on a specially treated paper. I mean it was really something. We spent about twenty-five thousand just on the preparation and the sketches. We talked to Stravinsky about the music and Vincent Price for the voice, but the Bishop said, "No dice." And this George Beverly Shea who does all the Billy Graham arrangements said it was too cute. Imagine a guy like him calling Walt Disney and Stravinsky too cute. Did anyone say DeMille's *Ten Commandments* was too cute? No, they didn't, but if it had been Walt Disney Presents *The Ten Commandments,* you can bet your ass the church would have been on our neck. DeMille had the reputation for handling big productions, and everyone thinks we can't do anything more serious than Mickey Mouse.

"Well, Adolph, you learn to do what you can in this world. The churchmen won't let us bring the saints to Sunday school, but they'll pack those kids into chartered buses and drive them a thousand miles to see a cardboard Jesse James rob a cardboard train and shoot up some plastic people. I can't figure it out, so I say, let's give 'em what they want. Right, Walter? How ya doin' back there?" In the rear of the helicopter Walt Disney lay upon three seats folded for him into a soft couch in the row behind his brother and the two bankers. "I'm doing OK, Will. When we get over the territory, let me know and I'll get up. I'm sure it's going to be OK, but I don't want to take any chances by sitting up too soon."

Will could talk, Will could deal. He could plan the sparkling future. Because of Will, Walt's sketches had taken on life. Animation techniques made the characters move in the eye of the camera, but Walt Disney knew it was his brother's determination that actually moved Walt Disney, Inc., and the millions of drawn animals therein.

There was no reason to argue when he knew that Will was right. This new place would probably be even better than Anaheim, and that one had made all their earlier achievements seem like the minor leagues. It took something to risk it all on one idea. If Disneyland hadn't made it big, the whole studio would have collapsed with it. But even though they made it, somehow Walt was sorry they had done it.

"I like the movies. I like the drawings," he told Will, when the original idea came to his older brother one night at the studio bowling alley. "Let's stick with what we like. You're talking about buildings and mechanics and bonds and stuff we don't know about."

Will sparkled like Tinker Bell and waved his magic hand. "Man is only dust and time and spirit," Will said, "but Disneyland can make him strong as an angel." He threw a strike, scattering the pins deep into the abyss. "Look at us, Walt, we've got Rolex watches and Bel Air mansions, Rolls-Royces and kids at Harvard, and still, Walt, there's more to it than what we've taken out. We've made people happy, haven't we? Who would you say has made more fun for more people, the Disney brothers or Shakespeare? Who has done more good, the Disneys or Queen Elizabeth and Harry Truman and Woodrow Wilson and all the politicians combined? We're not doing it for us, big Walter, it's for them. They need a place to take the kids. Where can a mom and pop in this great country go with the little ones? Oh, they can go for a picnic in the country with a thousand bugs or a dull ball game with a hundred drunks in the bleachers. The old man can't keep up with the kids in any of the games they play, and he hates their records and their friends.

"When we were kids, Walt, where'd we want to go, remember? You wanted to see the Mormon temple in Utah, and I wanted to see the Washington Monument. Maybe kids still want to see the nation's capital, I don't know, but if you had a choice now of laying out a lot of money for the White House or a place in California where you could enjoy the rides and the restaurants and the walks as much as the kids do, where would you go?"

Bowling pins were flying all around them. Walt just held his twelve-pound ball by three fingers while his brother went on about Disneyland, which was taking shape right there in lane number 11.

"I guess I'd go to Disneyland," Walt admitted, "but I wish someone else would build it."

Will motioned him to the seats behind the scorer's table. "Until this second, Walter, I never realized that America does not have her own national monument. Think about it. England's got dozens of places everybody has to see, France has the caves, the Riviera, the wine making. What did we skip over to India for—the Taj Mahal, right? Up to this minute, Walter, America has no spot that you have to see, and every rinky-dink country in Europe and around the world has one. We'll build a center for America. A place where you can stand and move the world from."

Walt Disney, powerless as usual before the brilliant energy of his brother, picked up his Brunswick Black Beauty and, aiming toward Anaheim, rolled one effortlessly down the middle.

# CHAPTER NINETEEN

*T*he Disneys made their headquarters at the Hotel Orlando. First they bought it. On the day of the announcement they put up a new sign on forty-four-foot stilts so it could be seen from the freeway: DIS-NEYWORLD HOTEL. It was the beginning.

Will was ready to roll. In his pocket he had letters of credit from BankAmerica and Chase Manhattan. Under his thumb he had the unions. The publicity was so good that he could have sold tickets to the construction sites. When he walked down the street people clapped.

"If you'd just get your ass over here," he told Walt, "you'd see how fine everything's going to be."

Walt was the only problem. Walt was down again. The blues had him. Sometimes it could last for months—Will had no patience for Walter's funk, even though when it was over, Walt sometimes came up with his best ideas. A long bout of depression led directly to Bambi. Even Pinocchio was preceded by weeks of Walt's brooding.

When his brother sank, Will urged him on like a cheerleader. "C'mon, big fella, folks in Florida are rooting for you. It's not that hard. Just get yourself to the airport, put that credit card in front of the ticket agent, and the whole world is yours. If you'd rather come by train, that's fine too. You can be here in three days, refreshed and relaxed. I'll take you down to Miami and show you a thing or two. There's lots more to see in Florida, Walt. We'll take it easy, maybe go down to the Keys, fish, take in the 'gators and the crocodiles, eat a little Cajun food. You'll like it here, Walt, you'll see. And if not, just head back to L. A., no hard feelings. No harm done."

Will wanted him there and Walt knew that it mattered. Just showing up would help. The world liked to see Walt Disney smile and wave and talk about the future. But Walt wasn't up to it, not just now. He'd been to Florida, had seen it, he'd disapproved, so what? Will did what he wanted to do anyway and it was just as well. Left to himself, Walt Disney would never have become Walt Disney.

"I'll be there," he told Will, "one of these days. You'll see. It'll be a surprise."

Walt hadn't left his house in two weeks. He awoke early but stayed in bed past noon. He couldn't concentrate on books. He didn't draw either. He just lay around and leafed through magazines and scrapbooks. One day he went through all his coins to see if there were any rare ones. He stared at the chandelier above his bed, first with his right eye, then with his left eye, amazed at the difference between them. When he did it fast it was like a home movie. He watched the tips of his fingers. Time passed. He went downstairs to eat dinner, or else Sharon the cook brought it up to him. If the colors of the foods interested him, he ate. He felt no hunger, even though once he called for orange sherbet because he wanted to watch it melt.

The staff thought Walt Disney was clever and up to something new; so did the boys at the studio. Will knew the truth and treated him sometimes like a bad boy, sometimes like a sick person. Walt knew he deserved it. He contributed so little, yet he was as well known as Coca-Cola.

He didn't dare tell Will, but on his mind these days was death. He wondered a lot what it would be like to be dead. He could imagine it pretty well. It would be like a change from his own body to that of an animated character, drawn by someone else. Everything would be so much smaller and time would go faster. He always conceived of animation as a way to think about death but he never told anyone. It would put it all in a different light if he said that. People would be sad, they wouldn't laugh if they thought about dying, though when Walt got in these moods he could think about nothing else.

It was almost like that before Bambi. But he was younger and had bounced back. He could leave the house, too. Every day he went to the beach. He rubbed white sunburn creme on his nose and the tops of his ears, then he waded out into the Pacific. He never went much beyond waist deep. He liked the waves to tickle his chin. He liked the aftertaste of salt water. He waited a long time for something to happen, for a fish to spurt from the surface or a lost float to bump against him. He thought of the salmon swimming upstream, looking for just the right place to die. And then one afternoon he put on his trousers right over his swim trunks and went to the studio. He drew some dots, he was thinking of the measles and of dot-to-dot puzzles, but his right hand was drawing a cloven hoof and then four long straight legs with knobby knees and pretty soon Walt Disney was looking at a baby deer. He was still thinking of a salmon's death, wondering exactly how it happened, but he was drawing deer after deer, panels of deer, and pretty soon there was a name, Bambi, and not long after that came Pinocchio so it turned into a good season and he almost forgot what it felt like when he was walking into the ocean.

But there was no Bambi now to take his mind off dying. Lying still in bed reminded him of it, so did his inability to concentrate or do anything. If it's all nothing, he thought, it's like a blank page. The mark on the page was life itself—animation. He thought of himself drawn by God's finger, the finger he knew from Michelangelo's painting. God didn't need ink. A few drops—there was the life of Walt Disney—a few over there, the Ice Age, or the end of the world, or Moses—everything happening at once on a big canvas that God drifted over, like steam over Chinese food. Walt wondered what happened to the erased lines. He took up a light No. 4 pencil, made some lines, then erased them with an art gum eraser. He played with the eraser's dirty rubber residue, then he blew it away. Where were the lines? Not on the rubber, not on the page, not in the air, not in his pencil. They were gone, like Lucille, like everyone who ever lived, who ever would live. He took up the pencil, drew random shapes, then circles, then round happy faces. He drew a few mermaids, some frogs, a Spanish onion. He drew clouds and a storm at the corner of the page. Then Walt used the art gum hard, all over the page, and the only thing left was art gum frizzle. He played with the eraser's mess, used his fingernails to try to shape it, but with those droppings he couldn't even make a circle. Yet that eraser so easily removed what was so vivid, so well drawn, so present a few minutes ago. Walt threw the eraser out the window. Then he looked out to see where it had landed. He noticed his gardens, his swimming pool, the blue tile around it, and the red rooftops of his Beverly Hills neighbors. He could not see the eraser. That powerful destroyer was itself a nothing—a speck hidden by a few blades of grass. He looked at the erased page and wished his drawings back as they had been. He closed his eyes. He touched the paper. He said a prayer. Then he felt foolish. He put on his brown felt hat and left by the garden door so he wouldn't see any of the help.

In the grass he looked for the eraser and found it under a brown leaf beneath his window. The window looked far away now. He put the eraser in his pocket and walked down the hill to crowded noisy La Cienega Boulevard. He felt as if he was melting—like orange sherbet heading toward the bottom of the bowl, getting soft and liquidy.

The temperature was 102 degrees. When Walt got on the bus a young man rose to offer him a seat. Walt turned down the offer but the man insisted. The man was chewing gum and seemed to be left-handed. He did not recognize Walt Disney sweating beneath the brown rim of his felt hat.

Whenever Walter went anyplace he needed at least a modest disguise. People knew his long pale face, his big ears, his mustache. They wanted a handshake, an autograph, sometimes only a hello. They wanted him to know they were alive. By the thousands they told him how much they loved Mickey and Donald. He smiled. What else could he do? Mickey? Donald? What were they to him? Lines. Ink blots that he had not crossed out. Someone else gave them names, wrote stories. How could Mickey and Donald matter to millions of people? He knew how—nothing mattered. That was the curse upon all things, the dread that Will wouldn't recognize or even let Walt talk about. Lucille used to tell him that it would pass, that it would disappear. It didn't disappear, but Lucille did. Walt wondered if he had drawn Lucille would she still be as alive as Mickey and Donald. Did ink blots always outlive flesh?

Somewhere in or near downtown, he got off the bus. He was watching a group of Mexican boys. When they arose he followed. They all wore high black basketball shoes. They ran away. Walt Disney looked around the bus stop. He recognized nothing familiar. The signs were all in Spanish. Because of the heat the streets were deserted. Walt Disney looked at the sun, decided to walk to the east. Trucks rolled by. Walt looked at the wheels, then at the tires, the miracle of roundness twice. It still fascinated him. He could watch a wheel across hundreds of frames—set it to music, put a face on it, give it a personality. Yet here were all these dull tires and arthritic spokes gliding past like unadorned bachelors who had given up, faded into anonymity. Content to roll silently across the world.

A wheel, a square, a triangle, plus a little violin music—that's all you needed for a cartoon, even a full-length feature. Who needed stories? Say one triangle brought home a cake that his wife, a circle, didn't want—there was a lot of throwing and chasing, a few tears, a happy ending, a few hundred more stories just like that one and then Disneyland and Disneyworld and Walt and Will themselves, wheels rolling across the world, falling off, finally not spinning, not drawing, just falling off into absolutely nothing. It didn't make any sense.

"We can help," the woman said. She was standing in front of Walt Disney. Either she had moved to block his path or he had bumped into her. She wore a white cap. Behind her he saw a mobile home. "The Red Cross is here," she said, "not only to take blood—we're here to help any way that we can."

Walt knew that she meant it.

The sun was too strong to look up at her face but when she spoke he could see that she kept her ankles straight. "The Red Cross is not interested in history or morality or politics or religion. We're just here. We just want to help. If we're going to help we need your blood."

She helped Walter off with his jacket. "It's too hot for this anyway, isn't it?" she asked. "I'm Miss Rubin. This is my station. I'm trying to collect thirty pints of blood today. Do you think I'll make it? So far I only have six. People think it's too hot. But inside the trailer it's air-conditioned."

Walt Disney stood his ground. He did not allow her to lead him into the coolness. Miss Rubin stood at the step leading up to the bloodmobile. Though middle-aged, she looked back like a bride, tugged lightly at his fingers. Her legs were in white tinted hose, even the bottoms of her shoes were clean.

"No," Walt Disney said.

"Silly me," Nurse Rubin said. She gave him back his hand, then his jacket. She went to the doorway of her trailer, stood there so that the cool air flowed across her back while she scanned the street for donors. The blown air puffed her short sleeves, the back of her uniform filled out. Her glance, darting up the street, took in the heavens. Walt Disney stood before her, transfixed. When she saw no others coming along the pavement, Miss Rubin returned her gaze to Walt Disney who looked up at her as if she was a painting in a museum.

"OK, sweetie," she said. "I think I understand." She stepped back into the heat of the day. "When's the last time you ate? Do you know?"

Walt Disney shook his head.

"You don't have to be ashamed," she said. "I told you we're in this neighborhood not only to collect blood but to help. In the suburbs they only need the Red Cross when God throws them a flood or a hurricane. For you it's disaster every day, isn't it?"

Walt Disney nodded.

"We understand, sweetie, we really do."

She took his hand again. "You know what? There's not likely to be anyone walking along Pacific Avenue when it's 102. Why don't I close up for a bit and take us out to lunch?"

She turned to pull the trailer door shut. Then she led Walt Disney along the row of shops, dry cleaners, used books, religious items, into a tiny Mexican restaurant.

She told her companion to order whatever he liked. It was inexpensive but very clean. That's why she stopped on this particular block. She felt safety in the presence of Carlos Huaracha who smiled at both of them. She ordered tortillas. Walt Disney found himself unable to speak to the waiter.

"Cat got your tongue?" Miss Rubin asked.

Walt Disney nodded. He saw it happening as she said it. A gray and black tom peeked around the corner, ran beneath a parked car, stopped for a quick sniff at a trash can lid, and then made a beeline for Walt Disney's tongue as the executive sat quietly in a charming cantina in the barrio of Los Angeles. Carlos and Miss Rubin smiled at the cat. The cat gloated, took the tongue and returned to the other side of the street while his family lounged and scratched and sunbathed and napped, all in Technicolor.

"It's OK," Miss Rubin said, "the Red Cross knows. You don't have to talk, friend. Enjoy your lunch. I can keep myself busy. See?"

Miss Rubin pulled a tiny book from her purse. She held a

cryptic page up for her companion to look at. "It's not a foreign language, it's eye exercises. I do them when I'm on hold on the phone or in a restaurant, or waiting for a client. You'd be surprised how much eyes are begging for exercise."

She put the booklet in front of her. Her eyes rolled upwards, then downwards, seemed to follow the motes in the air. Her eyes zigzagged, made U-turns, acted with the speed of the cat that took Walt Disney's tongue.

"Surprised by this?"

Walt Disney shook his head.

"Most people are, though. I guess you've been on the street enough to have seen everything. If I did this in a restaurant in Glendale or in the Valley they'd probably throw me out."

Her glances cut the air. Walt saw her following invisible lines. Perhaps the ones he had erased that morning. Her eyes reached their limit on the right, then stopped coyly as if asking directions, as if not knowing what to do next. He was afraid they were going to fall right out of their sockets into God knows what. Then they zoomed to the other side of their little world and did the same thing on the left.

"Nobody's ever watched so carefully," Miss Rubin said. "I see you're really interested." She blushed a little from the attention. Her gray-green speedsters paused, her lids came down for a bow, a curtain call, then the racing orbs took him on another tour of the world, to the northern rims, the watery south, to the edge of darkness on either side. They were fearless eyes. Their muscles held him for long counts in positions other eyes never knew about. Walt Disney saw them count and label and catalogue the emptiness, the erasings, all the things that should have still been there.

When the tortillas came and Miss Rubin carefully put her exercise book back into her purse Walt felt as if the lights had been turned up in the theater. There they were, regular eyes again, looking at what was in front of them. A dish, a glass, a cigarette butt on the table, a coffee cup.

Carlos put a plate of tortillas in front of Walt too. Miss Rubin's eyes made an unexpected exciting dive, a curtain call.

"Not really a prayer," she said, "just a reverent pause. I don't know how to pray." She was embarrassed by his silence. If the cat would bring back his tongue Walt could have told her that he understood the pause, even the inability to know the words of prayer. He was thinking of "The Battle Hymn of the Republic," but he knew that wasn't what he wanted to say.

He watched Miss Rubin eat in small clean bites. She instructed him to pick up his tortillas and eat. He did. He ate as if learning to do so. He watched her first, then he followed. She nodded her approval.

"I'm not even going to guess when you last ate. It's a good thing you didn't try to donate. Your fuel tank was too low. Don't let that happen again. Just trot in to Carlos and say fill 'er up." She looked serious. "A good meal costs less than a bottle of wine. Promise me you're not going to get down to empty again."

Walt Disney nodded. Maybe he was on empty. He remembered watching the sherbet melt but not any food that he'd eaten recently. He thought of the studio cafeteria and all those revolving trays of desserts, the lazy Susans of condiments, the steaming casseroles. He thought of all the openings and closings, the bitings and chewings of all those mouths, the wetness of lips, the menacing overhang of the nose. In the midst of all that commotion of chewing there was a sly hidden figure, the tongue, trying to stay out of the way of all those teeth grinding flesh. He had never before seen so clearly the mystery of the tongue, the silent witness at every feast, the one that lived in the same territory as the teeth but for other reasons. The one who spoke and sang and twisted and cavorted, the one who sliced breath cleaner than meat.

As he thought about tongues his own was back, right there in the center of his mouth. It raised itself in terror before all his chewing—it reared back like a horse before a snake. It ran every which way but it was back, safe and sound where it belonged but did not want to be.

"Are you all right?" Miss Rubin asked.

Walt Disney nodded. "Yes." The tongue, mollified by the words, squatted down, crept into its watery bed, curbed itself and let the onslaught of eating continue.

Walt Disney ate and Carlos and Miss Rubin were satisfied. Carlos slapped the old gent's back. Miss Rubin took his pulse. When he reached for his wallet she said, "Don't be silly. And don't be embarrassed either. This one's on the Red Cross. Life's little emergencies are as important as the big ones. In fact, they're worse because they happen only to you. You know the old saying, misery loves company; it's true."

"I agree," Walt said.

"But when there's misery there's little company, right?"

"Right."

He thought of his company, Walt Disney Inc. For Will company, for him misery.

"Would you like anything else?" Miss Rubin asked.

Quietly, modestly, Walt Disney asked if she would do her eye exercises again.

"Silly you," she said. Before she could stop them the speeding beauties did a fast U-turn forward and back before she reared them in as if she was the state police.

"It's back to work for me," she said, "and on your way for you."

When they emerged from beneath Carlos's fan to the overpowering sun the whiteness of Miss Rubin's uniform almost blinded him. Walt Disney pulled the brim of his hat lower and followed her back to the Red Cross bloodmobile.

"I've really gotta get back to work, sweetie, honest. If there's no traffic here I'll just get on the freeway. I've got nine specific stops. It's up to me to decide how long to stay at each one."

They were the only ones on the street. Walt Disney took off his jacket and rolled up his sleeves.

"You sure you want to? You don't have to pay for lunch, you know. This is the Red Cross, not a mission."

He held out his arm, palm up.

"OK," Miss Rubin said. "You packed away the carbohydrates."

In the cool dark trailer she became businesslike. She handed him a form to fill in his name and address, his age and his weight, then she pulled out the needle and placed it on the table. Nurse Rubin put a tiny pillow under his head. She looked at his form. He had filled in only his age.

"Sixty-six is a little older than we like to take. But there's no danger if you feel up to it. Better than being out in the heat, isn't it?" She pulled the flesh of his arm tight with a rubber strap and sat down beside him carefully. Nurse Rubin placed the needle into the skin of Walt Disney's left arm.

He barely noticed the needle. He was feeling her strong fingers at his biceps and her breath at the crook of his arm. He tried to raise his head to look at her now intent eyes.

"Lie down, sweetie, I've gotta poke around here for a vein. Hurt you?"

"No," Walt Disney said. He saw the jeweled bobby pins that kept her white cap in place. Her hair was curls, tight springs, circles again. Walt remembered a whole series of drawings he had done, all curls pulled one by one, stretching out as far as they could, then rolling back to their original shape. He had done curls of all colors—pop—they all rolled back.

"Just relax, sweetie. Sometimes those veins just don't . . . there, I got it, I think."

As Nurse Rubin plunged her needle into his flesh, Walt Disney thought of the gravedigger's shovel breaking in on a party of dancing worms. The worms were happy, safe in their dark place, not expecting Mr. Shovel. But it wasn't Mr. Shovel's fault, either, he was just doing his job. He could have chosen another spot, disturbed other worms, old Mr. Shovel just kept at it, getting himself dirty and then clean again in nice smooth strokes. The old in-out . . . another rhythm like the circle. With a railroad locomotive you could have both at once, the round wheel, the horizontal bar. Add them up and you had the world. One plus one . . . that's always the answer, the answer Miss Rubin was discovering too.

"Nothing," she said. "I'll be darned, I've got the vein, but nothing's coming out. If I wasn't seeing it myself I wouldn't believe it."

She waited for the gush of Walt Disney's blood. She took his temperature and his blood pressure while the needle stayed taped in place. Nurse Rubin touched the crook of his arm, poked, tickled, shook her tight curls at the naughty vein. When nothing helped, she looked at Walt Disney doing his best, but a disappointment as usual, even in a Red Cross trailer on a hot afternoon.

"I'm sorry," he said.

Nurse Rubin patted his shoulder, pulled out the needle. She touched his arm to make sure he was alive, warm, still there.

"It must be a kind of false vein or something," she said. "I think I'd better stop trying. But don't worry, your vital signs are just fine. It's probably all my fault."

Walt Disney saw vital signs, the plus sign, the minus sign, dancing in a circle. Ring around the rosy. Mickey, then Minnie, then Donald and Goofy, were vital signs too. Dancing blocks. One plus one plus one plus one, yet nothing added up. He looked at the dry needle hanging beside his arm, the arm itself hanging from his shoulder. He sat up.

"Can I do anything for you?" Miss Rubin asked.

"The eye exercises, please."

Mr. Disney knew what he liked. Speed in a narrow place. Tight curves. Small, unexpected miraculous motions. He wanted to see the flash of light at least once more.

"Please," Mr. Disney asked. He took off his hat, smoothed his thin straight hair. He reached for his wallet and showed Nurse Rubin his driver's license.

175

All by themselves her eyes raced. They were getting their screen test. A fantasy come true. Walt Disney looked only at her eyes. Nurse Rubin might have had wooden legs and whale blubber. She could have spoken Chinese or chewed on crushed glass. Walt Disney would not have noticed. He stepped clear of the offering table. The blood roared in all his veins. He took the arm of Nurse Rubin. The Red Cross had come through again.

# CHAPTER TWENTY

$\mathcal{T}$he day Disneyworld construction began was a holiday in Orlando. The mayor declared Walt Disney Day. The mayor spoke from the reviewing stand decorated with flags like the Fourth of July. He declared this day the beginning of a new era for Central Florida.

After the mayor's speech and a prayer from Reverend Bumpers, the workers marched, two thousand of them, each holding a paper flag with a red emblem of Tinker Bell. For sixteen blocks Orlando came out to give its thanks to Walt Disney. Dutch Henderson in two days sold eleven thousand mouse caps. The mayor himself wore a mouse cap. So did Will Disney. The mayor called him Will but everyone thought of him as Walt. There was only one Disney, Walt, one mouse, Mickey, soon one big Disneyworld right there in Orlando.

Will Disney took off his mouse cap and held it near his heart. He wanted the people of Orlando to know that they were close to his heart. "We could have picked a lot of different cities," he told the crowd, "Just about any Southern spot would do for us. But we didn't want just any place, that's not the way this organization works. We've always looked for what's special. Don't forget that all of this didn't start with any old mouse, it was . . ." He waited. The crowd roared it out to him: MICKEY!

"That's right, my friends, my brother Walter knew right from the start that if you're going to entertain people, you'd better be ready to give them the best of everything, and that's what we've always done. As some of you might know, we've got a mighty fine little operation in Southern California. The only reason I call it little is in comparison to what you're going to have down here."

The crowd didn't let him finish. Two high schools bands began to play the Mickey Mouse theme. Will held up his hands for quiet. It was like a presidential convention.

"I guess you're all ready to begin." The crowd cheered. The workers looked ready to drop the Tinker Bell flags and pick up hammers on the spot.

"There's one thing I don't want you to forget." His voice became quiet, serious. The drummers slowed their rhythms, finally stopped completely so that everyone could hear what Mr. Disney wanted to tell them.

"Don't forget that this time it's not Disneyland, it's Disney *World.*"

The mayor gave the signal. The firecrackers went off. Three thousand Mickey ear balloons rose then spread out over the skies of Orlando County. From the speaker's stand Will Disney looked at his workers, his town, the landscape that would soon blossom in rides and profits. He had never much cared for parades. He didn't see what pleasure there was for folks to stand ten or twenty deep waiting to catch a glimpse of something they wouldn't see anyway. That's why he wanted the balloons sent up, so at least everyone would get to see them. That was always a spectacle. High school bands he could do without.

"Mr. Disney," the mayor said, "two years ago when I ran I said that I would achieve a ten percent growth rate for Orlando. You know what you've done? You've made me a liar."

From his tiny office next to the locker room Bones Jones could hear the bands.

The season was over and everyone now understood that the Pirates were through. The players moved out. They took everything, even the half rolls of adhesive tape and the pinups in the lockers. Someone took the scale and the carton of resin bags and the leaded bat and the plastic on-deck circle. Even the bases were stolen. So was the foul-line chalk and the winter-green rubdown. Nobody talked about next year or the hope of new lights or maybe a strong-armed right-handed kid who would be the next Walter Johnson. The Pirates understood that next year they would all be building for Disneyworld.

"It's a damn shame," Earl Ramsey said. He walked in to say goodbye to Bones. Even Earl had gone to the parade. He knew Bones Jones hated the Disneys but what the hell, Earl was curious. And he only worked for Bones part time. In the off season he sold sporting goods at the big K Mart off I-4. The rest of the players didn't even try to say goodbye to their boss. Why should they? For the last month of the season he had treated them as if they were mosquitoes. He stopped keeping the league records. He stopped announcing the lineup to the fans. He stopped mimeographing scorecards. The players never knew for sure if there would actually be a game the next day. They thought Bones Jones might cut the electricity. They didn't know what had gotten into him. From the moment of the first Disney announcement, just when the rest of Orlando got pumped up, Bones went into a big slump. He still paid them and showed up at all the games. He started bringing Al and Hal, the two midgets who ran the Orlando Kiddieland, down to the dugout with him. At first the team thought he was going to use the midgets as pinch-hitters the way Bill Veeck had used a midget with the old St. Louis Browns, but Bones never put Al and Hal on the roster. They circulated in the clubhouse, some-times they brought in a case of Coke, and a few dozen comic books. They were decent little fellows. They told jokes. Not Bones. He stopped talking baseball. It was like the world had ended. Luke Simpson, a relief pitcher who had worked in an old people's home, said he thought that Bones had had a silent stroke.

"I used to see them get like that lots of times," Luke told his teammates. "They just change overnight. First they stop doing everything they used to do and pretty soon they're shitting in their pants and you have to feed them. It breaks your heart, even when it's some old geezer in the home, but when it's Bones Jones it's a genuine tragedy. Not a thing you can do though."

The boys did bring Doc Collins, the team physician, into the dugout to observe Bones. Collins was a chiropractor. He didn't believe in strokes. He said Bones needed his spine adjusted twice a week and he needed Ace bandages on both knees, tight. But who could tell Bones Jones anything? Doc Collins had tried for years. "This man is out of alignment," Doc Collins told the team. "If he was a set of tires you'd be opening your trunk looking for spares."

"Can't we do something?" Earl wanted to know.

"The man knows his problem," Doc Collins said, "and he chooses to ignore it. You can't lead a horse to the rubbing table."

Just before the season ended, after an extra-inning loss to Raleigh-Durham, the boys had a team meeting. They all stood in the doorway of Bones's office.

"You've been like a father to us," Earl said. "You saved the whole damned league. Without Bones Jones there wouldn't be Class D ball in Central Florida. We know it's all over now, Bones, but we've been together. The Pirates have meant something. What happened, can't you tell us?"

Bones looked at his team crowded together in the doorway. There were sore arms and slow reflexes out there, not even one quick bat, but he'd loved them, they were his boys, his Pirates, the only family he had.

It was so quiet you could hear the showers drip. Nobody popped their bubblegum. Earl's voice quivered. "Can't we help you, Bones? We'd do anything . . . We all owe you."

Bones Jones shook his head. The Pirates were disintegrating now, just as Perky Parrot had disintegrated in the flames. Even if he didn't sell Disney his land, who would come to see a shabby baseball team when they could go to Disney's park a few blocks away? The Pirates were through, the league was through, Central Florida was through. Bones Jones was through. Soon the little bungalows he had built over the years would all be torn down to make way for hotels. Everything destroyed a second time—twice without a trace. Not even an insurance company to complain to this time, just Al and Hal, the midgets whose Kiddieland was being wiped out. Pony rides, a merry-go-round, duck pins and cotton candy couldn't compete with Disney either.

The midgets and Bones Jones couldn't do a thing to stop Disney. They could go bankrupt and shut up. The Pirates standing at his doorway wouldn't understand. Or maybe they would; everyone in the room was as much a failure as he was. They failed not only as ballplayers, but as salesmen, or construction workers, or truck drivers. They hung around baseball because it had given each of them the only triumphs in their lives. They remembered their moments. Billy Diggers talked about his pinch-hit triple in Birmingham in AA ball in the 1956 playoffs. Earl once took batting practice while Johnny Mize watched, Laverne Coleman had a minor league contract with the Cubs. Maybe everyone had their version of Perky Parrot, but nobody else had one single human enemy who caused it all to happen and was coming to strike again.

Bones was about to tell his story, to explain it all to the Pirates, but his mouth got dry. He remembered the cartoons, even his wife. He remembered the draperies and the nice yellow carpet in his little building. He remembered the Coca-Cola sign outside his window and his swivel chair and the 16-mm. projector clicking away and the black tape he kept on hand for the slivers of light that peeked through the venetian blinds. It was all still there for him and Perky Parrot that gray-green prophet talking away as chipper and full of life as Bones Jones himself once was.

"Good luck, boys," was all Bones could get out. They had their cleats slung over their shoulders or tucked away in their gym bags. They left the clubhouse quietly, only their rubber shoes squeaked on the linoleum. In the empty locker room there was not a ball or a bat or a glove in sight. Four wooden benches, two rows of lockers, a grandstand that could burn in ninety seconds and three light towers needing bulbs. "My second empire," Bones Jones said. He turned out the lights.

# CHAPTER TWENTY-ONE

*T*he bitch was causing trouble. Treat Gilbert had promised that he would handle her. Will had gotten to Gilbert early—trusted him. "I should have known better than to put my faith in a lawyer," Will Disney told himself. He was sitting at a table between the mayor and the chairman of the city council. The unions expected him to pay the six thousand workers he'd hired even while they were idled by that bitch's disturbing-the-peace charge. It could run to $30,000 an hour. She said the construction noise was bothering her. She brought in a team of lawyers from New York. They filed petitions every day—disturbing the peace, unfair labor contracts, incomplete sewer lines, not enough highways to accommodate traffic, no safety and evacuation plans. Hell, he wasn't building a bomb shelter he told the mayor, he was building an amusement park. This was the third time in less than a month that she got an injunction to hold up the construction. Even a rainy day hurt the schedule—her delays were killers.

He told Treat Gilbert to find out her price. Gilbert laughed. "She doesn't want money. She might be crazy enough to spend as much fighting as you would spend on building."

Will Disney went to the fucking governor and the mayor. One person, no matter how rich, shouldn't stand against Disneyworld. The politicians were on his side but there was nothing they could do here. You couldn't pass out some autographs and sweatshirts and make everyone happy. You couldn't even pay for anything. She had private detectives watching every move. If a worker threw a cigarette butt near the lumber or turpentine she called a city council meeting and wanted a new ordinance with a thirty-day waiting period. He knew what she was trying to do—make it so slow and expensive that he would just move the World someplace else. This woman might have her millions but she did not know Will Disney. Come hell or high water Disneyworld was going ahead and going ahead right here in Orlando.

"Cinderella will dance on her grave," he told Mayor Greener. The council meeting dragged on. Her lawyers called in an expert on noise level. The expert showed a big drawing of the inside of a human ear.

Walt would like that, Will Disney thought, discussing a drawing of the human ear while six thousand workers sat on their asses next to unbuilt rides and castles and restaurants. And little brother, Mr. Personality, still hiding under the blankets in his bedroom.

He's a sick man, I know, Will Disney thought, and a genius too. And a kindhearted soul. But one of these days I'm going to pull him by the ears all across the Southwest if I have to and get him down here so people can see that there is a Walt Disney —that all of this is not just contracts and laws and who can spend more money on lawyers and detectives.

The mayor lit a cigarette. "I know this is aggravating to you, Mr. Disney. I know it's costing you a fortune too. Just don't hold it against Orlando. You know where the blame lies. You know that Orlando wants Disneyworld."

"I know," Will Disney said, "but you're gonna have to prove it. You're gonna have to change those goddamn nitpicking laws. Give me some kind of right of way. What the hell did you do during the war down here? Did you let the Japs and the Krauts sue you?"

"She's an American citizen, Mr. Disney."

"Then why doesn't she act like one? Any city in America,

any city on earth, would turn upside down for a Disneyworld and here I am getting bled to death by the Orlando city council."

"By one person, Mr. Disney, the rest of us are with you. Don't forget that."

"What the hell kind of democracy is this when one person can hold up six thousand workers?"

The expert folded up his ear and left. They called Will Disney to the witness stand.

Her lawyer had a hunchback and a big nose.

"You seem upset, Mr. Disney," he said.

"Yes," Will Disney said, "The prospect of losing $30,000 an hour does that to me."

"But some things, Mr. Disney, matter more than money."

"Name 'em."

The crowd laughed. They were with him but it didn't make a bit of difference.

"Peace of mind is more important and doing the right thing is more important. After all, money is a means not an end. We're here to talk about ends."

"Cut the sermon," Will Disney said, "and get on with it."

The lawyer wanted ninety decibels less noise. "We can't use rubber hammers," Will said. "We can't get elves to build it with silk threads. When you've got construction you've gotta have noise. Nobody needs an expert with an ear to tell him that."

When his testimony was over Will went outside for a smoke. The hearing dragged on. The mayor promised that the council would meet all night if necessary to change the law so that construction could begin again in the morning.

When Will came back into the council meeting room two midgets were giving testimony. They shared a chair. They said the noise bothered them too. He sat down next to Gus Harris, his chief lawyer. "We're bogged down with the midgets," Gus told him, "and the old geezer who owns the baseball field. We could use the ballfield for parking but it's not crucial. We've made him a good offer—who knows what they want? Greed brings on change in all people. The small fry are only an annoyance—but she's so rich that she can cause real problems."

"Get the midgets and the ballpark guy," Will Disney said. "We'll isolate her, and then we'll do whatever we have to do."

# CHAPTER TWENTY-TWO

*B*ones hired Raymond R. Harsch to represent him. Harsch came to him to offer his services. Harsch had gone to Mrs. Merriweather too, but she wouldn't even talk to him. Bones took Harsch up on his offer. He would need a lawyer. The Disneys had sent Bones a contract and a cheerful letter. He was about to make a nice profit, they said, and join in a history-making venture. They offered him sixty thousand for the field in as-is condition, plus five thousand more for the good will established by the Pirates. Sixty-five thousand for the second half of his life and all nice and cheerful, not even a threat of arson.

Lawyer Harsch didn't know Bones Jones's reasons but he understood Disney-hating. So did Al and Hal. Their Kiddieland was already closed. Already kids started saving for Walt Disney's big admission fees. At birthday parties their parents already gave Disneyworld certificates to be redeemed later, rather than take their kids to Al and Hal's the way they used to on nice weekend afternoons. Al and Hal had already sold their ponies and Bones let them store the merry-go-round under his grandstand. Al and Hal and Bones Jones and Raymond R. Harsch, they were the opposition. Mrs. Merriweather and her lawyers ignored them, but Disney had to fight them too. When Hal told Bones Jones that the Disneys wanted a meeting, he was too stunned to turn it down. He didn't know if he could bear it.

"Don't be nervous," Al and Hal told him. "We'll be there. We'll do the talking."

Bones told Raymond Harsch that he would never sell, not for a million. The Disneys didn't believe it. Will Disney and his lawyer drove up to Harsch's office in a construction company jeep. Bones was expecting Walt Disney. He'd never seen Will.

Will Disney wore coveralls and a straw hat. He looked like a farmer. "Howdy, fellas," he said. "I've come to make a deal and settle things nice for everyone." He thought he was dealing with real rubes. Al and Hal were teasing Raymond R. Harsch's secretary while she typed invoices. Will Disney gave everyone a Mickey Mouse sweatshirt and a mouse cap. Al and Hal put on the caps and ripped the ears off one another.

"Cute, fellas," Will said. "Real cute. I want you to know I'm sorry about your merry-go-round business. I want you to know that there'll always be a job for you in our park. After all, you're experienced businessmen, right? We're all in show business."

Al and Hal bowed from the waist. "We're just little birds," Hal sang, "far from our nest." Al accompanied him in a slow soft-shoe.

"Very good," Will Disney said, "a nice touch you've got there." Al and Hal went on to do their imitations of Al Jolson's "Mammy."

"Boys," Will Disney said, "if the day of specialty acts was not long gone I'd say you had a future. But let's get down to business. Mr. Jones knows why we're here."

"And you have my answer," Jones said. "No sale. No interest in a sale."

"Let's not be too hasty," Will Disney said. "I've come to talk. Our offer is just an opener."

"No dice," Bones Jones said.

Will Disney turned to Raymond R. Harsch. "Can't you tell your client what we're getting at here? We're prepared to recognize the value of your holdings as well as the necessary costs of relocating."

"But we've just now found us this wonderful hollow old tree trunk, Mr. Disney," Al said, "and we moved all our cute little things in already. And we met a talented squirrel who offered to make us custom-tailored suits. And an owl to give us legal advice."

"And we've stored up acorns against the frost," Hal said, "and there's good schools and cable TV."

"Much have we wandered," they sang in unison, "much have we roamed. And any way you look at it, there's no place like home."

"Enough monkey business," Will Disney said. He reached into his pocket and handed Bones Jones a blank check. "Just write in the amount you want and we'll cut this shit out right now. I don't like being here any more than you want us." Jones looked at the big green check with its engraved heads of Mickey, Donald and Goofy. His hand shook as he drew a Perky Parrot over them and returned the check.

Will Disney looked at the check. He saw no numbers. He didn't recognize the parrot.

He turned to Raymond R. Harsch. "Can't you talk some sense into your client?"

"Mr. Disney," Raymond R. Harsch said, "I wouldn't sell you the sweat off my balls."

"What the hell is all this hostility? Am I a Nazi for offering you all a fortune? Has the old witch bought you off already? If she keeps it up the only thing that will happen is that she'll kick the bucket fast and we'll stick her in the wax museum. The percentage is to go along with us. Disneyworld will be no small potatoes. The President will start the first ride—we might even bring the whole U.N. down here for a little vacation. We're not talking, you know, about the Ferris wheel and the roller coaster. This is international. The Japs, the Arabs, the Greeks, they all want in."

"Mr. Disney," Raymond R. Harsch asked as he slowly chewed a mint, "what do you notice about me?"

"You're mean and stubborn," Disney said, "you're narrow-minded and have poor business judgment."

"The first thing," Raymond R. Harsch said, "the first thing you notice about me. The truth."

"You talk like your mouth is full of shit," Will Disney said. "Excuse me, but it's true."

"And you know why it's true?" Harsch moved his face close to Will Disney. With his fingers he pulled up on his upper lip, exposing in the meat of his gums a bright array of scars. Will turned his head away.

"Don't be disgusted, Mr. Disney, by a plain old harelip like me." He exaggerated his voice and blew out his cheeks. "Huey, Dewey, and Louie, get in here, boys, it's about to rain."

"That's good," Will Disney said, "that's one of the best imitations I've heard."

"I'm glad you liked it, Mr. Disney," Harsch said with exaggerated cordiality. "But how would you have liked hearing it every day of your life, all through school, on playgrounds, on buses, on tennis courts, even in student council meetings? How would you like to be concentrating on something and all of a sudden you hear someone behind you whimpering in that voice your duck created, 'Get this shit out of my mouth, it's all wrapped around my tongue'? Do you think you'd like to hear that from friends, relatives, strangers?

"Many a night I have laid awake in my tearful bed thinking, Why did Walt Disney choose to pick on harelips? Why only us? He didn't put Donald in a wheelchair or give him epilepsy or diabetes or a hundred other funny little problems. He just made him a harelip; that's really hilarious, isn't it, Mr. Disney?"

"You're not going to let childhood nostalgia get in the way of good business, are you?" Will asked. "Holding a grudge is like holding a two percent bond. Cut your losses. Start out clean. There was nothing personal intended to any unfortunate in the world. Some voices and accents are just funny, that's all there is to it. Kids, and grownups too, have laughed at that voice for thirty years. If everyone felt like you there'd be no comedy anywhere, we'd all be a bunch of sensitive flowers afraid of hurting someone's feelings.

"Anyway, if it makes you feel any better, I can tell you that Donald Duck is washed up. He hasn't been in a cartoon for five years. He will have minimal space in Disneyworld, not even a ride of his own. The comic books, the lawn sprinklers and drinking cups and all that stuff is out of our hands. We sold secondary rights in the forties."

"We'll sell you the land," Raymond R. Harsch stated, "if you'll redo all the old Donald Ducks in the voice of Charles Laughton."

"He's crazy," Will said aloud to the room. "I came here to talk business and I'm surrounded by lunatics on all sides. I ought to just leave them here and sell admissions to watch these nuts."

Will Disney stood and motioned for his attorney to rise. "Keep your fucking ballfield," he said. "We'll put a pestilent swamp on your borders and a garbage dump at your gate. We'll blockade you behind plumbing and air-conditioning equipment. When the Disneys finish with your place, we'll buy your outfield for landfill."

He took off his straw hat and walked out. "Keep an eye on your midgets," he turned back to say, "because if I catch them in Disneyworld we'll stuff them for our freak museum."

"Goodbye, Mr. Disney," Raymond R. Harsch bellowed in his best Donald Duck voice. "Thanks for coming to see us. The nephews and I think you're just terrific." For the first time since the fire, Bones Jones thought of Walt Disney and laughed.

## CHAPTER TWENTY-THREE

*W*hen the first court order stopped all work at Disneyworld, the workers had no unemployment relief. The crews had barely been in place for a week. There were no union halls in Orlando, hardly any gathering places at all. There was the Civic Auditorium for concerts, the Bank of Orlando auditorium for business meetings, two small VFW ballrooms. Six thousand unemployed, most of them new to Orlando, roamed the downtown streets. They squatted in front of Woolworth's and spit chewing tobacco. Kroger's hired security guards because some women were afraid to walk past the groups of tattooed men.

Bored carpenters leaned in doorways, cleaning their fingernails with jackknives. Hod carriers dozed in the sunshine. All through the downtown, strong men waited like soldiers knowing they might be called to the front at any moment. They had only collected a single paycheck. Disneyworld was a billboard, some surveyors' ropes, a ditch and a few hundred scattered planks, nothing beyond knee height.

William White came to Margery's house. She had never met him. He was a local attorney she had hired over the phone. He had brought her successful invasion-of-privacy suit against Disneyworld.

In court Attorney White demanded the letter of the law against the Walt Disney Corporation. He successfully upheld Margery Post Merriweather's assertion that her right to privacy was being infringed. The judge accepted the proposition that two or three million visitors next door was a credible threat to anyone's privacy.

But Attorney White's pleasure did not last long. The next day he saw the clusters of the unemployed, he listened to the breakfast crowd at the Big Boy worry about the end of their brief boom. He decided that the $5,000 retainer was not worth it. He went to the Post mansion. In Margery's presence he was weak and apologetic, but firm in his conscience.

"I can't continue working for you," he said. "I want the other side to win. I'm sorry, Mrs. Merriweather, but that's how I feel. I was born in Orlando and I can't continue to try to stop the best thing that's ever happened to us."

Immediately Margery liked him. He was no Treat Gilbert. She could see that White was suffering, that he had a conscience. "I was betrayed by my first attorney," Margery told Mr. White. "If I have a strong enough case to convince the judge, why can't I convince you?"

"Because this town is more important than both of us. You should move, Mrs. Merriweather. If you don't like what's coming, you can go someplace else."

"You mean because I'm rich and I can afford to go elsewhere I shouldn't cause trouble. Should all the Negroes go back to Africa too? Should everybody stop defending their rights? Just not cause trouble?"

"It's not the same, Mrs. Merriweather. You're just one person."

It hurt Margery to be reminded of this even by a stranger who could hardly know how single she was. Yes, she was one person, not a mother, not a wife, not even an aunt. Just one person.

"But aren't the rights of a single person at the heart of democracy? How many people, after all, is Walt Disney?"

William White sat down on the couch opposite Margery. "You have a strong legal argument and if you want to pay for doing it you can cause Walt Disney a lot of delays. You may even have a moral argument. But all I have to do to know you're wrong is walk downtown and see the looks on the faces of the men who are out of work. Who's right isn't always the most important question. This time I don't think it matters that much." He handed Margery her $5,000 check.

"Keep the money," Margery told him. "You represented me once. You've earned it."

"I know," he said. "That's why I want to give it back. It makes me feel guilty for what I've done. Believe me, I don't go around returning fees. It would take me a half-dozen divorces to earn this much and divorces are no picnic."

That Margery could guess although hers had never even happened. She had filed the papers. The story made the news and then they delayed the court date because Merriweather was in Africa and after that neither of them had ever scheduled another date. Merriweather had no claims to any of her trust and she wanted nothing from him. The divorce she should have gotten was from Clarence Birdseye. He was the one who made her pregnant, the one she even loved. From Clarence she wished she had an official document stating the end of their union, but instead of a divorce she gave him a check. It would almost have seemed reasonable to her to marry him merely in order to divorce him—if only to have something tangible between them, something other than Birdseye Foods, something that was personal. If her father hadn't died, if she had been less confused, maybe she would have decided to bear the child and maybe even to marry Clarence. It might have been possible. Eventually he would have moved to a house. She could have built him a basement laboratory, surrounded him with the trinkets he loved. Instead she had the abortion—decided to start again—without her father, her husband, Clarence, without Battle Creek and vegetarianism. She wanted to be an average person, not the Queen of anything, and she did try.

She bought a house on West Jackson Boulevard in Chicago. She rode the streetcar. She went to the grocery store. She washed dishes, she listened to the radio, she sat on her front porch. Her neighbors knew she was Mrs. Merriweather. Nobody cared who she was. Only the postman, by the volume and nature of her mail, might have guessed that this was no ordinary Mrs. Merriweather.

Chicago was not Moscow either. Maybe just being apart from Merriweather made it better. She liked to listen to the talk in restaurants. In Battle Creek she had never even been to a restaurant. In Russia the cabbage smells bothered her and the sound of the language made her feel as if the foreigners were spitting at her.

In the first months after Margery returned to Chicago she expected Birdseye to show up at her West Jackson Boulevard house at any time. She thought he would come in with some new idea and she would watch him draw it for her on typewriter paper the way he had drawn her a picture of the teeth on the orange peeler and then pulled his fingernails down her back to let her feel the idea, sharp, but gentle too at the same time, and after a few more demonstrations she didn't care to think about the juice and wanted to put her arms around him. But Clarence never interrupted his work. You could not distract him. He never ate lunch or breakfast. He woke up thinking, he said. When he stopped thinking, then he would eat or sleep. The position of the sun in the sky, he said, had nothing to do with him. He was biology, not astronomy. "People are insignificant," he told her while he held her in his arms. "Bundles of energy, like fireflies." She had to tell him sometimes to shut up, but not always. Usually when they made love he could stop being the cranky inventor and lie next to her and she could feel the shivers of pleasure in him and wonder if even C. W. Post had been able to feel that way with her mother.

But he never came to her home on Jackson Boulevard or to the Birdseye Frozen Food Company. Never a card or a phone call, no sign that he was even alive until he cashed the check more than two years later, and even then she couldn't know for sure that it was his signature. He cashed it at a bank in Seattle, Washington, but by the time the check cleared he was not in the Seattle telephone directory and he had closed his account at the bank.

The attorney, William White, brought her back to the moment. She shook his hand, thanked him. He was an honest man. She knew how hard it was for him to return the money. She let him stand in her hallway for an extra few seconds so that he could remember the setting and his own pain and have in his memory for the rest of his life the bittersweet feeling of moral triumph. She envied him going back to his wife and children the hero of Orlando. He was right. Five thousand dollars was a small price for such a glowing fragment of a person's life.

He was right, but still a fool. Margery said "Fool" aloud as she closed the front door. She was tired of monkeying around with Treat Gilberts and William Whites, tired of other people's triumphs. The issue was between herself and Walt Disney. If she was going to fight Walt Disney she wanted the best generals there were. She called Biff Alexander in New York. Biff Alexander had handled her separation from Merriweather and her buyout of Birdseye. In those days he had needed the business. Now his secretary kept her waiting five minutes, even after she had given her name.

When the police called her about Merriweather's body, it was Biff Alexander who had kept the news out of the paper, arranged for the dispersion of the African ladies and the quiet burial of her husband.

He was still polite. He apologized for keeping her waiting. "I was talking to someone from the White House staff," he said.

"Biff," she told him, "you sent a whoremaster down here to take care of my property. He sold me out to the Disneys."

He reminded her that Treat Gilbert had already resigned from the firm. "I don't think you can blame the Disney business decisions on Gilbert, but I know, Margery, that he didn't do the right things . . . it's what happens when these firms get so damned big. Some rotten fish slip through. I am sorry about Gilbert, I made a mistake—he fooled a lot of us. How could we guess it? He was *Yale Law Review*."

"I want you to do this job yourself, Biff."

Biff Alexander hesitated for a few seconds. Then he chuckled, a loud self-conscious chuckle. Margery could imagine the eminent legal mind pulling himself upright in his chair—maybe even looking at a secretary near him or a junior partner learning the business by watching the master. She knew that the chuckle meant that she was embarrassing him, that he wished she would leave him alone now that he was too distinguished to remember that he had spent several weeks in the company of pagans who had beheaded a man. He had done this at Margery's request and he had not laughed at that. Now he chuckled. The peace of her last years was a joke, she thought. Because she was Margery Post she had already missed almost every other aspect of what most humans considered a happy life. Why did she have to miss living quietly where she wanted to live? If she couldn't even do that what was all the fuss and bother about her fortune? What did it mean to be so powerful if your old clerks now chuckled and told you that they had been on the phone with the White House?

"Biff," she said, "don't laugh at me. And don't remind me that you're an important lawyer these days. I know that your name is in the paper, I know there's talk that a Republican president might appoint you to the Supreme Court."

"That may be an exaggeration."

The way he said it convinced Margery that it was a sure thing. He was so busy now thinking of himself in black robes marching into history that he could chuckle at problems that did not aim at the heart of the Constitution.

"There isn't likely to be a Republican president for at least four more years. You'll have time to do this for me."

"You know I'll do anything for you, Margery."

She could hear his voice move to sweetness and understanding now. "But the kind of case you have down there now is not difficult. You could run your finger down the yellow pages in the Orlando phone book and pick any lawyer. Chances are he'd do just as well as I could. I hope you believe that, because it's true."

"I do believe it, and I think the President could use the same yellow pages for his Supreme Court appointment, but that's not the point. I want to win this case. I want you to do the legal work. Whoever else could do it is beside the point."

"Margery, I can't leave a busy office in New York to fight Walt Disney over local ordinances in Orlando."

"You mean you're too important for that?"

"I mean it's a local thing, it needs a local attorney."

"Someone like Treat Gilbert?"

"I already apologized about that, Margery, Gilbert is gone. There won't be any more rotten apples."

"Biff, either you represent me or I'll hire another firm for all my work."

"Don't threaten me, Margery. You know that your personal stuff is not important to the firm."

"The first thing I'll do if I hire a new firm, even before I get after Walt Disney, I'll sue Hedges and Knowles for sending a whoremaster and dog-track owner to manage my property."

Alexander was silent.

"You can call me later," Margery said. "I'll wait one day."

"You know," Biff Alexander said, "the Disneys are going to have their hands full. Anybody who crosses you doesn't know what they're in for."

He was in Orlando at the end of the week.

And it was exciting. This was not the kind of legal business Margery was used to. This was not merely walking into an office on Park Avenue and drinking coffee from china cups and signing your name in all the places that a beautiful secretary had marked.

This was more like a revolution. The workers were out in the streets. When the court closed down their projects, they sat on the curbs and drank beer. Margery could see them through her telescope. At night too she could pick out their figures with her infrared scope, small groups of men standing in front of bars, holding bottles of beer in their hands, men wanting to tear Orlando apart and build a Kiddieland next door to her. She felt no sympathy for them.

It surprised Margery how much she enjoyed being their enemy. For the first time in her life she had a starring role. To her father and Clarence she had been the supporting actress, but now in Orlando it was Walt Disney vs. Margery Post. She had been in the news virtually all of her life, but not in this way. Her birthday had been a front-page item in Battle Creek because she was C. W. Post's daughter. No more. The Orlando *Times* wrote a long editorial exposing her as a spoiled brat, a woman who had kept her silver spoon in her mouth all her life, a woman who traveled the earth seeking thrills, a woman who cohabited with a hobo while married to an ambassador, a woman who had spent her life in excess and debauchery, a woman who had never done a single thing for the good of society. "Give Orlando a break," the paper urged her directly in a front-page editorial. "Don't stand in the way of Walt Disney. For the first time in your life look at yourself in the mirror and feel good."

Margery did it. She looked at herself. The Orlando *Times* was right. She felt good. Taking on Walt Disney was a good thing. She was having a good time and she wanted to win, felt that she would win. The issue was not just her solitude, it was peace and quiet everywhere, privacy itself.

"Cut the bullshit," Biff Alexander told her. "You don't need it for me. You want your own way. You're used to it and you're willing to pay for it."

"Of course."

"And so does Walt Disney."

"But he wants profits, my argument is more subtle."

"We'll see about that in court."

She could tell that Biff Alexander was beginning to have some fun at this too.

"I never read local building codes before," he said. "They're hysterical."

Margery liked Cynthia, Biff's wife. On their first weekend in Orlando, she invited the entire legal staff to her home for dinner. Cynthia told her she understood why Margery was standing up for herself.

"Most older people, especially single women, are pushed around by everybody. They can steal our houses, our pensions, sometimes even our husbands. They keep us waiting an hour for a restaurant table. Nobody stands up for us. The kids have the future, the whole damn world, why can't they leave us alone? We'll be dead soon enough and then they can play all the games they want."

It was during Margery's party for the legal staff that the cablegram arrived. Margery went to her room to read it. She was not alarmed. What did she have to be alarmed about—no news could surprise her. She expected another direct moral solicitation to stop her Disney suit, perhaps from the combined clergy of Central Florida. God's crowd had already endorsed Disneyworld. They were at the head of the bandwagon.

Though the cablegram came from a stranger in Vienna, it struck her like a letter from the dead, a letter from her father.

"Fourteen crates of paintings belonging to C. W. Post, Battle Creek, Michigan, located in storage at Praterstrasse #386, Vienna. Some question continues as to whether the paintings are property stolen during the Nazi era. If you wish to exercise your claim to these works of art, please reply at your convenience. The crates have been in storage since March 11, 1938, or earlier."

After Madrid, C. W. Post had never mentioned art again. Of course Margery told her father what she had overheard in the Hotel Del Prado. She told him that very evening, but C. W. Post was not concerned.

"Artists are not murderers," he told his daughter. "They are merely blasphemers. Meat packers, butchers, hunters, those are the murderers."

And that was that. C. W. Post returned from Madrid, and announced that Europe was hardly any different from Battle Creek.

"I walked through the land of Columbus," he told his colleagues in Battle Creek, "and nothing surprised me. The people have eyes and noses and fingers just like ours, though more of them are left-handed. They speak a different language, but what does that matter? Their mouths are as delighted by Grape-Nuts as our own." C. W. Post had seen the world and pronounced it fit for Grape-Nuts.

Margery heard him say that so many times that she stopped remembering the dark nervous streets, the shops full of things she had never seen, the looks in men's eyes, looks that were not Battle Creek looks. Her father said there was no difference, and what could she do finally except believe him until the day that she would escape from Battle Creek to see for herself.

The trusts, the property inventories, the will. Nothing had mentioned paintings. C. W. Post kept track of his belongings. He specified who was to receive the lace tablecloth, his floor safe, his cedar chest, his cracked enamel dishware, but he never mentioned fourteen crates of art. On the walls of his home he had only one decoration, a Post Cereals Company calendar that he gave to all employees and suppliers at Christmas time.

Before she returned to her guests, Margery cabled her claim to Herr Joseph Schmitz of the Austrian Art Council. She recalled, after all these years, Robinson the art critic on his knees

aboard the *Mauretania*. She remembered his plea, that she inter-
vene with her father in order to save Western art from vegetarianism. She could recall the sweat on his upper lip, the silly
image of that tall distinguished man on the deck of the rocking
ship, kneeling before her begging as if he were a peasant and
she royalty when in fact to her it seemed the other way around.
Robinson had been everywhere, seen everything. She and her
father were Battle Creek innocents. On their first night aboard
the ship they heard the disaster signal. She and C. W. Post put
on their life jackets when they heard the sequence of bells. C.
W. Post said a quick prayer and took his daughter by the hand.
"The sea is opening up for us," he said, "the Leviathan awaits.
Do not fear the voice of the Almighty." She was too frightened
to breathe. C. W. Post pounded on the walls of their stateroom
in case their neighbors hadn't heard the distress signal. They
ran up the stairs to the main deck ready to go overboard.

"It's God's will," her father said. "I'll stay with the captain
until everyone else is on the lifeboats."

On the deck men in tuxedoes and ladies in long gowns were
standing in groups drinking and talking. Margery and her father had removed their shoes and put on rain slickers over their
life jackets. Robinson, biting his cheeks and laughing in spite
of his efforts, told the Posts the ship's bells were not an emergency signal, they merely signified the dinner hour.

"Thank the Lord," C. W. Post said. He returned to the stateroom, put on his shoes, and went to dinner where on that day
and throughout the trip he ate boiled rice and lentils for his
evening meal. Margery felt so humiliated that she stayed in her
room all the rest of that day. Yet a few days later, there was the
famous art historian, the man from New York and Paris, kneeling before her and crying and looking as foolish as she and her
father had looked when they mistook dinner for disaster.

She wished that Robinson were still alive so that she could
call him and perhaps quickly find out what this cablegram from
Vienna meant. But he died, she knew, in the 1950s. She had

read the obituary in *Time* magazine and wondered then if her father had ever had any contact with Robinson after their trip to Spain.

Now she would find out, perhaps. Now, as she struggled to save the peace and quiet of her retirement from the world, her father was sending her new signals, new distractions. She was excited about the discovery, but afraid too of what C. W. Post might have done. To C. W. Post life vs. art was no contest. He would have defaced the *Mona Lisa* to save a single rooster.

As she sat in her room remembering her father, the staff of Hedges and Knowles admired her telescope and sunbathed near her swimming pool and envied the flora and greenery in her enclosed gardens. They wondered what it might be like to be Margery Post. One of the young female lawyers told her so while she was on her way upstairs to read the cablegram.

"You'd be disappointed," Margery told her.

"I guess so," said the young woman. "Still I can't help wondering."

Neither could C. W. Post help wondering about anything. Margery remembered that way her father had of starting a conversation when she was trying to study. He would tilt his head sideways as if he was looking at a bug in the corner of the ceiling. He would smack his lips together and Margery would think about going into her room to study at her sewing desk, but usually she wouldn't do it because when she did that she felt sad for her father all alone in the kitchen and wanting to talk and having nobody in the world except Margery who knew about the kinds of things that he liked to talk about. And if she did go to her room, C. W. Post went to bed as soon as it got dark and then she felt sad and sorry and wished she had listened to him even though what he said usually caused her to wish that Post Cereals and Battle Creek would disappear in a sheet of flame while she slept so that in the morning she could be just like all the other girls in her class.

When he told her about his plans to buy Swift and Company

he was wondering as usual about God.

"What if the Almighty is an animal?" he asked Margery. She was studying geometry. The Pythagorean theorem sat in front of her. She was measuring angles with a steel protractor. She was not thinking about the shape of the Almighty, didn't want to. But C. W. Post was drinking his hot wheat broth and thinking about eternal matters, and like it or not, there she was trying to do geometry and listening to her father wonder if the Lord might be a red heifer or a waterfowl or a honeybee.

Margery reminded him that we are made in His image, and "we don't look like red heifers or waterfowls or honeybees."

Her father was disappointed by her literalism. "I'm not talking about outsides," he reminded Margery. "I'm talking about insides. Inside we're all kin, you and me and the waterfowl and the mosquito. Squash a bug and see it bleed. If you look long enough you'll see the kinfolk come for the body and cart it off for burial. The beast in the field is mute, the insect can only chirp, but how do I know that the very chirp is not the voice of the Lord? How do I know? How?"

Margery heard the pain in her father's voice; the urgency of his question was itself a prayer. C. W. Post never knew what it was to be a mere mortal. Her grandfather had created a Nazarite, a man who walked in the footsteps of the Lord, and wondered with every breath where that breath came from.

"Daddy," Margery told him, "the Lord is all shapes, all things, all in all."

He looked at his daughter, proud of her understanding. He sipped his hot broth. "I can give you this world," he told her, "but you are earning the next one."

He hugged Margery, touched her brown wavy hair, and told her he was going to buy the Swift meat packing company.

"Swift alone slaughters eleven thousand cattle and sixteen thousand hogs every day. Every single day those four-footed creatures walk through a torture chamber. We devour their flesh, even unto their eyebrows. The tongue that a mother cow uses to lick her young graces a human table. How can the Lord return to such a bloody earth? How can mankind hear the cry of one another when we don't lament eleven thousand cattle and sixteen thousand hogs every day from Swift and Company?"

Margery didn't care if her father bought every cow and chicken and pig on earth. She just wanted to do her homework and go to sleep and wake up without thinking about the sixteen thousand hogs that were being slaughtered that day in Chicago.

When her father's anguish for animals was at its peak, Margery tried to change the subject and turn C. W. from religion and animal ruminations to the subjects of her schoolbooks.

It was easy to do this because C. W. loved facts, was easily deflected by them. He liked learning facts, though he had only gone through sixth grade before Abraham Post told his son that he could no longer spare his daily labor. C. W. could read and write easily, but nonagricultural subjects were mostly new to him. He kept an open mind.

When Margery taught him a little algebra and geometry, C. W. acted as if the curtains of the universe had parted for him alone. He respected numbers. He liked columns and rows. He marveled at the neatness of addition and subtraction, how time after time those sums could be done in exactly the same way. He wondered what was behind numbers, how they worked with such simple perfection.

Margery told him that Pythagoras, the Greek who invented geometry, wondered the same thing.

C. W. Post went to the big Webster's dictionary in his room, the only book he owned besides the Bible. He did not find Pythagoras there. Margery spelled it out for him and told her father how Pythagoras and his friends drew the shapes of the visible world and measured the angles, how they figured out what equaled what. Her father listened like a child in Sunday school. He seemed both a saint and a fool to his daughter. Tears came to his eyes for Pythagoras.

"All those Greeks and Romans and Philistines, all the Jebusites and the followers after Moloch and Baal, what choice did they have?" C. W. Post worried and wondered. "What happened to the souls of pagans?"

Sometimes he thought that the souls of pagans inhabited the animals and that one day when mankind had stopped slaughtering animals and one another, then the beasts in one spontaneous outcry would reveal their past souls and the glories of the Lord would be known without any further miracles. We would look and finally see, finally understand what had always been in front of us.

C. W. Post would not talk to the men from Swift and Company, nor would he allow meat packers to enter his home or the offices of Post Cereals.

Reverend Mullins, a man of God, did the negotiating, and offered his church as a meeting place. The clergyman reminded Mr. Post that the Lord forgave everyone, that the Lord's house was a house open to all. The meat executives waited in the first row of pews. Reverend Mullins sat on the platform above them. Margery sat beside him. It was just after school. She was doing her homework on a prayer stand. Reverend Mullins prayed for wisdom and patience. He prayed out loud so that the Swift people would hear him too. He prayed for all souls from the beginning of time, above all for the souls of the innocents led to the slaughter. Margery looked up. Her hands were folded on her schoolbooks. The three men from Swift did not seem to be praying. They looked worried. She felt a little sorry for them. They had on light topcoats because it was spring, but it was still snowing in Battle Creek. Reverend Mullins didn't turn the heat up on weekdays.

Margery kept her gloves on even while writing her lessons. Reverend Mullins wore a sweater under his cassock. A black curtain was drawn at the side of the platform on which Reverend Mullins and Margery sat. Mr. Post sat behind that curtain so he wouldn't have to look at the Swift people. "I'll buy from them," he said. "I'll exchange money but not glances."

C. W. Post believed that the soul glimmered through the eyes, that it was vulnerable, especially in daylight, and when you were engaged in business. He wouldn't trust his soul to the glances from the packers. Margery, an innocent, could learn what he meant. He thought she was old enough to witness corruption. He told her to avert her eyes whenever she felt threatened. Reverend Mullins, also under divine protection, looked and spoke and offered hot wheat broth to warm the Chicago executives. They were moving their arms back and forth, rubbing themselves to stay warm. Reverend Mullins served the broth. C. W. Post sat behind the dark curtain atop a large cardboard shipping carton labeled POST'S CORN FLAKES.

When Reverend Mullins finished praying aloud, one of the Swift men asked to see Mr. Post.

"He is among us," Reverend Mullins said. He pointed to the feet which were barely visible beneath the curtain. He didn't see why it was necessary to explain C. W.'s wish to protect his eyes. Reverend Mullins himself did not understand it. C. W. Post liked to add things to religion. His fear of stray glances was not church theory, but Reverend Mullins knew Brother Post acted out of sincere convictions.

Margery kept her eyes on the Chicago men as Reverend Mullins read them the contract. They did not look like killers. One of the Chicago men stood up and talked. He said he wanted a face-to-face meeting with Mr. Post.

Reverend Mullins said that it was not possible. Mr. Post would not face a carnivore over a matter of business.

The Swift man said they were all wasting their time on this cold day in Battle Creek. All three got up and stamped their feet.

Margery closed her history book.

"I'm Margery Post," she said. "I can talk for my father."

C. W. had not empowered her to do so. Reverend Mullins was confused. She didn't even look at her father behind the curtain. She ascended the pulpit, asking the executives to be seated. She looked at their eyes, only a little worried about what she would see there.

They looked up at the fourteen-year-old heiress in her navy blue pleated skirt and middy blouse.

"Miss Post," the head man said, "we've come to talk business, serious business, this is not a child's matter."

Margery stared right at him. "You came to sell your plant, the one that slaughters eleven thousand cattle and sixteen thousand hogs every day. My father is ready to buy it. Reverend Mullins has the contracts."

The Swift men looked at one another.

"No sir, no ma'am, that's not the way it's done. We don't just hand the corporation over to a child and a minister. We have stockholders to think about, preferred stockholders and bondholders. We have a tanning subsidiary and a soap-making operation and a gelatin factory as well. We are talking millions of dollars and the future of a great manufacturing concern."

Reverend Mullins kept his eyes lowered, as if all these statements from the Swift men were prayers. Behind the black curtain Margery heard her father shuffle his feet. She waited in case he chose to speak but C. W. kept his silence.

"The Lord sent a child to rule the whole world," Margery reminded the gentlemen from Swift and Company, "and this minister has all the papers, and my father"—she pointed at the black shoes beneath the curtain—"my father has the money that you asked for."

C. W. Post arose from the cardboard case that had been his seat. He vowed to himself that he would say no word to these emissaries from Swift, that only numbers would cross his lips.

"Fifteen million dollars," he said from behind the curtain.

"Fifteen million dollars," Reverend Mullins repeated as if he was translating a foreign tongue. C. W. Post, using both his hands, pushed his cardboard carton toward Reverend Mullins.

Briefly his back, and his averted head, was visible to the Swift men.

Reverend Mullins lifted the large box and carried it to them.

They opened the box. Margery, looking down from the pulpit, saw that it contained money.

"Fifteen million dollars," C. W. Post said again from behind the curtain. "It's all there," Reverend Mullins said.

The Swift men touched the money and looked away as if they couldn't bear to see such a large amount.

Reverend Mullins gazed at the money. Margery looked at it and then started giggling. She was surprised at seeing all that money instead of rows of boxes of Corn Flakes.

"Gentlemen," said the Swift spokesman, "this is impossible. Nobody buys a corporation for fifteen million cash at four o'clock in the afternoon just like that. I wouldn't accept responsibility for such a large sum of money. Furthermore," he said, looking at the black curtain, "anyone who would buy Swift and Company without showing his face doesn't seem to be a reliable manager of our concern, or a person worthy of the great public trust our name has always carried with it."

"You're pig butchers," Margery said. "If you're not ashamed of that, what could shame you?"

The Swift men did not answer her. All three turned their backs on the box of money and walked out of the church into the twilight. C. W. Post came out from behind the curtain and, for a few moments, held his daughter's hand.

Reverend Mullins shut off the lights. The three of them carried the money to the Post cottage where it sat for a couple of days until C. W. Post called for a wagon from the bank. Swift and Company never became a part of Post Cereals. Hogs, cattle and sheep continued to die, in Chicago and elsewhere around the globe. C. W. Post milled bran and added honey to his wheat broth. He sold his recipe in the grocery stores in large jugs. He earned millions more on his Postum brew but in Chicago the slaughter never ceased and his heart remained heavy.

## CHAPTER TWENTY-FOUR

*T*he fourteen crates of art did not arrive easily. Negotiating with the Austrians slowed for a few days Biff Alexander's relentless pursuit of zoning, building and sewage violations committed by Walt Disney.

Biff did not complain even though Margery had promised him in advance that stopping Disney would be his only job in Florida.

"To do this is an honor. Anything directly connected with your father is an honor."

C. W. Post's name alone made this haughty lawyer meek. By not associating with people outside of Battle Creek her father seemed to the world a wizard, a saintly recluse. Biff Alexander had never met her father and didn't know that C. W. Post considered lawyers only slightly above meat packers on his moral scale. The lawyer was honored to work on behalf of the legend.

The Austrian government was more embarrassed than honored. Biff Alexander finally understood the difficulty. The Austrians felt that the fourteen crates contained stolen Jewish property from the Nazi era. Everything that resurfaced in Austria after the war was stolen Jewish property. It embarrassed the government, reminded them of how much actual stuff had been involved in the destruction of the Jews. The victims, the millions, were no longer a problem. Their individual names and lives were long forgotten. But property was always an embarrassment. There would be a painting traced to a recognizable owner on record in 1939 or '40 and then no owner and no relatives, the children, the cousins, the aunts, all possible kin vanished. It reminded the Austrians. It reminded everyone. It looked bad. It was bad. Things that survived so many people seemed suspect themselves.

Herr Schmitz told Biff Alexander that the government had opened the crates and would check each work against a master list of stolen property. It would take time. The paintings were not signed, named, or dated. A Viennese art critic had examined the find and declared the paintings worthless. He said he doubted that they were stolen, since the prewar Jews preferred oils, usually in somber colors, and these were bright watercolors. The critic had told Herr Schmitz that the paintings, if stolen, were more likely to have come from a greengrocer than a museum. Still, the Austrians had to be careful. They would be obliged to examine Mr. Post's death certificate and his will before they could release the crates.

Margery had the will, the original and only will C. W. Post ever wrote, removed from the vault in Battle Creek and flown to her. He had written it when Margery was fourteen, while she watched. He used a steel-nibbed pen and India ink and printed in block letters so it would look official:

EVERYTHING I OWN I LEAVE TO MY DAUGHTER MARGERY.
SEVEN YEARS AFTER MY DEATH
ALL DEBTS OWED TO ME ARE RELEASED.

Joyce Sullivan and Eileen Williams, two neighbors, signed as witnesses. Margery remembered Joyce signing, nervous about being a party to such a powerful legal instrument.

"It seems so easy," Joyce told Mr. Post. "Isn't there more to it than this?"

"No more," C. W. told her. "It's only this world."

Joyce Sullivan laughed. She could laugh. She could go home to her husband Harry and her children Irene and Sue, who were afraid to talk to Margery. She could go home and chuckle and wonder about C. W. Post, but Margery could not be amused by her father's scorn of this world. It filled the cottage, the factory, her own life. Her father hated the world, even the trees and flowers, even the very space she was growing into. He expected ruin and damnation as casually as other people expected sunshine or rain. What he left to his daughter, the world's greatest fortune, was of little concern to him. He wrote a will because he wanted it to be known officially that he was obeying the Biblical edict of a seven-year limit on debt. Had he owned slaves, he would have freed them too in the seventh year.

Margery was not surprised when after his death the cash started coming in to her. In each day's mail there would be a five-dollar bill, or a ten or twenty attached to a carefully printed name. C. W. Post had lent these small amounts of money to the farmers and merchants of Battle Creek. The money embarrassed her. She took out a full-page ad in the Battle Creek *News* announcing an early jubilee. She released all debts owed to her father.

Margery was surprised that so many of the debtors themselves were upset by her action. People wanted to pay. They wanted to pay up in the seven years that C. W. Post had granted in his will. They were not paupers. They also suspected her, suspected that years later she might make some secret claims against their land. She had to let the fools pay, let them sweat to send their money to the Morgan Bank in New York, a bank that didn't even know they were alive.

Copies of the death certificate in its simple black border and C. W. Post's will on lined paper torn from her eighth-grade notebook she sent to Vienna with Katherine Woodson, one of Biff's assistants. Ten days later Katherine returned with the paintings. The young attorney, anxious to impress her boss and Margery even more, rode in the back of the delivery van, baby-sat those paintings that had been languishing since 1938 in a Vienna warehouse. Katherine Woodson did not know what those crates contained as she led the delivery people toward Margery's observatory where she had been told to deposit the crates. She knew they were works of art and she knew that the Austrian government had written "fragile" on all sides of each crate and stuck official stickers all over the bills of lading. She had even met Herr Schmitz who had looked at her carefully and finally asked her, after the necessary documents were signed, if she was Jewish.

She had spent a week and a half of her life signing documents about these works without seeing what was inside a single crate. When Mrs. Merriweather entered the observatory and thanked Katherine for her work and asked Vince, the head of her security force, to use a crowbar to open each packing crate, Katherine Woodson, curious, asked Mrs. Merriweather if she could stay to see. The request stunned Margery.

"Of course not," she said.

They were both embarrassed.

Margery knew by her own quick and instinctive response that these paintings were strictly between her and her father, between her and that deceptively simple life of her childhood. That life was nobody's business, that life could mean nothing to a young woman on Biff Alexander's staff.

She was almost embarrassed by the strength of her recollections, by the memory of that cottage so empty of decoration and feeling and happiness. That emptiness was nobody else's business. She didn't explain a thing to Katherine Woodson and waited until the sound of the young attorney's high heels disappeared from the hallway before she opened the first crate. Margery felt as if C. W. Post, forty years after his death, was in the room wondering at all this splendor that the Lord had not seen fit to vanquish. Time had not stopped C. W. Post, nor had Robinson nor the Nazis nor the Allies nor the Russians.

Not war, not even death. C. W. Post got what he wanted and passed it on to his daughter, and fourteen crates full of his wishes sat in front of her.

She could no longer remember the sound of his voice, but she could recall his footsteps on the creaky floorboards, his morning cough, his lips smacking, the cereal dust that dripped from all his clothes, the sadness of his eyes, his one crooked eyetooth.

By the time she pulled the first painting from its heavy protective casing and with her fingers carefully tore off the brown paper covering the painting itself, Margery was already full of her father's presence. When she saw the first glimmer of red, and then quickly tore off the rest of the paper, Margery laughed and cried at once.

The fruit was like his signature, like a painting of himself, sent to Margery from another world in case she had forgotten. Only C. W. Post would have commissioned this painting. Her tears dripped onto the protective wrapping but did not touch the hard red fruit. "A pomegranate—only you, Daddy, only you."

How many hours had she listened to his musing over the pomegranate. With his Bible in front of him he counted pomegranates.

"All over the place," he concluded. "More than dates or figs."

Dates and figs he understood, milk and honey were crystal clear. But why was the Bible so full of pomegranates? It was one of the mysteries he never solved, one of the few projects that hadn't led C. W. Post to insight and then to profit.

"If pomegranates are important enough to be in the Bible, then they're important enough to be on our table."

In one spell, C. W. Post and his daughter ate pomegranates every day for weeks until even C. W. Post smacked his lips and admitted, among half a bushel of seeds which he had saved, that even he had had enough. At the factory he ordered pomegranates to be boiled, shucked, slivered and shredded. He even had them baked into pies and pastries. Nobody at Post Cereals could do a thing with pomegranates. The spoilage rate was high. The seeds took up 80 percent of the volume. The pigs refused the rinds. The juice was bitter. Reluctantly C. W. Post gave up.

As she looked at the solid curves in the painting, Margery remembered C. W. Post on his knees before the Lord asking to be granted the wisdom to understand the pomegranate.

By the time she opened the third crate, Margery had encountered five more large canvases of pomegranates, whole, sliced, quartered, pared—and a half pomegranate, squeezed dry. Each pomegranate was a thing of beauty. The painter had kept in mind the thick texture of the fruit, the darkness right in the fruit's deep vivid red. Even in the first pomegranate Margery understood that the Austrian art expert was wrong. These pomegranates could hang in any museum.

True, there was nothing original in the style or the execution, they were merely realistic portraits, but the world had never seen such fruit. The painter had rendered not the fruit itself, but C. W. Post's obsession. The dripping squeezed half, its pits scattered, its lacy interior eviscerated, struck Margery at that moment as a portrait of life itself. Looking at pomegranates, the painter had drawn people—round, hard, mysterious, pitted, tender, thick-skinned, above all useless. She put the six pomegranate paintings in a row against the blue-gray wall of her room that led to the stars. The telescope and its wonders seemed nothing to her, nothing compared to those six pomegranates, especially the squeezed bloody weathered one, the one that looked as old as history, as old as she herself now was, as old as C. W. Post must have felt, old as ancient Israel, old and useless as a pomegranate in a land of milk and honey. Though her father had been so childlike, old age was always his secret strength. He lived outside the valley of the shadow of death. He had passed through. He was beyond death. He had died when Margery was an infant, when his wife died, perhaps even sooner, when he married her and broke his vow, perhaps even before that, when he fell in love, or perhaps even when desire itself led him away from his father's promise to God.

C. W. Post lived without the clouds of human emotion, without the worry of purpose and meaning. He knew what every second on earth meant. He knew, he saw, he understood. He had heard God speak, but on earth all he could do was mill grain. He gathered his fortune but the money was dross. He distributed his grain to the four corners of the earth, everywhere mankind sampled his message, but they merely ate and digested and went on their way. The oceans did not dry up, the continents did not tremble. The Lord gave to him and he passed on to mankind the secret of life and they turned it into a breakfast food, a snack. They made him one of the richest men on earth, yet no one knew his failure. He had talked to God and the world still reeked. He had seen eternity in an ear of corn and then, as his punishment, the Lord had sent him backward to the fallen earth.

Margery's early life had been immersed in her father's great tragedy. The factories that produced his fortune were boils, pustules, matters of no significance. He packaged products for the body, but what did C. W. Post care about the body? He let his white beard grow to his chest. He made his shirts of flour sacks. The body was at best a nuisance. He took no delight in it. Even health was of little concern to him.

Though he was always kind to his daughter, Margery knew that in her own flesh she was the failure of C. W. Post. The daughter of a Nazarite—a contradiction. If he had remained pure, instead of producing a daughter, he might have given birth inwardly, secretly, to an angel, a divine being who might have swept the earth more completely than his cornflakes did. Within him there was a spirit glorious enough to move the stars from their orbits. God's own voice had slithered through his ears and still he sat in a cottage near the banks of the Kalamazoo River and watched his daughter do sums and his corn grow and his fortune mount and in his own eyes he had been dead for a generation and could hardly bear the smell of his own decay.

In that old thickened reddish-purple pomegranate Margery saw the glimmer of her father's crusted useless life, not the life the world saw but the one she saw, the one she lived, the one that still sat on top of her and depressed her even now in her gray-blue observatory that looked up to the heavens and across the orange grove to where the Disneys intended to build their world.

By the time Margery had looked at several crates of apples and grapes and figs and dates she knew that the same hand, the same spirit, had painted them all. None of the paintings had the texture of the pomegranates but she was surrounded by light in her darkened observatory, the light from within each fruit.

The painter had understood what mattered to C. W. Post, had understood that fruits and vegetables were the energy, the pumping force of life itself. If she had seen these paintings, this vision, when she was a young woman, she might never have gone off with Merriweather to sample the world and the meats and the pleasures that had been, after all, such a sad illusion for her.

C. W. Post had not shown her this light. He had shown her his failure, his sadness, his emptiness, his guilty tormented soul, a soul that longed to be, she suddenly understood, a pomegranate.

The old darkened, peeling, latticed, bitter fruit was a portrait of C. W. Post painted by someone who knew—someone who had intuitively understood as only genius can. The pomegranate in all its richness was not of the visible world. The pomegranate went back to that moment when the Lord had called to C. W. Post and ravished him there in the cornfield and poured upon him the secrets of rivers and trees and water and sunshine and then forbidden it all to him, put it out of reach, made him a prophet of no consequence, a Jonah who could arrive at Nineveh and deliver the word of the Lord and be honored for it and yet not save a single soul, so that men continued to roam as always, hungry, licentious, without grace or understanding, preying upon one another and also upon much cattle.

Exhausted and full of emotion and understanding, Margery lay down on her Oriental rug beside the pomegranate that was her father's biography and hers as well. Forty years after his death, C. W. Post had unveiled to his daughter the uses of the pomegranate.

# CHAPTER TWENTY-FIVE

*B*efore she hung up on the Governor, Margery knew that he too was in Walt Disney's pocket. He started out in his friendly Southern drawl talking in good-old-boy Chamber of Commerce style about the necessity of teamwork. He even called her a benefactor to all Floridians, but when she told him there would never be a Disneyworld in Orlando, no matter how much it might cost to stop the project, then the Governor said that he and all the State legislators would be right there in the crowd to tar and feather her if she did succeed in this blasphemy upon the economy and well-being of all the people of this great State.

She was in the bathtub when the Governor called, in one of the twelve huge tubs with gold-plated fixtures that the architects had put in the bathrooms. The tubs were all light gray— a payoff from some plumbing supply company, she guessed. In some of the bathrooms the tubs didn't match the elaborate color schemes but she liked the look of the water itself—blue-gray against the porcelain. She imagined herself soaking off the black tar and the white feathers. She laughed to think of three hundred State legislators and the Governor ringing the doorbell, pulling her out into a big vat of tar, loose feathers swirling in the air like the grain dust in Battle Creek. She wondered how it actually had been done, probably hot tar right on the back. Ah, what people didn't do to others, to themselves. And all this fuss over a playground, over stuffed animals and merry-go-rounds. What was it about Disneyworld that other people saw and she didn't see? Instead of all the bluster and the threats, why hadn't a single person been able to make her understand why Disneyworld would make Orlando better for all these Floridians? Why was a playground so much better than orange groves and meadows? She knew the financial argument—three million tourists a year, half a billion dollars—but why did the Orlandoites want that? She was not living in the midst of sharecroppers. Now and then she put on her sunglasses and borrowed Helen the cook's sedan and drove through the streets randomly, just looking at the houses of her neighbors trying to imagine what kind of lives went on inside them. The houses were all single-story bungalows, all had cars in the garage, many had a motor-boat as well. There were television antennas as abundant as trees, there were weed-free lawns and carefully tended flower beds around the bases of many trees. When she would park the car and walk through a neighborhood there was almost always a backyard clubhouse or tree house where children lived out fantasies that must have included much more than Mickey Mouse and Donald Duck. She had to be careful not to stay too long, not to observe the children too carefully. She didn't want to call attention to herself. How odd they seemed to her, these young creatures traveling in bands, on bicycles, wearing canvas shoes. All of them seemed so busy, there was so much coming and going, and yet what did they do? They weren't allowed to work, the child-labor laws prevented that. What did they do, then, when they weren't in school? Did they just run around on the streets like dogs, marking their territory? Were they observing nature, keeping diaries, growing wise in some mysterious ways she didn't know about? Were they talking to themselves, practicing their vocabulary, thinking, wondering what was to become of them in the future?

She sometimes had an overwhelming desire to pluck some ten-year-old with pigtails right off her red Schwinn bicycle and ask her what she was thinking, where she was going, what all this commotion was about.

Biff Alexander laughed when she told him that evening what was on her mind. After their second week in Orlando she allowed the legal staff to move into her home. The Ramada Inn had become too oppressive for them and dangerous as well. Every day there were threatening calls. Katherine Woodson said she knew she was being followed every time she went to use the Orlando City Law Library. It made it hard for her to concentrate.

Margery bought a complete set of Florida State ordinances and the Orlando City Codes too. She let the lawyers take over the house. Vince, the head of her security force, hired five extra guards.

Now that the lawyers were all in her house, she began to talk to Biff a little each evening. When she told him what she wondered about children, Biff answered her at once and easily.

"They're playing, Margery, you don't understand that, do you?"

He was probably right. Play was an abstraction to her, something she didn't remember doing very often. She did have a rag doll, she remembered that. She would put the rag doll beside her at the dinner table and her father would quiz the doll on Biblical facts—how old was Sarah when the angel came to her? Who was Samson's mother? What tribe did Delilah belong to? —simple facts that any rag doll would know. A lot of times Margery knew the answers but she didn't tell when her father carefully explained the answers to Marie, the rag doll. Was that playing?

Sometimes in the factory while her father talked to people in the glassed-in office she swept up a pile of grain dust and stepped in it, and jumped around just to feel how soft it was and how it stuck to her shoes. But someone always found her quickly and swept the dust up and usually even cleaned her shoes before her father came out of the office. And she had a bicycle too, and ice skates, some crayons and a wood-carving set. Of course she knew what playing was. But all these families in Orlando with their children and bicycles and TVs and boats, why did they want the Disneys, and all the extra free-ways and banks and restaurants and stores? They had so much already. She knew. She watched. Her telescope had a night-vision lens. After the lawyers moved into the south wing she spent more and more time each evening in the isolation of the observatory. The pomegranates hung there now. All six in a progression like the moons of Jupiter.

She knew what the people of Orlando had. She saw it every night. They had each other. With her night scope she could see inside the cars of teenagers who parked at the peripheries of her estate. She would watch the lovemaking teenagers until she became embarrassed and turned her scope away. They had their own young lives right outside her gates and yet it wasn't enough. In these very lovers' lanes they wanted Disney to build toll houses and roller coasters. Day and night Margery Post could look in on her neighbors, watch lives all pretty much the same. Lights out about 11, people up at 6:30. The meals, the kitchen, the bathroom, the television, sometimes a book. She knew what their lives were like, yet here was Biff Alexander, soon to interpret the Constitution, telling her that she didn't understand people. "But that's OK," he added, "you've been successful so you don't have to."

She didn't care what he meant by that. And what did success mean to her? Anything that didn't risk catastrophe couldn't be a success for Margery Post. The rest of the world could fool itself with money. Margery knew the only thing left her to risk was herself. And she *had* risked herself, first with Mer-riweather, then with Clarence, and after that hardly ever again. She didn't know why, but after her father died and Clarence disappeared, men stopped interesting her.

When through her telescope she watched the teenagers fon-dle one another, she tried to imagine herself sitting in Battle Creek inside someone's car or parlor—tried to imagine a boy with his arm around her, clutching her breast, sticking his tongue in her mouth. She couldn't visualize it. C. W. Post would not have allowed such a thing to come to pass. He wasn't crazy about marriage, though he allowed it. He was hoping that eventually people would couple more like plants with the aid of the wind, or like bees, in an open daytime way without lust or passion, just an easy natural fulfillment of the Lord's wish that they be fruitful and multiply.

Margery had not wanted to multiply, did not regret her abortion. The earth seemed far too full already. She had inherited her father's deep loneliness, an isolation she had never overcome. She and C. W. Post, a family in Battle Creek beside a cereal factory. She and Merriweather, a family in the new Soviet Union. She and Clarence Birdseye, a family on the frozen wastes of Central Asia. She didn't know what a family was, didn't want to know either.

Her father liked grain because it was predictable, harvestable. Only the weather could stop you. With children it was different. Who could predict anything? C. W. Post let her do as she pleased, never tried to stop her from marrying Merriweather, never gave her advice on how to live or act. He prohibited meat and warned her about intercourse, that was the extent of his rules. She was thirteen years old when he told her that the blood that flowed from her, and would now continue at intervals for forty more years, was a continuation of Eve's punishment. He told her that the blood marked Eve's sin and was a sign of warning. He told her that now she could copulate like the animals in the fields and begin to drop pups as they did, and it would happen all too soon if she forgot even for a moment that she was the Lord's vessel and that all life came from that source and not from a man, who would delude her, even as he had her mother. "What if mother had been a Nazarite?" Margery asked her father, hoping that she could find a way to avoid the blood curse.

"There are no female Nazarites."

"Why?" Margery asked.

C. W. Post checked his Bible as he liked to do at serious times. There were female judges, there were Biblical queens,

223

but not even in the apocryphal books was there a father who raised his daughter to the moon and promised that no wine would touch her lips and no man would know her flesh.

"Aren't nuns Nazarites?"

"No," he said, angry at his daughter for her mistake. He hated the Pope, thought him an Antichrist. "Nuns are the daughters of darkness. Put them out of your mind. You can't be a Nazarite and you can't help being a female. Bear your burden of blood with an open heart."

She had cramps and worries and still did not understand, but C. W. Post had said all he would say and in school, though none of the girls talked to her directly about it, she listened to them talk to one another and learned what she could about the mysteries of life that flowed from her.

When Biff Alexander and his staff moved into the south wing of her house she felt as if the Disneys had already taken over. She was not accustomed to all that activity around her. The lawyers were busy all day going through the hundreds of law books that now cluttered her library. Biff was enjoying the battle. He had a yellow pad filled with delaying tactics. He hired an Orlando architect and a structural engineer.

"You told me to go all out," he reminded Margery. "I have as many experts as they have. That poor judge doesn't know what to do. He's impressed by everybody. He calls us all sir. I don't think he'll be able to decide a thing. We'll have to do it all over again in a state court but every delay is a victory for us. Will Disney is going bananas. He won't talk to us in court. He keeps telling the judge this can't be happening in America, it must be Russia."

She was envious of Biff for having the pleasure of the battle. The day after looking at the paintings she became less concerned about Walt Disney. She was thinking about those pomegranates, about that day in Madrid and the man who came up behind her, touched her shoulders and told her that he would kill her father before he would destroy a painting.

She knew he must have painted those pomegranates, only Dali could have done them, and yet they were unlike any of his known works. And why, after all, would Dali have agreed to paint pomegranates for her father?

She wanted to know this, wanted to find Dali and ask him. It had crossed her mind more than once over the years whenever she was in Madrid to look up Dali just to ask him if he remembered her, but she was always a little embarrassed by that Margery she had been, the hayseed, so much her father's daughter, so much a girl of Battle Creek staying in a hotel for the first time in her life, having no idea what art or anything else was about.

She didn't like to be reminded of those years and that trip, the fool her father had made of himself. Once, not long after the Second World War, she did make herself go back to Madrid just to overcome her reluctance to revisit the city. To her surprise, she found herself sorry to learn that the Hotel Del Prado had been destroyed in the Civil War. She asked if Dali was by any chance in Madrid. The art dealer told her he lived still in Paris, and she was relieved because she had nothing to say to him except to tell him that he was a great genius which he already knew without another American tourist to tell him so.

If he had indeed painted the pomegranates why hadn't he said so or tried to locate them or have them mentioned in the catalogues of his work? His pen and pencil drawings were invaluable, his sketches on napkins were in the Museum of Modern Art . . . Dali was no fool. He knew the value of his work. He would not fail to mention fourteen crates of work, especially those masterpieces of pomegranates. It made no sense to Margery. Dali wouldn't behave that way. What other artist did her father know? It had to be Dali unless Robinson had located someone else, someone less committed to art, someone ready at C. W. Post's request to deface the past.

The lawyers were everywhere. They drank coffee all day. Margery even found Katherine Woodson sitting in her bedroom one afternoon. The young woman apologized, but Margery began to suspect she was a Disney spy.

There were the eight lawyers, the architect, and the engineer, constantly coming and going. The phone rang every few minutes. Only the observatory, across the house from them, was quiet. Like everything else she had attempted, the Disney battle was beginning to bore her too. The townspeople were beasts. They wrote graffiti every day on her gates. The lawyers who promoted her interests were dullards, monks drinking coffee and looking through lifeless books. Why should she save Orlando for herself or anyone, why not let the Disneys swarm all over her property? How much worse could they be than the lawyers?

She had an apartment in New York, a cottage in Bermuda, and a house in the hills behind San Francisco, but only here did she feel at home. Here in her quirky mansion in the middle of nowhere she had finally found a place she wanted to be, the place she had been looking for since she left Battle Creek with Merriweather, expecting the world to excite her.

Each day she realized that like her father she preferred pomegranates to lawyers.

In the second week of the lawyers' occupation she decided to leave. Biff Alexander was surprised but he told her that in fact it would be months, if ever, before she would have to testify. She just had to keep him informed of her address in case she had to return for an unlikely emergency hearing. He objected so little that Margery realized that he and his colleagues would be happy to get rid of her, to have the mansion and the staff all to themselves so that they could play their war games without being reminded that they were doing it all for her.

She had the pomegranates wrapped and put in storage. Let Katherine Woodson spy on all the rest. She made her plane reservations without setting a return date. She knew where she was going.

# CHAPTER TWENTY-SIX

*B*ones Jones put away the book on the 1964 Pirates. He kept the yearly accounts in individual notebooks. They were all stacked on a single bookshelf in his hotel room. This, their last year, was the worst ever. The Pirates had lost $16,000 more than Bones earned during the rest of the year. But he was not broke, far from it. Money losses alone would not have stopped the Pirates. He could have carried them a few more years, even appealed for community support, a civic loan of some type or the kind of support the Little League had, selling candy bars door to door. Bones would have done that himself. Nothing was too humiliating if you believed in it.

The day after the season ended he slept in his uniform. Then he took it off for the last time. He put it in a paper bag. On his way to the Sunshine Cafe for lunch, he dropped the uniform in a city trash can. He was thinking about going up to St. Louis for the weekend. They were going to build a new stadium in St. Louis. Just a few months ago he'd been thinking of maybe putting in a bid for a few of their old light towers, maybe renting a semi and hiring a few boys to load it up and bring those used big league lights down to Orlando. It had been a daydream but he might have pulled it off. What would Gussy Busch, the Cards' owner, ask for old light towers? Maybe he would have donated them to the Pirates. It was possible. In baseball there was generosity. It was the heart of the game itself. And he'd had the boys to help. Half a dozen usually worked for him in the off season as a construction crew. Tom Phillips, the backup catcher, was his foreman, as good a construction foreman as there was in Orlando. Tom was forty-five already, maybe older—he wouldn't say for sure. He handled the bullpen. For the last two years Tom could no longer crouch, but he was still all catcher. He wouldn't consider moving to first base. Bursitis in his knees got to him but he would still stand straight in the bullpen, hold up his glove, and give a big target to the erratic pitchers on the Pirate staff. He told the pitchers to imagine that his stomach was his head. Sometimes he even pinned a cap to his midsection.

In July, Tim Wilson, the regular catcher, split his finger on a foul tip, and then in the next inning Harold Oslo, the infielder who replaced him, missed a pitch completely and got hit by a curve on his Adam's apple. Bones had to call Tom out of the bullpen. Phillips was the only catcher left. The old catcher walked in from the bullpen to the plate, adjusting his knee guards. Bones and the umpire had moved the injured Harold Oslo to the bench. The seams of the ball marked Oslo's neck. He looked like he had a goiter.

"I can play," he whispered. "I just need to get my breath."

"Take it easy," Bones said.

Tom Phillips arrived at the mound. There were tears in his eyes.

"If I squat down, Bones, I won't be able to get up."

"Play ball," the umpire said.

Tom Phillips stood six foot three. You couldn't see the umpire behind him. Bones called him to the foul line for a conference. The pitcher came over too.

"Can you just sit down?" Bones asked him.

"You mean on the ground?" Tom asked him.

"Yeah."

"You mean on my ass?"

"Yeah. Just sit down with your legs stretched in front of you."

"I won't be able to get any pop flies."

"That's OK."

"And I won't have any zip on my throws to second base."

"That won't matter. We won't let 'em get on base, right, pitcher?"

The pitcher, Ken Kashewski, reminded Bones that if Phillips stretched his legs out, he would be interfering with the batter in the box.

"He'll get spiked, too," Kashewski said. "Be a bloody mess up there."

"You can cross your legs, can't you?"

"I think I can," the old catcher said.

Tom Phillips went behind the plate. Four hundred fans howled as he dug into the ground like a dog making himself a comfortable hole in the shade.

Bones explained the matter to the umpire as Phillips settled into his groove. He crossed his legs in front of him like a Buddha.

"Nothing against it in the rules," the umpire said, "so long as he don't block my view."

Tom caught four innings like that. Made the news wires. The St. Louis *Post-Dispatch* sent down a photographer two days later who got Tom to pose in the catching position he had assumed. The Pirates even won the game. Bones wondered if maybe Gussy Busch had seen that photo and would remember Tom Phillips and the Orlando Pirates.

Bones wouldn't need the lights now, but he thought maybe seeing a good ball game would cheer him up. It usually did. He went to St. Louis for a weekend at the end of the Pirates season most years. It was his vacation. He stayed downtown at the Fairbanks Hotel, same place as the visiting teams stayed. It cost him a bundle, but where else could you read the *Sporting News* at breakfast and know that a lot of people in the hotel were going to the same place you were going? He wanted to see Bob Gibson pitch, too. There was nothing like a fast-ball pitcher to cheer a person up. The sound of the ball against the catcher's mitt made you know you were alive.

"Why go?" Bones asked himself as he drank his bitter coffee at the Sunshine Cafe. "Why go to St. Louis or anywhere else?" He didn't know for sure what else to do. He couldn't just get on a bus again. He owned four building sites west of town, had planned to put up four stucco two-bedroom houses and sell them before next summer, same as he always did. If you bought a house from Bones Jones he threw in two season tickets to the Pirates. If he built four houses he earned enough to pull the Pirates through another season.

"Might as well get to it," he said. He walked down Monroe Street from the Sunshine Cafe and then up Second Street to Tom Phillips's house at the corner of Second and Hill. Tom Phillips had a big screened-in porch usually full of kids playing war. When they had found termites Bones and Tom put a plastic tent over the house and sprayed it themselves. Tom's wife Ethel came to a lot of the games. Bones was best man at their wedding. Tom came to the door, shook his hand; Ethel brought him iced tea. The kids must all be playing outside. You could hear the grandfather clock tick in the living room.

"Well," Bones said, "we can start on the houses any time you're ready. I guess I'm not going to see the Cards this year. Lost too much to spend another dollar on baseball."

Tom Phillips didn't say a thing. He sat there as if he was behind the plate waiting for a pitcher to pull up his socks and adjust his cap.

"When shall we start?" Bones asked. "I can order the lumber today if you can get the boys together. Even if there's no next season we've got those four houses to do, then we'll see . . . we'll just wait and see."

Ethel was standing at the doorway that separated the living room from the sun porch.

"Ain't gonna work for you no more," Tom Phillips said. He didn't look at Bones.

"Tell him why," Ethel said.

"It's nothing personal, Bones."

"Tell him, Tom."

"Got a steady job working for Disney. They're gonna be building for a long time. The pay is good. I knew there wasn't gonna be any next season . . . I'm sorry, Bones."

"I always counted on you, Tom. Every September we got started . . ."

"I know, but I was just working the off season. Now everything's gonna be the off season."

"He needed full-time work," Ethel said. "We got to have the income, the job security."

"Didn't I pay you better than the union?" Bones said. "Didn't I give you a bonus on every house? Didn't I let you keep all the scraps to fix up your own place?"

"It's nothin' against you, Bones, I just needed a year-round job, that's all."

"What about the rest of the crew?"

Bones had put down his iced tea. He knew what was coming.

"They're all going with me."

"Just like that?" Bones said. "Without talking to me?"

"Who can talk to you, Bones? You've been nuts the last month of the season. Who could tell you anything? It's not like we didn't try. You stopped listening to anybody. We didn't know for sure if you'd ever build another house. Even an old catcher has to take care of himself."

Bones understood that it wasn't easy for Tom Phillips to leave him. Ethel was still standing in the doorway. She must have convinced him, Bones thought. Or maybe Walt Disney himself came to the house loaded with souvenirs and turned the kids against Bones. Maybe that's how it started. All the crew had kids. The dugout was full of them at home games. Every player had his personal batboy, his own son or daughter. They sat on the dugout floor and played with their toys. The little ones didn't know baseball from training pants. Bones let them sit there. Their dads protected them from foul balls. Now Disney had turned them against him. Kids were Disney's meat and potatoes. Perky Parrot had not been for kids. He was something altogether new. He didn't talk much but what that bird said mattered. He sat up there in his tree and watched the crazy world underneath him. Bones spent a lot of frames just moving Perky from one tree to another. Perky could spend up to a minute just looking for the exact place to settle in, a strong major branch but a little hidden from the sun and the other birds. A little covered by foliage. Then when he did say something it came from almost nowhere. You could barely see him and he had been silent for so long that you forgot he was a talking bird.

Perky Parrot was no Mickey Mouse baloney. Perky watched human beings. He was like a judge in a divorce court, except he didn't say too much. Bones didn't bother to draw the people, just voices. Who needed to look at animated humans? The parrot knew people too, only by their sounds. Their voices were normal everyday voices. Bones himself did most of the men. The people didn't say much, either. They asked what time it was, or how someone was doing, or whether it was gonna rain soon. And the bird heard it all and moved around on the branches, and pretty soon something big just happened for no reason at all and the bird got interested, or maybe he just moved away to listen somewhere else. They were risky cartoons. Bones never tried to make them funny. They just came out that way. What the humans did was funny to the bird.

"Bones," Ethel said, "you've done a lot for all the Pirates. This had nothing to do with you. Everybody has to look out for himself, his family."

Bones looked at her the way Perky Parrot might have. He didn't say a thing. He moved to a different chair. He took a sip of the iced tea after all. The kids were back on the porch now. The noise hit him all of a sudden as if someone had turned on a radio in the middle of the night. A catcher who couldn't squat was leaving him. So were those four bungalows with red tiled roofs and squared-off sodded little yards. The bungalows were nothing. Without the Pirates to support there wasn't even much reason to build them. Bones could sell the land or grow tomatoes on it, it didn't matter.

He was thinking to ask Tom Phillips how a person decided what to do next. There must be a secret that other people knew and he didn't. He only knew how to do what he'd been doing for so long. To get the Pirates through the season and then build a few bungalows.

"You can get other workers," Tom Phillips was saying. "There's people coming from all over. My brother-in-law and his family are moving down here from Illinois. Hell, he might even go to work for you right off until he gets settled and all."

"Don't you promise James," Ethel said. "My sister's already put up with enough from that man. He's gonna work steady or else they might as well stay where they are."

"I didn't promise nothing," the catcher said, "I was just thinking."

"Well, then think of something reasonable. There's other people besides old ballplayers and their brother-in-law for Bones Jones to hire. There's a whole world of people out there."

Bones listened. He was already in the trees. They were just human voices, less interesting to him now than the wind he could hear through the open windows and in spite of the noise of the children. There must have been at least six children on the porch and a dog, too, rolling around. Bones wondered how they knew what to do next. He didn't remember being a kid at all, hardly remembered being manager of the Orlando Pirates. He was just sitting in Tom Phillips's house listening to voices and other sounds, and then in the dark little room with the green carpeting where Tom Phillips kept his television, someone turned on that 16-inch Philco. Bones Jones heard a closing rat-a-tat-tat from Woody Woodpecker and then the bouncing jingling voice of Mickey and he listened more carefully than ever and moved to a higher branch far away from everyone in Tom Phillips's house but with his eyes right on that Philco and hearing everything that happened, to the mouse and to the catcher and his wife and to the porch crowded with children. Bones Jones moved around and kept his lips sealed. He was beginning to understand.

# CHAPTER TWENTY-SEVEN

*M*ost of the time
Margery could sleep on an airplane as well as she could in her
own bed. For this trip she even bought the seat next to her so
that no burly salesman plotting his European itinerary could
keep her awake. But even this quiet smooth flight did not make
her drowsy. Her mind was too active for sleep, too curious now
about what might have happened so many years ago. Like the
Lord, the ways of C. W. Post sometimes took generations to
decipher. Margery had been looking at the pomegranates after
having dinner with Biff and Katherine Woodson when it came
to her, like an intuition of revealed truth, that her father had
done it. That he had somehow taken the meat and wine out of
the *Last Supper,* that he had cleared up other masterpieces as well
—that his fortune operating independently of his life roamed
through Europe in the 1920's and 1930's, transforming art the
way Fascism and inflation and the Depression were transforming people. She had no proof of this, only her powerful feeling,
as strong as her feeling that Walt Disney was a fraud, a charla-
tan, blindfolding the people of Orlando with dollar bills so that
he could steal their children. How could she have such a feeling
and not act on it? There was nobody to battle in this feeling,
she only had to overcome her own skepticism, the passing fear
that perhaps she was getting senile or deranged. It worried her
enough to make her keep her thoughts to herself. What she did
was her own business. Nothing strange about Margery Post
going to Europe. Nothing strange about anyone going to

Europe. Just going for a visit, a talk with the natives, a look at the town, those were the exact words her father used when he took her to Arizona. She didn't even remember the exact year. Sometime after he failed to buy Swift and Company. Maybe because of that he decided to build a perfect city. Why he chose Arizona Margery never understood. He had not mentioned Arizona, never talked about Utopia until he told her one Friday evening after cleaning the machinery that the next Monday they were going to Arizona and that he needed her help. She had taken two years of Spanish in junior high and he needed a translator.

"I don't know that many words."

"It's OK," C. W. Post told his daughter. "Mostly we'll be talking in numbers."

C. W. Post kept no records, no receipts. He liked to do his personal business in cash. Margery knew the system. In Arizona she helped him implement it.

They bought a whole town. It was going to become a vegetarian community in the wilderness. Margery and C. W. Post went door-to-door to the farms and shanties and talked to the owners. C. W. Post told the farmers about his dream of a vegetarian Utopia. Most of them did not understand. They were Mexicans. They lived in Arizona and walked across the border for a weekend in the old country. They raised turkeys and hogs and a few thin cattle. Margery spoke to them in Battle Creek Junior High Spanish.

"Usted quiere vender su casa?" she asked. "Mi papa quiere comprar."

She made the deals. She carried a typed page with the Spanish words for numbers since she tended to forget past ten. C. W. Post did not carry the money with him. He left it in the hotel in Douglas. He set the price and gave each person a solid handshake. Later that day he packed the money in big manila envelopes. Carl Simmons, a Post Cereals bookkeeper, went out to pay and to collect the deeds. The Bank of Douglas took care of the paperwork. In less than a week, in pidgin Spanish, Margery bought a town of two hundred families.

When they went back to Battle Creek, Carl Simmons stayed behind to manage the community. Carl sent for his wife and children. Carl named the town "Post" and as far as Margery knew his wife and grandchildren still lived there.

C. W. Post ordered the destruction of the Catholic church. But Carl Simmons never did it, and after C. W. died, Carl Simmons forgot too about turning the waste places into watering places. In the town where her father thought the longhorn would roam as free and as safe as the holy cattle beside the Ganges, the people ate hamburgers and chewed on salt beef.

Still, when she had translated for her father and shaken the hands of the farmers and sipped water from their chipped cups, Margery felt she was doing something. Buying a town was doing something. Talking to strangers in Spanish was doing something. Then, after they bought the town, it was back to Battle Creek, the noise of the factory, the clouds of cereal dust, and C. W. Post reading the Old Testament aloud after dinner, walking beside her to church, and calling aloud in his sleep some nights asking to be forgiven.

If he in fact had altered the world's greatest paintings, Margery did not know if he would be forgiven. Forty years after his death, when nobody remembered the man, his work might now turn out to have robbed the future not of meat but of art.

On this trip Margery did not pay attention to Milan. She did not notice the Piazza Mercanti and only glanced at the Duomo, wondering what it would be like to believe in a god of structures. She checked into the Hotel Venetia, then went directly to the Church of Santa Maria delle Grazie.

She walked through the fifteenth-century arches toward the small refectory where the priests once ate. The idea of changing the *Last Supper* struck her at that moment as an impossible desecration, but she knew that C. W. Post would not have called it that. In his mind he would have been doing holy work.

237

C. W. Post wouldn't trade a box of Grape-Nuts for a painting, not for any painting. He even considered color a form of idolatry. He didn't impose his own dark intuitions on Margery, but she grew up knowing that clothes were meant to be black and brown and gray. There were no pictures in their home, not even decorated wallpaper, and for all his love of animals and grains, C. W. Post never stopped to admire a flower. He could have taken the wine out of the *Last Supper* as casually as other people drew a hair out of chicken salad.

Margery was slightly out of breath when she reached the refectory. She had walked through the church as fast as she could. The ticket taker warned her that the chapel would close in ten minutes but she didn't want to wait one more day.

Because it was so late, she was almost alone with the *Last Supper*. A guard sat in one of the cloisters counting ticket stubs. A young gypsy boy seemed to be watching the guard.

The fresco was about six feet off the ground but obscured by scaffolding. Margery asked the guard when the scaffolding would be removed. He shrugged his shoulders. "Maybe one year, maybe two. The *Supper* peels from the wall sometimes." He returned to counting his tickets.

Margery stood across from the wall. She tried to ignore the scaffolding, though it did obscure the lower portion of the fresco.

She scanned the familiar windows behind the head of Jesus, noticed the sky dropping over the green hills, the cluttered table, the stricken faces of the Apostles. She did not look at the entire painting, only its parts. She was like a busy hostess counting silverware, as immune to art at that moment as the guard killing time with his ticket stubs.

Margery took off her bifocals and moved closer. She wanted to look below the tablecloth, but the scaffolding blocked her view. If she could get on the scaffolding then she could look right at it, scan the entire fresco. They might let her do that, she thought, if she made some elaborate arrangements and waited endlessly for the bureaucracy, but by chance she was virtually alone with the masterpiece. She did not even decide to do it, it just happened, her legs were on the stepladder and she was walking along the scaffolding looking at the faces of the Apostles as they turned away from their master to forever protest their innocence.

She stopped for a few seconds to contemplate the blue garment of St. Peter and to steady herself on the narrow planks. She was wearing low heels but not low enough for such footing.

The gypsy boy had seen her. He stood below her. Margery waited, but he did not call the guard. He watched her as casually as he might have stared at her in a cafe. Margery turned her back on the boy and sat down facing the *Last Supper*. She looked quickly below the cloth. She saw the brown legs of the table, the feet of the Apostles. She looked at the color and the darkness that Leonardo painted and the five-hundred-year-old cracks and then she saw beneath the figure of St. Bartholomew what she was certain was a cantaloupe, a round gray-brown veiny shape that blended into the background but looked as if it had fallen from the tragic table, perhaps pushed by the saint as he announced his innocence.

Only C. W. Post would have added a cantaloupe to the *Last Supper*. Perhaps unable to delete the wine, C. W. Post had settled for simply adding fruits and vegetables to balance the destructive influence of meat, to make art at least neutral. She knew that would be the way he would conceive of it. Two wrongs did not make a right but they balanced each other, just as the world itself stood in balance, barely holding on between heaven and hell, just as mankind hovered at the edge of sin and death thirsting for eternal life. A melon, a spot of grace at the corner of a painting, might save Leonardo and anyone through the millennia who looked at his work.

She was herself inches from the fresco, proof that it could have been done. If she had paint she could do it right now, add whatever she liked. The gypsy boy might even help her.

She leaned to look closer. She noticed the blue stripe in the table covering, the fringe at the corner of it, and then again the cantaloupe. She was sure.

"Signora," the guard yelled. He blew a whistle and suddenly there was an alarm bell.

"I'm sorry," Margery said, "but I had to see something. I'll come down now." She wanted to stand without touching the painted wall. She got to her hands and knees on the planks.

"No, signora," the gypsy boy said, but it was already too late. Her heel caught on the side of the scaffolding and she fell, face first, toward the wall. Her arm hit the wall, then her fingers slipped down it and she fell from the scaffolding into the arms and chest of the gypsy.

She could smell the boy's breath. The guard pushed a billy club against her chest.

"I saw it," she told him, "a cantaloupe."

He blew his whistle again. In a moment she was surrounded by police. The gypsy boy vanished before she could thank him.

# CHAPTER TWENTY-EIGHT

*H*er purse was gone. She had no identification, no money. Her head ached. Everyone was concerned about the painting. None of the guards cared if she was dead or alive.

"Help me up," Margery said. No one came to her aid. She raised herself to a sitting position. Her left forearm was cut, and blood from a cut eyebrow dripped into her left eye. Two guards grabbed her by the armpits and pulled her to her feet. They asked for her passport, which had vanished with her purse. As she fell toward the painting she had seen the cantaloupe again, it was unmistakable. The veined skin, the greenish tone, it was there, a half-ripe Mexican cantaloupe. She suspected that pomegranates were there too. Somehow her father had done it.

"The painting is damaged," someone was saying. "The surface is marred; you can see it in the texture."

"The painting was damaged long ago," Margery said. "The painting has been tampered with."

She was dizzy but standing now on her own. A policeman snapped a handcuff over her wrist.

"Don't be absurd," she said, but he spoke no English and would not listen to her bits of Italian and though she could hardly believe it was happening, Margery was led out of the church into a white police Fiat.

"Take me to the Hotel Venetia," she told one of the three policemen who surrounded her and pushed her into the back seat.

"Why not the Ritz?" one of them asked.

"Because I am staying at the Venetia."

"You're going to be staying somewhere else for a while, Madam."

The police turned on a terrible siren, the kind she hated most, not a wail but a three-cycle burst that made her headache worse. She could feel the noise in the fillings of her teeth.

"Take me to the Venetia," she said. "I don't feel well. I'll explain everything as soon as I can rest for a few minutes."

The police car moved through the narrow streets of Milan, past La Scala, past the castle of the Sforzas, toward the Hospital for the Criminally Insane.

There, a nurse took her blood pressure, a doctor bandaged her eyebrow. A policeman stayed in the examining room, then ushered her to a small private room with bars over the tiny windows. The officer led her toward the bed. Margery saw that the windows looked out upon an air shaft. Without her purse, her passport, her money, even her name, Margery was helpless. When she told the doctor who examined her that she was Margery Post Merriweather, that she was an American tourist who possessed a great fortune, he nodded, hardly listening. She knew he thought her a lunatic. Most of the patients around her probably thought themselves eminent personages as well. To him and to the police, she was merely a deranged old lady who had attacked a public treasure. At the moment she could not prove otherwise. Once he had taken her fingerprints, the policeman became more cordial. He allowed her to rest. He brought a pitcher of water and a plastic cup and placed them beside her. He locked her into her tiny cell. The doctor had prescribed rest.

"We will return in the morning," the policeman said. "Perhaps everything will be more clear to you at that time."

Between exhaustion and desperate alertness, Margery examined her surroundings, recognized that this room was almost a replica of her childhood bedroom. Add a sewing table, a wooden chair and the Post Cereals Company calendar with its photo of a box of Grape-Nuts, and she was at home, missing only a cereal factory off the front porch and a small city literally down the street.

Her head still ached, and she could hear the footsteps of nurses and guards in the hallway, but it felt exhilarating, too, not to be Margery Post, to be just somebody in a hospital room, somebody who could scratch a painting or check into a hotel anonymously, someone who could be insignificant, someone who finally, even after fifty years of atheism, could feel the eye of an angry God turn aside from her. She looked at the bars and felt strangely free.

"The Madwoman of Milan," she said half aloud. "Who would believe it?"

It occurred to her that she could call Biff Alexander but she didn't want to disturb his Disney work, and besides, she didn't want to contribute to his already elevated notion of himself by making him the rescuer of a helpless heiress.

There were Post Cereals representatives in Italy, but she didn't know any names, hadn't attended a board meeting for more than twenty-five years. No Post employees would know who she was. And since she personally controlled less than 5 percent of the company's stock, they wouldn't even know if she was alive. Perhaps some young employees didn't know there had ever been a C. W. Post and his daughter, Margery. To the world she had become, even while she still lived, merely a name.

She could leave this place in the morning, pay for the repair of the painting, even pay for an entire restoration if need be. Getting out of this mess was a small matter. She wanted answers to the cantaloupe and the pomegranates.

She tried to sleep, thinking of herself as the Madwoman of Milan, a homeless wanderer who roamed the streets, who entered libraries and museums merely to find shelter from the cold, who surprisingly, after years of such roaming, had become a perceptive art critic, saw into the heart of things. Her fall at the *Last Supper* was the swoon of appreciation, and she was old, too, that could explain it. She didn't need to tell the police any elaborate stories about C. W. Post and Salvador Dali and James Robinson. She could let the Milan authorities think she was a crazy old lady and leave it at that. Unless they asked for a huge bail bond—then of course she would have to identify herself.

What sort of bond would they ask for the destroyer of the *Last Supper?* She didn't even know if they had a bond system in Italy. Perhaps they would just keep her in this place for months or years, a prisoner led to a shower twice a week, a small allowance for snacks at the vending machine, two hours a day of television, supervised walks alongside nurses in white hose and starched caps. It could be a long time before anyone missed her. Eventually Biff Alexander would need her, maybe in a year to pay his bill and in two years to testify about her need for peace in her neighborhood. She laughed to herself. How foreign the words peace and quiet were to her now. In this cell she had all she wanted of those commodities. "I've given up the Disney case," she could tell the judge. "I've found what I wanted in a small prison outside Milan."

What would they charge her with? She didn't even know, and what had she done? Slipped, fallen face first into a 500-year-old portrait of Jesus or a 50-year-old fake—that one too would have an aura of antiquity by now. Five hundred years from now it would be indistinguishable from the original, maybe it already was, what difference did one cantaloupe make to Christ, to Leonardo, to the police?

Nobody would understand. Nobody else had spent her youth in that cottage, nobody else had seen art and wealth and family and home all ground down to a thin dry powdery being —her father, himself a cornflake, the distillation of a kernel of grain—the most simple form of life, not even life but a moving imitation, something like a painting, now and then colorful, seen by others at certain hours and from certain angles as valuable, but nothing at all in itself, dust, flakes, fifty million boxes of fuel for the bowels—wishes planted in the grain, in the guts, and at the corner of Leonardo's masterpiece too, where she had seen it. If that was craziness and crime, so be it. In her prison bed, Margery slept an innocent peaceful sleep and awoke refreshed and hungry.

At 8 A.M. they took her to a courtroom where she waited all morning on a hard bench, first for the judge to arrive and then for a more important criminal to be arraigned. The police guarded the doors but they let her sit by herself. She could not hear what the judge was saying to others in the front of the room. She felt tired as the morning wore on and found herself falling into short naps. She wondered if they had drugged her breakfast.

She had decided to keep her fortune a secret. Her identity, Mrs. Merriweather, was obscure enough if she let herself be just that, Mrs. Merriweather, a slightly berserk American woman, a widow from Cincinnati or Des Moines who was just overcome by beauty, had to get close and then simply swooned in front of the *Last Supper*. It must happen all the time in Mecca and Lourdes, the judge might understand, might be an aesthete or mystic himself. The extent of the court's interest in her, she decided, would depend exclusively on the damage to the painting. If it was serious, if its damage made the news, then even a widow from Des Moines would not remain obscure.

At 2 P.M. a lawyer finally came over to Margery.

She asked about the painting.

"Your concern is touching," he said, "but rather unconvincing in this circumstance." He spoke fluent English.

Margery wanted to fire him on the spot but she restrained her temper and reminded herself that she was going to remain as anonymous as she could.

"Are you not going to consider the possibility that I'm innocent?" Margery asked.

"It won't matter," the lawyer answered. "Only your motives could be innocent, that is you might have fallen or fainted as you stated yesterday." He was looking through a police file— her record, she assumed. "But the painting was hit and the guard was a witness. Of that you cannot be innocent, can you? You did strike the *Last Supper*"—he smiled at her—"though apparently you believe it to be a forgery."

Margery was embarrassed hearing it said aloud in the courtroom. "Yesterday in the heat of the moment I was overcome. How badly is the painting damaged?"

"It's being examined now by experts. The preliminary indications are that the damage is not too great. But you embarrassed the Bureau of Antiquities. They have talked for years about more sophisticated security equipment but they haven't done a thing. And you confirmed their worst fears. You showed that anybody who wants to can climb up to a painting and damage it. You're quite remarkable, you know. You don't look the part of a vandal at all."

The judge was not sympathetic. He had a preliminary report that the damage was slight. But he hated lack of respect for art. He accused Margery of attacking Italy itself, of storming the very soul of the nation. Then he went on to accuse her more broadly of attacking European civilization.

She asked to be released from prison. The magistrate ordered her held until the American consulate gave her a new passport and cleared her record in the United States. He told her that he was going to levy a very large fine, several million lire. Then he translated the fine for her, $10,000. Margery bent her head. She wished to appear contrite. Her lawyer accompanied her back to the hospital prison. He apologized for the steep penalty.

"It looks as if he wants to make an example of you."

"If I paid the fine and the painting was not damaged, then would he turn me loose?"

The lawyer looked interested now. "There will be my fee as well."

"Of course."

The lawyer became suddenly more active, more willing to help. "Perhaps I can find out today if the painting has been extensively damaged. If not, perhaps the church won't even press charges."

It was happening again, the old familiar rhythm. All she had to do was mention that she could pay and everything changed. The lawyer became sweet, full of hope and encouragement.

In her cell Margery slept the rest of the afternoon—her body became accustomed to the new time zone. When the guard woke her for dinner, the Church of Santa Maria delle Grazie had already reopened. Her lawyer had reduced her fine to $1,-000 and presented her with a bill of $3,000 for his services.

The American consulate had identified her, and the Consul arrived with her new passport and many apologies. The Consul and the lawyer took her back to the Hotel Venetia. The concierge had a new American Express card waiting and offered all the cash she desired from the hotel's vault. For one night she had been a vagabond in a prison, now she was Queen Ceres again. In her comfortable bed in her luxurious hotel she didn't even mind being herself. She had had a taste of anonymity and poverty, enough for her to recognize that it carried with it its own kind of boredom. She considered tracking down the gypsy who had stolen her purse in order to thank him but decided instead to find Dali, the only one who could have altered the *Last Supper*.

# CHAPTER TWENTY-NINE

*N*urse Bloom lived alone in a bungalow in the valley. She had a hooked Indian rug on her wall and a round-screen TV. She collected stamps. She subscribed to the *Saturday Evening Post.* Walt Disney crossed her threshold into happiness. He lay down on her flowered couch. She covered him with an afghan she had knitted. Her hands reached into his armpits as she pulled Mr. Disney into a higher, more comfortable position.

He had told her nothing. She parked the bloodmobile in her driveway behind her maroon Chevrolet. She knew he was Walt Disney but she asked no questions. Walt Disney himself was an elderly man in need. She had a bloodmobile, a house; she knew how to make a body comfortable. She brought a bottle of white lotion to her coffee table. She helped Mr. Disney remove his brown hat and his shirt. She pulled the suspenders from his thin shoulders.

"A little rubdown will cool you off, sweetie. I think all you need is a rubdown and a few more square meals and a good night's rest."

The liquid she rubbed on him felt like Alaska.

"It's OK, honey, you're gonna be fine. Who would believe —Walt Disney showing up in my bloodmobile? In this town you never know. Although you'd be surprised how few stars donate. A lot of 'em are afraid of a needle. You know how it is, they get used to being pampered. But not you, you poor sweet man, you came out into the heat and did your best, even if it didn't lead to anything."

Walt Disney rolled over onto his back. He tried to tell her something but he didn't have anything to tell her.

"I'm sorry" was all he could say.

"Don't you be sorry for anything," Nurse Bloom said as she turned him over to return to plying his back with dry-skin ointment. "After forty we need lubricity. After sixty the sun is a major enemy. In our seventies we should stay indoors except at night. I love all your films, Mr. Disney, I've seen *Pinocchio* four times. How did you make that long nose look so real? You don't have to answer. I know it's hard for you to talk. Do you have a family doctor or someone you want me to take you to?"

He nodded his head again. In the bloodmobile he told her he wanted to go to her house. She wouldn't have taken a bum off the street home with her, but this man was Walt Disney. The driver's license was real. Once she knew and looked closely, she recognized him too. He was on TV every Sunday night, although on TV his hair wasn't gray and he looked younger.

The man on her couch seemed semi-comatose, but Nurse Bloom liked his underlying condition, his 120/80 blood pressure, his pink skin, his ruddy fingernails. She couldn't locate veins, but what was pumping was OK. Blood pressure was her favorite reading. She knew, of course, that it could be elusive. When she worked at the Veterans Hospital she was used to 120/80s dying left and right, but they were mostly cancer. A 120/80 who could walk along the street as Mr. Disney did and eat a big Mexican lunch was OK and would get better with a little more lubricity.

Heat stroke, she thought, a little dehydration, maybe a swollen prostate. Probably a little diabetes, too—fairly common at his age. Still, he could be worse. Nurse Bloom had seen all kinds. It took all kinds. The Red Cross took all kinds, but with

Walt Disney himself at her mobile, and now on her good chintz couch looking pretty relaxed, who would believe it?

"Mr. Disney," Nurse Bloom said as she rubbed along the edge of his spine, "Mr. Disney, I believe you're a little under the weather, is that right?"

Disney nodded, mouthed the same words: "under the weather." That was exactly what he was; the weather was right on top of him, suffocating him.

"You relax awhile, then I'll take you home."

"No," Walt Disney said. He said it so firmly that he surprised the nurse. "I'll stay right here."

"OK, it's OK with me, Mr. Disney, but don't you have a great big house somewhere and a studio and a family and all kinds of people who need you all the time?"

"No," Mr. Disney said. He reached backward to point out a place on his shoulder that itched. Nurse Bloom rubbed along his spine, hard long rhythmic strokes. In a few minutes Mr. Disney, cool and lubricated, slept on the couch. His eyelids twitched a little. He breathed through his mouth. Every now and then his body jerked like a grasshopper. Nurse Bloom watched him sleep, then to be sure everything was OK, she gently pumped up the blood pressure cuff that was still on his arm. Asleep he was 110/70. Nurse Bloom relaxed. He had been with her almost three hours without going to the bathroom, so she considered his bladder fine. There was no wheezing, so the man had decent lungs. An emergency room, she decided, would never keep him once the paperwork was done. But her living room was no emergency room; she let the man sleep. She didn't like the idea of strangers in her house, but Walt Disney was no stranger. She pulled the afghan up around his neck and went to her room to remove her white oxfords and support hose.

"Be good to Mr. Disney," she said to Snow, her cat. "Let him get his rest. When he wakes up he just might make you a movie star."

The next day Nurse Bloom stayed at home with Walt Disney, but after that he seemed fine and for her it was back to business. She climbed into the bloodmobile and returned to the barrio. Walt Disney stayed in the guest room and watched the TV that she had moved into the room for him. Walt liked walking the neighborhood too, although at first it embarrassed her. What would the neighbors think of a man staying with her?—even if it was Walt Disney, which none of them knew. But it happened before she thought it would. One day, while she was working, he just took a walk. After all, you couldn't tell a man he had to stay indoors all day—that alone could make him sick; and here was Walt Disney, not so sick at all, moving along and acting interested in her neighborhood and in her house.

One morning he walked to the hardware store, bought some putty and a knife and filled in the area around each of the windows. He did such a neat job, too, just like a professional. Lillian was grateful, even though in her sixteen years in that bungalow she never once suspected that the windows needed caulking. Those were the kinds of things Mr. Disney noticed, things other people didn't notice. He was a genius. Why wouldn't he go home?

Nurse Bloom offered him a ride home each morning, but he said he was content where he was. Finally she stopped suggesting. Maybe he was in trouble at home, trouble that Nurse Bloom couldn't know about. Maybe some people just couldn't stand being rich. Maybe he was on some kind of quest and had to live a humble life for a certain number of days. She asked him if on the day they met he was out in the world seeking a kind stranger and was she being tested? Was she in a fairy tale? Was she the kind woodsman and Walt Disney the cursed prince, and was there some secret thing they had to do before he could emerge to his full strength and energy?

"Not bad," Walt Disney said when she asked him that question, "not bad at all."

He gave her his wallet which she refused to take. Rich or

poor, you didn't take anyone's money from him. And what did it cost to keep Walt Disney anyway? She cooked her own dinners and there were always leftovers; and for lunch he liked a baloney sandwich and lentil soup. The man could live on three dollars a day without a peep. He never even wanted to go to the movies, which Lillian liked to do every week or two just to get her out of the house on the weekends and into a crowd where she could see what other people looked like on Friday or Saturday night—mostly young people on dates, the kind she rarely saw because her bloodmobile had no school or college routes. She knew they sent the younger personnel to those places.

After the second day, she did insist, though, that Walt Disney telephone his house so that people there, whoever they were, wouldn't worry that he'd been murdered or kidnapped or got amnesia somewhere. "It will be in the papers if you're missing," she told him. "Kids all over the world will start looking in alleys. Walt Disney can't just disappear. At least he can't do it in my house."

So he called his maid and after that his brother knew where he was and called Walter every day. Lillian talked to the brother too. What a fellow he was, Will, so busy, so concerned, too, about Walt. "My sleepyhead little brother," he told Lillian, "he needs somebody to look out for him. Sounds to me like he's mighty lucky to have run across you. I should have thought of it myself. A nurse is what he's always needed."

Walt listened to everything but didn't say much on the phone. Lillian heard the whole story from Will—how that awful woman was singlehandedly holding up Disneyworld with nuisance lawsuits, how workers were going hungry and all Florida was literally going to become a second-rate swamp if she won.

She was a kind woodsman in Walt Disney's fairy tale, and Margery Post was the evil witch in the Florida saga. Maybe both brothers had a curse on them, a destiny that Lillian Bloom could hardly begin to understand. A destiny that had led them to make the cartoons and Disneyland and then to suffer and stumble and fail and lose all the fruits of their labors.

"It could be," Walt Disney said when she told him what she was thinking. "It could be."

He went to his room and stayed there until dinnertime. When he came out he kissed her cheek oh so gently.

"I think you figured it out," he said. "I think you really understand."

She was proud and happy but not too happy because what she had figured out was that the Disney brothers were going to lose everything no matter what they did. While they ate she thought about it some more.

"Walt Disney, you must be teasing me. I just made up a story like a fairy tale and you told me I figured it all out. I don't believe in curses and witches and neither do you."

He nodded.

"Then why did you tell me I figured it out?"

"It makes as much sense as anything else."

He ate his soup quietly and Nurse Bloom, who had enough trouble understanding the simpler things that happened to her, decided to leave Walt Disney's fairy tale to Walt Disney. He could stay as long as he wanted. He was a kind and decent man who kept to himself. She told Will that, too. He kept urging her to bring Walt to Florida. He offered her money to bring Walt.

"Just take him by the hand. Take him to the airport. Get on the plane with him. When he gets here, I'll take over."

"Your brother's not a baby, Mr. Disney, I can't lead him around like that. He has a mind of his own."

"Then why doesn't the son-of-a-bitch use it? We're down here pissing millions into the ocean and he won't even come to take a look, to get things moving. The fucking governor, the mayor and every Congressman from Florida comes down to support us, and Walt Disney, the one everybody wants to see, is too busy playing house in the San Fernando Valley to even look at the trouble he's in. And believe me, he's in trouble. We've got land and signed union contracts and options with specific performance clauses. If we have to pack it in and write off all of this, you can tell him he can kiss Disneyland goodbye too. Just send it over to the Bank of America. It's gonna be all theirs, they hold all the mortgages and, believe me, they don't want us to fail. Can you believe that just one person is doing all this? I've gotta have Walt here. All Florida needs him. We want him to confront her, one on one. We want to sidestep all this legal crap and let Walt Disney himself, accompanied by maybe five hundred little kids, come up to her door and take off his hat and say, 'Mrs. Merriweather, how can you do this to the children of America?' and then let her slam the door on him while the cameras are rolling and fifty thousand people are watching from her front lawn and the whole world on TV. She won't even talk to me, but nobody can sidestep Walt Disney and that's what it's gonna take. But I've got to get him here first before I can plan a thing."

Nurse Bloom was sympathetic. She didn't like to think of all Florida becoming a swamp. She felt sorry for the workers and the Disneys too, though Walt seemed so content in her little bungalow. "He's not mine," she told herself. "He belongs to the world. I can't be selfish." She prodded Walt a little each day, but not as much as his brother wanted her to. Will Disney started to call at the Red Cross office too, leaving messages to call him when she checked in.

"Of course I could just drag him down here," Will said when Nurse Bloom suggested that maybe he, not she, was the right person to accompany Walt to Orlando.

"My brother is a stubborn man. You know you can lead a horse to water but that's all. He's gotta be willing. If Walt Disney is willing he's a different person. Have you ever seen him willing? The big smile, the enthusiasm, the ten drawings in five minutes. He can charm the pants off someone anytime he wants something. That's what's driving me crazy, he's gotta *want* to do it."

"I'm not a doctor, Mr. Disney, but it seems to me that Walt is depressed. He told me that his wife died."

"She died three years ago. Believe me, that's not why he's depressed. He'd get like that in Kansas City when we were kids. He'd sit in the basement and make funny noises and it would be my job to get him to come upstairs for dinner."

"Maybe he needs treatment," Nurse Bloom said. "Maybe I could help him to get it."

"Don't you dare. That's all we need, Walt Disney in a looney bin. He's gotta be OK. He's Mr. Normal, Mr. What's-Good-for-Kids. That's our bread and butter, sister, and don't you forget it. Anyway, the man is not a nut. He's the most stubborn creature on God's earth. He's been going against me from the start. He's doing this to torture me. He doesn't give a damn about the money, you can see that. He'd be satisfied to eat Spam at a mission and spend the cold nights sleeping in the bus station. But now it's more than what he wants. Everything is riding on Orlando. Tell him to forget about Will Disney. Tell him to do it for the kids; they're the ones who are going to be the real losers. Like it or not, Walt Disney belongs to the kids. He's public domain. He's Shakespeare and Zane Grey rolled into one, and he's got no business hiding out in the valley and waltzing around your house in his little woolly slippers and tinkering with your plumbing and your windows and acting like an old farmer when we've got six thousand unemployed roaming the streets every day. I mean Orlando's burning and he's fiddling. This can't go on, nurse, we need him. With him leading an army of kids she'll have to give up. We'll go right up to her private guards. Those Pinkertons won't tear gas nine-year-olds. It'll be their own children and grandchildren. You can't pay security guards to do that. They'll put down their arms. The kids will storm the fucking palace. I'll have a film crew to get it all down. We'll market it later as a documentary.

I'm telling you, there will be nothing like it in the history of the world. What happens in the court won't matter, but I can't do it without him. I'm on my knees in this phone booth, Nurse Bloom, whoever you are. I'm here in the Orlando County courthouse just to the left of the clock and I'm on my knees, hoping nobody can see me, and there are tears in my eyes because I'm desperate and helpless without him. Drug him, lie to him, tease him, do anything you have to do, only bring him here in a good mood, ready to smile and talk and lead the charge."

# CHAPTER THIRTY

*W*hile she rested at the Hotel Venetia everyone continued to apologize. The police called and her lawyer returned to personally express his regret for the whole incident. Someone in the American consulate had obviously told them who she was. And since the painting wasn't damaged either, nothing got into the newspapers. A minor incident, forgotten already. Everyone hoped she had no hard feelings toward the authorities. Of course she had merely tripped or fainted, overcome by her long journey and her devotion to art. What other elderly tourist flies from the United States and then without resting rushes to look at a masterpiece so that she won't have to wait even until the next morning? An art addict, a simple explanation. Her love of art they had mistaken for crime. Who could know? She let the policeman and the director of the Bureau of Antiquities rattle on. She promised the Church of Santa Maria a donation when she retrieved her checkbook, which also embarrassed the director. The gypsies were after all always a problem, what could you do about gypsies? You couldn't ban them from the chapels, some of them were Italian citizens, even artists themselves. Some were honest, they came merely to steal ideas, designs from antiquity.

Margery ate and rested. But merely being released from prison did not satisfy her. She wanted to know about the cantaloupe, about the pomegranates, about what had happened in European art after 1950. She phoned Henri Tremonds, the leading Paris art dealer, someone she had known for many years. Tremonds handled many Dalis, he would know where the painter was.

Tremonds didn't hesitate to tell her. Suspecting a purchase, he offered to accompany her, insisted that he do so until she told him that it was private and personal and then Tremonds felt guilty for giving out the address when it would not profit him. "The maestro doesn't like to be disturbed, unless it's an important sale. Even then sometimes he says, 'Henri, leave me alone.' " A personal visit, Tremonds said, seemed a great waste.

"Between you and Dali," Tremonds said, "there must always be some exchange. Perhaps it will come to pass."

In the morning Margery flew to Paris. She merely dropped her bags at a Windemere Hotel where she was known, then took the taxi across the Pont-Neuf, toward the sixth arrondissement. She wondered if the art dealer had given her the correct address. Would Dali be working in a shabby neighborhood? She expected him to be living in a villa in Normandy, but instead Tremonds had given her the address of a third-floor apartment on an ordinary street near the Sorbonne. The driver had to circle the block twice to find the obscure building. In the lobby Margery found an elevator barely big enough for one adult. On the third floor there was a single door. At least, she thought, he has the whole floor.

When she knocked no one came to the door. Tremonds had promised that Dali would be there. "He never leaves the building when he's working, but when he completes something, then he may not be there again for years. He has six apartments in Paris that he uses that way, like mistresses. He's been in this one now for three months. I haven't seen him but I know he's there. The checks are cashed."

No one answered her knocks, although she heard footsteps and music coming from the apartment. She pounded on the door with her fists. Finally a voice came from a speaker above the door that Margery had not noticed. "Go away," the voice said in French, then in English, then Spanish. It was a recording. She could hear the hiss of the tape.

She pounded on the door again. "I won't go away. I came from Florida. I am C. W. Post's daughter."

The tape continued its message. Margery took off her shoe and smashed the speaker with her squat heel. Then she used the shoe to hit the door as well.

Dali came to the door himself. He wore a red turtleneck shirt with rolled sleeves. There were colors smeared thickly on his forearms, as if he'd been painting his own flesh. The apartment looked empty. She recognized him, and the artist seemed equally familiar with her.

He opened the door as if he was expecting her, as if they had seen one another yesterday rather than in 1917. Dali kissed her hand, led her through the empty rooms to an interior salon furnished as a sitting room. There was a fireplace. A servant brought them wine. Dali apologized for the recording. "I rarely see people." He smiled. "They are a distraction."

"I won't take too much of your time," Margery said. She did not feel any awe in the presence of the great one. She remembered Madrid, and the touch on her flesh.

"So," he said, "we've both had full lives now. What has it been, a half century?"

"47 years."

"You know," he said, "in spite of what you think, I liked your father. We never had any disagreements. I was very sad when he died."

"Let's not beat around the bush. I saw the *Last Supper,* I saw the cantaloupe, and I have the pomegranates and all the other fruits and vegetables. They've been in a warehouse since 1938. I'm not certain that you know about any of this, but Robinson is dead. My father kept no records. If you know anything, tell me the truth."

The painter sipped his wine. He seemed delighted. He offered a toast to the longevity of art, once it was crated in a warehouse.

"So they survived. Good. Of course I know, though I can't be sure either. Your father was unpredictable. Robinson was impulsive. He might have commissioned dozens of pomegranates. I'll have to see yours to be sure."

"What about the *Last Supper?* Did you climb the scaffolding —did you bribe the guards?"

Dali shrugged. "I'm no Leonardo. I painted fruits and vegetables."

"Did you ever paint a cantaloupe into the *Last Supper* for him?"

"Your father wanted fruits and vegetables. I gave him a happy savior, a vegetable god." Dali laughed. "Lemons. I remember them most of all. Your father thought Christ should be pictured among lemons.

"Listen," Dali said, "I can laugh now but you remember what it was like. Your father wanted vegetables, he actually wanted to buy and change the paintings. You remember.

"Robinson is the one who saved the day. Robinson sold him on the idea of substitutes. Substitutes that would be better than the originals. I did most of them. I had in those days a facility for such things. And your father paid me very well. Do you know that he was the first person who ever paid me? He wanted exact copies. He told Robinson to pick fifty or a hundred great paintings that contained wine or meat and then to make better versions. Your father thought it was not particularly difficult to improve on Rubens or Leonardo or Michelangelo.

"What can you tell such a man? I laughed. Robinson was close to death. He said he was going to commit suicide. He would leave a note to *Le Monde* explaining all. He would die a martyr. I think he wanted to die for art but he saved himself and the paintings by telling your father the substitutes would be better. Robinson never expected Post to believe that.

"I was 20 years old. If you mentioned Rubens or Leonardo to me at that time tears still came to my eyes. I too lived in awe, just as Robinson did. Great art, the glories of the past, the mysteries of every brush stroke—you know the whole story. It intimidates the young. There are your great-great-grandparents growing more powerful over the centuries, strengthened by death, accumulating a whole army of commentators and owners, each masterpiece becomes like a state over time, with its own citizens, its own language, it has rights and privileges. Then along comes your father, C. W. Post of Battle Creek, who recognizes none of this, is not affected by any worship of the past, considers it all idolatry. But he was no mere fool, he didn't want to rob the past, he wanted to improve it.

"I remember one day when I walked through the streets with your father. He wanted to know how the sewers work, and at what hour the gas lamps were illuminated. I told him that he had the eye of an artist, that it was art, his way of being exact about things that do not seem to matter at all.

"He said all things matter equally, but the living took precedence. 'Spit into the gutter,' he told me, 'go ahead, you have done what Michelangelo can't do. Every breath, every motion, is the glory of creation.'"

Dali put down his wine glass. The veins on the back of his hand were filled with color. "I remember every word he said at that moment. I still thought he was a crazy American but when Robinson asked me a few days later if I would begin to imitate the masters, and draw vegetables, I agreed.

"'You'll be a hack,' Robinson said, 'but you'll be the richest young painter in Madrid.'

"And as I did it, you know what I learned? I learned that your father was right. Living spit was more valuable than the marvels of Leonardo. I painted a Utrillo, a few Rubens angels, rough, inadequate copies. Mere exercises. But the more I did it the more I saw what was not life. Angels and the divine infant and round beautiful females were nothing to me, as dead as the trees that made the wood in the floorboards. Your father's commission cured me of forms, of worship of the past. He didn't save the world from idolatry, but he saved me from it."

Dali raised his glass in a toast. "To C. W. Post." He said it in his loud full tones. "The man loved life.

"Do you think I have forgotten him? Look." He walked into the next room, signaling Margery to follow him into a bare white kitchen. Dali opened the pantry. Grape-Nuts and Post Toasties sat side by side.

"Every day," Dali said, "I honor his memory."

"He would like that," Margery said.

The painter took two bowls off a high shelf and two large silver spoons. He poured Post Toasties for two and covered them with thick Parisian milk.

"In one of the crates you'll find this, too. It was my favorite, just a landscape, a meadow, some bending trees, and cornflakes coming, not like raindrops, but sideways like the wind, the way everything happens in this life, sideways, not up and down or backwards and forwards. That one I wish I could see again. I think it was the beginning of something. These things to collectors would be worth a pretty penny. To me they are only memories—you know what I mean by sideways?" the painter asked. "I mean like this."

He cocked his head parallel to the spoon and tried to dribble the soggy flakes into his mouth. Most fell to the table. He laughed. "Sideways. I painted for your father Leonardos and Davids and a Fra Lippi and you know what it led to? To this, sideways cornflakes. That's what I learned from all those masterpieces. I didn't want to paint any more up and down things, I lost interest in the face from the forehead to the chin. I stopped caring for triangles, for any forms that are always there."

"You mean my father's commissions influenced your style?"

"Your father made me puke over the masterpieces. He made

me see meat where I only wanted to see color. He made me understand that the world is sideways, always sideways."

"The *Last Supper* has a cantaloupe," Margery said. "Did you put it there?"

"It was all but a half century ago. I can't remember every fruit."

"If you painted a cantaloupe onto the wall of the Church of Santa Maria, you would remember that."

Dali laughed.

"That I never did, but I painted several *Last Supper*s. I practiced on that one. The composition is perfect but fairly easy to copy. Perhaps one of those copies came into the wrong hands. For your father I never desecrated anyone else's work. I told you I would never do so and I did not."

"So there are more paintings somewhere, more things you made for him."

"Who can know? There have been two wars, there are thieves everywhere. Dali has not always been Dali. Anyway, none are signed."

"How many paintings did you do for him?"

"Who counted? On and off I did it until he died. How sad I was. I had moved to Paris when Robinson sent me a cable saying that Post was paralyzed and that the project was over. Your father had wanted enough work for a vegetarian art museum. I think Robinson hired other painters as well, but was too embarrassed to talk about it. I never learned what happened to any of the work. To me it was exercises, school, learning; I was paid well to go to school. I learned to use up the past very quickly instead of lingering half my life over it."

The painter turned to her. "Enough of me. What did the angry little girl do with her half century?"

Margery stared at the soggy flakes in her bowl.

263

# CHAPTER THIRTY-ONE

*T*he last thing Margery
wanted now or at any time was a conference with Howard
Johnson. But Mildred called and made her request so meekly
that Margery agreed to do it. The meek were her weak spot.
Who knows, if Disney had come asking for a charitable donation, if he looked and acted like Mildred Bryce, maybe Margery
would have given him anything he asked.

Margery knew that Howard Johnson and Mildred were still
in Orlando. They were waiting along with everyone else for the
outcome of the court cases. She wasn't worried about the rest
of them, once Disney left he would take all the profit vermin
with him.

It was an odd coincidence, she realized, that she and Walt
Disney and Howard Johnson were human beings, that big busi-
ness had taken their names without wholly taking them over.
Even Walt Disney was just a man.

Maybe it lasts exactly one generation, she thought—actually
in her own lifetime, Margery had watched the Post name disappear into generality. The company was no longer Post Cereals; that had become General Foods, and she certainly was not
General Foods. When Howard and Milly were dead they would
become General Motels, and after the Disneys, there would be
General Amusement Parks. All the big industries eventually
became general. Howard Johnson and Walt Disney, by their
very success, were insuring that they too would become anonymous. Nobody thought of C. W. Post anymore when they ate

Grape-Nuts, and her father's hot drink, Postum, had become a general name, like coffee or tea.

She told Milly that she had nothing to say to Howard Johnson, and Milly just sat at her end of the phone, not saying a thing, letting Margery feel as if she was betraying one of her dearest friends. Margery tried to outwait Milly but she was no match for Milly's patience. After a few seconds Margery said, "OK, Milly, for you I'll do it." The appointment was for noon. Margery expected them for lunch; she had told Gabriella, the housekeeper, that there would be two guests.

But only Milly came to the door. Margery greeted her.

"Tell Howard to come in." Margery even waved her hand toward the car. "And invite the driver in, it's too hot to wait outside."

Mildred went into her meek act again, saying so quietly that Howard preferred to meet elsewhere that Margery didn't hear her friend the first time and had to ask her to repeat it.

"That's just the way he is about certain things," Milly said. "He wants to see you in the car."

"What does he want to do, take me on a date?"

Mildred blushed.

"Milly, you're wonderful." Margery hugged her old friend. "Only you could get me to do this." She told Gabriella to cancel luncheon, she was going out with Mr. Johnson and Miss Bryce.

Milly opened the back door and gave her own seat to Margery.

Howard Johnson was there, leaning against the window, his head down, sound asleep. The driver started the car as soon as Margery sat down. If not for Milly's presence in the front seat Margery might have thought she was being kidnapped.

Since Howard Johnson had asked her for this appointment, Margery decided to wait for him to begin the conversation. After about five minutes in the car, and several loud coughs from Margery, Mr. Johnson was still asleep.

Margery finally knocked on the glass separating her from

Mildred. Milly took so long responding that Margery thought both of her hosts must be asleep, leaving her to take a leisurely ride with the driver. Finally the glass partition came down.

"Howard must be dying to talk to me," Margery said. "He just won't shut up."

Milly smiled.

"I don't mind, Milly. I'd even enjoy it if you'd come back here so I'd have someone to talk to."

"We'll be there in just a few minutes," Milly said, "so I'll stay in front. I thought Howard would be awake—he was so alert this morning—and he does want to talk to you. It's important, Margery, you'll see."

Howard Johnson remained asleep even when the driver parked in front of the Rexall drugstore on Broadway Boulevard. The driver opened the doors for Margery and Milly but made no attempt to rouse Mr. Johnson. Margery didn't ask, she just followed Milly into the drugstore. They went right to a red vinyl booth beside the soda fountain. A cardboard poster of a tuna fish sandwich and a Coke swayed back and forth above them. Milly sat down and pulled open the plastic-covered menu.

"I don't know if we should order without Howard. Are you hungry yet?"

"Milly, I had lunch waiting at home. We didn't have to come to a drugstore."

"I know," Milly said. "Of course we could have been your guests. But Howard is funny about certain things. If he wants to discuss business, it has to be in neutral territory. He wouldn't talk to you in your home. I know it sounds silly, but that's the way he is."

"Well, at least you brought me to a good restaurant."

"We could go anywhere else you'd like," Milly said.

"No, this is fine."

In a way Margery couldn't be happier. She remembered envying people in Battle Creek who ate in the drugstore. She

266

couldn't remember ever having eaten in one in her life.

"Howard likes this particular luncheonette. We've been coming here every day. It's very clean."

"Does Howard eat at places he likes, or does he only nap in front of them?"

Margery was sorry as soon as she said it. "I know I shouldn't criticize him, Milly, I can doze off as easily as the next person. I can't stay awake for an hour of TV anymore. Does he sleep well at night though? Sometimes all the little naps keep people awake at night."

Margery looked around the drugstore. It was all so tidy, all the little boxes arranged on shelves, Band-aids and Mercurochrome and suppositories and deodorants, all those answers for life's little problems. A drugstore was so much better than a hospital. Here sickness seemed bearable, just part of everything, like the lunch counter and magazine rack and the cards chronologically arranged from birth to sympathy.

Just looking around the drugstore cheered her up. The pharmacist in his white jacket was busy filling a prescription for a customer. Otherwise she, Milly, the driver and the counterman were the only ones in the store. The driver sat at the soda fountain, writing.

"Doesn't he ever join you?" Margery asked.

"No, he's new, young, he likes to be by himself. It's a hard situation for him. He's a very careful driver."

As they were speaking, Mr. Johnson appeared between the rows of greeting cards. He nodded to the counterman, who was serving a Coke to Mel Briggs. Mel had finished his postcard. He showed it to Mr. Johnson.

"Dear Uncle Otis, tire pressure 32 psi. Oil OK, fuses and fan belts checked by me personally today. No crud on the battery cable. Love, Mel."

Mr. Johnson looked at the card as if it was written in a foreign language. To Margery his eyes seemed glazed as if he was sleepwalking, but he came slowly toward the booth, bent down and kissed her cheek. He looked so ruddy that Margery wondered if somehow he had shaved and showered in the car without completely waking up. He recommended the club sandwich but Margery ordered only a cottage cheese salad.

After they ordered Howard Johnson got down to business at once. He told Margery that he wasn't speaking to her as Milly's friend but as Margery's potential ally.

"No one person can stand in Disney's way," Howard Johnson said. "I couldn't either. But I now know what to do. We don't have to stop Disney, we don't have to beat him, we just have to do something better."

"Howard," Margery said, "I'm not interested in business or vengeance or profit or anything. I just want to be left alone. What I want is privacy, quiet. Can't you understand that?"

"Of course," Howard Johnson said in a low voice. "I've always tried to provide that."

"But I don't need a motel room. I have my house which is very peaceful and I want it to stay that way."

"I am not thinking of motel rooms," Howard Johnson said. "I am thinking of a place like Busch Gardens, tropical, lush, with real coconut and banana trees, with all natural rides, with a trip down the Amazon with big half-naked women, and Caution, Cannibals signs just for the fun of it."

As he spoke, Milly smoothed his white hair, a gesture so tender that Margery decided to listen a bit longer to Howard's travelogue.

"Nature," Howard Johnson said, "has its own kind of beauty. We came here for houses but the land calls out for parks. I hear it while I sleep. When I doze the trees sing. Wherever I look I imagine a dark cabana-lined sea. This is not a place for motels. This is a place for Bryceland."

"Howard," Margery said, "don't get angry at me for this. God knows we're in the same boat, but aren't you too old to be thinking of new projects? I know I am. I just want to be left alone."

"Yes," Howard Johnson said, "you're right. Serenity is a goal of old age, but not the only one. There is still room for adventure too. The mind craves it even when the body is tired or limited. Walt Disney does not know this. I understand Walt Disney. You cannot stop him, but you don't have to bother. Left alone, he'll wear out. He counts on novelty. He is like a wind-up toy. Once you stop winding, there is no energy, no movement. I have a different idea."

"Howard, I'm not interested in hearing any more of this."

Howard Johnson held up his hand, and Margery was surprised to find herself continuing to listen. He was certainly right to get her out of her house. At home she would have walked away at this moment. Here it was easier to let him go on.

"Take Holiday Inn," Mr. Johnson said, "they sometimes provide an adequate bed. But don't expect to get good room service from them. Your coffee will be cold, your toast will be stale. Once at breakfast they even brought me a day-old paper."

Howard Johnson and Milly both smiled. Margery could see the pleasure they took in the failures of Holiday Inn. She envied them. If only she could have hated Kellogg's she might have had a happy life crusading against Rice Krispies or Sugar Smacks. Milly sat there gloating over her club sandwich while Howard talked about the chipped Formica trays at Holiday Inn and the plastic water glasses and the industrial-strength disinfectants on the maids' carts.

"I have optioned two pieces of property at both ends of the freeway ramp," Howard Johnson said. "These are limited parcels for ice-cream stores. The corporation has OK'd this—it's a small investment and sure to be successful.

"But the corporation has not and will not OK Bryceland. Bryceland is a new concept. It will require large initial capital for the raw land and there will be no high-density buildings to guarantee a return. Bryceland will be a big risk. I'll have to finance Bryceland independently."

Margery picked at her cottage cheese. She still had no idea what he meant by Bryceland. But she liked to see her old friend Milly beaming at Howard Johnson. "This is what it must be like to love someone," Margery thought, "to feel proud even while he bores your friends. And Howard Johnson could certainly bore anyone." He was now listing ancient travelers to Mecca.

"Would you travel to Mecca," he asked Margery, "if there were good rest stops along the way, places free of Bedouin robbers, places where you could stop for a warm bath and a rubdown in clarified butter?"

Margery burst out laughing. She gagged on her cottage cheese and fruit cocktail. "Who gets rubdowns in clarified butter?"

Howard Johnson looked surprised. Milly also saw nothing funny about a butter rubdown.

"In Arabic countries," Milly told her, "a rubdown in clarified butter is as common as a shower is to us."

"Between Mecca and the Philippines there are no rest stops, not one," Mr. Johnson said, "no clear deep wells, yet upwards of eleven million people make the journey each year. They spend their life savings. They slaughter a sheep, then return home satisfied."

Margery bit her cheeks to keep from laughing. She was thinking of herself coated with butter and about to slaughter a sheep.

"Howard, I may be missing something, but these people who go to Mecca, don't they do it for religious reasons? Isn't it a holy pilgrimage?"

"Yes," said Howard Johnson, "internationally pilgrimages are 25 percent of all travel. Milly and I have never done any international business. We meant no slight to foreigners."

"But what are you getting at, Howard? Why do you need to tell me this, not that it isn't fascinating."

"So you'll understand that Bryceland will be like a pilgrimage. It will be a place to go when you're older, a place that will be a shrine to old age.

"Who," Howard Johnson asked her, "has ever tried to thrill the old? Disney invests in hardware, games, rides, thrills for the eight-year-old. Everything that you don't want, the noise at your gates, is Disney. At Bryceland people won't need mechanical contrivance. They will have living memory. At Bryceland people in their seventies and eighties will have, say, a comfortable warm replica of Antarctica. They will have the exotica without the fatigue. At Bryceland grandparents will come to kiss the black stone of experience.

"I have been looking at Florida," Howard Johnson said, "I have been observing couples cooking out at trailer parks and retired fishermen on small ponds. Laughter and surprise do not belong exclusively to ten-year-olds. The old are already dominant in Florida. They are like the twelve tribes wandering in the desert. Bryceland will open the Promised Land for them."

Margery saw Milly almost swoon.

"It's a great idea, Howard," Margery said, "but I think you should build it in Arizona."

## CHAPTER THIRTY-TWO

*T*he signs that Walt Disney was getting better were all over the place. Nurse Bloom saw them day by day as soon as she came home from work. Her boarder had turned the household chores into decorations. She knew for sure that he was getting better when she found a floral design in her Formica kitchenette. Mr. Disney had gathered flowers and spread single petals of roses and lilacs and wildflowers from the neighborhood across the gray surface of the table.

"Lovely," she said.

"Do you recognize it?" Walt Disney asked.

"A football and a curved line," Lillian Bloom said. She was thinking about taking his blood pressure and then beginning to bake some fish for their dinner. "It's lovely, Walt, it brightens up the kitchen. All those colors."

"It's a goose," Walt Disney told her, "a goose just floating along."

The next day he switched from flowers to pencil and paper and she saw the genius at work. The drawings didn't seem that good to her. He was drawing people, not animals. All the people seemed a little out of proportion, short and fat. Nobody's hair was combed. Maybe he's just not that good at drawing people, Nurse Bloom thought. She phoned Will Disney in Orlando to tell him what was new.

"I'm actually smiling now, Lillian," he said, "you are helping my poor little brother. You are bringing Walt Disney out of his funk. Don't think I'm going to forget you for this either. There's not going to be a No Room at the Inn for Nurse Lillian Bloom, no sir, not from the Disney brothers. You are going to get royal treatment, believe me. Have you ever been to Disneyland?"

Nurse Bloom admitted that she had not.

"You live right there in the Valley and you haven't been there?" Will Disney could hardly believe it possible.

"I'd send you a pass today," he said, "but I don't want to rile little brother, not now when he seems to be coming along. So you just wait until he's himself again and then you just see what kind of treatment you'll get at Disneyland. There'll be no standing in line for Nurse Bloom, you can bet on that."

Will cautioned her to go slowly but to suggest every day to Walt Disney that he come to Orlando. "Nurture him with the idea. Promise to come with him. Remember, you are dealing with a stubborn man but someone who is a hero, too. Someone who is about to do battle with a monster. He has to be ready."

On the day that Nurse Bloom called to tell him that Walt Disney was drawing elves and other little people Will Disney went into action. He bought a black suit and read the television announcement himself. He chose the day and the terms. He said that on September 15, 1964, Walt Disney was going to confront Margery Merriweather. The cartoon king was going to march right to her mansion and flush her out. He was going to present a petition signed by every resident of Orlando, stating that the people wanted Disneyworld.

"Walt Disney is not going to beg, not going to demand. He's going to show Mrs. Merriweather that this is the United States of America, the land governed for the people and by the people, the land where the people speak no matter what the courts and lawyers say.

"Walt Disney is going to challenge Mrs. Merriweather in simple good citizenship. He is going to ask her to come out from behind her locked gates and her private army. He is going to

273

challenge her to walk the streets of the city she claims to love, challenge her to walk beside him and tell him face to face that she wants unemployment and substandard housing, that she wants sad faces on children, that she wants this town to miss the opportunity to become a paradise for children from all corners of the earth."

After Will spoke, the mayor declared September 15 Walt Disney Day in Orlando. The workers had been idle for twenty-five days and there was no end in sight. Day laborers who started flocking to Orlando as soon as the announcement was made had no place to live. The trailer parks were full, campgrounds as far away as southern Georgia were clogged. There was money, there were jobs, there was a glorious thing to build. "Let's come out to support Walt Disney," the mayor said, "let's vote with our feet, with ourselves. Let's make September 15 the day Disneyworld becomes a reality."

Walt was coming, Nurse Bloom promised. She told Will that little brother didn't even resist when she read him Will's long letter. He just said, "Order the tickets, please."

"He's OK," Will Disney said. "When it comes to the bottom line, when the stakes are big enough, Walt's finally all there. The man is hard to figure, but look at it this way, when's he ever lost on anything? He lets old Will do the worrying, he's a sly one all right, then he comes out and clears the field. Watch, Walt Disney will have that old witch eating out of his hand. She'll probably throw her arms around him and thank him for all he's done for Orlando. She'll probably donate her mansion for Cinderella's castle. It could happen. People sometimes need a little push to open up and show you what they really believe."

Will knew it would be all or nothing on September 15. He didn't even consider failing, but just in case, he was in preliminary negotiations with Vero Beach. He had to be practical. It either had to happen by September 15 or not at all, there was a limit to pissing away millions. Maybe for her there wasn't, but for Will Disney there was and he had pissed it away long enough. He was not cut out for courtrooms. He was a man of action. There were six thousand workers ready to punch in at one hour's notice and in the courtroom the lawyers stood around and told jokes while the judge went into the back room to call his wife or jack off or whatever the hell he did back there. Will Disney was sick of it. He'd rather fold up his losses and move on than take any more of that. He just needed Walt this last time. It was all nerve but he felt confident. When hadn't it been all nerve? When had selling moving drawings of a mouse been anything but raw nerve? When had the world needed cartoons or cried out for them? If it wasn't for Walt and him there might never have been animation. It was not written in stone, it wasn't evolution, it was something *they'd* thought of, at least Walt had. He had to hand it to that crazy little brother, he was the one who did it, not that it would have amounted to a hill of beans without Will to make it worth something. And it had always been nerve, bravado, daring. The public liked that, too. September 15 was going to be it.

Walt Disney packed his new drawings in a cardboard suitcase that Lillian loaned him. He had only two shirts that Lillian had bought for him at J.C. Penney's, and an extra pair of trousers and some underwear and socks. She bought him all of it on the second day that he was with her, the day that he told her he didn't want to go back to his house. He packed in five minutes. While he had been her guest, Walt Disney had not shaved. The night before he left Walt agreed to let Nurse Bloom help him. His beard was gray and grew in tufts that he never combed. He liked to push at it, squeezing all the hairs toward his chin.

"I like beards." he told her. "I wish I'd grown one when I was young."

"Yes," she said, "but everybody expects you to look like the Walt Disney on TV. You don't want to have an old gray beard down in Orlando."

"OK," he said.

Nurse Bloom shaved him as he sat in her red leather chair. She brought a basin of hot water into the living room. She was used to shaving people, not only faces, but chests, tummies, anywhere. She lathered him up and cut the hair away from his pink skin.

"There," she said, "you're a handsome fellow."

She handed him his bright yellow sport shirt and helped him tie his shoes. He left his brown hat in the closet. On the way to the airport he looked more and more like Walt Disney. She handed him a Dramamine at the gate.

"One once with the eyes, Lillian, please."

Nurse Bloom did her eye exercises. Walt Disney smiled, entered the walkway. As the plane moved out over the Pacific and then curved back toward Orlando, Walt Disney held his nurse's hand.

"Thank you," he whispered in her ear, "it's good to be back."

# CHAPTER THIRTY-THREE

*W*ith Lillian beside him, Orlando didn't seem so bad to Walt Disney. It was her first time in Florida, first time south of the Mason-Dixon line. Will promised her a nice long ride through the Everglades when all of this was over. It was going to be a special present. He winked when he said it. Walt knew what the wink meant.

People were coming to City Hall by the thousands every day to sign the petition for Disneyworld. They lined up as if they were waiting to vote. Everyone who signed got a free mouse cap and a map telling them the time and place, September 15 in front of the Post mansion.

The mood in town was good. The people were happy. Now there was at least a feeling that there was something they could do, they could sign the petition and then come to the gates of the mansion. Will said they were going to blow her out of the water. He said the people were finally going to get what they wanted. This was the truth of history.

Walt was not only up and about in Florida, he was drawing again. Not just on scraps of paper, but in his mind, too, Walt Disney was once more seeing things. He saw a great big piñata of Margery Post, maybe forty feet high, made of cornflakes and papier-mâché. When he told Will, Will hugged him and kissed his forehead. They were at Mayor Greener's house.

"He's here one day and the world changes. What a human being. Walt, you brother, you, what an idea."

He used the mayor's phone and ordered the crew to begin the

piñata immediately. They still had two days to go.

"A stroke of pure genius. We'll have that big cornflakes doll hanging there and right on camera we'll let the kids knock it to pieces. The Mexicans may have invented the piñata, but leave it to Walt Disney to make it something wonderful."

Walt never knew for sure when Will would like an idea or not. He didn't think the piñata was much, it just occurred to him, that was all. Like Goofy had at the very beginning. Who would have ever thought Goofy would be a hit? Walt actually drew Goofy first, long before the mouse, before he ever thought he was going to be a real artist.

He modeled Goofy on his dad, Ralph Disney. Dad had big floppy ears that young Walt liked to play with, especially the soft lobes.

Ralph Disney was a mail carrier, a civil servant. Will hated those two words, was ashamed that his father walked through town wearing a little black bow tie and saying thank you to people who offered him a glass of water. Will wanted a more successful dad.

Walter always knew his brother was going to be a rich man, that he was going to leave Kansas as soon as he could.

"I'll take you along, kiddo," he told Walt. "I'm not gonna leave you here to be a junior mail carrier."

Walt never saw anything wrong with delivering the mail. Neither did his parents. To everyone but Will the post office meant a secure job.

And Ralph Disney liked his job. At the post office they had a letter from President McKinley telling the men what good work they did. When Teddy Roosevelt took over he made the Post Office even more important, made it seem like the Army. Sometimes young Walt got out of bed at 5 A.M. just to watch his dad put on the gray uniform, tie the bow tie, pick up the leather bag and leave for his long day's walk.

Walt remembered when Ralph Disney had a chance to get a new route outside of town, a route that would give him the use of a car. He talked it over with his family. Will was all for the car. Walt and his mother had no opinion.

"I guess I'll stay on foot," Ralph Disney said. "I've been using my legs for so long that I feel like a dog or a horse. Can't say as I'd take to using an automobile."

When Walt drew Goofy, he drew the character as his dad said he imagined himself, a combination dog and horse. His original Goofy had long horsey ears and a frisky tail. The horse-dog carried a mail bag and wore a black bow tie and was always ready to bark. Will wanted Walter to draw some dirty pictures, the kind he could sell at school, five for a quarter.

"If I could draw like you," he said, "I wouldn't be drawing horses."

When he was eighteen and Walt fifteen, Will Disney left home. He was out of school and he had a job. He took a room at the Turner Street boarding house about six blocks from the Disney house.

"Will you still come home for meals?" his mother asked.

"Now and then," Will said, "but when I do, I'll pay restaurant prices."

Tears came to her eyes. Will was already making good money as a feed salesman. He drove a Model T and covered more territory in a day than his father did in a month.

When Will moved to the boarding house Walt had a workplace. Will's old bedroom became the first Walt Disney studio. Walt set up a permanent easel. He liked the space but missed his brother.

It was worse for Ralph Disney. He didn't say much, but now and then when he was reading the paper or listening to his wife chatter, he would say, "My firstborn has left the roost."

Walter helped his mother with the dishes.

"Dad misses his firstborn," she said, "but what would I do without my baby?"

"Mom," Walt told her, "I'm fifteen."

"Still, you're my baby. At fifteen, what do you know about

the world? What do any of us know? Look at your father, forty-six now and suddenly missing a boy he hardly noticed for eighteen years."

"You work hard," Mrs. Disney said, "you scratch out a living, you have some children . . . a few good times . . . I don't know . . ." she said. "I hope it will be different for you, Walter."

His mother's sadness always got to Walter. Her hands were almost up to the elbow in dishwater. Her gray-black hair hung down loosely over her ears. She wore mannish brown oxfords except on Sundays, and her face, though it was still the face of a youngish woman, showed deep lines of worry. She washed the dishes. Walt dried. Will never let himself be burdened with the dishes or his mother's sadness. He took walks to the corner tavern to hear what was going on, to learn where there was money to be made. He impressed everyone as an up-and-coming young man. He wanted Walter to accompany him. "She can do the dishes herself," Will said. "It's not like we're such a big family and Mom has so much to do. She's not busy enough, that's why she sits around moping. You'll never see me doing that."

It was his mother's sadness that made Walter stay so close to her. While Ralph Disney read the newspaper and readied himself for his eight o'clock bedtime, while Will roamed the streets looking for opportunity, Walt and his mother, amid the clutter of greasy pans, traded melancholy looks.

She told Walter that he resembled in his habits her own father, Samuel Steiner, who had been a Kansas farmer but also a maker of fine woodcuts.

"I wish now I'd saved everything he made."

Walt had heard this story so many times, had heard those woodcuts described so often, that he felt he knew them better than if he could have seen them. The only woodcuts his mother had were unillustrated moral maxims. The Root of All Evil Is Greed and The More Flesh the More Worms hung on the kitchen wall.

"Grandpa Steiner drew lots of pictures," she said. "I don't know why I have those two that are only words. But you got all the artistry from him, that's for sure. If he didn't have to work so hard on the farm he might have become an artist. Who knows? He never had the chance."

"Did the work kill him?" Walt asked.

"Not the work," Mother Disney said. "I think he died so young out of disappointment."

"Disappointment with what?" young Walt always asked his mother when the Grandpa Steiner story got to that point.

"Disappointment with anything. You don't need a reason to be disappointed. Look at your dad. He's disappointed now that Will's moved out but it's more than that, too. Your dad's always been a disappointed man."

Young Walt Disney didn't need his mother to tell him that Ralph Disney lived with disappointment. It was always right there in his father's face. His ears never perked up. They were more like a soft dog's ears than the horse's ears Walt had drawn on Goofy, and Ralph Disney had the postman's slow and careful step and the gentle manner. He was used to seeing ladies in robes holding feather dusters. He appreciated small, everyday favors. He never complained about the heavy load that over the years had bent his shoulders and caused the arches in his feet to disappear. But when you looked close you could see that this tired man was not content.

His eight o'clock bedtime cast a pall over the entire household. Will and Walt never went to bed much before ten but Dad, a light sleeper, walking so many miles a day, needed his rest. They had to be careful about noise after eight. They didn't have friends over and for years resisted a telephone.

Mrs. Disney believed that her husband drove Will out by going to bed so early.

"It's not his fault. If he doesn't sleep eight hours he can't deliver the mail."

Ralph Disney wore a sleeping cap to help against the noise

and he glued black paper around his windows to keep out the long summer sun. He put support pads into each of his black shoes, and every day before he left the house he leaned his weight first on one foot, then the other, to be sure the supports were in the right places. He did everything as slowly as he opened the mail slot to drop in three letters and a postcard. During the week he rarely saw his sons except at the dinner table. They ate at four, almost as soon as the boys came in from school.

"Your dad is hungry earlier than other folks are," Suzanne Disney continually had to explain to an angry Will.

"Why can't we eat by ourselves later—when we're hungry, not when he is?"

Finally it came to Will eating alone at six or seven. He simply refused to come home at four and his mother had no choice but to feed her elder son late. Ralph took his son's rebelliousness at the four o'clock dinner as a great personal affront. By the time Will was twelve his father was his enemy.

Walt kept his seat at the mailman's dinner table, but no great affection flourished between Ralph and his younger son either.

"It's not just the early meals," Mrs. Disney told Walter. "Lots of families get along without eating together or even without enough on the table. I'm grateful that we've got plenty of food. What's missing here is some respect between you boys and your father."

"I respect him, Mom," Walt said, "I know how hard he works. I want to talk to him more and everything but you know how hard that is."

Ralph Disney came in and collapsed on the couch six days a week at 2:30. First he elevated his legs. He wouldn't even take a glass of lemonade until three. From three to four he soaked his feet in Epsom salts. Mrs. Disney kept a special blue porcelain dish which she brought into the living room for him, then filled with warm water from the tea kettle. Walter's strongest memories of his father were of Ralph Disney's feet. As a little boy he played quietly beside the porcelain bowl. In his coloring books he tried to draw the blue bowl with the white spots. He grew to enjoy the aroma of Epsom salts. While soaking his feet Ralph Disney usually fell into a light sleep. He wiggled his toes. His closed eyelids sometimes trembled. Walter drew his father's feet.

He also drew dogs chasing mailmen, and cats hiding under porches. He drew the rising sun and the white picket fences around some of the nicer houses on his father's route. Finally one day while Ralph soaked his feet and Mrs. Disney baked spare ribs in the oven, Walter put the feet and the ears together. He drew Goofy. He named the character instantly. Years later when he drew the mouse it was Will who named him Mickey. Everyone thought that Mickey was the first, but Mickey was only the first cartoon. Goofy was the first character. The long ears, the big teeth, the disappointed expression, were copied from Ralph Disney. But above all, Goofy's feet were exactly those of the mailman. The feet were the source of the livelihood and of the pain; large, awkward, soaking in Epsom salts, those feet paddled across Walt Disney's pages, moving a character.

"I don't know why I call him Goofy," Walt said when he showed Will a whole group of sketches of the big-footed man-horse-dog. "Goofy just seems like the right name."

Will, in his rooming house, was already beginning to encounter women.

"Listen, kid, don't worry about your pictures. In a year or two I can get you in at the grain company. There's always need of a young man who isn't lazy and you get more than a salary." Will winked. "You'd be surprised how many women like to be called on during the day."

"Do you like these Goofy drawings?" Walt asked. "I thought you might want some to decorate your room."

Will Disney laughed. "You don't think I want anything that

looks like Dad hanging from my walls, do you? Even if it's a kind of dog. No sir, I've had my fill of civil servants. Goofy, though, is a good name for him."

Walt was a lot older now than his dad had been when his son drew Goofy, and Will had come so far from Kansas that they never even talked about the old days anymore. Will wouldn't even listen to Walt reminisce. He said it was likely to get Walt blue but it wasn't so. Lillian Bloom liked to hear Kansas stories. After the first couple of days she never even asked about the movies and the cartoons.

Yes, with her Florida was OK, though Walter still didn't care if the project worked or not. And since Goofy was now on his mind, he made a note to himself to tell Will that a Goofy pavilion or a ride might be a good idea. He didn't know if it was a good idea or not. To Walt it seemed a lot better idea than a cornflakes piñata.

While he thought about Goofy, Walt Disney was walking in downtown Orlando with Lillian Bloom. It was two days before what Will called D-Day. Around town people were starting to recognize Walter. He wanted to take a long slow walk with Lillian but on every block a few people stopped him. Walt had just ducked away after signing a half-dozen autographs. He and Lillian turned off Main Street, there were too many people there. He was starting to get a little tense. He hated to be Walt Disney in public. He and Lillian ducked into the drugstore to buy a long-billed cap they saw in the window, a cap that would hide Walt Disney's face.

The pharmacist did not recognize him as he bought the dark-blue long-billed cap, but Mel Briggs, looking up from his cross-word puzzle, knew who the man was and ran over to tell his two bosses in the red booth where Mr. Johnson was talking away like Mel could hardly believe.

Margery Merriweather looked up just as the man was putting his cap on. She didn't see the face full, neither did Howard or Milly.

"That's him," Mel Briggs said, "believe me, that man is Walt Disney sure as I'm standing here."

Howard Johnson doubted it. Margery slid across the booth and walked toward the drug counter. She had no idea what Walt Disney looked like. But if fate had tossed him to her in a drugstore without his brother and a gang of lawyers, she was anxious to see him. The man she looked at seemed worried, maybe even a little hungry. He was with a dowdy woman who looked like she might be from Battle Creek.

"Are you Walt Disney?" Margery asked. The man nodded but looked toward the exit.

"I thought the hat would help. Forgive me," he said, "I don't want to sign any more autographs."

"I don't want any," she said, "I'm Margery Post Merriweather."

Walt Disney did not seem to recognize her name.

"Your enemy," Margery said. "I'm having lunch at table number 3 in the corner. Would you and your wife . . ."

"Friend," Nurse Bloom interrupted, introducing herself.

"You are welcome to join us."

Walt Disney put his cap back on.

"I am ready for lunch," he said.

"Good," Margery told him. "This is the best place in town."

# CHAPTER THIRTY-FOUR

*W*alt Disney ordered a tuna and swiss cheese. He seemed relaxed in the company of Margery Post Merriweather. He told her about the forty-foot piñata they were going to build.

"Now that I've seen you," he said, "I can help them sketch in the features."

Lillian Bloom found it hard to talk to the woman who Will said caused all the trouble.

But as Walter ate, it was Howard Johnson, not Mrs. Merriweather, who attracted his attention. Probably because he had just been thinking about Goofy, he noticed Mr. Johnson's horsey face. He hated to stare, but he couldn't help himself. On a whim, he asked Mr. Johnson if he had ever worked for the U.S. Post Office.

"No," Howard Johnson told him, but he seemed pleased by the question.

"Do I act like Public Enemy Number One?" Margery asked Walt.

Walt would have preferred to just sit in the booth and not talk any business. He wasn't supposed to do a thing except stand at the gate and hand Margery the petition. If he had the damned paper with him he would give it to her right now.

"You're not my enemy," he said. "I don't believe I have any enemies."

Walt noticed that Howard Johnson had such wonderful slow movements. When Mr. Johnson reached for a napkin, Walt wanted to set it to music, violins, maybe. And the tiny woman beside him was perfect. Howard Johnson was a bald eagle and she was a sparrow. Walt wouldn't have been surprised to see her nibble bread from Mr. Johnson's lips.

"We do not compete directly," Mr. Johnson said, "but your Tahitian Treat would never make it on our menu."

Walt Disney didn't even know what Mr. Johnson was talking about. He was watching the man's smooth lips, the way the words came directly out of the wrinkled face. When Howard Johnson spoke it was like a statue talking. And the little bird lady was hovering around it, bringing in words out of the air. They were a couple, all right. Everything he said flickered across her face. Walt Disney wanted to draw them right there on the thin "Frank's Rexall" napkins, peeking, one at a time, out of their holder.

Margery could hardly believe that this man who chewed lettuce so quietly was the creator of such noisy entertainment. Walt Disney praised the sandwich, dabbed at his lips with a napkin. She could imagine him sitting down with Howard Johnson for a clarified-butter rubdown. Together the two tycoons seemed to have about enough energy for one nap.

"Walt Disney," she said, "tell me the truth. Don't you hate me? Don't you want to strangle me for all the obstructions I'm putting in your way? Everyone in Orlando thinks I'm Satan and here you are eating lunch with me, acting like nothing's wrong."

"What you do is your own business," Walt Disney said. He wished she would stop talking to him so that he could concentrate on watching Howard Johnson eat. Mr. Johnson looked at every forkful. If everyone ate that slowly, Walt Disney was thinking, it would be good to decorate forks all along the tines.

Lillian explained to Margery that Will Disney was much more up to date on the project than his brother.

"Still," Margery said, "you've got to have some pretty strong feelings about all this. Believe me, I do. When you pack up and move somewhere else, it will be the happiest day of my life."

"Really?" Walt Disney asked.

He had her. "No, not really. But at least for a while I'll be relieved."

"All feelings are temporary," said Howard Johnson. "On the other hand, certain structures can last for millennia. Take the pyramids."

Margery didn't know how Milly could stand him. He was like a tour guide.

"Howard," Margery said, "the pyramids were tombs."

"Yes," said Howard Johnson, "but they were also houses. The Egyptians believed that housing the dead king was the most important priority."

It took Mr. Johnson some time to say it. He stopped between words just the way Walt wanted him to.

"You know," Lillian Bloom said, "maybe if everybody could just sit down peacefully like this in a booth and talk we could settle the whole thing without any more squabbling."

"Of course," Margery said, "all you'd have to do is move your park somewhere else."

Howard Johnson was not interested in the battle between the Disneys and Margery. He wanted to know whether in their planning the Disneys had ever considered the aging tourist. Had such an individual ever crossed their minds?

Walt Disney thought about it, tried to remember if Will or anyone else ever said a thing about older vacationers.

"I don't think so," Walt Disney said. "The theme park came right from the cartoons which are for children. I don't think we plan anything for adults."

Howard Johnson nodded, looking at Margery to make sure it registered. He hadn't asked yet, but she knew it was coming, his request that she join him in building Bryceland. How many millions would he want, not that it mattered. Even if Howard Johnson could promise her the gratification of creating another frozen orange juice, the last thing Margery wanted now was to spend her time running a geriatric day camp. That might be fine for Howard and Milly, cooing at fast room service and praising grilled cheese sandwiches. Anyway, listening to Howard Johnson would be enough to drive Margery back to Battle Creek.

"You can tell your brother that his rally won't work. Tell him that he can bring every ten-year-old in America to howl and beg outside my fence if he wants to, but I won't change my mind."

"There will only be two thousand official marchers," Walt Disney said, "although the crowd will be much larger."

There seemed no way to get to this man, Margery thought. He was as unlikely a Walt Disney as she could imagine. How could all of those cartoons and games come out of this old man in the baseball cap sitting next to her. When he was younger, maybe, she thought, but looking at him she doubted it. In her father you could see the fire in him, muted, kept down by the love of God. In Clarence she had seen and felt it too as it passed between them.

Howard Johnson and Walt Disney were talking about the only thing on Mr. Johnson's mind, Bryceland. If Margery wasn't interested, he just went on to the next listener, this time Walt Disney. And Walt was licking it up. When Howard Johnson started on Mecca again, Margery excused herself. She asked Milly to accompany her on a walk down Broadway Boulevard. Milly did not seem anxious to leave the side of Mr. Johnson though she must have known his speech by heart. After making sure that the driver's Coke was included on their bill, she joined Margery.

"Do you want to shop?" Milly asked her.

Shop—it had never occurred to Margery to shop in Orlando, Florida, and yet right in front of her, literally across the street from Frank's Rexall and on both sides and all along Broadway Boulevard there were nothing but stores. And the people walking along, some carrying packages and pushing children in buggies, they were all shopping.

"Do you shop?" she asked Mildred.

"Of course; not often, but when I need things I do."

Briefly in Chicago Margery had tried shopping but it was too confusing for her. She found herself reading the labels, unable to choose between brands of ketchup or milk or shampoo. There was too much of everything. She had gone straight from C. W. Post's cottage to Russia. There was little shopping in those two outposts of civilization. Later, in Chicago, without any practice at it, she found herself either buying large quantities or unable to make choices. After a few weeks she hired a cook to buy household supplies and a personal shopper at Marshall Field's to choose all her clothes. Someone was still doing that. Three times a year a large package arrived from Marshall Field and Company, the styles of the season.

Of course in cities all over the world Margery bought what she wanted, whatever caught her eye, but she never thought of shopping as a thing to do, a way to spend time, a social activity. She didn't like going into stores. She didn't like people asking her what she wanted.

In Battle Creek it had not been possible for Margery to shop. Even when she needed something, a winter coat or some other item of clothes, whether with C. W. Post or as she grew older by herself, no merchant would take her money. Whatever Margery wanted, store owners and managers insisted on giving to her. The storekeepers thanked her for taking from them. She was embarrassed by the fact that she needed socks or underwear or wanted a skirt. Her father told her it would be a sin to refuse natural generosity. She had to be as grateful for charity and kindness as the poorest soul. Her father gave everyone a job, made the city—who wouldn't give his daughter a wool coat? So she took what she needed and left quickly and in her heart knew that she was never grateful.

At the corner of Pearl and Main Margery saw the end of the line of people waiting to sign the Disneyworld petition. The front of City Hall was now painted light blue and a gigantic model of Tinker Bell floated from the top of the Doric columns. People dressed as Goofy and Mickey and Donald and others circulated in the line, handing out leaflets that said "Make the New World Happen Now."

Margery looked at the front of the line. It was more than a block long, filled with shoppers and children. Everyone who could walk or hobble or was lively or clever enough to grab a pencil was there to vote for noise and greed. For the last thirty years Margery had made it a point to avoid most people. Looking at this line of Disneyites, she had no regrets.

# CHAPTER THIRTY-FIVE

*I*t was Mildred who decided impulsively on the morning of September 15 that she and Howard should go to the event in front of Margery's house. She was watching on television. It looked like everyone else in Orlando was already there. Only the desk clerk remained at the Holiday Inn. All morning the local TV station had been on the air, covering the story. The cameras showed Walt Disney waving as he put the rolled petition with 200,000 signatures under his arm and left City Hall. Will Disney said nothing like this had happened since the people of England presented King John with the Magna Carta, an event that Walt had chronicled in *The Adventures of Robin Hood,* and was now reenacting.

The Governor had called out the National Guard just in case but so far, everything was orderly. There were not even traffic jams—most people had gone by foot. Margery's house was a three-mile walk from the center of town. Families came out early and picnicked in the meadow outside her gates. Disney was giving out free Cokes and salami sandwiches. On television you couldn't see over her high walls, but a female lawyer finally came out to talk to the people. She said Mrs. Merriweather had just returned from a long trip and had no reason to see Walt Disney. She said the crowd and the cameras could do what they pleased, it was a free country. She hoped the people enjoyed their picnic. Walt Disney could ring the gate bell if he chose but Mrs. Merriweather had no obligation to see anyone she didn't want to see. Mrs. Merriweather was tired and resented this publicity stunt.

It was already 11:30, only a half hour before the scheduled confrontation, when Mildred decided that she and Howard should go. After all, Margery was her friend and might need her support when so many thousands had ganged up against her. Mildred hated crowds, even on TV, but she planned to stay in the car, then drive up to the gate after the throngs cleared and maybe stay for a quiet afternoon with her friend. Howard thought it was a good idea. He wanted to time the patience of the crowd. He was anxious, too, he said, to see Walt Disney in action.

Mel Briggs could hardly wait. He had been thinking of going by himself but he didn't like to leave the two of them in case they needed the car for something, like going to the drugstore or someplace like that. You never knew what Mr. Johnson was up to. Most of the driving seemed silly to Mel, they never went anyplace. At least this Walt Disney stuff was something exciting. Everybody in town would be there. Mel was starting to wonder why he had even taken this job. At first he thought it would be terrific, going everywhere in the black Cadillac, but all he did was cruise the malls and drugstores of Orlando, the way he used to do in his town when he was sixteen and driving a lowered '51 Ford. But at least then he was with his buddies out looking for pussy, not just sitting around in drugstores and motels going nuts.

In his mind he was already writing a letter to Uncle Otis telling him why he was going to quit. Telling Otis, that would be the hard part. Leaving these two would be nothing at all. They were nice enough and all that, but he was ready for some real talk and some action, too, and a few people his own age.

Mel liked the mood in town now, though. Everything was jumping, had been all week. There were reporters from the networks and from lots of newspapers. Most of them were staying at the Holiday Inn. Mel listened to their talk in the coffee shop. They all treated it like it was a pretty funny thing. "Like two elks locking horns in a forest nobody even knows exists"—that's what Mel heard one of the news people say. They called it the Battle of Orlando on TV. It didn't seem like any kind of battle to him. He didn't care one way or the other, and he sure didn't see what Howard Johnson had to do with any of this stuff. What he really wondered was how all these people got so rich without doing any real work.

Bones Jones was there, too, in the crowd outside the high brick wall. He had been there since before eight. He'd walked too. He had been waiting for a long time, waiting to see Walt Disney. Walt Disney hadn't bothered to come to see him. There were no peace talks, no big crowds when Perky Parrot was at stake, no petitions, no cameras, no National Guard. Just a cigarette lighter and a can of gasoline, a casual flame. A fire under control in thirty minutes, no big news to anyone except Bones Jones.

In the crowd, though most of the people were white, hundreds had locked hands and were singing "We Shall Overcome." Bones moved away from the swaying lines of singers, he didn't care if they overcame or not. He came to catch a glimpse of the one who had overcome him, the one who had torched the Parrot.

The Parrot was up in the branches, watching as the National Guardsmen stood along the sides of the two-lane pavement. The soldiers were boys carrying riot sticks. They looked like Little Leaguers to the parrot, kids out to play, waiting for instructions on what to do next. "Hard to see them fighting a war." The parrot was laughing. He heard the human voices, saw the thousands on the grass filling the meadow, many of them with picnic lunches. Disney had given everyone a mouse hat. All you could see were mouse ears, all stamped with the date, September 15, 1964, in gold letters—souvenirs so that everyone could say they'd been there, so that everyone could know what they had been doing at 12:00 when Walt Disney would walk up to the gate and hand over the names of every citizen of Central Florida. Perky climbed into a tree to get a good seat. The high branches and the leaves were a bit in the way, making things a little blurry, a little hard to see exactly what was happening. All those thousands of ears were moving toward the gate, but Perky could see what he had to see. He saw the car coming along the road, slow, as if it was in no hurry at all, as if it had been planned and this was the way it was supposed to be, the only way it could be, which was true. Perky always knew the truth, knew right from the start that he would be burned out, ruined, a bird without a bush, because there wasn't room for everybody, even in the good clean forest of Mr. Disney.

It was 11:45 as Mel Briggs moved the limousine between the lines of National Guardsmen who were trying to look serious about all this, but Mel could see in their faces that they wished they were part of the crowd, hanging out on this fine, sunny day waiting for the band or the parade or whatever to begin. He was just taking a drive. There was no traffic. All the cars that were coming had been there for some time, and it felt a little strange for Mel to be so alone on a state road—to have thousands of people on the grass and nobody on the road. Mildred was looking up at the house, wondering if her friend had any idea what was going on outside, wondering too if she and Howard ought to take on the kind of energy the Disneys were demonstrating here. To compete with them took more than money and patience, you had to be able to stand up to all these people and tell them to take off those ridiculous beanies and act like adults. And who could do that when the Orlando Lions Club Bugle Corps was playing "Charge" only a few yards ahead of them and the crowd on the grass seemed to be moving toward the gate.

Margery watched the crowd gather in front of her gate through the telescope. She was looking at the limousine, wondering where Milly and Howard Johnson hoped to go from here.

Their car was moving along with the mob. Margery had never seen a car move so slowly; the long black limousine was like a person almost in step with the crowd. It even drove off the road onto the grass. The Disneys and the television crew had blocked the public road. Biff Alexander phoned the county road commission and the state police to protest, but this time he could not stop them. This time Will Disney had taken out a parade permit. By now he had learned his lesson. He followed the letter of the law.

"He's being careful now, but we'll get him on another statute," Biff said. All the lawyers except Katherine Woodson were in the library watching the proceedings through their binoculars. Whenever they saw anything suspicious they checked it against the city and state ordinances.

"Even if Disney manages to pull this off," Biff said, "what's he gained, a little publicity, that's all. Maybe he can make us look like meanies for thirty seconds on the CBS news but it won't help him. Publicity or not, we're going to put him through the wringer on plumbing. If he's going to go ahead with his park he'll have to dig up all the sewer lines and replace the half-inch pipe."

Through the telescope Margery could see individual faces in the crowd if she wanted to, but she preferred to look at the whole thing, the whole snakelike progression that seemed to come out of the grass and the trees and was moving toward her electric fence. She had ordered the charge shut off, not to help Disney, she just didn't want anyone shocked by the voltage. She knew it would not be possible to keep everyone from touching the fence no matter how many warning signs she had posted. The charge was ready if she needed it.

Margery stepped away from her telescope and watched the crowd for a while with her naked eye. She could see characters in mouse hats and duck heads mingling in the crowd and bigger than all of them, hanging from a cheaply built plywood gallows, was the papier-mâché piñata.

Walt Disney had not done a very good job. The face did not resemble her, it didn't look like anyone, but it must have been hard to cut careful features into cornflakes. Here was an art in grain her father might have liked. There she was, Queen Ceres, five times as big as any of the Disney characters, hanging in the middle of the festival. She wondered if they had filled the belly with candy. Everyone looked happy. Were revolutions like this? Did the people storming the Bastille have a good time? Here there was no politics, no one ready to throw bricks or shoot flaming arrows, but they were all there to show Margery up as the enemy to progress, to show by their presence, by their bodies, that they, the citizens, were on the side of Walt Disney and noise and profit and fun. They were there to prove that Margery Post should make way for Cinderella and Prince Charming and everyone who would pay a few dollars to watch that triumphant couple live happily ever after.

Disney's such a simpleton, she thought, Cinderella is so tame —a wicked stepmother, a prince, a ball. If Disney was smart he would animate the story of C. W. Post. Now that would really be something, the voice of God coming in an ear of corn, the souls of pagans arising within domestic animals—that was the stuff for a theme park, the world she knew, with Stalin and Merriweather as a pair of odd godfathers and Clarence Birdseye popping in to surprise everyone. And she would be not Cinderella, but Queen Ceres, old now but still wondering what had happened to Prince Charming and the chariot and the horses and all the activities that she had lived through before taking her stand at the fountain of youth—alone against Walt Disney and the world's children.

The TV people outside her fence were probably telling her story now, as much of it as they knew, the simple version, a rich old woman who stands in everyone's way.

Margery had an urge as she looked at the festival to hit the happy crowd with tear gas and water hoses. It was all there. Vince had what he called the war material just in case. She

realized how pleasant it would be to destroy the enemy—
except how could she think of them as her enemies? They were
such fools, they didn't want to murder her or rob her, they only
wanted to play, to bother her. When she turned on the intercom that connected her to Vince she could hear the voices at
the front of the gate. Amid the noise and the stage directions
she heard a Mickey Mouse complaining that his head was on
too tight. "Keep it on," someone said, "the cameras are rolling.
Keep it on fifteen more minutes."

"I'll choke," the voice said, "they made the neck too tight.
The head fits OK, but the neck is getting me."

"Take deep breaths."

The band started playing, drowning out the mouse's complaints. Margery heard the voice orchestrating it all, the voice
that must be Will Disney's, the voice that stayed near the
microphone that was planted at her gate.

"I want this to begin exactly at 12. It's going to go live at
12:03 on Mutual radio. By then, Walter, you're going to be
reading the proclamation. Clear everyone else out of the way.
I want Walt right here at the front and the children behind him
and then plenty of space at the edges. Keep the rest of the
crowd back. I want to give the cameras a good long shot of
Walter and those two thousand kids behind him. And then a
lot of space. And I want it all framed. Yes, Walter, believe me,
Lillian will be right here behind me, she can't be in the action
shots but we'll have her in the documentary—we'll interview
her close up."

Margery shut off the intercom and went back to her telescope. It was better to watch than to listen. The two thousand
children did look impressive. Disney had lined them up at the
top of a hill and they were marching, now slowly, toward the
gate. They all wore white shirts and blue shorts and those
mouse caps. She could see their faces, too, they were as solemn
as if they were in church, marching down the hill toward Walt
Disney, full of expectation like tiny little brides and grooms,

marching toward Walt Disney who would marry them two by two. They were grouped according to size, three- and four-year-olds in the front ascending to twelve-year-olds at the rear. The phrase "as to war" came into Margery's mind. She hummed the song "Onward Christian soldiers, marching as to war." That was one of C. W. Post's favorite hymns. He liked the "as to war" phrase—not real war, he told her, "spiritual war, the most important kind."

And finally here she was in a spiritual war, against children and rides, a war against amusement. General Disney against General Merriweather, his children against her lawyers. Biff Alexander wouldn't go out to face the cameras. He didn't want to jeopardize his claims to the Supreme Court by taking on children. Biff was clever. He sent Katherine Woodson, who now stood next to Vince. She looked very beautiful in her white linen dress. Katherine Woodson would have been a credible Snow White or Cinderella. Margery did not trust Katherine Woodson. When Disney confronted them, she was not sure that Katherine Woodson would not walk through the gates to join the children and go running into the trees with her long hair trailing. It would look good on TV.

Margery and Biff had made their decision as soon as Disney announced his plans. Neither of them would go out to meet Walt Disney. Let him present his petition to Katherine, get his thirty seconds of publicity, then disperse the crowd.

If the crowd caused any trouble it would be on Disney's head, not hers. The people of Orlando could have their say, they could picnic right up to her property line and call her whatever names they wanted. They could praise Walt Disney from noon until midnight if they wanted, but as soon as someone crossed the boundary of her property, Vince and the rest of the security force were ready to repel them.

# CHAPTER THIRTY-SIX

*E*xactly at noon it grew silent. Margery could hardly believe that so many thousands could stop just like that. Since early morning the noise of the growing crowd had been all around her. It reminded her of why she was fighting Disney. Then suddenly everyone was silent. She switched on the intercom to see if it was that silent at the gate as well, and it was. Only a few staticky coughs came to her. There wasn't even any noise of crying babies.

She heard Walt Disney speaking softly into the microphone. "We the people," he began. Margery shut off the intercom and took another look at the scene through the telescope. They were all standing like sheep listening to Walt Disney read his pathetic proclamation. Why was she hiding from them? She wasn't afraid to look into the eyes of a cartoonist. She was not awaiting a Supreme Court nomination. If ten or twenty thousand people were standing outside her gate, why didn't she just go down and tell them to leave? She was laughing at Biff Alexander and his staff with their binoculars, but here she was, at her telescope, watching Walt Disney move his arms mechanically to illustrate what Margery guessed must be a patriotic speech.

The suggestion that she not go down was Biff's. Margery had nothing to lose. If everyone could see the cornflakes piñata on television, why shouldn't the people see her as well?

Margery went to the library to tell Biff that she had changed her mind. She decided to go down after all.

"Don't do it, Margery, they're looking for a confrontation. If you stay in the house they can't have it. You may not even be safe out there. Some of those people may be dangerous. Disney has been telling them for months that because of you they won't have jobs, because of you their children will be poor. He's got it set up like a peasant revolt."

"The National Guard is out there, Biff, and Vince has tear gas. Anyway, Walt Disney is nobody to fear."

"You'd be surprised."

"No, Biff, I think you would be." She decided not to tell Biff she had met Walt Disney.

"Nobody who's done what he has done is meek, Margery. Anyway, Will Disney is running the show and he'd let them scalp you, National Guard or not."

"I'm going down, Biff. Why should we let Katherine Woodson have all the fun?"

"Don't be foolish, Margery, we're talking about a mob out there. This isn't courtroom litigation where things are under control, this is war. This is what we've talked about avoiding. On the legal issues we'll stall them to death. Will Disney knows it, that's why he wants mano a mano, you against Walt. If you go down there you're giving him just what he wants."

"I won't give him anything. I'll stand on my side of the fence and tell him to pack up the crowd and get out. I'll tell him to take his elves to Arizona."

"You've heard what I have to say, Margery. If you stay inside your position will be well represented by Katherine."

As soon as he mentioned Katherine, Margery knew she was going to the gate. Why should a thirty-year-old honey blonde who had probably smiled her way into a fancy job be a stand-in for Margery? The world wanted an old witch, she would give them one. Walt Disney meets Katherine Woodson had no drama. The silence was still out there drawing her, intriguing her. At least for a few minutes she wanted to see what was out there, all of it, all of them.

She walked quickly down the stairs to the golf cart that Gabriella used to drive to the mailbox.

Walt Disney was reading names aloud. She wondered if he was going to read all two hundred thousand of them, but as she drove closer Margery realized that Walt Disney was not naming people but games or events. He was reading to the crowd a list of what they would not have. He was teasing them with unknowns called Sky Screamer, Lucky Lady, Minnie's Mine, Pirates' Treasure, The Black Hole of Calcutta.

Katherine Woodson, just as Margery had suspected, was smiling through the big black bars, waving as if she was Miss America visiting the penitentiary. Vince was several yards away from Walt Disney. He was holding a walkie-talkie and looking at the crowd. She felt safe just seeing Vince stroll toward the electronic switches and making signs to the security guards whom he had placed all along the length of the fence at about twenty-yard intervals. There were at least forty strong men and the National Guard. She had nothing to be afraid of. Margery stopped the puttering golf cart and walked to the gate. The crowd remained quiet. Nobody even knew who she was. She told a surprised Katherine Woodson to go back to the library.

"Are you sure, Mrs. Merriweather?"

Katherine was deflated. After one hour as Cinderella she now had to go back to the law books.

"He asked us to tell him why we are standing in the way of Disneyworld. I already read the statement that Mr. Alexander gave me. There's really nothing more to do except ask him to leave. I've already done that once but the crowd, as you can see, is being very respectful."

Disney continued to read the names and events. Two thousand Mouseketeers in white shirts and blue shorts formed a chorus behind him. It was a striking scene, all those thousands picnicking in the meadow behind their solemn leader. There was even the fragrance of oranges in the air, one of the things

Margery liked best about Orlando. No wonder the Spaniards thought it was the Fountain of Youth. Maybe today, from 12 to 1, it actually was.

Margery waved to Vince. Her presence didn't seem to have any effect on Walt Disney or upon the crowd. Walt Disney was still reading names: Screaming Serpent, Lickety Split, Rolling Thunder, each name strengthening Margery's resolve.

The man who fell out of the tree broke the hypnotic silence. Margery saw it happen before any of the Disney crowd. She was looking out and up, and she knew it was the baseball man, the one with chewing gum in his pockets. He came feet first out of the tree, but flapping his arms as if he expected to fly and was deceived by gravity. He landed on the soft grass a few feet from Walt Disney. He made no attempt to stand up. On all fours he crawled toward Walt Disney. Walt Disney looked at him. For a few seconds nobody moved.

"Bite Mickey Mouse's ass," the baseball man screamed. He stood up then and went, not for Walt Disney's ass, but for his throat. Walt Disney dropped the scroll of two hundred thousand names. Will Disney grabbed the microphone.

"She did it"—he pointed toward Margery—"she sent an assassin to get Walt Disney."

The crowd moved. Nurse Bloom, first to the rescue, began hitting the baseball manager in the face with her purse. The National Guardsmen came running. Walt Disney's pale fingers gripped the fence. Walt was right in front of Margery, and the madman did not seem to loosen his grip. Margery pressed the electronic lock on the gate and pulled Walt Disney toward her, then she pressed it quickly again, letting the horsepower of the electronic gate loosen the grip on Walt Disney's throat. Lillian Bloom continued to batter the baseball man even though he held only the iron bars. He was crying. In a few seconds the National Guardsmen had him.

Walt Disney stood next to Margery. He touched his throat. He coughed. Then he smiled at Lillian Bloom through the bars.

"I'm OK," he said quietly. "Thank you," he said to Margery. He shook her hand.

Will Disney at the microphone continued to work the crowd. He motioned Walt to get away from Margery. He pulled his hair when Walter shook hands.

The crowd was unstoppable now. Only the ones in the front actually saw what had happened. The rumors spread quickly. Most beyond the first hundred feet thought Walt Disney was dead. Everyone wanted to see. Some people ran away in fear of their own lives but most surged towards the Post mansion. The teenaged National Guardsmen could not hold the crowd back. Walt Disney stood next to Margery and watched the people come toward her. Vince came running. He paid no attention to Walt Disney.

"I've got to turn on the fence," he said. "They'll storm the house if I don't."

"No," said Margery, "look who's right against it." The youngest of the Disney brigade, the white-shirted three- and four-year-olds, were holding the bars with their chubby fingers and had their beautiful little faces against the iron bars.

Margery pulled Vince's hand from the switch. "You can't do that to children," she said.

"You're the boss," Vince said.

"Forget the tear gas, too," Margery told him.

"Some general I've turned out to be," she said. There were hundreds of hands and faces on the fence now, but she looked only at those white-shirted three- and four-year-olds. One after another, they were gorgeous, poster children. Did all children look like that, or had Disney hired professional models? While Margery looked at those beautiful children, while Vince put in his emergency call to the state police, Walt Disney pulled the switch to electrify the fence. He did it calmly, slowly. If she had not seen his hand with her own eyes Margery would have suspected that Vince did it from a remote location, or Biff Alexander from inside the house. But it was the hand of Walt

Disney that easily pulled the black steel lever, the one Margery herself had never touched. First there was a three-second warning siren. Then all at once the red lights that were built into the fence began to whirl, as if two hundred police cars suddenly came out of the ground.

"Don't do it!" Margery screamed, but it was too late. The current had already hit the iron. Margery saw those angelic faces contort, those pudgy fingers cling briefly and then fall free. It was like a scene from a concentration camp film. Those little bodies fell to the ground. Margery couldn't stand it. She looked at Walt Disney three feet from her, his hand still holding the switch.

"How could you?"

"Look," he said. He pointed to the children.

The youngest ones were on their feet, shaking the bewilderment from their limbs. The older children were now being shocked. She saw the five- and six-year-olds writhe, then rise, and brush themselves off. Quickly lines began to form at each of the flashing red lights. Parents were taking snapshots of their children as their gums rolled up in shock.

The crowd was getting orderly again. Everyone began moving toward the back of the line. She heard some of the fallen ones saying that they could hardly wait until their next turn.

Margery did not notice the baseball manager or the piñata, only the lines of children awaiting their chance at the fence. In the distance she saw Howard Johnson's limousine turn away from her house.

"I can't believe my eyes."

"Yes," Walt Disney said, "that fence is really something, better than Cinderella's Castle. I think we'll leave it just as it is."

Nurse Bloom approached the fence as closely as she dared. She had to yell to get Walt Disney's attention.

"Let me in, I want to have a look at your neck. There might be bruises to your windpipe."

Walt Disney did not answer. He kept one hand on the lever, with the other he waved Nurse Bloom away.

Margery could not take her eyes from the spectacle, the way the children grabbed the iron and fell backward and were then replaced by others. Their screams were like childbirth and Walt Disney stood there as helpful as a midwife.

"Nothing can stop you," she said.

"You can," Walt Disney said. "It's your fence."

Margery wanted to tell Walt Disney to let go, to leave her property, leave Orlando, but she couldn't do it. As awful as it looked, as awful as it was, he was giving them what they wanted.

"They're yours," Margery said.

Walt Disney showed no emotion. Glum and businesslike, he kept his hand on the lever.

"I'll move," Margery said. But even as her lips formed the words, she did not know how to turn away from what she saw.